The Way We SCORE

USA TODAY BESTSELLING AUTHOR

TIA LOUISE

This book is a work of fiction. Names, characters, places, and incidents are products of the author's imagination or are used fictitiously. Any resemblance to actual events or locales or persons, living or dead, is entirely coincidental.

The Way We Score
Copyright © TLM Productions LLC, 2025

Cover Illustrator: Laura Moore, LCM Designs
Cover design: Kari March

Printed in the United States of America.

All rights reserved. No part of this publication can be reproduced, stored in a retrieval system, or transmitted in any form or by any means—electronic, photocopying, mechanical, or otherwise—without prior permission of the publisher and author.

Playlist

"Always Gonna Be" – Dan + Shay
"If I Could Change Your Mind" – HAIM
"Fireball" – Pitbull, John Ryan
"Sin Wagon" – The Chicks
"Under My Skin" – Nate Smith
"Chasing After You" – Ryan Hurd, Maren Morris
"Wildflowers" – Miley Cyrus
"Shivers" – Ed Sheeran
"Steal My Girl" – One Direction
"Lifetime" – Justin Bieber
"Be My Baby" – The Ronettes
"Don't Give Up On Me" – Andy Grammer
"a thousand years" – Christina Perri
"I Don't Want To Miss a Thing" – Aerosmith
"Unsteady" – X Ambassadors
"Work It" – Missy Elliott
"LEVII'S JEANS" – Beyoncé, Post Malone
"Easy Silence" – The Chicks

Dedication

For the book girlies who prefer their Heroes very tall, very handsome, with a big personality and an even bigger… *heart*.

And who isn't afraid to hop up on the bar and shake that ass. Ready to dance?

"Be nice until it's time to not be nice."—James Dalton

Prologue

Garrett

"You're still reading that book?" My little sister Dylan plops down beside me on the lawn separating the two buildings of our high school. "You've had it a month."

"I thought it would be more interesting, you know, being monsters and all." I groan, turning the skinny paperback copy of *Frankenstein* in my hands. "It's all thoughts and feelings and boring as hell."

It's spring, although it's still early enough in the year to be cool in the afternoons in south Alabama—meaning it's mid-80s with a light, coastal breeze. I've got my back against a sprawling live oak that's probably one hundred years old, and I look up at the two-story, brick buildings surrounding us.

On the south side are the seventh through ninth-grade classes, and on the west are the sophomores through seniors.

Dylan's finishing her freshman year, and she's acting all superior. She's at the top rung of a mid-level holding pen just waiting to move to the bottom again.

I'm at the very top, graduating senior, fielding offers from colleges that will give me a free ride, regardless of my grades, just as long as I join the team and take them to the national championships.

Hell, some are even offering me under the table deals.

None of it matters, though. I'm going to Tuscaloosa, where I'll be a starting offensive lineman for the Alabama Crimson Tide.

I glance at the door-stop in her hand. "What's that you're reading?"

"The newest Dragon Lovers book." She does a little shiver, opening the black book covered in gold, swirling letters and elaborate borders to the middle. "It's not boring *at all.*"

I hold my skinny book next to hers, and she's already read two times as much as I have. "Damn, Dee. What makes you such a nerd? If you came at me with that thing, I'd run."

"I'm not a nerd!" She shoves my shoulder as hard as she can, but I don't move.

Dylan is five-foot-four, and with all the ballet dancing she does, she weighs about fifteen pounds soaking wet. I'm clocking in at six-foot-four, 250 pounds if I don't stop eating.

I never stop eating.

"Is *Frankenstein* even 200 pages long?" She squints an eye at me. "Wimp."

"I'm not like you and Zane. I don't like to read."

"I think you haven't found the right book." She gets on her knees getting all excited like she does. "Reading is like movies in your head, only you get to decide how everyone sounds and looks and—"

"Whatever."

She exhales a little laugh. "You're graduating soon. Just DNF it."

"What's that?"

"Did Not Finish."

"What? I'm no quitter. I'm going to finish this thing." I lift the skinny book and slowly read each word on the page. "He's so damn whiny."

Nothing is so painful to the human mind as a great and sudden change...

Shrugging, I guess that's true for some people, but I've always been one to roll with the punches, like the tide.

And our family has been hit with some hard changes, starting with the death of our mom a few years ago. It hurt like hell, but watching her suffer through cancer hurt more.

We held onto each other through that big wave. Then our dad died of a broken heart soon after, although there were pretty clear signs of chronic traumatic encephalopathy or CTE, the "football disease." We didn't realize how much Mom had covered for him until she was gone.

He was never officially diagnosed, but our dad spent years as the star quarterback for the Texas Mustangs. He took a lot of hits before he retired and moved his little family to this small town on the coast. My two youngest siblings weren't even born yet.

Losing both of them so fast was like trying to survive a Category 5 hurricane, which we've also done here. Our little community banded around us like they always do, helping our family stay together through the storm surge.

When he was alive, Dad passed his football legacy on to all of his sons, teaching us the game and opening doors for us where he could. Our oldest brother Jack took his place as the star quarterback for Texas.

He's there now, but even three states away, he still manages to keep his youngest siblings back home in line.

Our second-oldest brother Zane, is being courted by all the big teams, while I'm gearing up for college. My little brother Hendrix is only a year older than Dylan, but he's the most like Dad when it comes to the love of the game. He's a cocky little shit, but he's got a heart of gold, which he hides behind a swagger that sends panties flying.

Good thing he has me to give him a wake-up call when he needs it.

When Hendrix was a little boy, he'd sleep with his head on a football as a pillow. Now he's a star on our high school team along with me, and I expect he'll be joining me in Tuscaloosa in a few years as well.

He's a damn good tight end. It's a lot of fun to work the offensive line together. I make an opening, and he runs right through it for the touchdown.

Dylan's back is against my side, and she's turning pages twice as fast as I am. I'm about to pull her long brunette pony-tail, when I hear the voice that warms my body from my stomach to my toes.

"It came!" Olivia "Liv" Bankston runs up the sidewalk holding a large, white envelope over her head.

Her strawberry blonde hair waves around her shoulders in soft waves, and she's wearing a tennis dress in her signature color, cherry-red. You'd think it wouldn't work with her hair and skin so fair, but she looks really hot all the time.

I fell in love with her freshman year, when she came back from drill-team camp four inches taller, curves in all the right places, and legs for days.

Okay, looking back, I fell in lust, I'll admit it. We'd known each other since we were kids, but she'd never looked like that. A little while later, she noticed me, and well, the rest, as they say, is history.

We've been inseparable ever since, sharing everything, all our firsts, all our hopes, all our dreams and fears. Nobody but Liv saw me cry when we lost Mom and Dad. She held me in her arms, kissing my temple and soothing me with her cool hands and her warm body.

Nobody comforts me the way Liv can.

We're the corny, stereotypical football player boyfriend and dance-line captain girlfriend. Hell, I see myself marrying this girl, and I feel fine.

She skids to a stop, dropping to her knees in front of us, and Dylan jumps up just as fast, leaning in to see what my girlfriend is holding.

"It's the big envelope." Liv's hazel eyes are wide. "That's a good sign, right?"

"That's what they say." Dylan is at her shoulder, her brown eyes blinking excitedly. "Open it!"

"What is it?"

"I hope it's my invitation to audition, which essentially means I'm in. I got my college acceptance letter last week."

I scoot forward so her slim body is in the cave of my arms as she tears the top off the envelope. I'm frowning, expecting to see the signature crimson *A* logo. Instead I'm confused to see purple and gold.

The pages are out, and she jumps up so fast, I barely have a chance to register the glossy photo of a girl with long blonde hair in a white one-piece leotard with a sparkling gold fleur de lis outlined in purple on the front.

"This is it!" she screams, jumping up and down, her face shining with tears. "It's my invitation!"

Dylan is on her feet as well, jumping up and down beside her, holding her arm. Liv is three inches taller as she leans down to hug my sister.

"I have to submit a video audition no longer than one minute…" She's reading the requirements, but I'm confused as hell.

"Switch leap, switch arabesque…" Dylan reads along with her. "I can help you with all of this. Pirouettes are easy."

"Easy for you, Miss Balanchine."

"I don't think there was ever a Miss Balanchine." Dylan's nose wrinkles, and they laugh.

"This is for LSU." My brow furrows, and I feel like a rug has been pulled out from under me. "Why are you auditioning to be a Golden Girl?"

Liv blinks wide eyes up at me. "Because I want to join the Mustangs' professional cheerleading squad after college."

"So be a Crimsonette."

"Garrett." Her chin pulls back, and she grimaces like I suggested she go to clown college. "The Golden Girls are the best, most historic precision dance line in the SEC."

My stomach twists as my lips curl in disgust. "But it's *LSU*."

Dylan gives Liv's hand a squeeze before stepping back and grabbing her book, and I'm pretty sure she can sense my mood. She's leaving us alone.

"I've got to meet Craig. We're supposed to be practicing this afternoon. See ya, Liv. See ya, Grizz."

Grizz. Short for *Grizzly*, because I'm a bear. Only, I don't feel like a bear. I feel like a dog who's just been kicked. Hard. I've got the wind knocked out of me, and I'm wondering if I'm the last person to know my own girlfriend's college ambitions.

"How long have you been planning this?" I hear the confusion, the pain in my voice.

Liv blinks up at me, her pretty hazel eyes wide and pleading. "I applied to all the state schools back in November, but Grizz, you've known what I want to do. It's never been a secret."

Reaching up, I trace my finger across her cheek, moving a lock of strawberry hair behind her ear. Her palms are on my chest, and I move my hands to her waist, pulling her closer to me.

"I never knew you wanted to go to Baton Rouge."

"You could come with me. You have your pick of teams."

I almost laugh. "I can't play for the Tigers. I grew up hating those guys."

"You don't have to hate them. It's only football."

It's like I'm in *The Twilight Zone*. It's like I've spent the last four years believing one thing, and I'm waking up to discover everyone else believed something completely opposite.

Liv has been a given in my life so long, I can't even imagine myself without her.

"What about us?" My voice softens. "Don't you love me?"

I think about every time I've held her in my arms. I think

about all the times I've devoured her lips, the taste of cherry lip gloss on my tongue. I think about her long legs straddling my waist, sitting in the driver's seat of my truck, her beautiful hair falling around us as I pulled a hard nipple into my mouth. I think of the two of us holding each other so tight as she came apart on my cock, and I lost myself deep in her warm body. So many times, I've lost count.

Beyond that, I think of being wrapped in a blanket with her at a bonfire with all our friends, cheering for our home team, prepping for the big games, homecoming, state champs.

I think of her soft lips whispering in my ear, *I love you…*

She's always been my forever.

"Of course, I love you." Her eyes flicker to her hands, and she blinks fast. "It's only four years. If we're really meant to be together, we can make it work long distance."

"But it's the best four years." My voice is soft, pleading. "I don't want to make those memories without you."

Her eyes lift to mine, and it hurts so much. My dream since I was a little boy—or a smaller human, since I was never really little—was to play for the Tide. I grew up in a house of black-and-white houndstooth and crimson.

Her dream has always been to be a dancer. Not like Dylan's dreams of New York and the American Ballet Company. No, my girl wants to be a show-stopper. She's fierce and sexy.

She's leaving me.

Lifting her hand, she puts a cool palm against my cheek. "I promise, we can make this work. We just have to believe we can."

I don't want to believe. I don't want to work hard. I want her with me always. I don't want to let her go.

Dropping my chin, I know that makes me sound like a child. "Of course I believe we can. We'll FaceTime and call and text and do what it takes."

"We'll both be so busy, you with practice and games, and me with practice and games." Her lips tremble as she forces a smile, and a crystal tear hits her cheek when she blinks. "You have to believe we can do this, Garret. If you don't believe in us…"

An ache grips my throat, and I slide my hand in the back of her hair, pulling her closer into a tight hug.

"I'll never love anyone the way I love you, Liv." Thickness is in my voice. "If that doesn't mean we can make it, I don't know what does."

"We'll be together when you join Jack and me in Texas. It's only for a little while."

It's only for a little while.

That's what we promised each other…

Chapter 1

Olivia

Present Day

THE MONT BLANC PEN GLIDES SMOOTHLY OVER THE STIFF WHITE pages. I sign my name, *Olivia Cherry Bankston* in a decisive script on the last page of the divorce decree.

I feel heavy. I feel free. I feel… so ready for this to be over.

Mason Clark, my divorce attorney's expression matches mine in solemnity. "Initial here…"

I follow his instructions, adding a swift *OCB* on the short line, exhaling my emotions over the reality of it. The finality.

"And here…" He turns the page, and I scribble once more. "And that, my friend, is that. You're done."

"That's that." Straightening, I screw the top on his fancy pen and hand it back to him.

Frustration, failure, and annoyance, all of it twists in my chest. I've spent six months rehashing all the "how did I let this happen" and "how did I get here" questions.

It's been a long, difficult road, and I've finally landed on acceptance. I've accepted that I made a mistake. I've accepted I did my best, and I've accepted it was never going to be right, especially after I found out my ex had been sleeping with other women.

"You never think about the end when you're at the beginning." My voice is quiet, and my memory trips back to the day four years ago when I married Warner Oberon III.

It was an unusually hot day in October, and we stood in front of a massive gathering of mostly his friends and family at his parents' estate in Mountain Brook.

I wore white lace. He wore a powder-blue suit. The humidity was unusually high, and I was uncomfortable, hot, and itchy. I looked out over that crowd, and I couldn't find a single familiar face outside of my mother's. She never stopped crying.

Ignoring the unease in my stomach, I focused instead on Warner's smile. He looked like he'd just closed a deal.

"I guess not." Mason's tone has all the cynicism of a seasoned divorce lawyer as he calmly collects his things. "Yet almost half of them end."

"I hate being a statistic."

But didn't I always worry that for Warner I was merely another successful acquisition? Love was never part of the equation for him. Was it for me? Surely I loved him at some point.

Mason reads my face and places a warm hand on my shoulder. "Stop." Our eyes meet, and he continues. "Nothing has changed, Liv. You're still a smart, successful lawyer, and this is merely a bump in the road of life."

My eyes narrow. "It feels more significant than a bump."

"If you knew how many of these cases I handle in a week, you wouldn't fixate on it. You'd accept it and just keep swimming."

"Sorry, it's my first divorce." A hint of sarcasm laces my tone, and I walk to the window of my law office.

I have a stunning view of Birmingham, facing Red

Mountain, which is topped by the monument of Vulcan, the Roman god of fire and forge, holding his spear to the sky in defiance. A burly, bearded, bare-bottomed old god who refuses to lay down his weapon, instead lifting it to the sky. *I defy you, stars.*

The knot in my throat makes me wonder what I'm truly mourning. I've navigated one failure after another since I met Warner Oberon, from my lack of promotion to partner, to discovering our infertility issues, to discovering he was cheating on me, to now, standing here with freshly signed divorce papers.

I'm at my lowest point, but my urge to fight is strong. He humiliated me, but he won't win. I'm not a failure.

Blinking down, I quickly swipe a hot tear off my cheek.

Mason lifts his deep-brown leather messenger bag onto his shoulder. "It's an adjustment, but I think you'll realize once the dust settles, you made the right decision."

I almost laugh. "I made the only decision after I found out what he'd been doing."

"Warner Oberon is not a loss for someone like you." Mason continues. "You'll bounce back. Hell, I bet there are eligible men all over town marking their calendars for an appropriate time to give you a call."

"You're sweet." My insides are heavy. "You'll see that he signs those?"

"Yep, I'll take care of it." He starts for the door. "I'll get his signature and file this with the judge. You've been separated for six months, so it won't be an issue. Take care of your mother, enjoy your friend's wedding, and when you get back, you'll be ready for a fresh start."

"Thanks, Mason." I go to where he stands at the door, extending my hand. "You're a good friend."

"And you're a smart, capable woman. You're a survivor. Don't let anyone tell you any different."

"Right." I nod, exhaling a laugh.

"I miss my babies." Mom leans heavily on the arm of her walker, staring out the small kitchen window with the white lace curtains. "I miss feeding them, talking to them, listening to their little clucks."

I've been home a week, and my stomach is still a jumpy mess. The entire Bradford clan is filtering into town for Dylan's wedding, which means I've been hiding out here since I arrived.

Still, for all my efforts, of course I ran into Garrett on my first attempt to be sneaky. It was at his family's restaurant Cooters & Shooters. Mom was craving Dylan's spicy food, so I called in a to-go order. I crouched in the shadows near the pool tables, behind the mass of dancing people, and still he spotted me like I had a homing beacon on my forehead.

Towering over me, with all his room-filling personality, he'd asked how I was. With a wavering voice, I'd answered fine, which wasn't entirely true.

Then I said he looked really good. *He did…*

I managed to get away without too much interaction, but for the rest of the night I was flustered. I lay awake in my bed thinking about him, analyzing every word, wondering what he was thinking about me—if he even *was* thinking about me.

He looks good. He looks like he always did, big, strong, handsome… square jaw, muscles for days. Knowing grin, big hands, full lips. I denied the attraction that still pulled me to him. It's been years. That's all over now.

Lies. It's still there.

He was on the bar dancing with Craig, moving his hips like he always did. You'd think someone that tall and big would be awkward. You'd think he'd clod around like some kind of Frankenstein's monster. You'd be wrong.

Garrett Bradford thrusts his hips and moves his body with a rhythm that should be sinful. Every woman in that bar was licking her lips and watching him work. My stomach tightened as the onslaught of memories hit me hard.

I remembered climbing onto his back, wrapping my arms around his broad shoulders. I remembered burying my face in his neck and inhaling his warm scent of citrus and soap. I remembered his oversized personality, his laugh, his oversized everything.

I've never felt so safe as I did when Garrett Bradford held me close. I've never felt so broken as I did when that relationship exploded.

Exhaling a low growl, I remind myself there's no point trying to dig up the past. Life goes on, and going backwards only brings you back to where you started. I'm not running in circles.

Standing in the living room of my mother's small house, I lift a framed photograph off a mahogany end table. It's me in high school, captain of the drill team. I'm wearing a royal-blue sequined bodysuit with gold accents, thick nude tights, and tan dance shoes.

My hair is ironed stick-straight, which was the style then, my posture is perfect, and I look like I've just popped my neck to face the camera. My eyes are flashing, and the smile on my face is laser-sharp, red lips perfectly glossy.

Beside it is another picture of me in college, in my white LSU Golden Girls uniform with the large purple and gold fleur de lis on the front. It's another action shot, and my hands are on the waists of the girls on either side of me. We're getting ready to do our precision kicks, all the way to our noses.

Studying this girl I used to be, my brow furrows lightly. I was so certain back then. I knew exactly where I was going and how I'd get there. I knew what I wanted, and I was going to get it.

At least, that's what I thought.

"You need a more recent picture of me." I return the frame to its place on a hand-crocheted doily.

"I like the one on your law firm's website." Mom calls from the kitchen.

She's talking about the professional headshots my associates and I all took on the same day. I'm in a light gray pantsuit with a white shirt unbuttoned at the neck. I'm focused, serious, my lips barely lifted in a Mona Lisa smile.

"It's very formal." Nodding, I decide that might be the best approach. At least, it's the approach I've been using for six months—protective, professional, boundaries. "I'll see about getting one for you."

I go to where she's leaning on her walker, still looking out the window at the wire-walled henhouse. It's a charming little chicken coop, and I'm pretty sure she built it herself.

The frame is sturdy two by fours painted white. The tin roof has a rooster turret on top, and it reminds me of a children's playhouse with wrought iron climbing frames propped against the sides and large flower pots filled with vegetation.

Pale, fleshy plumeria blends with lacy ferns, and a group of six specialty chickens roost in boxes like bunk beds safe from dogs or raccoons or opossums or any other predators.

"The doctor only said you shouldn't do all the bending and feeding and cleaning. You can still go with me and talk to them while I do all that stuff." I slide my hand over her tissue-soft one. "You have to be careful, though. Isn't poking around the coop how you fell?"

"No, it was that dog Gladys was sitting. It went crazy, chasing Henny Lane and Mother Clucker up the ramp. I was trying to catch him when my clog got caught under a crate."

She tries to demonstrate how it happened and almost loses her balance again.

"Easy there." I grab her arm. "We won't have any excuse if you go down on my watch."

Her lips purse, and she shakes her silver head. "I'm not going down."

Mom always had dark red hair, but now it's all silver. She likes to say there's no point in dying red hair. I wouldn't know.

Mine's only ever been strawberry blonde—*pink*, as she calls it, which isn't as hard to maintain.

"I wouldn't have gone down the first time if it weren't for that darned dog," she continues grousing.

"That's good, because you're not as young as you used to be."

Which is why it's taking her break so long to heal. Knowing she'd fallen and broken her leg with me three hours away in Birmingham had been hard. Every mile, every minute it took to get all the way down here had felt like an eternity.

It got me rethinking everything.

We take our time descending the short flight of stairs at the back door. My childhood home is a small beach cottage with only two bedrooms and one bathroom.

When I was growing up, Mom liked to say it was enough for us. Wanting more than we needed was greedy in her book.

It's a very old-school Newhope attitude, considering the town was founded by utopian populists who owned all the land in common. It's an attitude that's quickly disappearing as the old-timers die out and rich young couples filter into the pristine coastal community.

"This henhouse is about the same size as my bedroom." I lightly tease.

"And it houses six chickens." Mom lifts her chin as if she's proud of her communal thrift.

"I thought you only had three chickens."

"Don't question the chicken math. It happens."

My eyes narrow, and I hold back the quip on the tip of my tongue. I don't care how many chickens she has, as they clearly make her happy.

Being back here makes me happy, even if I'm hiding from a certain someone. The scents, the sound of the water lapping against the bay, the smiles of neighbors and friends, the familiar roads and paths, all of it is a balm to my aching insides.

It's giving me all sorts of ideas like remote work or even

something crazier, hanging out my own shingle, doing wills and estates and being a simple, country lawyer.

Forget the big city. Forget trying to make partner. What has it brought me? A lot of money and a lot of heartache.

"I think that dog really upset Henny Lane." Mom leans heavily on her walker, gesturing to her favorite little white hen. "She's been acting strangely for the last two weeks."

The chicken in question has long, white feathers that almost seem like hair blowing in the breeze. Her face is tiny under her massive, white mane, but she's proud.

"She seems okay to me." I give my mom's arm a nudge. "Just look at that expression. I think she knows she's named after a famous Beatles song."

The chicken jerks her beak side to side as we get closer.

"Honestly, Liv." Mom scoffs. "How could she possibly know that?"

My mom has never gotten my sense of humor.

"Hey, Henny." I soften my tone as I gently lift the small bird into my arms. "You okay, little girl? It's going to be all right now. That bad old dog is gone."

The hen makes a low cluck-cluck noise as I cuddle her under my arm.

"She used to be one of my best layers." Mom's tone is forlorn. "Now she stands and gazes at the horizon."

"Maybe she's pining for the fjords."

"What?" Mom's nose wrinkles as she pulls back her chin.

I'm about to explain it's a Monty Python reference when a high, cheerful voice greets us from the sidewalk leading around the house from the street.

"Hi, Ms. Plum! Hi, Liv!" Dylan Bradford skips up waving one hand while balancing a glass dish in the other. "How are all the hennies doing today?"

"Dylan!" Mom cries, smiling and waving. "What are you doing here?"

"Well, I'll tell you." Dylan stops at the door, and I notice she also has a brown paper bag under her arm. "I was reading an article, and it said chickens love hot peppers! Can you believe that? They can't taste capsaicin, and apparently peppers are really good for them."

I've known Dylan my whole life, and I'm always glad to see her. It's the giant cautiously strolling up behind her who sends my stomach flipping like a stone to my feet.

Garrett's a foot taller than his sister, and so much broader. His hands are in the pockets of his jeans, and he's wearing a navy henley that clings to his toned chest and muscular arms.

When his blue eyes meet mine, a hint of a smile curls his lips, and electricity flashes through my body, sending my heart thumping like a rabbit.

"I brought all my scraps for you to feed them." Dylan is always so excited to share her love of deathly hot peppers. "I heard Henny Lane isn't feeling so good. Maybe they'll give her some pep?"

"Well, I don't know." Mom turns her walker, carefully lifting it over the obstacles as she picks her way to the door. "Let me see what you've got. I might not want to share."

Dylan happily complies. She knows how much my mom loves hot peppers—unlike me.

Opening the bag, she gives it a shake. "I've got the tips and stems of black hungarians, poblanos, jalapeños, a few red habaneros, and a serrano."

"My goodness!" Mom's at the door, lifting her walker over the threshold so she can join Dylan at the small picnic table.

I'm left alone with the chickens to face the man who was my first love. The man who holds my history, my hopes, my fears. The star of all my high school dreams.

I swallow a gulp and do my best to fade into the background, trying to seem very busy inspecting the row of empty chicken boxes. Two large Cochins are on their nests, and I return Henny Lane to hers. I don't think he can see my fingers tremble.

"You doing all right, Ms. P?" Garrett's voice is pure warmth, and my body tenses. "I hope it's okay that I tagged along to check on all the girls."

"Garrett Bradford, you are always welcome here!" Mom exclaims loudly. "I haven't seen you in a raccoon's age."

"You know, raccoons only live about two or three years." Garrett's eyebrows crinkle as if he's apologizing for bursting her bubble. "So I guess that old saying is wrong—unless you mean it *hasn't* been a while."

"Is that so?" Mom frowns. "It always seems like those pesky little robbers hang around way longer than three years."

"Now a naked mole-rat lives thirty years." He holds her thin arm, helping her maneuver her walker across a square paver.

"Garrett Bradford!" She scolds, giving him a little swat on the arm. "I would never call you a rat, especially not a *naked* one." She whispers the word *naked*. "It's undignified."

I bite my bottom lip to keep from snorting. Garrett's one of the few people in Newhope who always shared my goofy sense of humor and loves giving my too-serious mom a hard time.

It's part of the reason I loved him so much. For so long.

"To be fair," he continues, "raccoons aren't much better than rats, naked or clothed."

"What in the world are you two talking about?" Dylan cries, hopping over to assist my mom in her slow pilgrimage across the small yard. "We're here to help my favorite fancy chicken feel better, not talk about naked rats and raccoons!"

My head ducks as I swallow a laugh. Mom allows Dylan to help her scooch her way to the table where the glass casserole dish and the brown bag of peppers wait.

"Olivia, bring Henny Lane over here and let's see if she'll eat a pepper." Mom pauses to turn back, not seeming to notice my fluttering hands and squirming stomach. "Garrett, you can help Olivia… Oh!"

Her walker folds, and I bolt from behind the chicken bunks at the sight of my poor mother going down again.

"Mom!" I nearly fall as I try to lurch around the ramp extended from the top chicken bunk to the ground.

Then I almost turn an ankle as I step in a water trough, sending it flipping and slinging water everywhere, all over my legs and feet.

"Shit," I hiss, my hands flying through the air for anything to break my fall.

"Easy!" Garrett's large hands catch me, swooping me up before I break my own leg.

"I've got you!" Dylan holds my mom around the waist, re-opening her walker. "You've gotta take it easy, Ms. Plum!"

Mom shakes her head, lowering herself slowly to the bench beside the table. "I don't know when I turned into such a klutz."

"You okay?" Garrett's voice is low, his strong hands gripping my upper arms.

He lifts me as if I'm a rag doll, which at five-foot-seven, I am definitely not. He doesn't let go until he's sure I've regained my balance.

"Thank you… Yes, I'm okay." My hands are on his biceps, and I take a step back, eyes watering and my ears burning red.

"You'd think we were putting on a comedy show!" Mom calls from where she sits, exhaling a heavy laugh. "Maybe we should move that ramp, Liv. I think it's a hazard right there."

"I think you're right," I mutter, glancing around the cluttered space. "This whole place is a hazard."

My fingers thread in the chicken-wire wall, and I'm completely flustered as I shake the water off my drenched foot.

"I can help move things around if you need me to?" Garrett has to duck so his head doesn't hit the roof of this little shelter.

"It's okay, I'll do it." Bending down, I straighten the plastic water troughs. "I need to refill these."

"I can definitely help with that." He smiles.

Nodding, I look down at the clumsy, damp mess I've become. "Thanks."

An awkward silence falls briefly, and Dylan hops to her feet, taking the glass dish off the table. "We should probably refrigerate this—it's poblano peppers stuffed with black beans, corn, and rice and topped with shredded cheese. And don't worry Liv, poblanos aren't hot at all."

Mom hesitates a moment, her eyes moving from me, up up up to Garrett, and she seems pleased with Dylan's suggestion.

"That sounds delicious, and I've got fresh-squeezed lemonade." Mom wobbles to her feet again. "Garrett and Liv can take care of the chickens. See if Henny will eat one of these peppers, Liv!"

Dylan keeps pace as my mom slowly makes her way to the back door.

"But, I don't know how much to give her…" I try to protest.

"Make sure you fill the feeder and don't forget the oyster shells."

With that, they're climbing the short steps. The screen door slams, and I'm left in the small shed with the man I've been doing everything in my power to avoid.

Garrett clears his throat, looking down at the plastic trough. "That was pretty sneaky, leaving us with all the chores."

Blinking up to his blue eyes, I exhale a huff. "Ever since her accident, she's been ordering me around like she's the Queen of England. It's like I came here to wait on her hand and foot."

A deep laugh rumbles in his throat, and it squeezes my stomach. He's so familiar. Four years in high school we were together. Four years in college, we painfully fell apart. But right here, I can only remember how happy I used to be.

"Well, now I'm here to give you a hand." I watch as he turns and goes to the side of the house where the garden hose is wrapped around a black metal wheel designed to be decorative.

His faded jeans hug his ass, which I can't help noticing hasn't changed a bit since high school. It's square and tight, and his muscled thighs stretch those pants just a bit, just right.

"Thanks." I turn in the opposite direction, going to the square wooden feed bin on the other side of the coop.

A bag of ground oyster shells is inside it along with a scoop for refilling the chicken feeder. The feeder is designed like a picnic table, with a trough on top. It has high sides to prevent waste.

Garrett is back with the hose to carefully refill the water troughs while I prep the food, scatter the oyster shells, and check their litter.

It doesn't take long before we're done and standing around, hands on our hips watching the small birds prance around eating and squawking.

Some of them have soft feathers that remind me of little alpacas, while others have flat feathers that are black or brown with white tips that make them appear lacy. Their eggs range in color from light blue to dark brown, and they usually lay about one a day.

"Those are some fancy chickens." Garrett walks back slowly from where he finished wrapping the garden hose around the wheel again.

"Mom could tell you the different breeds." I keep my eyes on the hens. "I have no idea what they all are. She's added some new ones since I was here last."

Garrett stays outside the small house, reaching up to slide his hand over the back of his neck. "Are you just in town for the wedding?"

"I'll probably stay until Mom's a little stronger." My nose wrinkles as I look up at him. "You?"

"I don't know." He drops his arm, looking down at his boots.

The chickens cluck and peck, and the wind ruffles their feathers. I look up at the house, wondering what Mom and Dylan are doing. I imagine them standing at the window spying on us.

"This is weird." Garrett's voice is low. "Things have never been weird between us."

My shoulders lift in a shrug. "Things change."

"Not this much. This is new, and I don't like it."

"I don't like it much either."

Henny Lane hasn't gotten out of her nest to eat, so I walk over to lift her off the straw. She lets out a low, fussy cluck, and I carry her to the picnic table. "Let's see if she'll eat a pepper. Dylan seems to think they're the cure for everything."

"Want me to hold her?" He lifts a hand as I approach.

"Sure." I carefully pass the small bird to him, and we go to the table.

She looks like a stuffed toy compared to him, and I open the paper bag, peering inside to where the pepper scraps are all mixed up. Instead of reaching inside, I tilt the bag and shake out a few pieces. I know better than to get capsaicin oil under my fingernails.

"Hello, Miss Lane." Garrett holds the chicken up to his face.

"Oh!" My hand flies out to clutch his arm. "Don't get her too close to your eyes."

His brow furrows, and humor narrows his gaze. "You think she'll peck my eye out?"

"I don't know what she'll do."

"She's not a BB gun, Liv." Still, he lowers her to the table near where the pepper scraps are waiting. "She's a sweet little bird."

"Mom said she's been acting weird." I use a stick to slide a deep reddish-green tip closer to the chicken.

"She's no Henifer Lawrence." He nods. "Or even Henifer Aniston."

"What...?" I'd been watching as Henny Lane carefully inspected the pepper pile, but he got me with that one.

"I mean, if we're handing out awards for acting."

My smile tightens, and I nod. "She's very noisy. She might be more of a singer than an actress."

"She's the Yolko Ono of the group." I can't hold back any more, snorting a laugh, which makes him smile. "That's better."

His tone is a mixture of pride and warmth, and my chest squeezes. "You always made me laugh."

"They say it's the best medicine." He stands, wiping his

hands together. "I'm okay with making house calls, but you should come around more. Don't be a stranger. It's your hometown, too."

Squinting one eye, I look up at him. "Okay."

I don't know why I'm still nervous, but it feels good to say yes. It feels good to remember who I used to be. Maybe it's who I still am?

"I've got to get on back." He walks backwards along the path to the front of the house. "Maybe I'll see you at the restaurant one night."

My gaze lingers on his face, his smile, his broad shoulders and narrow waist. The confident way he moves like an athlete.

I nod. Maybe.

Chapter 2

Garrett

LIV IS STILL SO DAMN BEAUTIFUL.

Watching her standing in that chicken coop, in that red dress with her pretty strawberry blonde hair falling around her shoulders, squeezing herself as hard as she could behind those silly rows… For a minute I forgot how to form complete sentences.

I had to get my bearings by talking to her mom. Ms. Plum has a familiar way about her. She takes everything way too seriously, so it's easy to tease her.

It was difficult to see her struggling with that walker, seeming older and more fragile, but Dylan said she's getting better. It's just taking longer because of her age.

Breaking a leg is never great. I've done it more than once myself, so I've got a lot of empathy for that old lady. Still, her eyes sparkled, and she's determined. She was all ready to put me in my place, wheeling around that yard like one of those fussy little chickens she keeps.

It's the same defiance Liv always had. Steel magnolias,

nothing getting them down. Only something's got Liv down, and it's not just hiding from me.

She reminds me of a receiver who's missed one too many passes. Her eyes are discouraged, like she needs a pep talk, a reminder of what she can do if she puts her mind to it. I've seen what she can do. I can remind her.

"Remember when I told you I wanted to date Dylan?" Logan brings me back to the present.

We're walking from the house down to his radio station along the wide concrete path along the bay. His question almost makes me laugh. It was so long ago that summer month when he fell in love with my little sister.

"How could I forget?" My brow lowers, and I can't resist giving him shit. "A player like you telling me you wanted to date the best girl in Newhope?"

Not counting Liv, of course.

"I was never a player."

"Still, you were talking about my baby sister."

"And I had no idea what you were going to do." He laughs, rubbing his hand over his scruffy chin. "You could've seriously kicked my ass if you'd wanted to."

"Still could." A smile curls the side of my mouth, and I look down at my friend.

Logan and I've known each other a long time, which is part of the reason I had to give him the speech two years ago. The truth is everyone loves Dylan. I'd have had to take a number and get in line to kick his ass if he ever hurt her.

"Good thing you've never given me a reason."

"What's the reason with Liv?" He cuts blue eyes up at me, and I clear my throat.

Tightness is in my chest, and it's a page of my history I don't want to revisit. "I don't know what you mean."

"Yeah, you do." He shoves my shoulder.

It doesn't move me.

When we played together for the Pirates, Logan and I were

like a well-oiled machine. He was the wide receiver, and I was the offensive lineman knocking down every player who tried to block the pass or take him down.

We set records. It was fun, the best years of my professional career. It reminded me of when I used to play with Hendrix in high school, another golden time in my life.

Then he met my sister.

Now he's a sports radio host and producer, retired from the game, and getting married in a week.

"What happened with Liv?" He's not letting me off the hook, and I stop walking.

We've reached a copse of live oak trees, and the city has placed a nice wooden bench in the shade. It's not awfully hot yet, so I walk over and take a seat. He follows me, doing the same, and we look out at a boat across the bay, headed down to one of the barrier islands.

"I haven't thought about this in a long time." My voice is quiet. "I haven't wanted to think about it."

Logan's dark brow furrows, and his square jaw tightens. "Did she cheat on you?"

"What? Hell, no." I huff a noise, leaning forward and placing my forearms on my thighs and clasping my hands. "Liv was always true blue. At least that's what I realized when I finally got my head out of my ass. When it was too late."

"So what happened?"

"She went to LSU. I went to Bama."

"What?" Disbelief cuts through his tone. "I don't believe that for a second. It was more than just that old rivalry."

Lowering my chin, I rub the back of my neck feeling all the guilt and shame all over again. "Yeah, it was more than that." *A helluva lot more.*

"How much more?"

My throat is dry and achy. "I thought we'd be like my parents. They went to the same school, graduated together, got married, had babies. I thought Liv would go with me when I went to the pros."

"She didn't feel the same about you?"

My hands are clasped in front of me, and I hang my head. I know she did. She wanted to stay together, but she didn't want to give up her dreams for my football career.

"I was hurt when she left. I thought we were on the same page about our plans, and we weren't. I wanted her by my side all the way, but she wanted her own things."

"Things like what?"

Scratching my chin, I exhale slowly. "All through high school, I'd only ever had my sights set on one college. The only college in Alabama for football."

Logan's lips twist. "If I remember correctly, there are two SEC teams in Alabama."

"I'm talking about serious football."

He laughs, holding up both hands. "So it's like that?"

My eyes lift to the bay, and I nod. "It's always been like that for me."

"You let a football rivalry come between what might've been your one true love?" He's joking around, but he has no idea.

"It was worse than that." My stomach is a hot ball of tension. "We tried to stay together. She wanted to do long-distance, but damn, she was so fine. You should've seen her on that field in that skimpy uniform. Every guy wanted her."

"But she was yours."

A low growl rumbles in my chest, and I rub my fingers over my closed eyes. "You might've noticed I can be a bit of a hothead."

"Not you." His tone is teasing. "You're the best guy I know."

"I've had a lot of time to grow up."

"Before you did all that growing up, what did you do?"

Inhaling, I straighten my back, feeling like I'm in confession. "I started picking fights over stupid things. I was jealous, and there was this one guy… He went after her hard. He talked a big game like they were so close."

"Was he on the team?"

"He was one of the band captains, so they spent a lot of time together. They practiced together, traveled together. The Golden Girls go with the band." Lifting my chin, I look out at the water. "I was never there, so I didn't know what all they did."

"You broke up with her over a band captain?"

"Worse." Clasping my hands, I shake my head. "I gave her an ultimatum."

"Wow." Logan rubs his hands down his thighs, exhaling a low noise. "Dylan said Liv always wanted to dance for the Texas cheerleaders, America's Sweethearts. She said it had been her dream since junior high, that she had posters all over her walls."

Clearing my throat, I shift in my seat. "Yeah, and I made it all about me. I understand that a lot better now than I did when I was nineteen."

Logan shakes his head. "That sucks."

"Tell me about it." That old shame twists hard in my gut. "When I realized how bad I'd fucked up, I tried to push it all down. I tried to pretend like it didn't matter. I'd keep track of her through friends and on social media, and I saw she never got with that guy. I saw she was moving on with her life. She didn't go to Texas to dance. She went to law school instead—at Cumberland."

"Good school."

"Yeah." I exhale a bitter laugh. "I convinced myself she was happy, and I got on with my life. I moved to New York and never looked back."

Logan studies my profile. "All this time I thought you were just trying to find the right girl. I didn't know you never got over your first love."

"It doesn't matter. There's no going back."

"Says who?"

"Says everybody."

"I don't believe that. You can totally go back." His voice rises. "In fact, I think you'd be foolish not to see if something's still there. You're here and single. She's here and single…"

"She won't go down that road again with me." Shame tightens my chest. "I should've trusted her. I should've told her how I was feeling. I should've talked to her, but I was proud. I hurt her. Bad."

I'll never forget the tears in Liv's pretty green-hazel eyes. I'll never forget that night and the wind blowing in her soft hair as she told me I was breaking her heart. The truth is I didn't just hurt her.

Yeah, I never got over it.

"So talk to her now."

Shaking my head, I study my palm. "It's too late."

"Is it?"

He's optimistic in a way that tells me he's happy with his life. Everything is going right, and he sees every problem as having a solution with only the best possible outcome.

I'm glad my sister has made him so happy, but he doesn't understand how bad I fucked up in the past.

"Yeah, it's too late."

"Do me a favor." He reaches over to grip the top of my shoulder. "Try."

"Tell me what you've got lined up." Dylan is wearing clear goggles and plastic gloves, and her long, dark hair is twisted up in a high ponytail on her head as she stands in front of the large, metal work table in the kitchen at Cooters & Shooters.

Tonight my baby sister is mixing up her last Dare Dish before she goes on her honeymoon, and it's a doozy—Blueberry Trinidad Scorpion sauce to be served over those little cups of vanilla ice cream they buy in bulk for emergencies.

She said it's meant to be a pre-wedding treat, but Trinidad scorpions are second to the top on the Scoville heat scale, right under the Carolina Reaper. I read eating one can cause the muscles in your stomach to break out in spasms they're so hot.

I can't wait to try it.

The tiny fruits are red and shriveled, and I watch as she carefully cuts a long strip down the side of one.

Craig is all the way on the other side of the room holding a towel over his nose and mouth as he reads from his phone. "Grilled poblanos with nacho cheese sauce, Muhammara…"

"Muha what?" Dylan's brow furrows.

"Muhammara," he shouts. "It's roasted red peppers, bread crumbs, walnuts, and pomegranate molasses."

"Roasted *red* peppers?" Dylan's voice goes high. "As in red *bell* peppers? They don't even count!"

"And you call yourself her sous chef." I walk over to where our lifelong friend and former across-the-street neighbor is standing.

"I never called myself Dylan's sous chef. Why do you think I stand all the way over here with a towel over my face? I don't like touching Satan's fruit!"

Nudging his shoulder, I laugh. "You'd touch Satan's ding-dong."

"Not if it had the same effect as one of those peppers." I arch my eyebrow in a disbelieving look, and his lips twist. "Okay, I *am* intrigued by the thought."

"Cause you're a kinky motherfucker."

He holds a finger in my face. "I'm easily distracted."

"You two are gross," Dylan sniffs, continuing her careful slicing.

"He set me up," I defend.

Craig fights a laugh. "I won't mention this to Clint. It might be a bit much for him at this point in our relationship."

"I need to get to know Clint better, make sure he's right for you." My brow lowers. "Has he come out of the closet yet?"

"He's escorting me to the wedding."

"That's a good start."

Holding up a hand, we high-five as he returns to my sister. "You asked me to cover for you, and I told you, I'm not preparing any recipes that require me to wear goggles and plastic gloves, Danger Girl."

"That's Dylan Danger to you." Logan saunters in the room with my older brother Zane right behind him.

The two of them host a sports-talk radio show every Thursday at Logan's radio station, and they've been pre-recording episodes all day for the next two weeks while Logan and Dylan are on their honeymoon in Mexico.

Logan chose the location so she could scout out new hot-pepper recipes. It's the birthplace of her hot pepper passion. She helped chaperone a high school senior cruise a few years back and came back obsessed.

He wraps his fist around Dylan's ponytail, and gives it a tug so he can steal a kiss. It's their standard greeting, but when he sees her protective gear, he hesitates.

"You're not going to kill me, are you?"

"Not tonight." She winks, poking out her lips for a kiss. "But don't touch *anything*."

He kisses her briefly, lifting both hands before going to stand on the other side of Craig. Those two wimps melt like snowflakes just thinking about capsaicin oil. Come to think of it, Olivia was always the same way.

"I like the idea of serving it over ice cream." Zane's voice is low as he inspects the dark blue sauce my sister is simmering in a large pot on the stove.

She carefully slides in the diced peppers and gives it a slow stir. "It's festive, and the ice cream will help cut the heat so more people can try it. Also, the blueberries and the lime juice will make the capsaicin less potent."

"Sorry I'm late!" Allie, our summer waitress and one of Dylan's best friends breezes into the kitchen, grabbing an apron off a hook. "You wouldn't believe how crowded it is out there tonight! They must know Captain Vanilla's taking over for a while."

She elbows Craig, and he sniffs. "I am hardly vanilla."

"I bet you don't have a single hot pepper recipe on tap. Show me."

"I will not." Craig's tone is defensive, and Dylan snorts a laugh.

"He doesn't."

"I knew it!" Allie cries.

During the school year, Allie works as the librarian at the high school, and she helps out on Dare Nights, which have gotten busier and busier as the word has spread about my sister's deliciously dangerous hot pepper nights.

Now that it's summer break, she'll be working full-time at the restaurant.

"I'm worried we don't have enough hands." Allie peeks through the double doors leading into the restaurant. "Maybe we should charge a cover?"

Dylan serves her dishes for free, but we more than make up for the small cost with the increase in bar sales on Dare Nights. Not to mention the repeat customers.

"I can't charge a cover!" Dylan's nose wrinkles. "It's bad enough I try to melt their lips off every Thursday night."

"I can help out." Grabbing an apron, I pull it over my head. "What do I do?"

"Pull the lids off ice cream cups." Dylan lifts the large bowl of fiery blueberry sauce. "I don't want any of y'all touching this stuff. Experts only tonight, Allie."

"I've got the perfect song." Craig starts for the door. "I expect you to dance with me, Grizz! I don't care how helpful you're being."

I spot my sister as she transfers the bowl onto a cart with wheels, and we head for the kitchen door. The crowd bursts into cheers as we emerge, and they've decorated the place with balloons and streamers. Several people are holding signs that say *Congratulations* and *Best Wishes*, and my little sister stops walking, lifting her hands as tears flood her eyes.

"Oh, y'all!" she cries. "What have you done?"

"Don't touch your eyes!" Allie cries, grabbing a tissue and blotting the tears away for her.

Rachel holds Miss Gina's arm as she reaches for my sister. "Miss Gina!" Dylan's voice cracks. "Did you know this was happening?"

"I don't know what's happening!" Miss Gina laughs, her blind eyes lifting to the ceiling. "I only know you deserve it. You give so much joy to everyone."

My sister leans her head on the old lady's shoulder. "My hands are all covered in pepper juice or I'd squeeze you."

Liv helps her mom scoot up behind them to give Dylan a hug, and my insides tighten. I want to go to her and pull her into my arms like it's old times. I want to tell her all the things Logan said I should.

But I don't know enough about her story yet. I can't bulldoze into her life like I'm the only thing that matters. Like I used to do.

I'm not a toddler, and she has feelings and a life. I want to know more about all of it. This time it's not all about me.

"I can't wait to taste this." Ms. Plum points at the bowl in front of Dylan. "I love that dark purple color. And over ice cream?"

"Hold that thought." Dylan holds up a finger, her brown eyes shining. "Allie's going to give you the scoop."

Liv's nose wrinkles, and she laughs. "This is so fun. Last time I was here the whole place turned into a dance party!"

"Let's do this." Craig slides by in his shoulder-length, curly blond wig, looking like he's about to sing "Sandra Dee" from *Grease.*

He goes to the PA system, and I lean into her ear. "Stay close."

Her greenish-brown eyes blink wide, and I give her a wink before following my sister to a long table stocked with ice cream in coolers, spoons and napkins.

Allie is already there, primed to make the usual announcement.

"Okay, y'all, this is an experts-only night!" Cheers interrupt Allie's speech, and she holds up a hand, waving at them. "Trinidad scorpion is no joke, but tonight in honor of the future bride and groom, we've got a special blueberry-lime sauce served over vanilla ice cream. If you're lactose intolerant, you can try it on a slice of tomato. I know that sounds weird, but it's really good. And in honor of the couple, we have special Fireball shots two for one at the bar. Let's do this!"

The lights switch to the flashing, rainbow disco-swirls, and Craig hits the music. It's Pittbull's "Fireball," and he's on the bar at once with the girls, rocking his hips and shaking his ass.

I'm beside Dylan, ripping the tops off tiny vanilla ice cream cups, and just as fast she spoons a dab of Blueberry Trinidad Sauce on top. Allie passes them a wooden spoon and a napkin, and the customers dance away.

My brother Zane follows as Rachel leads Miss Gina to her favorite booth in the back of the restaurant, away from the noise. I watch as he kisses the side of her head before leaning down to hug the old blind lady.

He whispers something in Rachel's ear, and her eyes light. The satisfied smile curving his lips really fans my optimism. It's kind of awesome to see my broody second-oldest brother so content. After all the nights I spent worrying about him following his injury, it's been a long time coming.

She rises on her toes to kiss his lips, and he crosses the room headed for the pool area. I figure he's going to check on her younger brother Edward, who they keep now. He's got some special needs, and all the noise and partying of Dare Night is a bit too intense for him.

I'm reaching for another cup of ice cream when Dylan

touches my arm, rising onto her tiptoes to yell in my ear. "I think we're good for now!"

My attention returns to the room, where the line is gone and the brave customers who dare to try the pepper from hell are taking careful bites and fanning their mouths or watching or dancing. Dylan's right. A cover charge would be dumb, considering the number of folks who just come to join the party.

Not to mention, the girls are selling Fireball shots faster than we ripped the tops off vanilla ice cream cups.

"Sin Wagon" by The Chicks starts up, and boots are stomping.

Craig yells at me. "Get up here!" And I look up to see him shaking his ass with the girls to Praise the Lord and pass the ammunition.

Holding up a hand, my eyes scan the room until I spot Liv at Miss Gina's booth, hovering over her mom, who appears to be on her second cup of ice cream with the blueberry fire sauce.

"I can't tell you what I'd give to see you and Liv dance together again." Dylan is carefully rolling the plastic gloves inside-out from her hands and depositing them into the trash behind the bar. "You two could set the room on fire. You were hotter than anything I could cook up."

Huffing a laugh, I try to play off the surge her words provoke in my lower stomach. "I haven't danced with Liv in years."

"I bet you remember how."

She goes to the sink behind the bar, and I watch as she takes out a tub of coconut oil to slather all over her fingers and fingernails. My eyes drift again to the back booth, and this time, Liv's eyes meet mine.

A careful smile curls her lips, and my feet carry me in her direction without even being told. I cross the room, through the stomping, singing, and laughter. When I get to their table, I lower to a squat, so I'm not hulking over them.

"Hello, ladies, can I bring you anything?"

"Garrett Bradford, have they got you waiting tables?" Ms. Plum reaches out to squeeze my forearm.

"I offered to help out, but don't get excited. I'm not much of a waiter. Can I bring you some drinks while you still have taste buds?"

"I'm safe!" Miss Gina waves her hands, laughing. "I'm too old for all this spicy food. I might not survive it!"

"I don't think it matters how old you are." Liv leans into her side. "I'm not having any either."

"I ate all of theirs!" Ms. Plum waves a hand over three empty ice cream cups in front of her.

"You didn't eat mine!" Rachel cries, and I lean to the side to inspect the two partners in pepper-crime.

"Purple lips." I nod, like I've cracked the case. "A dead giveaway."

"What!" Rachel's eyes widen. "Are they…?" She taps her phone camera to inspect the damage. "Oh, no! Zane can't see me like this. I look like I drank all the grape Kool-Aid!"

Ms. Plum only laughs. "I don't have anybody to impress. I'm only sad it's over."

Leaning closer, I speak out of the side of my mouth. "I bet I can get you some more."

"Would you?" She bounces in her seat, eyes sparkling like a little kid at Christmas.

"Is my brother over here asking Liv to dance?" Dylan skips up behind me, wrapping her arms around my neck.

"Ahh," I stand, and she holds on, gripping my waist with her knees and moving to a piggyback. "Get off me, banshee!"

I swat at her like a sasquatch.

"Please dance with Liv for me!" Dylan's head tilts to the side. "It'll be just like old times."

"You and Liv danced together?" Rachel's eyes widen, and she looks from me to Liv.

I can't help noticing Liv's cheeks are bright red, and she

appears to be sinking lower into the vinyl beside Miss Gina as if she's trying to hide.

"Are y'all having a party back here without me?" Allie runs up, climbing into the booth behind Rachel on her knees. She puts her elbows on the back of the seat and leans forward. "What'd I miss?"

"Apparently Garrett and Liv are some kind of dancing duo!" Rachel shouts over the strains of Disco Inferno.

"What?"

"You should've seen them," Dylan coos from where she's still on my back. "They were like Johnny and Baby. It was hot."

"Are you saying they didn't leave room for Jesus?" Allie's brow arches, her hazel eyes flashing.

"Only if Jesus were really, *really* thin." Dylan laughs.

"I dance better than Baby." Liv sits a little straighter, seeming offended.

"You'll do it?" Dylan's entire body bounces higher on my back.

"That's enough." I reach around and poke her in the ribs, which makes her squeal and hop off me. "Liv doesn't want to dance with me."

"I don't believe it." Dylan sits on the edge of the booth beside my ex. "You love to dance, just like I do. I remember how happy you were dancing."

"I stopped dancing a long time ago." Liv's eyes drift to her lap.

"But why?" Dylan's voice is soft, and I know my former prima-ballerina little sister can't imagine anyone would give up something she loved so much unless she was forced.

"It's a cut-throat, misogynist field." An edge is in her tone.

My little sister hesitates, then she wrinkles her nose. "Nothing like practicing law."

Liv's lips twist, and she narrows her eyes playfully. "Touché."

"Oh, Liv." Dylan shifts in her seat, hugging her. "It'll make you smile, I just know it will."

My chest is tight as I look down at her. I can't think of anything I'd like more than to hold Liv in my arms and sway to the music like we used to do, but I'll be damned if I'm about to pressure her to do anything.

"What do you think?" Her eyes lift to mine in a hesitant question.

"I'm not cutting any throats, and I have only the utmost respect for women."

Her green eyes roll, and she shakes her head, laughing. "If I even remember how."

"I bet you remember."

I bet she remembers a lot of things.

Chapter 3

Olivia

WE DON'T GRIND.

Garrett puts a hand on my waist and clasps my hand in his other in a respectable pose. I hold his muscled shoulder, and we leave plenty of room between us for Jesus.

Dylan and Craig were clearly in cahoots to make this happen, because all the hot disco songs have suspiciously changed. There's no more Pitbull, no more Chappell Roan or Donna Summers. In their place is slow-dance, heartstrings-pulling country.

We're currently moving in time to "Under My Skin" by Nate Smith. My eyes are fixed on Garrett's chest, and his large hand holds mine so gently. He's not forcing me. He actually seemed as uncomfortable as I was by Dylan's persistence.

I'm not mad at her. Dylan might as well be my little sister for how close we were growing up, and we were both dancers, even if we were on different ends of the spectrum.

She was a classically trained ballerina on her way to the

American Ballet Company in New York—until an accident ended her career.

I was the precision dance line and drill team captain with my sights set on the biggest professional cheerleading team in America. Until I saw too much behind the scenes.

Still, we loved to dance, and Dylan is so nostalgic. Of course, she wanted us out here.

Now I'm listening to my heart thundering in my ears louder than the sultry song. I'm thinking about the bead of sweat sliding down the center of my back. I'm thinking about being in these arms I thought I'd gotten over years ago.

I'm not over them. They still make me feel safe, like I'm going to be okay.

Garrett's been walking around this restaurant all night in those jeans that show off his fine ass with that apron barely covering his broad chest. The short sleeves of the tan Cooters & Shooters T-shirt he's wearing stretch painfully over his biceps, and I steal a glance up at him only to get a shock from my chest to my toes when I meet his blue eyes.

His full lips curl in a careful smile, and he leans closer. "Is this okay?"

My chin lifts, and I'm nodding before I speak. "Dylan's so sweet. She just misses the old days."

Only something is different about my oversized partner. I can sense how much he's changed in the years we've been apart. When we were in high school, Garrett was the loud, boisterous, baby brother of Jack and Zane. It's a status that ended when Hendrix and then Dylan were born three years later, but he'd been the youngest long enough for it to be ingrained.

He was never afraid to speak his mind, and I fell in love with his big personality. I loved everything about him—his laugh, his brash fearlessness, his confidence, how he took what he wanted… Until it turned on me.

Until that night in Baton Rouge when it all fell apart.

A knot twists my throat and I lower my chin. The song

changes, and the strains of "Chasing After You" by Ryan Hurd begin. A noise of approval ripples across the room, and it doesn't take long before we're surrounded by lusty slow dancers.

They push and nudge, and with a gentle tug, Garrett pulls me closer, all the way to his chest. I don't resist. My eyes close, and I don't even question it. It's so easy to let go and let him lead me.

Moving to the music against Garrett's body is truly like riding a bike. Two measures, and I'm right back to where we used to be all those years ago. Every chance we could get we were together, touching, dancing, holding on like we'd never let go.

Our hips move in time, and we sway like an old love song our bodies remember. We're keeping it clean, but we're much closer than we were one song ago.

My cheek rests against his chest, and we let the music guide us. The scent of citrus and soap and memories wrap me in a spell, and I'm not the sad lady who came here with her tail between her legs to care for her injured mom. I'm that girl who used to have it all.

I'm the girl who knew exactly what she wanted and how she was going to get there. I'm that girl who loved so fiercely, she couldn't imagine it ever slipping away.

"I love chasing after you…" Garrett has a great voice, and it's a wash of warmth through my chest.

He always did that when we were in school. I'd jump on his back, and he'd walk on, carrying me and singing. I'd sing along, harmonizing if I could hear it. It makes me smile, when I think about how beautifully golden we were.

I could never forget something this good, this fundamental, this real.

The song ends, and I take a step back as if waking from a dream. My eyes rise, and when they meet his, he seems as affected as I am.

"Want to go for a walk? It's nice outside." His large hand still holds mine, and I nod.

"Sure."

I don't even notice as we pass through the bodies, heading for the screen door that leads to the small kids' playground out back. It faces the bay, and there's a little beach outside the fence leading all the way down.

He gives me a nudge, and I see he grabbed two Corona longnecks on the way out. Must've been when we passed the bar. The perks of owning the place, I think to myself.

"Thanks." I smile, looking up at him as I take it.

"Figured you might be thirsty."

He has no idea.

The water shushes quietly onto the shore, and my eyes lift to the sky. It's black with a full yellow moon right in the center painting the waves with silvery tips. I'm sure the sky is full of stars, but there's too much light pollution for us to see them here. If we were out in the pasture south of town, it would be a different story.

We walk slowly along the edge of the bay until we reach the end of the sand. We reach the point where a massive log stretches into the water and behind it is thicker foliage. It's probably leftover from one of the hurricanes, but the sturdy bushes keep us from venturing farther.

"Have a seat." He holds my hand, and I sit beside him on the log.

I expect water turtles climb up here during the day to bask in the sun. I imagine it's the same three turtles who gave their names to the restaurant. What did he call them? A laugh puffs through my nose.

"What?" He glances up at me from where he sits.

"I was just thinking about Snappy, Happy, and Earl."

"Oh." He takes a sip, grunting a laugh. "Kimmie loves those guys."

"That's Jack's little girl?"

"Yeah. Jack's a single dad, but he's really good at it."

"He always was." I think about his serious oldest brother.

Jack stepped up when their parents died and held the reins

on this crazy bunch of kids. He kept them close, like a good big brother. He was always so good at everything.

Garrett takes another sip of his beer. The air is heavy with all the words we might say to each other right now. It's not the first time we've been together since The Last Time, but it's the first time we've been alone together. I have no idea where to begin.

He's the first to speak. "I've been wondering why you're back here all by yourself."

I pick at the label on my beer. Nothing like getting straight to the point.

"I'm not by myself." I lower the bottle, giving him a wink. "I'm here with you."

He huffs a laugh. "You know what I mean. Last I checked you were married. Now it looks like you're not wearing a ring."

Looking down, I spread the fingers of my left hand, studying the third one. It's been over so long, it doesn't even have a suntan line. I don't even carry a trace of that mistake.

"It didn't work out."

"He must be a real loser." It's a low retort, almost lost in the sip of beer he takes.

Squinting one eye, I study my companion. "You don't even know him."

"No, but I know you. Olivia Bankston never gives up. She gives 120 percent, and she doesn't quit until she's sure it's a lost cause."

It's not teasing or judgmental. The last words carry a tinge of regret, almost like he's thinking the same thing I am. Almost like now after all this time he recognizes how hard I tried.

"I couldn't get pregnant." The words fall out of my mouth so fast, I can't stop them.

Like heavy marbles pressing against my lips. Like that old musical *My Fair Lady*.

"What?" He blinks up at me, stunned.

"I'm sorry." I cover my mouth with my hand.

"No, don't apologize. I wasn't trying to pry or make you tell me…"

"Of course you weren't." I shake my head, letting it all out, unable to stop it. "We couldn't get pregnant, and I didn't want to do fertility treatments. He said it was because I wasn't committed to our marriage, but it wasn't that."

"He sounds like a total dick." A growl enters Garrett's tone, and I almost love him for it.

"He was right. I didn't want to put my body through all that… that difficult, costly ordeal. I didn't want to do all that hard, emotional work to create a baby with a man I wasn't sure was my forever." I look at the bottle in my hand. "So I blamed my job. I wanted to be a partner. I was just getting established at the firm, and I wanted to be taken seriously."

"Nothing wrong with that."

"They gave the partnership to Graham Turgison." My eyes blink up to his. "They said I'd probably want to start a family soon, and I'd be glad not to have all the extra hours and work being a partner would require."

Garrett shakes his head, letting out a low whistle. "A whole bag of dicks… Dammit, Liv, that sucks. I'm sorry."

"The best part is I was right." I laugh wryly. "He was sleeping around, all over town."

"God…" Garrett pushes his hands against his thighs. "I hate this guy."

"Of course, he tried to blame me. He said it was because he wanted kids, and I wouldn't give him any."

"Now I really hate this guy. He didn't wrap it?"

"No, but don't worry." I hold up my hand. "I've been tested, and he didn't make it worse by giving me a lifelong parting gift."

"What a dick," he quietly fumes.

I feel weak and wrung out, like I've been holding onto this information, and I finally let it go. I let it go on the guy I always knew I could trust. The guy who didn't deserve to hear it.

"I'm sorry for dumping that on you." My voice is quiet, and my cheeks heat. "I don't know why I said all of that just now."

A large hand covers mine, giving it a tight squeeze. "Because I care about you, Liv. Your secrets are safe with me. They always have been."

Lifting the bottle, I take another long sip of beer. It's true, but it's still cringe.

"Do you know how humiliating it is to ask for an STI test when you're married? It's like admitting everything is fucked up. It's like a big *loser* stamp right on your forehead."

"You are not a loser, Liv, your asshole ex is the loser." A huff slips through my lips, but he's right. I won't argue. "As for being embarrassed, I bet that nurse didn't even think about it. Hell, they test us all the time for shit. It's just another day."

"Well, it's not for me."

We're quiet again, both with our forearms on our legs, our feet in the sand, looking out at the water.

"So it's over?" I can't tell if he's concerned or merely curious.

"Yep, I signed the final papers before I left town."

"I'm sorry."

"You don't sound sorry."

"Okay, I'm not sorry you divorced that jerkoff. I want to drive to Birmingham and kick his ass right now."

A laugh bursts from my throat, and I cough on my sip of beer, covering my mouth with my hand as I wait for it to pass. "I'd love to see that."

"You're too smart for a guy like that." He takes a sip of beer. "You're way out of his league."

"Oh, am I?" I sniff, not feeling it.

My eyes drift to his, and his expression has changed. The warmth I saw earlier, the care, has melted into something proud, maybe even a little possessive.

He looks at me like he's remembering something we stopped doing a long time ago. His brow lowers, and my core tingles to life. I remember a time when a look like that led to me climbing onto his lap. It was a time when doing what we wanted was as easy as walking around the block.

"We'd better get back." He stands, holding out his hand. "Your mom's probably wondering where you are."

I doubt she is. I'm sure she saw me walk out the door with Garrett Bradford, who has always been her favorite, and her night was made.

Still, he's right. We can't stay out here alone any longer.

Pushing off my legs, I stand. "You're right. We'd better get back. It's late."

I walk briskly, but he keeps pace. The awkwardness has fallen away, but I think we're on the same page about this not being a good idea.

It doesn't take long to be back at the screen door leading into the large dining area. The crowd has died down, almost like they know when it's time to start settling down. It's a Thursday night, after all, and Cooters & Shooters is a family restaurant, not a bar. It only has these moments of madness once a week.

Garrett catches my forearm before I step through the screen door, into the open room where our family stands around in a smiling, laughing circle. Rachel's brother is there, and they're all so easy and comfortable. So familiar and homey.

Hesitating, I turn to face him, and he puts a finger under my chin, lifting my eyes to his. "Chin up, Cherry. When you're at the bottom, there's only one way to go."

"Unless there's a shovel."

Shaking his head, he chuckles. He's happy, and excitement tingles low in my stomach.

He's touching me, getting angry at anyone who would hurt me… fanning the smolder still hiding deep in my heart for him. The painful flickers of a fire that never went out.

I'm afraid of this feeling, but I can't fight it. It's lingering in the air around us, and I know it'll only take one weak moment to let go.

Chapter 4

Garrett

"HERE YOU ARE. I THOUGHT WE WERE GOING TO HAVE TO SEND A search party." My little brother Hendrix weaves through the crowd of family, grabbing my hand and pulling me into a hug.

I say little brother, but it's only because he's almost three years younger than me. Hendrix is a six-foot-two rockstar tight end in Los Angeles, and trust me, he knows how to use it to get all the girls.

If my little brother's head gets any bigger, I'll be searching for a pin to prick him. The good news is, he's got a shit-load of our dad in him, which is why he's the best player out of all of us. The even better news is he's got enough of our mom in him to keep his feet on the ground and give him some heart.

"Hendrix finally got here!" Dylan rushes forward, grabbing him around the waist in a hug.

He only laughs and noogies her head, which makes her squeal and pull away. These two are eighteen months apart, and

I swear, if our mom hadn't been so determined to have a baby girl, they'd have stopped with me.

I'm glad she didn't, but it was pretty crazy having two little babies in the house.

"Can my honeymoon be staying right here in Newhope all week with my family all together?" Dylan holds onto Hendrix like she hasn't seen him in years, which I guess is almost true.

It's his first visit home since last Christmas.

"No." I glance over to where my best friend looks like he just swallowed a Trinidad scorpion pepper. "Bruh, you nearly gave Logan an aneurysm. He's finally taking some time off from the radio station."

Logan walks to where we're standing and pulls his girl into his arms. "All thanks to Zane. I'm finally getting to where I'm comfortable being gone."

Our tall, quiet older brother stands on the periphery watching us with a satisfied smile like he always does. Rachel's younger brother Edward stands beside him holding a gray cat. Miss Gina gave it to Dylan as a kitten, and now it lives at the restaurant eating scraps and mousing.

"I need to find my mom." Liv's voice is quiet, and she turns as if she'll leave.

"Wait!" Dylan catches her hand before I can. "Will you come to my bachelorette party tomorrow night? It's going to be here, and it's going to be so fun. Just Rachel, Allie, me, you, and—Oh, come meet Raven! Raven, this is practically my sister Liv Bankston."

"Hi, practical sister!" A girl a little taller than Dylan, but not as tall as Olivia steps forward. She has nice curves, and her brown hair has pretty golden highlights in the front. "I'm Raven Gale."

Liv laughs. "Nice to meet you, Raven."

The two shake hands. "You can call me Rave if you want. I'm testing out nicknames."

"That's fun—how do you two know each other?"

"Dylan and I chaperoned the senior cruise a few years back,

and we just hit it off. We've been swapping pepper recipes ever since."

"I haven't met the new addition." I walk over to where they're chatting.

Raven holds the back of her neck squinting up at me with a grin. "Dude, how tall are you? Dang, I've never met someone so big."

"Six-four, but there are guys bigger than me on the team."

"I can't even imagine how much they eat." Her sparkling brown eyes are laced in gold.

"I'm so glad you're here!" Dylan hugs her waist. "I hope it wasn't an inconvenience for you to do this."

"Are you kidding? I am so happy to be here!" Raven cries. "I've been wanting to visit ever since you told me about the restaurant and the Dare Nights. I'm so sorry I missed most of it."

Dylan's hand slides to Raven's. "Come meet my brother Hendrix. You'll be walking down the aisle together. Hendrix, this is Raven."

Hendrix is talking shit to Zane, and when he turns around, his eyes flash. It takes every bit of strength in my body not to make a wisecrack. That boy is as transparent as a window pane, and I can tell he likes what he sees.

Somebody should warn Raven, because she seems like a nice girl.

"That's a cool name." He puts both his hands around hers, giving her that panty-dropping grin. He even adds a wink. "What do you like to do for fun, Raven?"

I really am about to drag him away, but she surprises me.

"Call me Rave." Her chin lifts, and she shakes her hair back with a touch of defiance. "I'm a meteorologist, so I chase storms."

"You're kidding?" His voice rises. "Are you one of those poor reporters struggling to stand up in the hurricane while you tell everybody to evacuate?"

"That's me!" She nods, laughing and ducking her head. "I

almost ended up in the ocean one time, but as you can tell, I'm not so easy to knock down."

She motions to her body, and I guess she's trying to say because she's not a stick figure she can stand up to 100-mile-per-hour winds. I think she looks good. I'm about to counter that I'm not sure a guy as big as me could stand up to a hurricane, but Jack walks in with Allie's son Austin, distracting me.

Allie's eyes light, and she skips over to meet him. "Here's my guy! How was school? How did the extra practice go?"

Austin shrugs, making a noise as he glances around the room embarrassed. Total teenage boy.

He's gotten a lot taller since I saw him last, and he's filled out. He looks like he's been pumping iron. Hell, he looks like he's ready for college ball.

"Don't be like that." Jack's voice is barely audible as he gives the kid a nudge.

I'm surprised it makes me nostalgic. I remember how many times Jack guided us after our parents died. Well, all of us except Zane, I guess. They were too close in age for that kind of stuff.

"Sorry, Mom." Austin steps forward, leaning down to give his petite mother a hug. "It was good. Coach Jack helped me a lot."

"Okay!" She blinks up at him like he hung the moon, even though he didn't give her any additional information. "Are you hungry? Thomas has burgers on the grill, and Dylan made this deliciously spicy blueberry sauce to go over ice cream. Help yourself."

She tries to reach up and muss his hair, but he turns, headed for the kitchen. I want to say something, but Jack is on it.

"He's doing really good." His voice is low, and he gives Allie a tight smile.

"That's good!" Allie leans her arm on the bar, rising onto her toes in front of my oldest brother.

She hangs on his every word, sliding a lock of hair behind her ear, and lightly biting her bottom lip. The tension between them is palpable from all the way over here, but my oldest brother is all business.

"I think he's ready to be QB-1."

"Oh, Jack!" Allie gasps. Her hands clasp, and she raises them to the bridge of her nose. "You're so good to him."

I swear, if she cries…

"He's got a lot of talent." My brother wipes a hand across his jawline. As a high school football coach, he's accustomed to dealing with emotional parents, but still. "Austin's a good kid. He works hard, and he takes instruction well."

She's blinking up at him, and I'm about to groan from the pain of wanting to push them together, when I notice Liv slipping away.

Shit. I want to walk her to her car.

Turning to the group, I do a little wave. "Nice to meet you Rave. Save some of those hurricane stories for me."

"Will do!" she calls, and I hustle over to where Liv is helping her mom get the walker over the doorstop on the floor.

"I didn't think you'd be back so soon," Ms. Plum mutters fussily. "Your lipstick's still in place."

Liv's brow furrows. "I don't know what you thought would happen tonight."

"I thought I'd catch a ride home with Rachel and Miss Gina so you two could have some alone time, but they left while I was getting more spicy blueberry sauce."

"How many did you have?" Liv softly scolds, but when she sees me approaching, she blinks away fast. "Nevermind, I need to get you home. You're tired."

"I'm not tired." Ms. Plum sounds like Kimmie when she needs a nap, and I can't help but chuckle remembering what Liv said about her mom treating her like a servant.

"Can I offer you ladies some assistance?"

"Oh, no, it's okay—" Liv starts, and I wish it didn't feel like she was retreating from me again.

I'm pissed as hell over what she's been through, and I want

her to feel safe talking to me. I want her to know I've changed, and I wouldn't treat her like the clowns she's been dealing with these last few years.

Or like the clown I was in college.

"That would be lovely, thank you, Garrett." Ms. Plum puts her hand on my forearm, nodding overtly at her daughter. "You never know what might be lurking in a dark parking lot."

"I doubt there's much more than a opossum or a raccoon, but that gravel can't be easy for you to manage with this thing."

She exhales a frustrated huff. "I'll be glad when I'm off this walker."

"That makes two of us." Liv follows beside me, carrying all their things—her mom's purse and her sweater.

She's wearing a pretty red dress with a cherry pattern on the skirt and some kind of little ballet shoes with straps. I just noticed her in her signature color with her namesake fruit. Hell, I haven't been able to tear my eyes from her pretty face or her soft hair or her sad smile all night.

"Y'all just let me know if you need any help." I stop at the gold Lincoln Towncar her mother has driven for years. "It doesn't take me any time to walk to your house."

I used to do it all the time when we were in high school. I'd climb in her window after dark and sneak out before dawn. My stomach tightens at the memories, and I wonder if Liv still remembers. I wonder if it aches for her, too.

"We will!" Ms. Plum sings out, and I expect I'll get a call.

"Thank you, Garrett." Liv reaches out to touch my arm. "For everything."

It sounds so final. "We've got all weekend. Dylan's got all kinds of fun stuff planned."

"Right." She nods, helping me help her mom into the back seat before going to the driver's door. "I'll see you at the wedding."

"If I don't see you first." I don't want to let her go this way.

Luckily, she takes the bait. Her cute, upturned nose wrinkles, and she squints at me. "I've never understood that reply. Does it mean you're going to avoid me?"

Exhaling a light laugh, I shake my head, reaching up to slide my thumb along the side of her cheek. "Not me. I'd never avoid you, Cherry. I'll be looking for you."

Her cheeks flush, and she looks down to open the door. "Goodnight, Garrett."

I step back to let her go, softly bidding her goodnight. For several minutes after they've left, I stand in the parking lot watching the taillights fade. My stomach is tight and I can't decide if this was a good night or not. Was that a final goodbye or a longing one? How could I know for sure?

Laughter echoes from the restaurant, but I don't feel like going back inside. Instead, I turn and walk up the hill to our family home where Dylan and Logan now live, and where I'm staying for the wedding.

Zane and Rachel briefly lived with them as well, but now they have their own place with Edward a little farther north, closer to Miss Gina's.

I've just reached the door when my phone buzzes in my pocket.

Hendrix: You getting back with Liv? Fuckin A! Give her that BDE.

Jack: What's BDE?

Hendrix: Something G's got in spades. When are you going to give Allie yours? It's literally painful to watch.

Jack: Don't start with that.

Does anybody say BDE anymore?

Jack: Don't make me google.

Hendrix: They should. Tell us about Liv.

Nothing to tell.

Zane: Big Dick Energy.

Jack: Is that still okay?

Zane: It better be, or Grizz is in trouble.

Hendrix: Why is there no Liv news? She's great. I remember how happy you were together.

She's been through a lot.

Zane: So help her heal.

That's rich coming from you.

Zane: Hey, I know what I'm talking about.

Logan: Where's the Grizz I know and love? Get that girl!

Hendrix: You want the woman? You take the woman.

Logan: The Three Amigos!

Hendrix: And G says I'm the dork…

Zane: Did you forget how? Need me to draw you a diagram?

Yo, Z? 👍

Jack: What's stopping you?

It's not what she needs, and I'm not fucking this up again. I've changed.

The chat falls silent, and I continue upstairs to get ready for bed. Energy is in my veins, and I'm sure I won't sleep. I only want to see her again. My arms ache to hold her, and I want to kiss her pain away, remind her how things used to be.

Truth be told, I want to do a little more than that. I want to see if we still have the chemistry we had so much of all those years ago. Back when we used to say *I love you*.

My phone vibrates, and I look at the screen.

Jack: How can we help?

Just be cool. Are we taking Logan out tomorrow night? Getting him shitfaced before the wedding?

Zane: Yeah, the girls are having another girls' night at the bar.

Hendrix: We might have to crash it.

Logan: Dylan will hate that.

Dylan will get over it.

Chapter 5

Olivia

"WHO NEEDS MORE PURPLE DRINK?" ALLIE DANCES BETWEEN US carrying a gallon jug of what I'm pretty sure is grape Kool-Aid mixed with Everclear.

I took one sip, and I was scorched from my throat all the way to my stomach.

"Me!" Rachel holds up her hand.

"Oh, me too!" Dylan waves, and I squint an eye at her.

"Remember you have to walk down an aisle tomorrow." I lightly note.

"Not until the afternoon—Good thinking, Dylan!" Rachel holds her glass up for a cheers.

"The golden hour is so beautiful at Miss G's. It was either late afternoon or early morning, and I know this crew."

Allie's right there like the true New Orleans lady she is. "You're definitely having another. It's your bachelorette!"

"Just as long as I don't barf all the way through the

ceremony." Dylan puts a hand over her eyes as Allie gives her a heavy pour.

Then she skips over to where I'm sitting on a barstool beside Raven.

After spending all day taking care of Mom's chickens, gathering the eggs, making sure they had food and gravel and water, she practically shoved me out the door.

"It's a short walk. You don't need to drive," she ordered. "Have fun with your friends."

"I'll have fun, but I can also drive." I tried to go back, but she held me outside.

"If you drive you'll have to be responsible." Mom shook her head. "I don't want you to feel like you have to come home early. Or even at all!"

My eyes narrowed. "Why do I feel like the only adult in the room?"

"I don't know, but stop it. Be young and have fun."

She closed the door on me, and my shoulders dropped. I shook my head and turned, walking the short distance that brought me here to my friends and the warmth of a small, close-friends bachelorette party.

Dylan wears a sash that reads *Mrs. Logan Murphy* in gold glitter. A tiara is on her head, and Allie pins a button on her that says *Same Dick Forever.*

She was not allowed to cook, so we all chipped in for pizza. Rachel brought a cooler of beer, but a few sips of purple drink has me reaching for a bottle of water from the refrigerator behind the bar.

"Are you really a storm chaser, Rave?" Rachel leans over the bar, batting her green eyes at the newest addition to our group.

Rachel's blonde hair is in crinkled waves down her back, and she's in black leggings and a long-sleeved, mint-green sweater. I'm just as casual, although I'm wearing jeans and a short-sleeved red tee. My hair is loose down my back, and I'd just washed my face before Mom shoved me out the door.

"I mean, not like in *Twisters*." Raven's pink lips twist. "Although, that looks like so much fun."

"Depends on how you define fun." Allie leans into my ear, and I shrug.

"I've never been much of a daredevil."

"I'm trying to get a job on the Gulf Coast," Raven continues. "I'd love to be somewhere around here, where the weather gets really intense. Atlanta's so basic, weather-wise."

My lips press into a frown, and I'm not sure what to say.

"Logan might be able to help you." Dylan's voice is thoughtful. "He really only does sports radio, but he might know somebody at the TV station."

"Really?" Raven grabs her hand. "I would love that so much! Can you imagine if I was here with all of you?"

"It would be a lot of fun, but now I'm nervous." Dylan makes a cringey smile. "I don't want to get your hopes up if he doesn't know anybody."

"I mean, it doesn't hurt to ask." Raven shrugs. "It's the thought that counts."

"Well, there are no hurricanes tonight—unless it's Hurricane Dylan!" Allie gets us back on track, cranking up the dance music. "Are you allowed to tell us where you're going for your honeymoon or is it a secret?"

"It's a secret—even from me!" Dylan hops off her chair, brown eyes dancing. "I only know it's somewhere in Mexico where I can pick hot peppers straight off the vine, and the chef is going to teach me some new recipes."

"Cooking on your honeymoon?" Allie's nose wrinkles. "That doesn't sound like fun. I swear, I don't understand all these people posting videos of them cooking on vacation. If I see one more post about homemade ravioli—"

"Don't be grumpy!" Dylan nudges her side. "You know I love finding new pepper recipes. I think it's very sweet of Logan not to complain."

"He is sweet." Rachel waves her hand. "Now it's time to play! I've got some good ones tonight."

"Tell me about this game." I take a sip of my drink, and Raven scoots closer to the bar.

"I've played it before," she says. "It's Fuck-Marry-Kill. You get three options, and you have to sort them."

"Only we make it harder." Rachel digs in the bag and pulls out a little plastic hourglass. "You only get one minute to decide. No flailing."

"A minute should be plenty of time—" I start.

"You'd think so, wouldn't you?" Allie's brow arches, and she nods, knowingly.

Dylan passes out slips of paper, and Rachel is right behind her with pens. "Write it down, so you don't forget when everyone starts talking."

Rachel wobbles her tipsy head. "We're just getting started. Mine are the best."

Digging in her bag, she pulls out a notebook. "2000s TV stars… Adam Brody, Jared Padaleki, Chad Michael Murray. Go!"

My nose wrinkles. "Can we throw them all back and try again?"

"Your turn is coming." Rachel sniffs. "Now go!"

"I'm done!" Allie cries.

My pen is still hovering over the paper, but I shrug. "I don't guess I can go with kill, kill, kill?"

"It's like that horror movie," Raven cries. *"Bodies bodies bodies!"*

"How's this?" Allie dives right in. "Fuck Adam, marry Jared, kill Chad. Am I right?"

Dylan's nose wrinkles. "I would kill Jared. He was so annoying on *Gilmore Girls.*"

"But he was Sam on *Supernatural!*" Rachel argues.

"Not as good as Jensen Ackles. Why wasn't he in the mix?"

We're about to devolve into arguing when I hold up my finger. "I have one we can do. It just came to me. Ready?" Everyone scoots around and nods. "Robert Pattinson, Taylor Lautner, Billy Burke. Go!"

"Ew, kinky." Allie wiggles her eyes. "Throwing a dad in the mix."

"I know who you're going to pick," Dylan murmurs under her breath, and Allie shoves her side. "Oh, Zaddy…"

Dylan waggles her eyebrows, and Allie squeals. "Shut UP!"

"Time!" I hold up a finger. "Who's with me?"

"It's all on the line, Liv. MFK is the true test of friendship."

"Fuck Taylor, kill Robert, marry Billy!" I toss my pen on the table, holding up both hands in triumph, but only Allie high-fives me.

"Seriously?" I study the group. "Who are you killing?"

"I killed Robert!" Rachel's eyes are bright. "But I married Taylor."

"He's such a baby, though!" I argue. "Billy's more mature."

"He is not a baby, and I bet he's got stamina. He's a were-wolf, after all." Rachel's smile is naughty, and Allie screams.

"Rachel is so kinky! First she wanted the pierced dick then she wanted Jason Momoa, and now she wants a werewolf. Does he change or stay in his wolf form when he takes you?"

Rachel's cheeks flame. "I don't know. Either way, it's still him."

"Okay, my turn." Allie continues the game.

I lose track of time amidst all the laughing and screaming and arguing. They're right about bonding over the game. I've had too much purple drink, Dylan's weaving as she gets more snacks, and I'm really, fucking happy here. I'm so behind at work—I shudder to think what my desk will look like when I get back to Birmingham.

Then I exhale a sigh, wondering why I'd even go back to Birmingham.

Three phones buzz at once, and I look around to see Dylan, Rachel, and Allie tapping on their screens. Raven and I exchange a glance.

"Wow, I've had FOMO before, but this is kind of next level," Raven laughs.

"Tell me about it. We are not cool."

"Here," Raven scoots around. "Give me your number, Liv, and I'll text you."

I lean forward with a little snort and hand it to her. She types in her number and quickly sends me a text. My phone lights up, and I grin when I look down and see what she sent.

> Raven: You're pretty. I bet you're good at chess.

My fingers fly over the screen as I quickly reply.

> You're really good at the weather. I bet you know all the storm names.

"Oh my gah! Look at them!" Dylan cries, oblivious to our teasing.

Running around to where we're standing, she shows us a text from Zane.

> Zane: Logan's getting a lap dance from two hot blonds.

She hits the triangle *Play* button on the face, and music blasts. My eyes widen, and I'm almost afraid to look.

Logan sits in a chair with a very uncomfortable expression on his face, but when they all burst into cheers and cat-calls, I lean closer to see.

Sure enough, two blonds in gold, metallic hot pants and shiny white-satin crop tops flank him. One twirls around behind the chair, holding his head back against her chest. The other in front straddles his legs and thrusts, hopping closer and closer to him in time with the music.

My brow furrows, and I notice they're shaped oddly for women. Their waists don't curve, and their shoulders are too broad… and one has a beard.

"It's Craig and Garrett!" I shriek.

They're wearing their blond wigs from when they dance on the bar at Thursday Dare Nights. Craig is behind Logan, sliding his hands up and down Logan's chest, and Garrett puts his finger on his lips, acting coy.

Logan's hands rise, and he looks like he'll try to escape by pushing them away.

Garrett is quick to stop him. "No touching! Those are the rules!" He's using a fake-feminine voice, and we're all screaming-laughing.

Garrett's knees bend, and he tries to sit on Logan's lap without success. "Don't sit on me, you big ape!" Logan yells. "You'll break my legs!"

"Rude!" Garrett's expression is offended, and he straightens at once, turning to shake his ass in Logan's face.

We're still cheering, and I wipe the tears from my eyes. "Oh, my God, I love him." I say it on a laugh-induced exhale, and the room falls quiet.

I look around, and four pairs of eyes stare at me expectantly.

"It's an expression!" I cry. "I just meant I love his sense of humor!"

"Oh, sure. It's an expression. Don't be uncool." Dylan's words are a little slurry, and I can tell she's hitting a wall. "But if you really meant you *love* him, that would be okay, too."

She leans hard into me, and I glance up at Rachel and Allie. "I'd better get the bride-to-be home before we all get in trouble when she can't make it to the wedding."

"We'll clean up, and I've got the keys to lock up the restaurant." Allie scoops up the paper plates.

"I can help!" Raven skips around to gather up the leftover pizza. "I'm staying at the house, so it's no problem."

"How will you two get home?" I pause, considering Allie and Rachel do not live in walking distance. "I don't think I should drive anybody anywhere."

"It's all good," Allie waves before collecting the empty cups.

"Austin agreed to pull chaperone duty for the night. I just have to text him."

"He's hanging out at our place with Eddie." Rachel adds. "Watching *Pool Sharks.*"

"In that case." I wave, pulling Dylan's arm around my shoulder. "I'll see you all tomorrow at Miss Gina's."

We're out the door heading up the hill when my quasi-little-sister rouses.

"Oh no!" She lifts her chin, looking around us in the dark. "Did I fall asleep at my bachelorette party?"

"No! You just had a little too much jet fuel." The path from Cooters & Shooters to the Bradford family home is white gravel illuminated by small lights close to the ground.

When we reach the house, I lean her against the wall as I inspect the yard ornaments. "Can you stay right there while I get the hidden key?"

"We don't use it anymore." She shakes her head. "Logan installed a special combination lock. Check it out."

Lifting her finger, she flips a cover back then circles it over the keypad before punching in six numbers.

"I think that's it." She mutters, and I hope the hidden key still works when the satisfying shush of a lock sliding tells us she was right. "There, see? I did it."

Her tone is slightly surprised, and I laugh as I hook my arm around her waist again, leading her inside. "Muscle memory."

"It got me through many performances." She waves a finger over her head. "You, too, I bet."

She guides me to the guest room across from the kitchen, and I stop at the door. "Can you take it from here or do you need me to help?"

"I think I've got it." She turns around in a complete circle before returning to where I'm standing at the entrance to her bedroom. "I wish I'd known you were going to be in town. I'd have asked you to be one of my bridesmaids."

"It's really okay." I smile, tapping her nose. "I won't hold it against you."

"Just imagine you walking down the aisle with Garrett."

My stomach twists, and I swallow the knot in my throat. "That would've been interesting."

Her lip pokes out, and she puts both hands on my shoulders. "Tell me the truth, Liv. Is there any hope for you and Garrett or is that all over… ancient history… lost treasure?"

"I'm not sure what you're talking about, but I'll bring you a bottle of water and some ibuprofen. You *do* have to walk down an aisle tomorrow."

And I need to get away from here and catch my breath.

"I'll wash my face." She stumbles back through the room to the bathroom, and I hear the water start as I return to the kitchen.

Opening the refrigerator, I grab a bottle of water. Then I dig in my purse for a small, plastic tube of pain relievers.

I put a brown pill on her nightstand with a water bottle beside it. I can hear her brushing her teeth, and I'm about to go when the water switches off and she returns to me.

"You can't walk home in the dark by yourself. Just spend the night."

"Then I'd have to walk home in the morning, when I'm feeling worse. It'll only take a few minutes, and you know Newhope is one of the safest places on Earth."

"Still, there are gators and opossums… And raccoons! Some of them have rabies."

"I haven't heard about any rabid raccoons." I pat her shoulders. "But I'll sleep on the couch for a few minutes. Now get in bed and go to sleep."

"Oooo, I love you, Liv!" She gives me one more, tight hug, then turns and goes into her bedroom.

I stagger over to the sofa, wondering how long I have to stay to fulfill my promise of staying a few minutes. I decide a few is two, and I sit down, taking out my phone to look at my emails from work. I told everyone I was taking a little time away to care for my mother, and I even set up a responder email.

Still, there is so much work piling up in my inbox. Leaning to the side, I don't even realize my eyes are heavy until I open them again. The house is pitch dark, and I'm comfortable and warm on the buttery leather sofa.

Someone put a blanket over me, and I blink hard in the darkness, trying to get my bearings. A noise from upstairs sounds like light snoring. The scent of citrus and soap greets my nose, and I have the distinct sense of a body nearby.

Sitting up slowly, the blanket falls, and I freeze when I hear the shuffle of something heavy moving around on the floor right in front of me. My heart beats faster, and my lips part. I'm about to say something when the body rises to a sitting position.

"Did I wake you?" It's Garrett, whispering.

"No!" I whisper back. "I think I just woke up… I heard a noise."

The soft snore sounds again, and we both look at the wooden staircase leading to the second floor, where all the siblings' rooms used to be.

"Logan didn't want to see the bride before the wedding day." Garrett tilts his head. "He's sleeping upstairs in Zane's old room."

My lips press into a smile, and I look back at him. "Why aren't you sleeping in your old room?"

"I don't know." He shrugs. "Jack and I showed up to crash the bachelorette, but you'd already left. I didn't want you to leave again without me knowing."

I'm quiet, unsure what to say. I think of him trying to find me, and affection warms my chest.

Exhaling a soft hum, I glance around the dim living room. "This reminds me of high school, when we'd get home late after away games, and I'd sleep on the couch."

It's his turn to be quiet, and I wonder if his mind has gone to the same place as mine. Back in those days, I'd start on the couch and end up in his bed.

My stomach tightens, and I move the blanket aside. "I'd better get home so I'm not completely dead at the wedding tomorrow."

"I'll walk you." He hesitates. "If that's okay?"

Another flush of warmth moves through my body at his gentle concern.

Tilting my head to the side, I smile. "It's okay."

Chapter 6

Garrett

THE MOON IS FULL TONIGHT, AND EVEN AT THIS HOUR, IT CASTS A silver glow over the wide path. It's a short walk to her mom's cottage, but we're taking it slow. We're taking everything slow, considering how much water is under this bridge.

In the past, when we were teens, she'd hop on my back, and I'd hold her legs as we made this walk. Her arms would be around my shoulders, and her cheek would be right next to mine.

Sometimes she'd tilt her head to the side to tell me something, and her lips would brush my ear or my neck. Sometimes I'd turn my face and kiss her for it.

Soft lips, cherry lip gloss. I remember her sleeping over at our house, starting on the couch and ending in my bed, her body draped over mine, kissing those lips again and again.

Now, walking beside me, she's like a beautiful vision. The moon tips her hair in shiny light, and I want to reach down and take her hand, thread our fingers.

The water washes against the sandy shore, and I look out at the bay. I think about the old sailors who'd been out to sea a long time seeing land for the first time. They'd fall to their knees and weep for joy.

In a way, that's me. I'd pushed these feelings down so far, I didn't realize how strong they were until she came into my sight again.

"Dylan showed us the video from tonight." She grins up at me. "You guys were having a lot of fun."

"Yeah," I nod thinking about the party. "Logan's a good sport."

"Isn't his dad some kind of billionaire, media mogul?"

"Yeah, but Logan's not like that. He likes a good joke."

"He'd better, considering the crew he's marrying into."

Exhaling a laugh, I remember Logan's protest at getting a surprise lap dance. First he tried to fight it out of consideration for Dylan, but when the music started and he saw us prancing out, everything flipped.

Being with my brothers and Logan and Craig, seeing how comfortable and easy they all are, having fun and enjoying life, it made me wonder why I'm still so far away. Only a few years ago New York felt like where I belonged. Now I feel like an orphan in the big city.

"It looked like you girls had fun, too." I glance over to where she's sliding a long piece of copper-colored hair over her shoulder. "Allie said all the purple drink was gone."

"Gah, that purple drink," she groans. "It's like straight alcohol!"

"I heard y'all got a little crazy."

"Not too wild." Her eyes dance up to mine, and they're almost pure green, outlined in gold. We're at her mom's house, and she turns to me. "I think Dylan'll be okay, and I'm planning to sleep in. You'd better get some rest, too. You've got a big day tomorrow."

"I walk down an aisle." I hold out my hands. "I don't have to say anything. I'm not even in the spotlight."

"You're always in the spotlight." A tease is in her tone.

She puts her hand on the ornate iron railing and takes a step up.

I take a step closer. "Maybe we can dance again… at the wedding." I want to keep her here with me a little longer, but I'm fumbling for what to say to make her stay. "I liked dancing with you the other night."

Holding her in my arms was pretty incredible.

She nods, exhaling with a wistful smile. "I liked it, too."

She takes another step up, and I take another step closer. "Liv?"

She hesitates, looking down at me confused. "Yes?"

"I was just thinking, it's really late."

"I know." Her brow quirks.

"I heard somebody say one time, what happens after midnight doesn't count."

I move closer, and now I'm on the step just below her. At my height, it puts our faces on the same level. I'm close enough to inhale the soft jasmine of her skin, to see the way her lashes flutter as she blinks down to my chest.

"What doesn't count?" Her voice is a soft whisper.

"Like if I kissed you goodnight… Would that be okay?" I'm holding the reins, but my voice cracks with the longing twisting in my chest. How would it feel to have one more hit of cherry lips? "Just for old times sake?"

Her thick lashes flutter, and I'm hanging by a thread.

"I don't know…" She seems to be filtering through all the reasons. "Is that a good idea?"

I swallow the air in my throat. "That's the best part. It's after midnight, so it doesn't count."

Green eyes capture mine, so serious. "I think for us it always counts."

Moving slowly, I put my hand on her waist, remembering how good it felt to hold her close when we danced, remembering how good it all felt.

"Sure, but this time…" My voice is quiet. "It'll be our secret."

She puts her hand on my shoulder, and I take another step. Now I'm all the way close, looking down at her bright eyes, her pillow lips, dewy in the moonlight. Her breasts rise with her breath, slightly faster, and I'm so tired of fighting. It's so late, and not so long ago we were both asleep mere inches apart.

"It's still night." I move closer. "Pretend it's a dream."

A wish. A memory…

Her body sways closer to mine, and we're chest to chest. I don't know who caves first, but another breath and we're together.

My warm lips cover her full ones, and they slide before parting. Tongues curl and caress, and breaths mingle. My arms tighten around her waist, and I pull her, lifting her fully against my body.

Her fingers curl at my neck before moving higher to trace into my hair. She whimpers softly and a low groan vibrates in my chest. My arms tighten at her waist, and hers wrap around my neck. We're clinging to each other like we can't get enough.

Faster kisses, my lips nip and pull hers before tracing a line to her jaw. Dragging my teeth along her skin, I could devour her. She exhales a whimper, and my dick jumps.

Fuck, I can't even let my mind go to sex. It's too much.

We're holding so tightly, but she's the first to break the spell. Her body stiffens, and her hands unclasp, sliding down to my biceps before stopping, gently pushing.

"We're really tired, and it's late. We shouldn't let things get… blurry." Her voice is thick now, and it's physically painful to let her go.

Nothing about this moment for me is blurry. It's sharp as glass. I want her.

Still, I can't force her.

Nodding, I don't speak through the ache in my throat. I lift my hand, lightly tracing the line of her jaw, forcing a smile, before turning away and practically jogging back the way I came.

"I don't say this much anymore, but I wish I could see right now." Miss Gina leans against my bicep as I walk her down the aisle to a vaguely familiar classical song. "Everything feels magical."

The elaborate gardens of Miss Gina's huge, Italian-style mansion on the bluffs north of Newhope are decorated with white twinkle lights in all the trees and shrubs. White flowers are wrapped around trellises and columns, and the towering crepe myrtle trees are adorned in lights and white ribbons.

I don't know much about decorating or throwing weddings, but this place looks pretty damned good. Craig is in the back in a suit, directing people to their seats, and somewhere his boyfriend Clint is overseeing everything happening today.

"It's something to see," I lean down to speak softly in Miss G's ear. "They've got white flowers all over the place, and some kind of sheer fabric over the arch. Those little white Christmas lights are strung in the trees and over the arches. They're pretty much everywhere."

"It sounds breathtaking!" Her blind eyes flicker to the sky, and her face glows with happiness. "I'm so glad they had it here."

"Dylan's been in love with this place all her life." I give her a nudge. "Then she met you."

"I don't know why she wanted an old maid in her wedding. Isn't that some kind of bad luck?"

I almost laugh. "I don't know how it would be, since it's her wedding. I think having you here is a little like having our mom with us."

Dylan's never said it, but I suspect she thinks of Miss Gina as her surrogate mom.

"Garrett, that's so sweet." Miss Gina lifts a slim, trembling finger to her lips. "I never thought anyone would think of me that way."

I hold her hand and wrap my arm around her shoulders, gently pulling her into a hug. "I think you'd be surprised how many people would like to think of you that way. If it wouldn't be too presumptive."

We're at the front with Logan, and I release her. He gives us a grin, and I lift my chin at my best friend. Who knew he'd come here and steal my little sister's heart? Who knew she'd steal his right back?

The music continues, and I watch as Hendrix escorts Raven down the short aisle. Their lips move almost imperceptibly, but their eyes dance. I can tell they're cracking jokes the entire way, and I grin. This is an interesting development I'll be keeping my eye on.

Next up is Zane and Rachel. His brow is set, his expression is serious, but Rachel holds his arm smiling at the familiar faces in the crowd. Her light hair hangs in soft waves around her shoulders, and she holds Zane's arm so tightly.

I'd think she was clinging, but when they get to the front he looks down at her with an intensity that removes any doubt. My older brother is in deep smit. I've never seen him so in love.

Jack and Allie are right behind them, and Jack's as serious as Zane. At the same time, he gives a little smile when he sees a face he recognizes.

With his square jaw, blue eyes, and straight white smile, I swear, our oldest brother is too perfect. He was a legendary quarterback before he walked away to take care of us. Now he's turning out legendary players at the high school.

Allie dips her chin, and her thick, dark hair slides in a shiny curtain across her cheek. She says something, and he covers her hand with his so fast. His brow lowers, but she shakes her head. Still his shoulders are tense and ready.

Twisting my lips, I have to fight rolling my eyes. My

brother might act like he's immune, but he doesn't miss a breath where Allie is concerned—or her son. One of these days he's going to crack. I'm only worried I'll be too far away to give him shit for it.

Kimmie is up next, skipping down the aisle in a little-girl white tulle dress with a big yellow ribbon. She has a basket of ivory petals she scatters along the way, and a black-and-white kitten chases after her. I'm pretty sure she's taunting it.

Edward and Austin follow her. They're dressed in suits and ties, and Edward's expression is dead serious. He leans down to grab the miscreant kitten, quickly tucking it under his arm. Austin only grins, like the blossoming first-string quarterback he is, cocky but sweet.

It's our family, and I study them all, thinking how each of us fits exactly where we should be.

The music changes, and everyone stands. My throat tightens, and I'm caught off guard by the surge in my chest when my baby sister steps into the aisle. Thomas escorts her, and his chin is lifted. He's so proud, and she holds his arm so tightly.

Fuck, I swallow the knot in my throat, doing my best not to cry. I knew this was coming. Dylan told us Thomas was the closest thing we have to our dad. They played ball together. They started the restaurant together. He works with her every day in the kitchen, helping with recipes, guiding her steps. At every major holiday, the two of them prepare all the meals.

Now he's walking her down the aisle, filling in for our dad, and it's exactly right.

Dylan lifts her chin, and she's beautiful. Her dress is straight, ivory lace, and over her head is a long veil extending to the floor in front and back. Her dark hair hangs in thick waves down her back, and her amber eyes shine as they focus on Logan. Cutting my eyes to my friend, I see his jaw tighten. He blinks a few times quickly, and his lips part.

He's seeing his future, and I can't lie, I almost feel like I get it. My eyes leave them to travel into the crowd, to find Liv.

She's tapping her eyes with a tissue, and she leans closer to her mom.

Pastor Conrad steps forward to conduct the ceremony, and I gaze around the perfectly planned venue. The sun is setting behind the house, and the sea breeze lifts the curtains and the ladies' skirts. It ruffles my hair, and when my eyes return to the guests, I watch it slide Liv's long bangs over her eyes.

She reaches up to move them away, and I remember the feel of her slim fingers in the back of my hair. I think of my hands around her waist.

Our kiss has been on my mind ever since it happened. I told her it didn't count, but damn, that was a lie. I don't think it was just me, either. The soft noise that slipped from her throat as I kissed her deeper haunted my mind all night. I had to adjust my fly every time I thought of it.

Now she's sitting out there beside her mother, and I'm trying not to wish this would all hurry up and finish. I'm so ready to touch her again.

The pastor asks for the rings, and I watch as Kimmie skips forward with her basket. Edward very seriously takes a velvet pouch from his pocket, placing it on the Bible before stepping back.

It's the final step in the process, and I glance down the row at all the girls dabbing their eyes. Dylan gazes up at Logan as they say the words, *With this ring, I thee wed.*

My sister raises her hands, helping her husband lift the veil off her face, and once it's gone, he looks at her like he's discovered a new land.

Devotion glows in his eyes as she steps forward. My sister gazes up at him with so much love. Their lips unite, and the entire place erupts with clapping and whistles, cheering and cat-calls. Everyone has been waiting for this moment.

They're pronounced husband and wife, and finally, it's time to party.

"Why did I drink so much purple drink last night?" Allie holds her small bouquet over her forehead, leaning hard on the table.

"You must've had more than I did." Liv slides a hand over her shoulders. "I'm not feeling too bad today."

"I was sampling the recipe as I mixed it." Allie moans.

"Here." Jack puts a plate of tiny meatballs and small, round toasts in front of her. "See if that helps."

"My hero!" she cries, grabbing the plastic fork and stabbing one. "Give me five more of these, and I might come back to life.

Clapping erupts from the other side of the patio, and I glance over to see Dylan and Logan emerge through the French doors leading to Miss Gina's elaborate foyer.

"Thank God they let us escape. I'm going to be green in every wedding photo." Allie squints at the crowd. "Is that Logan's dad?"

Sure enough, Kellan Murphy stands near the front of the group to the right of the doors. He's dressed in a clearly expensive wool suit, and his chiseled face is not smiling as always.

"We should introduce him to Aunt Thelma." Our grandmother's youngest sister is lurking around somewhere in her old lady brown dress and matching jacket.

She drove all the way down here from Birmingham, and I bet all she'll do is nit-pick everything.

"She brought Kimmie an American Girl doll." Hendrix snorts from where he's standing beside Raven. "Kimmie screamed and ran away crying."

"I told Aunt Thelma she doesn't like the eyes." Jack slides his hand down the front of his suit coat, seeming frustrated. "She never listens. Dylan didn't like them either."

Raising my voice, I lift a chin at my brother. "She needs to show Aunt Thelma her cooter."

Rachel leans forward, almost doing a spit-take, and Allie collapses on Liv's shoulder laughing.

"What other choice does she have?" Liv nods, and that does it.

I'm not letting this girl go without at least another kiss.

Everyone's lining up for food, but now that the bride and groom are here, the DJ cranks up the music. It's time to make my move.

"Are you hungry?" I lean down to take Liv's hand.

A hint of a smile is on her lips, and her nose wrinkles. "I had a little snack before we came, so I'm okay for now."

"Good. Let's dance."

The first notes of that old song "Shivers" begin, and I lead her to the dance floor. We're not the only ones skipping the line. Dylan's veil is gone as she squeals trotting over to join us in the patio space marked off as a dance floor.

"My favorite dance partners!" Her hands go over her head, and her hips twist.

White lace spins around us, but my eyes are on Liv. Our bodies are together, and we groove, closer than ever, letting the rhythm move us in time.

The knee-length skirt of her coral dress swishes around her long legs, and my hands are on her waist. Light sparkles in her eyes, and she smiles up at me like she's having as much fun as I am.

When the song changes to another old one by One Direction about stealing my girl, I can't hold back a laugh. "Really, Cray? Did you make this playlist?"

"With Dylan's help!" Craig struts onto the floor holding the hand of a tall guy in a tan suit, who I assume is formerly closeted Clint.

When Dylan sees them, she squeals and slow-struts in time to the music over to where they're dancing—if you can dance to this.

The three of them hold hands rocking their hips side to

side, until Logan leaves his dad on the sidelines and walks straight across the floor to pull her into his arms.

Leaning down, he kisses her nose. "Nobody's stealing my girl."

I glance back at his dad, and for the first time since I've known him, Kellan Murphy breaks into a smile. He's proud of his son, and Logan is so wrapped up in his wife and his new life, it doesn't even matter anymore.

"What's that look about?" Liv's hands are on my shoulders, and she's studying my face.

"Good things are going to happen tonight." My eyes return to her pretty ones before sliding over her shiny hair down her cute nose to her bright eyes.

"I'd say they already have."

"And we're just getting started."

The song changes to something by Justin Bieber, and the DJ comes on to announce the bride and groom's first dance as a married couple. It's something about a lifetime, and I catch Liv's hand, leading her off the floor. We go to where Allie and Rachel are standing side by side, arms around each others' waists as they wipe away tears.

"Stop!" Liv waves her hand at them. "You're going to make me cry, too!"

My brow furrows, and I feel like I'm missing something. "Why is everybody crying?"

"Uncle Grizzlaaaaay!" That little voice shifts the mood.

The slapping of small patent-leather shoes on flagstone announces my niece running at top speed in my direction. I drop to a squat, and little arms go around my neck as I lift her off the ground.

"You did a great job tonight, Peanut!" She's crawling out of my arms, and she nearly pulls my coat off trying to get onto my back. "Hang on."

"Let me help you." Liv steps over, adjusting my little

monkey-niece into her preferred spot. "You're just a natural at piggyback rides."

Liv stands in front of me with her arms crossed and laughter dancing in her eyes. I'm not sure anything could feel more right in this moment.

"Aunt Thelma brought me a Chucky doll!" Kimmie's pouty voice is in my ear. "I started crying and Daddy fussed at me. He said I was too big to cry over a silly doll, but Uncle Hendrix said those dolls come alive at night and I don't want that ugly doll chasing me when I sleep!"

She buries her little face in the side of my neck. My eyes meet Liv's wide ones, and I take a turn away from the sounds of music playing. I have a lot of plans for tonight, but they're going to have to wait.

Following the path, I walk around to where a raised platform sits under a flower-covered arch. The bay is visible through the posts, and with the sun setting on the water, it's peaceful and lovely.

"Come here." I sit on the platform, and she stands up behind me, walking around to sit on my lap. I take her little hand in mine. "You know when Aunt Dee was a little girl like you, Aunt Thelma gave her one of those dolls every year at Christmas."

Her little head nods, and her lips poke out. It's funny how much she looks like Dylan at this age.

"I hid them all in the closet, and when Aunt DeeDee found them, she screamed, too. Lightning McQueen said he would protect me, but he's too busy getting married."

I swallow my laugh, both at her variation on Logan's nickname and imagining my sister opening a closet full of American Girl dolls.

"I don't think those dolls mean to scare little girls. I think they want to play with you and be your friend."

"But Uncle Hendrix said—"

"He was making a joke when he said that." Her round

eyes lift to mine, and I can tell that isn't going to cut it. "Still, I bet that new doll would feel a lot better with the other dolls, don't you?"

Kimmie nods so fast and hard, I'm worried she'll give herself a whiplash. "She needs to be with all those other bad dolls!"

"I'm not saying she's a bad doll. I'm just saying we'd all probably be happier if she stayed in Aunt Dee's closet with her friends instead of going home with you. Yeah?" Again she nods hard, and I chuckle, giving her side a poke. "I'll talk to your dad and take that doll home with me, but you can't tell Aunt Thelma, okay?"

Another serious look, and she lifts her little finger, crossing her heart and lifting her elbow, doing her best to bring it to her mouth.

"What are you doing?"

"Trying to kiss my elbow."

"Well, stop. You look like something's wrong with you." Reaching out, I grab her around the waist, standing and holding her at my side like a sack of potatoes. "Now let's get back to the party!"

She lets out the happy little-girl squeal I was hoping for. "Uncle Grizzlaaaay! Put me down!"

"What?" I yell. "I can't hear you over the music!"

She starts kicking her feet, and I lower her to the ground. The moment her shoes touch pavement, she's off running at top speed. "I'll show Aunt Thelma my cooter!"

I chuckle watching her zoom straight to the dance floor, and Liv pushes off a column, where I guess she was waiting or watching, eyes narrowed with a smile.

"I didn't even tell her to do that."

She shakes her head. "Has anybody ever told you you're pretty good with kids?"

Reaching out, I pull her to me by the waist. "I've had a lot of practice."

"I know, I was there, but you're especially good." Her hands rest on the lapels of my jacket. "Not all men seem to get that message."

"What message?" My voice is low, and I lean down to catch her eyes.

They flicker up to mine, and she shrugs. "Being good with kids is sexy."

The charge between us flashes, and I nod. "Never thought of it that way, but good to know."

"Very good." She turns, stepping out of my embrace but sliding her hand down my arm.

I stand for a moment, watching the sway of her hips as she walks to the dance floor. It only takes a minute for me to snap out of my daze and hustle right after her.

Chapter 7

Olivia

WE'RE SO CLOSE, IT'S PAINFUL. GARRETT'S LARGE HANDS HOLD MY waist, and his hips move with mine. He's always been a good dancer, and it's always been fucking sexy as hell.

Our faces are close, and that kiss floods my memory. It started out gentle, but it quickly turned demanding and possessive. I was hungry—make that starving, and it was a big fat steak. The slide of his tongue against mine, the feel of his hard cock against my stomach, had me antsy and adrenalized.

All night I dreamed of what it would be like to go further. Is it possible? Would he want that? The way he's moving right now makes me think he would. It was his idea to start kissing after all.

A Beastie Boys song starts, and the guys rush onto the floor.

"Get over here, Grizz!" Craig yells out, and a frustrated smile curls his lips.

He presses his forehead to mine. "Hold that thought."

My lips tighten into a smile, and I nod up at him. We've

been dancing closer and closer to the fire and now the flames are tickling my inner thighs.

"Liv!" Dylan wobbles up, still in her wedding dress, and puts a crystal tumbler of amber liquid with a bright red cherry in my hand. "I had the bartender mix this just for you. It's called a hot cherry because you love cherries so much."

"Ahh…" I do a U-turn with the glass and pass it right back to her. "No thanks. You know I don't like your hot stuff."

"It's not pepper hot!" she cries, passing it to me again. "It's cinnamon—Fireball and cherry bomb. Try it!"

Wrinkling my nose, I take a careful sniff. "It's your wedding day, and I hate to disappoint you."

"Then don't!" she cries, holding my arm.

It doesn't smell like pure alcohol, so I figure one tiny sip can't hurt. I tip the glass slightly, and I'm surprised when it doesn't burn. It's actually pretty tasty.

"Okay!" I smile. "Thank you!"

Dylan squeals, putting her arm around my waist. "It's named for you, Hot Cherry, now get out there and bag my brother!"

"Oh, shit," I laugh. "Keep your voice down."

"Please. You've been eye-fucking each other all night. Everybody sees it."

My face flames red, and I look around the expansive patio. From what I can tell, the guests all seem to be pretty wrapped up in their own situationships. Even our group seems focused on their own significant others.

Zane has his arms wrapped around Rachel, who's happily sitting on his lap. Hendrix and Raven have completely disappeared. Kimmie is passed out on Jack's shoulder, and he's sitting at a table with Allie, who keeps sneaking swoony glances at him.

"I think you're the only one watching Garrett and me." I squint an eye at her.

"Logan and I are about to leave for the guest cottage. I just want to be sure all my guests are covered." She bumps my hip with hers. "Garrett will have the house all to himself tonight."

Chewing my lip, I glance over to where he's lifting Craig off his feet and shaking him up and down. I almost snort. "I need to get Mom home—"

"She's already home!" Dylan cuts in fast. "She left with Aunt Thelma a little while ago, and they dropped her off on the way to the hotel."

"Mom left without telling me?" I'm not really mad, I guess.

"I said I'd tell you, and she said she'd send you a text."

Lifting my phone I see her message glowing on the face saying she got back safely and to enjoy my night. My brow arches, and I sense cahoots.

"Won't Hendrix be at the house?"

"He likes to get a hotel when he visits. He says it's too crowded on the second floor with only one bathroom." Dylan leans closer. "I think it's because he doesn't want us to know his business."

My eyes narrow as I look down at her.

I'm about to say she sure covered all the bases when Logan walks up and catches her around the waist. "It's time to consummate, Wife."

"Logan Murphy, if you throw me over your shoulder, I swear…" Dylan laughs, gripping his arm.

He pulls her away, and a large hand slides onto my waist, lighting up my entire body. "Everything okay over here?"

She waves, and I turn to look up at him. "Yeah…"

His blue eyes lock on mine, and my breath disappears. Clearing my throat, I manage a smile, although now all I can think about is consummation and empty houses and this hot cherry drink has me all warm and horny.

"I could use some water."

"Come with me." He takes my hand, leading us in the direction he took Kimmie earlier, away from the crowd.

I follow him down a flagstone path lined with deep green

bushes covered in gardenias. They're mixed with camellia bushes that will bloom later in the season. If Mom were here, she'd be going on about perennial gardens and whatnot.

The only thing on my mind is the man holding my hand, who's walking with a determined stride to a small, unattended bar station on the other side of a glass greenhouse.

"How did you know this was here?" I stop as he goes behind the bar and retrieves a paper cup from the cabinet.

His suit coat is long gone, and I watch the way his white cotton dress shirt stretches over his muscled chest and arms attractively. I want to untuck it from those black tuxedo pants, unbutton it, and slide my hand over his body.

"I helped Zane move some trees around last year." He opens a silver bin and stabs the cup in what sounds like ice. "Check this out."

He brings it up and fills it with water before handing it to me.

"What?" My eyes widen, and I bounce higher on my toes, looking at the ice nuggets filling the cup. "How does Miss Gina have Sonic ice at her house?"

"Look at this place." He laughs, taking the cup after I finish and drinking a long sip. "She has the best everything."

"I'm not sure she has the best *everything*." I rest my elbows on the smooth wooden surface, leaning closer to him. "Her floor show can't top a Thursday Dare Night."

"Is that so?" He leans down, resting his elbows on the smooth wooden surface across from me and grinning.

It puts our faces on the same level, and I smile, taking the cup from him and sipping some more, crunching a soft piece of ice between my teeth. "And she definitely doesn't have the best cooter."

He puffs a laugh, dipping his chin to swallow the water he nearly spit out. My eyes shine, and I love that I make him laugh. He always made me laugh.

We're close, and a comfortable pause falls between us. He

puts the empty cup aside and reaches across the bar to take my hand.

"Hey, Liv." His voice turns soft, and I watch as our fingers lace.

"Yeah?" My brow furrows.

He rotates my arm, exposing my pale forearm. He studies my skin as his palm slides higher to my elbow. My bottom lip goes between my teeth, and my chest tightens.

His gaze follows the path of his hand, and my breath stills as he lightly traces his thumb along the crease inside my elbow. It's the lightest touch, and it sends a shiver through my stomach.

Curious blue eyes flicker to mine. "Still a sensitive spot?"

My lips press together, and I nod, blinking slowly. "You know them all."

Holding my gaze, he lifts his hand to trace his middle finger from the hollow just behind my left ear, lightly down the side of my neck to my collarbone.

It causes me to drop my chin, and a lock of hair falls across my cheek. My eyes close briefly, and with every heartbeat, energy pulses through my body. Longing squeezes my lungs as I study his large hand holding mine.

"I haven't felt like this in so long."

"How do you feel?"

Hesitating, I search for the right word to describe it. *Seen* isn't right. *Valued* is too strong. It's something more subtle, more important. It's how he's always aware of what I need, like he's watching me... the way I watch him.

A soft laugh huffs from my lips. "Like you care about me."

He rounds the bar, coming to stand in front of me. Placing a thumb on my chin, he lifts my eyes to his. "You already knew that."

Studying his face, dark blue eyes, fine lines, scruffy, square jaw. He's not a boy anymore. He's a man now, and I'm a woman.

"I guess I thought it might've changed."

The muscle in his jaw moves, and the pull between us is

so strong it aches. "I think when it comes to us, some things never change."

My throat tightens, and my fingers tremble as I reach out to place my fingers on his waist, hard skin beneath soft cotton. I think about what I want—removing this shirt.

It's reckless and bold, and I can't stop myself. "One way to find out."

Stepping closer, he threads his fingers in the side of my hair forcing me to look up at him. "Don't say that if you don't mean it, Liv." His voice is rough. "Because I won't lie. I want more than a kiss from you tonight."

My skin is electric, my nipples tight, and wet heat slips between my thighs.

Placing my hands on his broad shoulders, I curl my fingers as I match his heated gaze. "I want more than a kiss."

His mouth covers mine before I finish speaking, and a soft whimper slips from my throat. He turns my head, and warm lips part mine, tongues curling together. Another soft noise as I pull him closer. Our teeth bump as our kiss turns hungry, and orgasm spikes in my veins.

"Oh, fuck," I gasp as those feelings, those old, intense feelings rage to life. "Where can we go?"

A growl rolls from his throat, and he cups my ass in his hands, lifting me off my feet. I wrap my legs around his waist, and I swear, if he wanted to fuck me right here against this bar, I'd let him.

Instead, he carries me away, farther from the music and the lights, to a small building. I can't tell if it's a pool house or storage shed, and I don't care.

The door closes, and our mouths crash together again. I'm on my feet and his hands are under my skirt, sliding up my thighs as little grunts and whimpers echo in the semi-darkness. In a snatch, my underwear is gone, and I exhale a sigh as he touches me.

My fingers fumble over the buttons on his shirt desperately, starting at the top, and my mouth is on his throat, moving down to his chest as salt touches my tongue.

"Wait." He reaches behind his neck to pull the shirt over his head in a sweep.

I exhale a sigh, but he's wearing a damn undershirt. With a little growl, I grab the hem, shoving it higher, practically ripping it to expose his perfect body. Garrett has always been big and perfect, a lined chest and stomach lightly dusted with brown hair.

"This has changed." I glance up at him from where my lips press against the top of his chest.

Two hands cup my cheeks, and he pulls my mouth to his for another kiss, opening mine and tasting my tongue, sucking my lip between his teeth and groaning hungrily.

"Just older, Liv."

"Also harder," I note, which makes him chuckle.

"I could get pretty hard for you at sixteen." He pulls the straps of my dress down and lowers my zipper. "I jerked off so many times to this body, I'm surprised I didn't have blisters."

A rough moan scrapes from my throat as he lifts and kisses my breasts, pulling a hard nipple into his mouth. My fingers thread in his hair, and I'm kissing every place I can find as his hands travel lower, returning to that space between my thighs.

"When did you have time to jerk off?" I whisper, thinking about how insatiable we were back then. "Oh, fuck."

My hips jump, and I almost forget where I am when he slips a thick digit into my core.

"Did I mention I still do?" He lifts his chin from my breasts and kisses me long and hard.

Another finger joins the first, and he slides them in and out, circling my clit with his thumb. I'm on my toes, holding his shoulders and riding his hand as his face moves to the side of my hair, to my ear.

It's another erogenous zone, and my lips part as cascades of pleasure race down my arms.

He holds me in place, pinned against the wall by his hard body, and my orgasm is rising fast.

I want more than his hand. "Garrett…" Kissing him once more, I push against his arms.

He releases me, and I look around the dimly lit room. It's some kind of work room, with a low counter across from us. I go to it, placing my hands on the smooth surface and looking back at him over my shoulder.

His eyes are hooded, and he comes to me, lifting my skirt higher as I lean forward and close my eyes.

"Perfect." His voice is low, and my pussy clenches.

Large hands span my waist, and his thumbs circle my lower back before moving farther down. He squeezes my ass, parting my cheeks and opening my legs wider.

My lips part and I pant. I know what's coming. I've been here before, and I know how good it feels.

Unzipping his pants causes a light touch of fabric against my oversensitive skin, and I jump, sighing softly. His hand returns to my hip, and I push up on the flat surface as his body draws closer.

Turning my head to the side, I move my hair away so he can find that place behind my ear at the back of my neck that drives me wild. His lips touch my skin and a new sensation, his scruffy beard almost makes me scream.

"This body…" His voice is low, and I'm clenching and desperate.

One hand is on my breast, kneading and pinching while the other is between my legs, fingers circling my clit.

I feel him long and hard at my backside, and I can't wait anymore. "Please…" I gasp.

He reaches down, gripping his cock and sliding it up and down before finding the entrance. "You're so wet for me."

Turning more, I find his mouth, pulling his lips with mine, curling my fingers in the side of his hair.

With one firm thrust, he's inside me, and I moan loudly,

rising onto my toes with the force. He hisses a swear, holding still a moment, as I stretch to accommodate him.

My legs tremble, and I'd forgotten how completely full it is to be with him. My fingers curl against the wooden surface. His fingers stroke up and down my clit, side to side and up and around, urging my growing orgasm as his hips start to move.

"So big…" I groan, dropping my head back against his shoulder.

He kisses my neck, sucking and pulling the skin between his teeth as his face moves behind to the center of my back. Flutters break out from my core down my inner thighs, and I'm so close to coming.

I've never had a lover like Garrett, who knows my body this way and is so focused on my pleasure. His arms are around me, and we move the way we dance, primitive and hungry.

He moves faster, and I meet his thrusts, sending him deeper, to that place only he can find. The incredible tension, the twisting pleasure grows tighter until it's too much.

I whimper with every hit, and he groans. He thickens, going impossibly deep, until he stops, holding me firmly against his body, pulsing deep between my thighs.

He groans through his orgasm, bending forward, his fingers still moving until I fly over the cliff, breaking with a shuddering cry. We both fall forward, and my inner walls clench and pull, spasming with orgasm as his hand holds me secure.

"Fuck, you still do it." He gasps, lifting his chin and dragging his lips over the top of my shoulder.

I don't know what he means, and I don't care. I'm coming so hard, I don't want it to end. He wraps his arm around my chest, holding my back against his front.

Sweat slips between our bodies, and I clutch his forearm, fluttering until I'm boneless. His mouth presses to my head, my ear, my neck, covering me with kisses.

As soon as I'm able to move again, he picks up his shirt,

pulling it over his shoulders as he restores the buttons before helping me zip my dress.

"I have the house to myself tonight."

I squint up at him. "So I've heard."

"Seems a shame to waste it."

Maybe this doesn't count. Maybe it's after midnight, and we're only taking a quick visit down memory lane. Maybe we have our own lives in vastly different locations, and we just needed a little hit of something special.

I only know it's been a long time since I was in this place, and I'm not ready to leave so soon. "Waste is a terrible thing."

His hand covers mine, and he leads me quickly out the back way, down a brick path to a gate and out to his waiting truck.

Chapter 8

Garrett

Lying on my back, I study my phone, thinking about everything that happened after we got to the house last night. Rolling onto my side, I'm not going to lie, I'm pretty sure that's the only time I've passed up sleep to be with a woman.

When we finally collapsed from sheer exhaustion, it was early.

Then when I woke up, she was fully dressed, standing over me, and very apologetic.

My younger brother's not letting me off that easy.

Is it possible to walk bowlegged from having too much sex? Is there such a thing as too much sex? These are all questions I'd be asking the brothers in the chat, and yeah, I'd be a little braggy about it… But I don't think Liv would like it. She wouldn't want me discussing our sex life with them, so I won't.

I rub a hand over the back of my neck. What makes me think she even cares?

"What the hell?" Craig sits back on his stool when I enter the kitchen. "Why does your face look like that?"

The tall slim guy I didn't officially meet last night, but who I know to be formerly closeted Clint stands beside him. They're both dressed in jeans and T-shirts, and their hair is neatly messy. If we were in that kind of town, they'd look like hipsters on the way to a specialty coffee shop.

As it is, we're in the kitchen of Cooters & Shooters, and the only coffee here is drip.

I can't say for sure, but I think we're all a little tired and-slash-or hungover.

"Good morning to you, too." I walk over to the pot of coffee and pour me a cup.

"Why do you look like somebody kicked your dog? Did Liv throw you out of bed? Were you snoring too loud?"

My brows quirk, and I shake my head. "Actually, I think she was trying to slip out without waking me."

Clint's lips twist in an empathetic frown, but he doesn't say anything, thankfully.

Craig, by contrast, who grew up with all of us and who has known everybody since forever, including Liv, sits back and crosses his arms. "So what happened? Liv doesn't play games, and she was *all* up in your grill last night."

I take a long, slow drink of comforting, hot coffee, and I kick around all the thoughts that have been warring in my head since she said she'd better get going when I caught her with one foot out the door at five a.m.

She was so pretty in the morning glow. Her cheeks were scuffed from my beard. Her lips were swollen from all the kisses… all the many, *many* kisses. I ate her pussy, she sucked my cock, she rode me backwards and forwards. At one point, we came so hard, we made monkey noises. Yet, there she was, barely making eye-contact as she thanked me for a nice evening.

A nice evening.

"I think it was sort of a rebound-type deal. You know, for both of us." I put the mug down and stare at it, not wanting to meet their eyes.

Rebound. It's what I settled on after she left with a polite smile, and an even more polite kiss.

It was so fucking nice, you'd never have known I'd had the tip of my dick in her ass for a good ten minutes while she yelped like a puppy.

"What does that mean?" Craig's face squints with a disapproving frown. "Rebound from who?"

I take another long sip of coffee, thinking how this hot, dark liquid sort of helps. I'm not about to tell him I wasn't rebounding from anyone. I haven't seriously dated anyone since I moved to New York, and being with her last night had me thinking all kind of crazy long-term, rekindling thoughts.

I was all in. Still…

"I don't want to share her private business, but I think we all know she was married."

Craig shakes his head like *duh*. "So? She hasn't had a ring on the whole time she's been here."

"Well, she told me she'd just signed the papers before she came." The day she left town, she'd said.

"Doesn't it take a while to get to the signing papers part? She's had plenty of time for a rebound." Craig crosses his arms. "I'm not buying it. *You* are not a rebound, my friend."

"Look, all I know is if you went through a painful divorce, it makes sense that a reunion-type situation with an old high school boyfriend would be a good way to get over it. Right?"

"Wrong." Craig shakes his head. "That is not how you get over it. A hottie in the club with a big dick is how you get over it."

"You're thinking like a guy, and a gay guy at that." This coffee really is helping me focus on reality. "Liv is a woman. Women like to feel safe in their sexual relationships."

"What the fuck?" Craig cries. "When did you turn into Esther Perel?"

"That's a total stereotype." Hendrix strolls in talking like he's been here the whole time and goes straight to the coffee pot. "Some women love to be sexually adventurous, take it from me."

I'm about to take it from him—and stick it down his throat.

"It's closed-minded to think all women are looking for their daddy," he continues. "Also, what's this about her mom and the walker?"

"Yeah," I exhale a laugh, distracting my urge to pick up my younger brother and throw him in the dumpster. "Apparently, Ms. Plum pretended to be lame so Liv would stick around for Dylan's wedding."

She didn't explicitly say it, and I don't know for sure, but I think her mom wanted us to have a "reunion" weekend as well. Ms. Plum was always on my side. It's probably because I always mowed her grass and helped her move furniture around and cleaned the limbs out of her yard after storms. She would say I was the son she never had.

The thought makes me smile.

"The important question is did you give her that BDE?" Hendrix waggles his eyebrows.

Craig makes a groaning noise. "Incorrect usage. You *have* BDE. You slip her a BD… or a BBD, depending on your persuasion."

"I'm not talking about having sex with Liv with you two big mouths."

"Uncle Grizzlaaaay!" That little voice shuts down all our locker-room talk.

"Lord, I love that little girl, but somebody turn down her volume." Craig puts his hands on his face.

Small shoes slap against the tile floor, and my niece bursts through the double doors, heading straight to me. Bending down, I scoop her onto my back, feeling a lot better since I had a mug of coffee.

"You're up early, Peanut. What are you doing?"

"Daddy said Uncle Craig was making omelets, and he said everybody was coming here for breakfast, and Aussie gave me a ride."

"I don't know about omelets, but I'll scramble up some eggs." Craig opens the door of the industrial size refrigerator and takes out a cardboard box.

"You're here with Austin?" I glance over to the doors. "Where's your dad?"

Our phones light up with a text.

Jack: Roll call.
Who's around for breakfast?

I glance up to see my younger brother's fingers moving over the screen, so I don't worry about it. I bounce Kimmie over to where Craig and Clint are dragging out shredded cheese, a bag of minced onions, green peppers, spinach.

Hendrix: Garrett's here with me.

It only takes a few minutes for the rest to reply.

Zane: Still in bed with my lady.

I half expect my formerly dark-horse older brother to include a selfie, but if he did it would be one of those artsy-fartsy ones with the sheet billowing around their entwined bodies with nothing showing.

Damn, my brain is fucked-up this morning.

Rubbing my forehead, I don't want to think about Liv leaving. I don't want to think about how it was only a rebound for her. I don't want to think about how she smiled as she thanked me so politely for a fun night.

The fucking earth moved under my feet. It was a fucking Carole King song, and she was so cool about it all. Sure, she was annoyed with her mom, but she actually gave me a hug and a smile. She was sorry she had to get back, but she'd been out of the office for almost a month. She didn't even want to think about the pile of work on her desk.

She acted like last night didn't count. That was my dumb, made-up rule, wasn't it? I could kick my own ass. All of it counted, from that kiss to the dancing to every single moment.

Logan: Headed to the airport. Dylan said I can't text while we're on our honeymoon, so y'all have a nice two weeks.

My head tilts to the side, and I glance back at Kimmie on my back. "What do you want for breakfast, Peanut?"

"Eggs! Eggs! I want eggs!" She bounces the stuffed, red turtle on my shoulder with every word.

"I've got all the eggs coming right up. You two head out and set the tables."

"I know how! Miss Allie showed me!" Kimmie wiggles, and I put her on her feet as she takes off like a comet through the double doors again.

"If only there was a way to bottle that." Craig shakes his head, turning to the stove and clicking on the fire.

"I'll make more coffee," I volunteer.

Lord knows I'm going to need some more. I'm going to

need a lot more of a lot of things to get over last night, and the only person I have to blame is myself.

"I loved that Hot Cherry drink." Rachel's head is in her hands. "A little too much."

"Kinda like what happened when Zane got *your* hot cherry," Allie stage-whispers, leaning into her side.

"Oh my God, Allie!" Rachel gives her a push then immediately grabs her head. "I shouldn't have done that."

My brother puts his arm around her, exhaling a chuckle as he hugs her closer. "Have some toast."

She snuggles into his side, and I remember when I thought they were cute. Sunny Rachel who finally dragged my grumpy older brother out of his shell. Now they need to get a room and stop being all happy in our faces.

"Try the cooter special with a side of sherry," Hendrix teases. "Or skip the soup and just do a shot of sherry."

"I have three cooters!" Kimmie hops onto her knees in the chair beside me.

My little brother snorts, dropping his chin. "It's too much."

Kimmie's eyes sparkle like she knows she's doing something, and she tries to stand. "Miss Olivia said their names are Snappy, Happy, and Earl!"

Reaching out, I hold her waist, wondering when Liv might've told her that. "Easy there. That's not safe."

She crawls into my lap. "She said I was just like Aunt Deedee when she was my age." Her amber eyes sparkle, and I can tell that makes her happy.

"You are." I give her a little pat.

"Like Dylan on crack." Hendrix laughs.

Kimmie makes a face at him before scooting higher to put her hand on my shoulder. "Crack is wack, Uncle Grizz."

"Oh, yeah?" For once today, I don't have to force a smile. "Who told you that?"

"Uncle Hendrix."

"Well, he's right, but don't let him teach you all his grandpaw slang. He looks slick and edgy, but he's not. He's a dork."

Hendrix flips me the bird. "I'm auramaxxing. You should try it."

"I'm afraid to ask."

"Develop an aesthetic. Sit in nature." He locks eyes with me. "Make eye contact."

"Knock it off, freak." I lift my hand as if to ward him off.

"Have a social life outside your love life," he continues.

"Pretty sure I'm already doing all that."

"If Garrett gets any more aura, he'll explode," Craig calls from the other end of the table.

"That's my boy Cray." I lift my hand to do an air high-five. "Always got my back."

Looking around, I notice Jack talking to Austin at the back of the room near the pool tables. Rachel's brother Edward is holding Smokey, the resident gray kitten, while he watches his friend Benji shoot pool.

"I think I'll head back to the house." I collect all the plates around me, while Kimmie climbs into Hendrix's lap.

"Snappy has aura." She crosses the red turtle's legs. "He's doing an athletic."

"Aesthetic," Hendrix corrects her. "It means your vibe."

"He has a vibe." She crosses the turtle's leg the other way.

"Don't teach her that crap." I give him a nudge.

"I don't have to teach her. KJ's smart."

"I make all fives in school." She nods, looking up at him.

"Good work." He pats her back. "Now, let's just get this straight. You don't have permission to like any boys until you're an old lady… except your dad, Uncle Zane, Uncle Garrett, and me."

Her little face scrunches. "What about Uncle Logan?"

"And Uncle Logan… Oh, and Uncle Craig."

"Uncle Craig only likes boys. That's why he's so gay."

Holding my nose, I do my best not to snort.

"That's correct, little queen, and don't you forget it." Craig touches her shoulder as he passes with Clint, and she nods.

"I'm going to marry Aussie." She lifts her chin with a confident smile.

Hendrix shifts in his seat, looking to where Jack and Austin are talking. "Does Austin know that?"

"I think so." Kimmie shrugs. "He takes care of me, and he's a quarterback like my daddy."

"Ahh… that doesn't necessarily mean—"

I decide to leave my youngest brother to untangle that mess, and I head for the kitchen. I'm halfway there when Jack catches up with me, holding the door so I can carry the plates to the industrial dishwasher.

"You okay?" His brow lowers. "I saw Liv on the way out of town. She was driving pretty fast."

"I guess she had to get back to Birmingham." I don't know what else to say, and I don't really want to talk about it, even though it seems everybody knows.

My oldest brother crosses his arms, watching as I finish loading up the dishwasher. I know he's waiting to walk with me to the house, and I'm tempted to clean the pots and pans as well just to see if he'll give up and go away.

I know he won't. Jack's took over the role of dad after we lost ours years ago, and he's not going to let any of us off the hook if we're hurting. Looking around, I decide to get it over with and head for the screen door down the hall from the kitchen.

He follows me out, down the short flight of steps to the path leading to our home.

"I'd say that was a pretty interesting development last night, but you don't look too happy about it." He cuts those blue eyes up at me. "It didn't start with Liv, though, did it?"

This guy. He doesn't miss a thing.

"I don't know." I shove my hands in my pockets, taking the path at a slower pace.

I said Liv used last night as an escape from the things that were troubling her back home, but hell, I did the same damn thing.

"What's on your mind?"

We take a few steps, and I guess if anyone would understand how I'm feeling, it's Jack. He didn't retire because he was injured. He was at the top of his game. He was a superstar on the way to being a legend when he walked away and moved back to Newhope with a little girl and a shitty divorce.

"I've been thinking," I start. "In a few short months, I'll be looking at another season. I'm not so sure my heart's in it anymore."

His hands are in his pockets, and he looks down at his boots. "You have one season left in your contract. Have you thought about what you might do when it ends?"

"I've actually thought about it a lot."

Glancing up at me, his brow quirks. "Radio?"

"Nah, that's Logan's thing. And Zane's. And yours, I guess."

"Not mine," he laughs. "I'm glad to stop in and chat every now and then, but I don't want to have to talk for ninety minutes every week. I can't believe Zane does."

"No shit. I couldn't believe it either." Looking up, we're almost at the house. "He's good at it, though."

"So what are you thinking?" He stops, turning to face me.

"I got my degree in criminal justice." Reaching up, I scrub the back of my neck. "I kind of always wanted to work in law enforcement. Maybe be a sheriff here in town. I just need to do the training. Hell, maybe I could even do it on the job."

His brows rise, but as he thinks about it he starts to nod. "I can see that. You'd be a damn good sheriff. You're intimidating as hell, but you're actually pretty even-keeled and fair."

"Thanks, bro."

Nodding, he takes a step and we continue up to where his

old Ford step-side is parked in front of the house. "I'll talk to Rodney and see what you'd need to do. I bet in a year we could have something lined up if that's really what you want."

An unexpected weight lifts off my chest. It's so surprising, it actually makes me want to laugh. "Sounds like a plan."

"All right." Jack smiles, smacking his palm against my shoulder. "Now you're looking more like my baby brother."

"Baby brother, my ass."

"For a few minutes you were a baby."

"Now I'm the man."

"You've still got some training, and I'm pretty sure there's a test at the end."

"I'll be ready. I was born ready."

"Okay, big shot."

"I'm also ready for you to do something about that Allie situation. Need me to help you like I helped Zane?"

"*You* helped Zane?" He makes a scoffing laugh, and I can't resist.

"Need me to draw you a diagram?"

His jaw tightens, and he doesn't say a word as he climbs into the truck. Still, I'm pretty sure I catch the hint of a grin.

Chapter 9

Olivia

"ARE YOU STILL MAD AT ME?" MOM'S VOICE SOUNDS CAUTIOUS through the speaker on my phone.

"No, Mom, I'm not mad at you." I transfer the call to my headphones as I sort through the new files on my desk. "I just don't appreciate you tricking me like that. I do have work to do, and you took advantage of the situation."

"I did, and I'm sorry." I can almost see her shoulders droop. "I just didn't want you to miss out on an important family event."

"It would've been easy for me to drive down for the weekend. The wedding was on a Saturday."

"Yes, but you wouldn't have done it." A tone is in her voice, and she's got me.

I can't argue with her.

I wouldn't have done it because Garrett was there. Hell, I spent the whole week after he arrived in town hiding at my mom's house and doing everything I could to avoid him.

I knew what would happen, and here I am, dealing with

the achy aftermath. Every time I move, I can feel how hard and how many times we screwed down memory lane.

He kissed me rough and demanding, then soft and savoring. He wrapped me in those muscled arms and held on as we soared through space again and again.

We collapsed back on the bed smiling at each other as the sheet descended lightly over our glistening bodies. Then we fell asleep in each other's arms, only to wake up and do it all again.

We revisited every position we'd ever liked as young lovers, back when we were learning what to do and how to touch each other for maximum enjoyment.

It was sexy and decadent, and I'm afraid to try and remember everything we did too much… I think at one point, the word *love* might've been uttered.

"Oh, God." Leaning forward, I put my face in my hands. I am *shooketh*.

It was arguably the best night of my life with a man who knows exactly how to turn me on, and when the light of day came shining through those windows, I ran as fast as I could.

I couldn't face the aftermath. If he'd wanted to shake hands and act like it meant nothing, I don't know what I would've done. The only thing worse would've been if he'd suggested we try to do long distance.

I'd have said yes.

Finding a video on Instagram of my mother dancing at a friend's birthday party the week before was my one escape, especially since she'd told me she was going to a church bingo game that night.

Garrett's eyes were still closed when I texted her to get to the bottom of that surprise reveal.

> How were you doing the chicken dance at Marnie Pickle's birthday party last week if you had to use a walker?

> Mom: New phone. Who dis?

You're too old for that line. You lied to me.

Mom: I only did it for your own good.

Shaking my head, I didn't have another word to say. She'd played me like a fiddle, and I had to get out of Newhope.

Not to mention, my heart was seriously melting for Garrett Bradford, and that was *not* a path I planned to go down twice. I'd already been to the end of that road, and it was slick with my tears.

There is no world where Garrett and I can be together. He's in New York, and I'm here. I'm not going there. He's not coming here. The end.

Now I need to work. Focus.

"Well, you have to come back," she continues pouting. "You lit out of here so fast, you left behind a dress and two pairs of shoes."

"I'll drive down and check on you in a few weeks, and I'll get whatever I left then."

"I love you, Olivia." Her pout turns defensive. "I only want you to be happy."

"I know, Mom. I love you, too." My tone is all business.

"Henny Lane misses you. She's still acting off, and I'm sure your sudden departure didn't help matters."

"Tell her to keep her beak up. I'll be there soon." *When it's safe.*

Looking down, I'm in my professional gray suit. My red-cherry dress is far behind where it belongs, with the childish hopes and dreams I put away years ago.

Or at least I thought I did.

The next time I go to Newhope, I'll be sure the coast is clear. I am not falling in love with Garrett Bradford again, no matter how good he is in bed.

Three weeks later

Dylan: Logan said you left pretty quick after the wedding.

Allie: Pretty sure she didn't even say bye. Not that I'm salty.

Sorry, Al, I was a little salty.

And running scared.

Dylan: What happened? Dammit! Did Garrett mess everything up again?

Oh, if only, then I wouldn't be tossing and turning in my bed every night. As hard as I try to block him out with work, I catch myself sitting at my desk, staring out the window at Vulcan and daydreaming about Garrett's mouth on my body, my mouth on his body, his mouth on mine…

Not at all! We had a really nice time.

Nice. I hate that word. It's what I said when I left him, and there was nothing nice about the night we spent together. It was dirty. Very dirty and very… *disorienting.*

Raven: Ew, I don't like the sound of that.

Dylan: What happened to you, Rave? You disappeared early.

Raven: I'll never tell 😏

Dylan: Oh, yes you will! Don't make me resort to blackmail!

Raven: I have no idea what… Oh. Not that. You wouldn't dare!

Allie: Well, now you have to tell us.

Raven: She swore an oath never to tell. The Aztec gods will know.

It happened on the cruise?

Dylan: Off the cruise 😈 A certain pepper farmer named Joaquin…

Raven: I'm leaving the chat if you say it.

Allie: Sounds like we need another girls' night to get to the bottom of this.

Dylan: That would be so fun! When is everyone coming back to Newhope?

I'm so behind right now. Give me a few weeks.

Raven: Logan wanted to talk about a job, so ask your husband.

Dylan: Hey… My husband! I like the sound of that.

Allie: As much as the sound of My Wife?

Dylan: Fifty-fifty

> See you soon, spice girls.

Dylan: Love it! Craig already calls me Pepper Spice.

Rachel: Don't go! I just got here! I was in the pool with Miss Gina.

Allie: Grape spice.

Rachel: You're Bookish Spice?

Allie: We'll workshop it. Cherry Spice for Liv, Stormy Spice for Raven—unless Sr. Joaquin changes things…

Raven: Joaquin is dead to me.

Dylan: He did not wash his hands very well 🤭

Raven: Goodbye, spice girls.

> Same—time for me to be a lawyer.

Dylan: Boring spice.

> Cherry kisses 😘

I put my phone down, but I don't go back to being a lawyer. Instead I slide my laptop into my messenger bag and pack up whatever I can take home for the day.

"Headed home?" Bob Semple, one of the head partners, stops me in the hall as I start to go. "Been through a divorce myself. I know it can be rough."

"Ah, no." I straighten my spine, giving him a confident smile. "My divorce was the best decision I've made in a while."

"Oh, I'm sorry, I…" He looks down.

"No worries." I continue, faking it til I make it. "I came in yesterday, so I've caught up with my desk. The rest I can take care of at my house."

"I see." He nods, seeming uncomfortable.

Instead of apologizing, I reach out and pat his upper arm briskly. "See you tomorrow, Bob."

Then I turn on my heel and stride to the door. As soon as I reach my gray metallic BMW, my shoulders fall. I pull the handle and toss my bag onto the passenger's seat.

On the way home, I make a quick stop at a Safeway to grab a pint of Ben & Jerry's Cherry Garcia, and when I get to my apartment, I pull on my plaid pink flannel PJs and pull up the old Cher movie *Mermaids*.

Curling up on the couch, I wrap a blanket around myself and eat my favorite ice cream as I watch Cher, Winona Ryder, and little Christina Ricci navigate life as a family of three girls on their own.

I remember watching it with Mom after my dad left us and moved to Tuscaloosa to start a whole new family. I didn't want to be Winona Ryder. She was so obsessed with the nuns and Jake Ryan, and I couldn't relate.

Instead, I wanted to be like Christina Ricci, the champion swimmer. That was who I'd be. I'd be the very best at something, and then he'd be sorry he walked out on us. He'd regret not wanting to be my dad. It's when I started dancing.

Only, he never saw me dance.

Then he died of cancer.

When I met Garrett and we became more than friends, Mom was so excited. She would tell me all the time Garrett was nothing like my father. He'd take care of me, and he'd never walk out on his family.

I believed her so much. I believed in him. Only she was

wrong. Garrett did walk away from me. The only thing that mattered to him were his own dreams, and when my plans didn't line up with his, he blew up everything.

He didn't realize I'd already seen what happened when my mom chose my dad's life over hers. She still ended up with nothing.

Lying on the couch, I don't know why I'm feeling like I'm going through that breakup all over again. I don't know why these tears are on my cheeks, and I'm eating ice cream and wallowing. I don't know why it hurts so much.

I got over Garrett years ago. It took a long time, but my broken heart finally mended.

Leaning my head on the pillow, I touch the tears away with my fingertips. I'm a strong, independent woman. I'm not crying over a memory of who I used to be.

Six weeks later

"Putnam and Barnes didn't disclose these new witnesses in time for depositions." I'm on the phone with Marcus Merritt in Chicago, my co-counsel on a pipeline deal gone wrong. "I'll have to request a continuation and get back to you."

"I'll tell my assistant to keep an eye out for your email."

I've always liked working with Marcus. He's a good lawyer, and he doesn't try to bulldoze everyone or be the biggest dog in the room. Possibly, because he's married to a successful fashion designer. Either way, he's a good co-counsel.

I do my best to be solid, dependable, and professional. If another lawyer is fucking up, I call him or her on it in a non-confrontational way. I approach everyone as if they're acting in good faith. If there's irregularity, I document it and put it before the judge.

I'm a peacemaker.

And I'm about to vomit.

"Olivia, I have this filing for the new platform off Dauphin Island." Graham walks into my office like he owns the place. "Porter is concerned we don't have the proper permits…"

He's halfway through his speech when I grab the can from under my desk and lean forward, barfing hard into it. It's loud and groany, and it takes me a minute to get a handle on myself.

"Oh my… lord," I gasp, reaching for a tissue box behind my desk. "I'm so sorry, Graham."

I take a moment to blot my eyes and cheeks, then I grab a few more and blow my nose before turning to face my horrified partner.

"Jesus, Liv, do you have a virus?" His hand is raised in front of his nose, barely hiding his scowl. "Perhaps you should take the rest of the day off."

Frowning down at my ruined trash can, I reach up to feel my head. "I don't have a fever. I wasn't feeling bad when I left the house this morning. Maybe I got some bad mayo on my sandwich at lunch?"

I'm so confused, but Graham is the exact opposite. "You need to go home. I'll let Porter know you're ill. Follow up tomorrow?"

"Definitely." Standing, I'm a tad dizzy as I move the briefs into my messenger bag. "I honestly don't know what just happened."

"It's okay." Graham holds his papers over his nose as he gives me a wide berth. "Don't come back until you're well."

The next day, I am not well.

After stopping by the drug store on my way home, I grabbed a box of Dramamine and another of Imodium just in case the vomit turned into something worse.

Racking my brain, I try to think of anything odd I've eaten, but nothing comes to mind.

I was at Mom's a few weeks, so I had to go grocery shopping

and purchase all new perishables. Not that I left anything in the refrigerator that could go bad.

I'm lying on my sofa inexplicably watching *The Muppet Show* on some streaming service when my stomach pinches with hunger.

Scrubbing my forehead, I don't know what to do. Hunger is a good sign, right?

I go to the refrigerator, and a luscious bosc pear sits on the top shelf taunting me. I'd bought a bag when I got home as a treat, and the first three were so juicy and delicately sweet.

I take it off the shelf and bite into the buttery soft skin. The cool juice is soothing to my dehydrated lips, and I'm loving it so much, when all of a sudden, my stomach twists like a sponge. It feels like it's turning itself inside out.

Dropping the brown pear in the sink, I run to the guest bathroom, barely making it to the toilet in time before the bite of pear shoots back out of my mouth.

"Ugh!" I sob, flopping onto my butt on the cold tile floor. "Why is this happening?"

I continue to vomit for three straight days—still no fever, no weird foods. Staring at my phone, I decide it's time.

Picking up the receiver, I dial my old GP's number and leave a message.

"Congratulations, you're pregnant." Dr. Beck stands in front of me scribbling in large, messy handwriting on a pad of paper. "Here's a prescription for prenatal vitamins, and I'll get you a prescription for Diclegis—"

"Stop!" My chest is tight as I shake my head. "Just stop right there for a minute."

Dr. Beck is an older fellow with a pretty decent sense of humor and a great bedside manner.

He sits back frowning at me. "What?"

"I'm sorry, but I am *not* pregnant. You've made a mistake."

"I have?" He says it in a tone that suggests he's wondering when I got my medical degree.

"Yes." I hold up both hands like he pulled a gun. "My ex-husband and I tried for two years to get pregnant until we were finally told it wasn't going to happen. I can't get pregnant. We have… *had* fertility issues."

The good doctor's eyes narrow, and he presses his lips together, nodding slowly. "Did your OB happen to say what kind of fertility issues you had? It could've been a situation where only one of you was the problem, say if your ex-husband had a low sperm count."

"I don't remember that part." I'm sure the doctor told us, but I'd gone into a kind of daze when he'd said *never get pregnant*.

It was the final nail in the coffin of my mistake, and I was already more than a little depressed and feeling stuck in a commitment I never should've made.

"I see." He glances down at the prescription pad, clicking his pen.

Somehow, I get the feeling he doesn't see.

"We can do this the old, *old*-fashioned way and order a blood test if you'd prefer." He glances at his notes. "Still, these days a urinalysis is almost 100 percent accurate."

My head is light. I can literally feel the blood draining to my toes, and I don't dare try to stand at the moment.

"We have to test again." It's barely above a whisper.

Hours later, I'm pacing my bedroom, arms crossed over my waist as I try to wrap my head around what happened. My stomach is in knots, and for the first time in days, the nausea is giving me a break—probably because of the prescription.

Dr. Beck said I'm somewhere between six to eight weeks along, and the only person I've had sex with, over and over, in all the positions, is more than eight hundred miles away.

It's Thursday night, and I walk over to pick up the remote

for my large, flat-screen television. Flipping it on, I bypass the streaming services and head straight to Live TV. It only takes a few clicks for me to find the game. It's a longshot, but there it is. His team is playing tonight against some other team out of Ohio.

I don't know how they decide which games to put on television. There must be a million teams—some states have more than one. I guess it has something to do with popularity or chances of going to the playoffs.

Two years ago, Logan and Garrett were the dream team. Even though it's only Garrett there now, they must still be pretty good for ratings. It's a testament to how popular they were.

Standing in front of the monitor, I chew on the side of my nail watching the players on the sidelines, straining my eyes for him. Damn these cameras focusing on the quarterbacks and the running backs.

It's just like Garrett to have a massively important role that people don't even realize is there.

Finally the cameras flicker to the sidelines, and I see him towering over most of the guys. I can't help a smile, a flush of emotion, of… something more.

My eyes are fixed on him, his confident swagger, his muscular physique accentuated by the tight uniform. His expression is serious as he studies the field, almost seeming frustrated.

In the past, when he played in college, he'd always be smiling and messing with the other guys on the sidelines. They'd do their fist bump routines or he'd do a little dance when something good happened on the field. He was always playful and light and so damn handsome. My stomach tightens when I remember us being together.

Now he seems almost dissatisfied. He definitely looks as uneasy as I feel.

I'm carrying his baby.

More emotion clogs my throat, and every muscle in my body is tense. This changes everything, and it has me on edge with what I have to do. I can't sit here watching him on television a thousand miles away.

Going to my room, I take out a small bag and fill it with a few toiletries and a change of underwear. Then I take out my phone, quickly tapping the buttons as I reserve a time slot.

Exhaling slowly, I'm not afraid. I've never been afraid to do hard things. I've just never wanted to do them alone.

Chapter 10

Garrett

Zane: Have you talked to Olivia?

I stare for a minute at the phone, wondering why my chest is tight, like I've been caught doing something wrong. All I've been doing is living my life.

About what?

Hendrix: Bruh, you still haven't called her? It's been two months.

Jack: You're supposed to call the woman after you sleep with her.

Hendrix: You're a meme.

I don't know what that means.

Zane: Need me to draw you a diagram?

Logan: Hey, it just hit me—we're really brothers now!

Logan: So good.

I should be happy for my former best friend turned brother-in-law, but instead I wonder if he'd look so smug if I gave him a wedgie.

Hendrix: What if Logan hadn't called Dylan?

Logan: I call my lady every chance I get.

Hendrix: Smart man.

Smart enough to know the four of us would've broken every bone in his body if he'd mistreated Dylan.

Logan: Don't forget Craig and Thomas. He's always got the shovel on standby.

Zane: Call Olivia.

Hendrix: Do or do not. There is no think.

Hendrix: Yoda had a killer aura.

He could also lift things with his mind.

Zane: Remember how to dial, Garrett? Put your finger on the button and press.

Hendrix: Damn, Zee. What's Rachel done to you?

Zane: None of your business.

Hendrix: Ruthless.

Glad you got your head out of your ass.

Zane: Now it's your turn.

Logan: Time to do the show, bros.

I put my phone down, turning to my laptop. Once a month, Hendrix and I join Logan and Zane on their weekly sports radio show, which has now turned into a simulcast on their YouTube channel.

We started doing it last year to help Logan grow the station, and it pretty much blew up. Jack joins us a few times during the year to talk about the rising high school players and which seniors to watch. The ratings have gone through the roof, especially when we're all together.

"Welcome to the Lightning and Thunder Weekly Sports Roundup." Logan's polished radio voice always throws me off a little. He's so good at it. "This week, we've got my brothers Garrett and Hendrix with the player's-eye view from the sidelines, and as a back to school treat, the one and only Jack Bradford shares his thoughts about the rising stars. Welcome to the show."

"Welcome back from your honeymoon, my man," I'm

always the one to bring out the personal side. "You're looking tanned. Are you allowed to tell us where you took the misses?"

"I took our favorite spicy pepper lover to an eco-resort in Mexico called Cuixmala."

"Eco resort? Did you see Maya Lopez?" Hendrix tries to be edgy, but I imagine one of those sad-horn sound effects.

"Dude, nobody watched that show. It was a big flop."

Logan is undeterred. "It has a biodynamic farm, so she was able to go out with the farmers and harvest the peppers. When they got back, she could join them in the kitchen to watch and learn how they made local dishes. She was pretty much in heaven."

I can't resist. "In the meantime, you didn't eat a thing?"

"They had mild dishes." He holds up both hands. "But she's got some new Dare Night recipes coming soon."

"For the locals," Hendrix notes.

"Let's get down to sports." Zane steps in to get us on track. "Looks like the Pirates' offensive line hasn't quite jelled this year. What's going on there, Garrett?"

"Way to go in dry," I tease. "Thanks, bro."

"My pleasure." He smiles, and I swear, he's so damn cocky since Rachel came along. "Johnson's playing a good game, but the receivers aren't quite where they need to be. At least one of them."

Charlie Johnson is the quarterback for my team the Pirates, which was also Logan's team before he retired.

His replacement Ricky Berke has never been a favorite of mine, and now that he's our new wide receiver, I'm forced to interact with him all the time.

"Have you stopped using the nickname?" Hendrix cuts me a look, referencing what I used to call Ricky—*the Dick.*

"Yes." I glance at my old partner in crime. "I'm working on camaraderie since we lost our MVP."

Logan holds up both hands. "Like I had a choice."

"You had a choice."

Thankfully, we pivot to discussing the highlights and low-lights of the past week's games. It's Thursday, and we're playing against the Admirals, which is Zane's old team. It's part of the reason he's giving me hassle.

When we're done wagering who'll win and which teams will move up or down, Jack comes in to talk about the high school guys. All eyes are on Austin Sinclair, who he's trained since he was a freshman in high school.

Austin's a junior now, but next year, it's going to be crazy around here with all the media and the scouts. We've all lived through it before, but they have no idea.

"He's got a lot of natural talent," my oldest brother notes, keeping his poker face intact.

"Some would say he's the next Jack Bradford." Logan cuts him a smile, but Jack doesn't take the bait.

"He's a good kid." It's all he'll give us. "He's under a lot of pressure, but he manages it well."

We wrap it up, and the music plays. The guys want to hang around longer and shoot the shit. They're done for the day, and Hendrix has an off night. I've got to get to the stadium.

I say goodnight and leave the Zoom, but I'm not even out the door of my apartment when my phone lights up with a text. I almost don't look at it, but it's not the brother's chat.

It's Jack.

Jack: You okay?

He's being Dad again, not letting me brood alone. Sometimes it gets on my nerves, but I know his heart's in the right place.

I'm good.

Jack: The guys are giving you a hard time, but you know…

Yeah, I know. I've earned it.

Jack: Especially from Zane.

Exhaling a chuckle, I acknowledge I'm usually the shit-talker, and I was pretty much the ringleader when it came to pushing our grumpy, loner brother into the arms of sunny Rachel.

He's a cocky old shit now, so I'll take that as my thanks.

Jack: You were pretty cocky yourself at the wedding. Why not give her a call?

And say what? Hey, Liv, I've changed. I'm not the same self-centered asshole who thought your whole life should revolve around me, and when it didn't I broke your heart?

Jack: It's not a bad start.

People don't want to hear that. They want to see you've changed.

Jack: So show her.

We're a thousand miles apart if you haven't noticed.

Jack: You can show her with your words, and if our plan works out, you'll be a lot closer soon.

Birmingham's still 300 miles from Newhope.

Jack: Try being her friend.

Pretty sure we graduated past the friend zone a while back.

Jack: Still, you can take it easy. Good things start slow.

Is that your excuse with Allie?

Jack: Not going there.

Give me one good reason not to call Allie.

Jack: I'm her son's coach.

So?

Jack: So I've been a high school coach a long time. I'm not taking advantage of a sweet single mom who gets emotional because her son has a mentor in his life who cares. Happens every year.

Allie is a lot more than that, and you know it.

Jack: Next year, he'll graduate, and they'll go where he signs. Or she'll go back to New Orleans. There's no reason for her to stay in Newhope.

So give her one.

Jack: I've been down that road. Not planning to do it again.

Allie is nothing like your ex. She's Dylan's bestie, Kimmie loves her. Hell, we all love her.

Jack: You're dodging the subject. Call Liv.

Just calling it like I see it.

Jack: Have a good game, little brother.

He's ending the conversation, and I can't help a groan. The thought of taking it slow with Liv after our night together feels impossible, but I know if I have even a hope of a chance, he's right. Especially after the way she practically sprinted from my bedroom.

It's possible I'm not a rebound, but based on her behavior, our reunion night was more than she intended it to be.

Studying my phone as the car pulls up to the stadium, I think about the game ahead. I think about the plans Jack and I've discussed and how much I want them to happen.

Still, even if I return to Newhope, Liv has her life in Birmingham. She has her friends and her law practice. Hell, she wants to be a partner.

Even if I think the lawyers in her firm are a bunch of douchebags for picking some other guy over her, I'm sure she's on their shortlist.

If that's her dream, the last thing I'll do is ask her to give it up for me. If I've truly changed, I'm not repeating history.

I'll show her I can put her first this time.

"Way to hustle, Rick, you're really improving." I hold out my hand for our wide receiver as we jog off the field.

Ricky Berke transferred from our rival team when Logan retired two years ago, which means we're the new dynamite duo. At least, that's what he wants us to be.

I've been working hard to stop calling him *The Dick*,

especially since Hendrix pointed out it's probably not great for team-building. It's just what Logan and I always called him.

"Thanks, Big G, you made it happen." He slaps my hand and we do a fist bump combination ending with a point. "You help a lot more than I realized out there."

It sounds like a dig, but he means it as a compliment. I hold back from saying Logan wouldn't have dropped the ball. It's true, but it won't bring us any closer.

Who am I kidding, I'm never going to bond with this guy.

"My man Grizz!" Our quarterback Charlie Johnson slaps both hands on the tops of my shoulder pads when I get to the sideline. "We're not where we were, but we're getting there!"

Ripping off my helmet, I take the Gatorade bottle from his hand. "I'm creating a hole. He just has to hold onto the ball."

"He's no Lightning Murphy, but I'm seeing improvement."

Charlie is good at being a motivational team captain. The question is whether I'll still be around when Ricky finally does get there. I think about my brothers after the show, taking it easy, laughing and hanging out, and I'm less satisfied than ever.

Glancing to the side, I see Johnson making a heart with his hands while he looks up at his box. One look, and I know he's not signaling his mom. Maddy is up there, and it's another twist of dissatisfaction in my gut.

Liv crosses my mind, and I wonder if I'd feel this way if she were up there smiling and blowing kisses to me right now. Would I still want to leave then? I toss the plastic bottle roughly, and walk over to sit on the bench, leaning forward on my forearms.

It's not even possible, so why wonder?

The rest of the game goes pretty much like it always does, no surprises. I take it back, Ricky actually completes a pass. That's a surprise.

We're in the locker room, and the guys are amped up and snapping towels. Even without our help, we still won the game, and my teammates are full of post-game adrenaline.

"You coming out with us tonight?" Ricky walks over with

his towel around his waist acting like he did anything to be proud of tonight.

I remember how Logan would get if he underperformed. Even if we won, he'd be in a foul mood, more ready to train at ten p.m. than go out clubbing.

I guess that's the difference between an MVP and a regular player. As much as Ricky likes to hot dog and say he's the next Logan Murphy, he's not. The years Logan and I played together were for the record books. Nobody's talking about what we're doing now.

"I think I'll head back to my place." I pick up my duffel bag and pull the bomber jacket over my shoulders.

"Hey, Grizz, you okay?" Johnson meets me at the end of the lockers as I'm walking to the door.

He's packed up to go home as well, but the difference is he's got a wife and a little baby waiting for him. His partying days are over, and his reasons for playing are very different from these guys.

"I'm good. What's on your mind?" Reaching out, I hold the metal door for him to pass through.

"I don't know. You've been sort of distant since we got back this year. It's like you're somewhere else or something. Distracted."

We walk down the wide hallway leading to the exit, where we'll be blinded by flashing lights. The cameras are all for him, since he's the star quarterback this year. There was a time when a few of those flashes would've been for me, too, but not anymore.

"You know how it is, thinking about the game, how to play better next time."

It's a deflection. I'm not about to tell him my visit home for Dylan's wedding pretty much cemented how I've been feeling about being here. It started the year after Logan left, then going home, seeing the guys with their families, and spending the night with Liv, confirmed everything I was already feeling.

Even if Charlie's a good friend of mine, it's too soon to tell him about my plans. We've got twelve more games this season, and I don't want to throw off his mojo. I also don't want to be dropped back to second string, not that I'm afraid they'd do that. I guess it depends on how mad they are.

He studies my face. "You'd tell me if something was going on?"

"Of course."

"Want me to see if Maddy has any friends you might like? Not that you need it, but she knows a few southern gals in the city. Might do you some good."

"I'll let you know if I do." *I don't.* Reaching for the door, I give him a tight smile. "Ready for this?"

"As I'll ever be."

We step out into the blinding flashes and shouted questions. Security is here to escort us to the black SUVs that will take us to our apartments, but it still feels like running the gauntlet.

With the help of my man Fred, I'm able to leave Charlie and the reporters along with his fans behind as I hop into my ride. I've just sat down and fastened my seatbelt when my phone lights up with a text.

One glance at the name and my entire mood changes.

> Olivia: Hey, I'm in the city. Would it be possible to get together?

My knee bounces as energy zips through my veins, and my stomach is tight.

Jack had me pretty much convinced, and all during the game, I kept thinking about ways I might approach calling her out of the blue.

I even rehearsed a few different opening lines. I didn't like any of them, but now it doesn't seem to matter. I should probably question this, but I don't. I'm too fucking happy.

> Hey—it's absolutely possible. What are you doing in the city?

Gray dots float on my phone screen then disappear. Then

they're back, and I wonder if she's about to send me a big long text or if she can't decide what to say.

I can relate to not knowing what to say. It's totally out of character for us, but a lot has happened.

Finally, her reply appears.

Olivia: I'll explain when I see you.

Short and sweet. Okay.

Sounds good. Want to come to my place? I'll send the address.

Olivia: Yes, thanks.

No thanks necessary. I'll be glad to see you again.

I wait, but she doesn't reply. So I send her my address.

She's probably here for work, and she wants someone to show her around the city. I can do that. We have another game on Sunday, and I wonder if she'll be here long enough to go.

I could offer for her to sit in Johnson's box with Maddy. I bet Maddy would like Liv. Maddy's from Atlanta, and she always likes to meet "home girls."

I imagine Liv in the box wearing my jersey, watching me play, and my chest squeezes. I like that a lot.

She could never do it in high school being dance captain and all. Not that I'm complaining. I never minded checking her out on the sidelines with the other dancers, looking like the finest thing I'd ever seen in that skimpy uniform, kicking her long, muscular legs all the way to her nose.

We're pulling up at my building, and I hop out at the curb, hoping I have time to prep the place before she gets here.

My apartment is on the top floor of a steel and glass high-rise in Midtown. It's one of the newer buildings, and I have a private elevator, which I shared with Logan when he lived here.

On the way up, I alert the doorman that I'm expecting a guest, but I also text her the code.

At the stadium, I took a quick shower and pulled on jeans and a white T-shirt before leaving. Hanging my jacket in the front closet, I hurry around, scooping up my discarded socks and jogging pants from earlier in the day.

I grab the shirt and jeans I left on the floor of my bathroom yesterday and throw everything in the laundry hamper. A cleaning service comes once a week, but it's been almost a week since they've been here.

While I'm in the bathroom I do a quick check, lowering the toilet seat and replacing the empty paper roll.

Crossing the wood floors through the living room, I lift my chin and sniff. The sofa is leather, as is most of the furniture. The kitchen is stainless steel with gray marble. I don't detect any funky smells, but I still dig in a drawer until I find a lighter.

Dylan sent me a basket last year at Christmas, and I pull out the pine-scented candle I've never used. It's barely fall, but I'd rather the place smell like pine trees than athletic socks.

I only have a few beers in the refrigerator. Scratching my chin, I look at the clock and wonder if I have time to order up a bottle of red wine or rosé or something. The only thing I saw Liv drinking at the wedding was that Fireball cocktail.

A bottle of Jack Daniels is in the cabinet, mostly because I'm not much of a whiskey drinker. I'm about to pick up the phone when a soft knock sounds on the door, and I decide beer and whiskey will have to do. Or I could offer to take her out... I wonder if she's had dinner.

Hustling to the door, I take a second to check my breath before opening it. It doesn't make a bit of difference, because as soon as I see her standing on my doorstep, she steals it.

She's dressed in jeans and a thin red sweater that hugs her breasts. Her strawberry-blonde hair hangs in long, smooth waves down her back, and her hazel eyes blink up at me quickly, a little worried, I think. *No need to worry, beautiful.*

Her cherry-red lips part as if she'll speak, and I shake my head, remembering how to form sentences.

"Hey, girl." Stepping forward, I give her a careful hug, not too tight, not too long. "Come on in. What are you doing in the big city?

"I… ahh…" She steps into the small foyer inside my front door, and her chin drops. She pushes a silky lock of hair behind her ear before looking up at me again, worried. "I had to come for work, and you're the only person I know here."

It's what I expected. "No problem, I got you. Want to stay with me? I've got plenty of room."

I give her what I hope is a welcoming smile, not a hungry, you-look-like-the-best-thing-I've-seen-in-six-weeks smile.

I must be successful, because the tension seems to leave her shoulders.

She exhales a shaky laugh, rubbing a slim hand over her cheek as she glances up at me. "That would be great."

Chapter 11

Olivia

When my eyes meet Garrett's, I completely lose my nerve. He's standing in front of me, all six-foot-four, in a white T-shirt that stretches across his muscled chest, and I swallow the drool in my mouth.

I remember very well how he looks naked. I don't know how, but his body is even more defined than when we were young. Lines of muscle cut across his abs, and his broad shoulders are round and defined.

The sleeves of his shirt stretch around his biceps, and his hair is slightly damp at the collar like he recently showered. It looks like he's either preparing to go out or he just got back, and now, standing here in front of him, I don't know what the hell I'm doing.

Booking that flight was a total, panicked impulse. We haven't talked since our wild night of sex after the wedding. Not that I blame him. I walked out—correction, I ran out. The onus was on me to call him if that's what I wanted.

Now I'm thinking I'll show up here and tell him I'm pregnant completely out of the blue? I should've written him a letter. Does anybody write letters anymore? I only know I should've figured out some way to give him the heads-up and feel him out.

I should *not* have jumped on the first flight out of Birmingham without even packing a suitcase. It's possible I was in shock. And completely freaked out.

"I'll be honest with you, I'm not really prepared for company." He puts his hand on the back of his neck like he always does when he's thinking or embarrassed or unsure, but his blue eyes are shining and warm. He's so damn appealing. "It's kind of late, but it's New York. We can go out for dinner, or we can walk down to the grocery store and pick up a few things. What do you think?"

"I think grocery shopping sounds fun." Blinking up at him, I force a smile, hoping it doesn't look as panicked as I feel.

I can't imagine what he'll say when I tell him. Part of me wants to believe he'll be cool and supportive. I have no idea what that will look like from a thousand miles away.

My throat tightens, and through sheer force of will, I command my body not to vomit.

"I'll put your suitcase in my guest room…" He looks past me, and my cheeks heat.

"I didn't bring one." I look down, trying to figure out how to explain my one small bag. "I just brought some personal items."

Toiletries and a change of underwear. Who packs this way?

His brow furrows. "What was it, some kind of legal emergency?"

"Something like that." I scrub my hand over my face.

Get a grip, Liv. I'm a lawyer. It's my job to look at all the angles, apply reason, and calmly make the right decision for all parties involved. I do it all the time, every day. I do *not* freak out over difficult situations.

All the vomiting has made me weak. And my heart. And

Garrett. And I will not cry, *oh my lord. I will not cry.* Is this pregnancy hormones?

Clearing my throat, I look around quickly. "Would you mind if I have a glass of water? Flying makes me a little dehydrated…"

"Oh, shit, of course." He hustles down the hall, and I follow him into an expansive, stainless-steel kitchen. "Here you go."

"Thank you." I take the glass and look down, away from his curious gaze.

His penthouse in Midtown Manhattan is absolutely gorgeous. It's completely furnished, and very masculine, all dark wood and leather.

The living room has an overstuffed, brown leather sofa and chairs with a polished coffee table and a massive flatscreen television. A wall of windows provides a breathtaking view of the city lights.

It's straight out of *Architectural Digest*, and I'm doing my best to breathe, drink the water, get control.

"Your place is really nice," I say, glancing at him over my shoulder.

"Thanks." He holds up my tiny bag. "Does this mean you're only staying one night?"

He actually seems disappointed, which I guess is an encouraging sign.

"I'm not sure." I return slowly to the kitchen. "I'm kind of playing it by ear."

"Okay…" His tone is justifiably confused, and he places the bag in a room across from the kitchen. "Ready to get some groceries? There's a Whole Foods on the corner, and I'm pretty sure they have just about everything."

"Sure." I place the glass on the bar, following him to the door. "I can help pay for the groceries."

"We'll figure it out later, and don't worry if you need to pick up anything, extra clothes or whatever. I bet we find anything you need."

He has no idea.

"Thanks, Garrett."

His large hand gently holds my upper arm, and I have to fight the urge to lean into him, to wrap my arms around his waist and break down and tell him. But I'll hold it together a little longer.

The Whole Foods market actually is right on the corner, down the block from his building. It's decorated for Halloween with corn stalks and pumpkins everywhere. He almost takes my hand a few times as we're walking, but quickly redirects to guiding me by gentle touches to my arm. It's a little zip of electricity every time.

A nervous laugh bubbles in my throat when he pulls out the small cart. "Let me push it. You look ridiculous with that tiny thing."

"I beg your pardon." He pretends to be offended. "I shop here all the time."

"I'm sure the workers love it." I give him a wink, and he straightens to his full height, looking around the relatively empty store.

It's after 10 p.m. on a Thursday, and we're almost the only people here.

"Shit, now I feel like Shrek."

I exhale a snort through my nose. "You're way better looking than that guy."

He smiles down at me, and a silly heat floods my stomach. This is the better approach, starting as friends. We'll warm up, have a chat, then I'll tell him what happened, and we can decide what to do.

My stomach clenches at the thought, but he's out in front of me loading up the cart. He grabs two Italian sandwiches he says are the best he's ever had—even better than Central Grocery in New Orleans, which I seriously doubt.

He picks out a bottle of wine, and I'll have to figure out a way not to have any without raising his suspicions.

Not that my whole appearance here and behavior aren't suspicious enough.

"They have the best gelato." He guides me to what looks like an ice-cream counter down from the deli section. "Check it out, they've got dark chocolate, pistachio, tiramisu, coconut, melon…"

"What's your favorite?" I blink up at him, and he shrugs.

"They don't have cherry, but the dark chocolate and hazelnut are really good together."

"Sounds good to me!" I grin, and we wait as the server scoops it into medium-sized plastic containers for us.

We watch as she weighs them before passing them to us, and he places them in our basket full of sandwiches and wine and chips and odds and ends. He directs us to the check-out area, and he doesn't let me pay for a thing, claiming I'm his guest.

Shaking my head, I take one of the bags, and we walk slowly up the block in the direction of his apartment. I'm thankful the prescription Dr. Beck gave me seems to be helping with my nausea. If I started throwing up, I don't know what I'd say.

He nods at the doorman, and I watch as he enters the code for the elevator. "Did you have plans for tonight? I hope I didn't ruin anything."

Leaning against the glass wall, he shakes his head with such a warm smile. "I was actually about to crash for the night. We had a game, and I don't know—"

"Oh, I'm sorry! I should've checked. Of course you had a game." I scrub my hand over my forehead, feeling awful.

"It's my job, Liv. I play every week."

"I know, but it's a lot with all the pregame and the post game and the *game* game." My smile is more of a cringe. "Did you want to go out with the guys? Did you win? Of course you won. Are you all amped up? Of course you are—"

"Take it easy, Cherry." He laughs, patting my shoulder. "I'm really glad you're here. I didn't feel like partying tonight."

It's a relief to hear him say that, but it's also worrying. This

is not the Garrett Bradford who gets on the bar at Cooters &
Shooters in a blond wig and shakes his sexy ass to the music—
or who gives his best friend a lap dance at his bachelor party.

"You've never been one to turn down a party." I tilt my head
up at him. "Are you okay?"

"I'm good, I just… I don't know." He shrugs. "Maybe I'm
getting older? I wasn't in the mood."

We've reached the top floor. The elevator dings, and I decide to put a pin in that for now. It's not like I have a leg to stand
on when it comes to uncharacteristic behavior, considering I
showed up on his doorstep with no notice, no luggage, and no
good explanation. He's probably thinking something's going on
with me—and he'd be right.

He enters the code, holding the door for me, and instead
of focusing on how awkward we're both acting, I decide to
lighten the mood.

"I wouldn't say getting older is a reason not to party." I give
him a little smile. "We're the same age, after all, and we partied
hard at Dylan's wedding."

"Are you saying you want to party with me tonight?" He's
teasing, and I carry the one bag he let me hold into the kitchen.

Shaking my head, I put it on the counter. "I'm just saying
it's lucky for me you decided to stay home."

"I'm feeling lucky to have such a pretty house guest." He
places the three bags he carried beside mine on the counter.

"We should buy a lottery ticket." This is better.

Our old banter is returning, and I'm feeling a little more at
ease about being here. My confidence is returning. Yes, it was
an impulsive decision, but this is Garrett. I can talk to him.

He puts the gelato in the freezer and pulls out the two sandwiches and the wine. "I don't know about you, but I'm starving. Let's eat these muffalettas and watch some *Road House*."

"*Road House!*" I cry. "What?"

"Yeah, but the old one. Not that new MMA, Jake Gyllenhall

bullshit. I want the classic, 'pain don't hurt,' Patrick Swayze *Road House*."

"Oh no!" I snort covering my nose.

This is the Garrett Bradford I know and… *loved*. Past tense. We're friends now. And potentially parents. *Oh, God. Confidence slipping.*

He takes out the wine and holds it up. "Can I pour you a glass?"

"Um…" I chew my bottom lip, searching for an excuse. "I think I'll just stick to something unleaded tonight. The plane kind of got me a little…" I wave my hand up and down, side to side.

"Hate that." He walks to the refrigerator and puts the bottle inside. "Turbulence is the worst. Let's see… I've got beer and one of these sparkling waters. We should've grabbed some ginger ale at the store."

"Sparkling water's good." I manage a smile, and he hesitates a moment, his brow furrowing like he might ask me something.

My chest tightens. We know each other so well, and I'm sure he's wanting to ask why I'm really here. I don't give him the chance.

"If we're going to watch *Road House*, then we have to watch *Dirty Dancing* to even it out."

"No!" He groans, putting a hand over his eyes. "Not Johnny and Baby."

"You said you liked that movie!" Now it's my turn to pretend to be offended.

"I said that because I wanted to get in your pants. I don't know a single guy who likes *Dirty Dancing*."

"Craig does!" He gives me a look, and I raise my eyebrows. "You said a guy."

"Sorry, a straight guy."

"I don't know why you're rewriting history." My stomach tingles at the memory of us as teenagers. "You didn't have to pretend to like *Dirty Dancing* to get in my pants."

"Tell you what." He steps closer, placing one hand on the cabinet above my head. "We'll watch *Road House* tonight, and maybe if you stay another night, we can watch *Dirty Dancing*."

Lifting my chin, I look up at him leaning closer. The pull between us is strong as ever, and now I'm here, surrounded by his scent of soap and citrus, the warmth of his body raising the hairs on my arms.

"Are you suggesting you might try something, Mr. Bradford?" I'm teasing, but his eyes darken.

I almost expect him to lean down and kiss me, but instead he pushes off and walks around the counter. "Not at all Ms Bankston. It's just nice to have you around."

His response sends me straight back to uneasy. Garrett has never put distance between us, and I don't know what to think. Then it hits me. It's so obvious. My body flushes hot then cold, and nausea creeps up my neck.

"Will it create a problem for you if I spend the night here?" I take a step back, wondering if it's too late for me to book a hotel room.

"What do you mean?"

"Is there… *someone* who wouldn't appreciate me being here all night, alone with you?" Looking into the guest room, I see my bag sitting on the dresser.

Of course, he has a girlfriend. Look at him. It's why he didn't call me after our red-hot wedding weekend. It's why he made a point to say it didn't count if he kissed me after midnight.

"Whoa, hang on." He rounds the counter, brow lowered as he charges into my space again.

I take another step away, ready to grab my bag and bolt. "I'm so sorry. I didn't even think—"

"Liv, stop." He puts his hands on my upper arms, holding me in place. "There's no *someone*. There's no one." His expression tenses as if that's not accurate.

"You're not dating anyone at all?" I want to be perfectly clear. "How is that possible?"

"No. I mean, sure I've had *dates*, like for awards ceremonies and charity events and stuff, but nothing serious." He shakes his head. "I'm not dating anyone."

Relief hits me so hard, my knees almost give out. I can't even imagine how that would've complicated things if he were. At the same time, it's not right for me to be so relieved. I have no claim on him. We had a crazy, passionate weekend, but we didn't make promises. He's not mine.

That thought sends another painful twist in my stomach. Turning away, I rub my hand over my midsection. My feelings are so mixed up and intense these days. It has to be pregnancy hormones. It's the only explanation for my roller-coaster insides and impulsive behavior.

"Okay." I nod, wrinkling my nose as I look up at him. "That's good, I guess… another lucky break?"

He huffs a laugh, releasing me. "Let's eat. It's getting late, and you're really going to like this sandwich. You'll see."

He returns to the kitchen to plate the food, then he leads me around to the living room and pulls up the movie. Plates on the coffee table, he tosses two large pillows on the floor in front of the couch and pats one for me to sit beside him.

"Ready for one of the best action movies ever made?" He grins widely.

"Pretty sure that's up for debate."

"You know, they modeled the whole thing after old westerns."

"Makes sense. I usually slept through those, too." I pick up the large, round sandwich and take a bite of ham, salami, provolone, and green-olive salad.

I hold my hand over my full mouth. It's an explosion of rich, salty, spicy, deliciousness with a touch of tang. "Oh my god!"

"Good, huh?" He nods, wide-eyed, and I can't argue.

"It's delicious!" I also haven't eaten since breakfast.

I'm starving and exhausted and emotional, and the movie

opens with a ridiculous fight at an over the top bar full of bad acting, bare breasts, and a band shielded behind chicken wire.

My mind drifts to Mom at home in Newhope with the chickens. Henny Lane was acting strangely, and I need to call and ask how she's doing. She's Mom's favorite fancy chicken…

When I open my eyes again, I'm lying on the couch. The living room is dark except for the glow of city lights shining through the large windows.

I'm not surprised I fell asleep. I'm more surprised I lasted as long as I did. Every day after work, I've been getting home, lying down on the sofa, and falling dead asleep. I must've been running on adrenaline.

Garrett is on the floor beside me sleeping, just like we did at his house, and warmth settles deep in my chest.

I want to reach down and slide my fingers through his hair. I want to slide off the couch and let him hold me in his big strong arms and tell me everything's going to be okay. Nothing can ever hurt me when he's around.

Instead, I place my cheek on the cushion, smiling gently as I close my eyes again.

Chapter 12

Garrett

A DUMB REDNECK IS TRAPPED UNDER A GRIZZLY BEAR, AND PATRICK Swayze is standing on the banks of a lake after ripping a dude's throat out.

Liv's head is on my shoulder, and I'm about to say *A polar bear landed on me*, when I hear a soft snore. It's really more of a snortle, and it's pretty damn adorable.

I know from experience Liv only snores when she's really tired, so I carefully reach for the remote and turn off the movie. Moving slowly, I lift her off the floor and shift her onto the couch.

She's not as skinny as she was when she was dancing off every calorie she ate in high school. She's more womanly, less breakable, and it's fucking sexy as hell. I've always loved her long body, her tall frame, her pretty strawberry hair.

I'm doing my best to walk the walk and be better than I was at nineteen. Hell, it's taking every ounce of my strength not to kiss her. I got close so many times tonight. The hardest was in the kitchen when she was being all sassy and saying I didn't need *Dirty Dancing* to get in her pants in high school.

Trust me, I remember how eager we always were back then—very well. And even though it was ridiculous, I was pretty stoked she got all jealous thinking I might have a girlfriend.

She knows me better than that. I would never have slept with her if I had a girlfriend.

My jaw tightens as I study the sleeping beauty on my couch, and I think it's probably better not to test that statement. When it comes to Liv, I'm sorry to say I just might. No one has ever affected me like she does. I'd probably do anything for her.

She exhales a little noise, and her slim brows pull together like something's bothering her, even in her sleep. The protective side of me surges to life, and I wish she'd tell me what's really going on. I know she isn't here for work, but what else could it be?

She's acting the same way she did when I saw her for the first time in Newhope at Dylan's wedding. She's guarded and anxious, like something's out of her control, and I know my girl well enough to know she hates being out of control.

Her fucking ex had better not be causing her problems again. Hell, if that's what's happening, and she ran here to me, it would be my pleasure to have her back.

I'll personally fly her back to Birmingham and punch that guy in his fucking face.

Okay, it's possible *Road House* has me a little riled up, but from what I've heard of Warner Oberon *the Third*, that guy's a world-class dickhead. He'd better not try anything around me.

Taking the blanket off the back of the couch, I place it lightly over her, doing my best not to wake her. I silently collect our plates and carry them to the kitchen, then I go to the bathroom and brush my teeth and change into something comfortable.

My girl is out, because when I get back, she hasn't moved. Her sweet face is less stressed, though, which makes me feel better. I rearrange the pillows and take up my usual spot on the floor beside her.

One thing Olivia Bankston can always count on—anything that might try to hurt her has to get through me first.

You can't really see the horizon in Midtown, but from this height, dawn shimmers off the smaller buildings, casting a golden glow across the high-rises.

I could sleep through it, but Liv exhales a noise, stirring on the couch. My eyes open, and I sit up from the floor beside her.

Her head drops, and she blinks hard, rubbing the sleep from her eyes. "I'm sorry I fell asleep on you."

Her voice is thick, and I smile, reaching out to move the hair behind her ear. "It's okay. It was late, and I guess you were pretty tired."

She nods, her hair falling over her cheek. "I've been so tired every day, I'm surprised I made it as long as I did."

My stomach tightens, and I study her face. "Are you sick?"

She doesn't look sick. She actually seems to be glowing.

"Just… working hard." She smiles briefly, placing her slim hand on my forearm as she stands slowly. I'm not reassured.

"I'd better change. Although…" She looks down at her sweater and jeans. "I don't have anything to change into, do I? I'm sorry I'm a mess."

Pushing off the table, I stand to my full height, which towers over her, even if she is tall for a girl.

"No more apologizing." I give her a nudge, and she blinks up at me. "You can crash here as long as you need to, and I told you, it's New York. We can find whatever you need, possibly even have it delivered."

She hesitates a moment before stepping forward to put her arms around my waist. I wrap her in my arms at once, leaning down to press my lips to the top of her head, inhaling the sweet flowery scent of her hair. I could stand here all day doing this, but it doesn't last.

Her arms relax, and she pulls away. Lifting her shoulder, she squints up at me. "At least I brought a toothbrush."

"I'll make some coffee." I follow as she goes to the guest room. "If you look in that dresser, I've got some old shirts and stuff I don't wear anymore. It'll all be too big, but you're welcome to try it."

She nods, giving me a little smile before closing the door. Hesitating a moment, I bask in that brief glow.

I've got fresh-brewed coffee and I cracked open a tin of cinnamon buns to pop in the oven. When Liv opens the guest room door, she's wearing an oversized T-shirt that says, *I have mixed drinks about feelings.*

"This isn't going to work." She looks down at the shirt that hangs to her knees.

"Hey, you make that look good." I've changed into my jogging shorts and a tee.

Her eyes light as they run over my shoulders and chest, and I know that look. It makes my dick twitch.

Diverting her eyes, she goes to the coffee pot to fill a mug. "Are you going for a run?"

"I'm headed to the stadium. I've got to do my morning workout. What are you planning to do?"

"I don't know." She turns, holding the mug close to her face as if she's basking in the warmth. "How long will you be gone?"

"You could come with me if you want. I'll just be lifting weights and running plays with the guys, but they won't mind if you're there."

"I can't go like this." She looks down at the shirt-dress she's wearing. "I only have what I wore last night."

"I've got something for you." Going to my room, I dig around in the drawers, coming back with one of my old cotton practice jerseys. "Put this with your jeans."

"You want me to wear your jersey?" She cocks an eyebrow, and I lean on my elbow beside her.

It's one of those moments where it's taking all my strength not to kiss her again. "You used to wear it all the time."

Lifting her chin, she takes it from my hands. "Wouldn't want to break with tradition."

Ten minutes later, we're riding down in the elevator. Her face is freshly washed, and her hair is brushed back in a ponytail. She's wearing my cotton, navy and red Number 50 jersey, tied at the waist, and she blinks bright hazel eyes up at me.

"Will I get to meet the whole team or just your group?" She's smiling and lighter than she was last night, which eases my concern a bit.

"It'll just be the offensive line, but I can introduce you to whoever you want. I know everybody."

"I don't know anybody." She laughs, looking down. "I'll hang out with you."

"We'll see who's there. You don't have to stay in the gym with me."

When we arrive, it's a small sausage party. A lot of the guys are still sleeping off last night, but we bump into Maddy and Charlie and their baby boy Paxton in the entrance hall.

"Hey, guys!" I greet them as we enter.

"Garrett!" Maddy skips forward, her arms full of wiggling six-month-old. "Who is this in your jersey? Have you been hiding a girlfriend from us?"

"Now I understand why you didn't want to go out last night," Charlie teases.

"No… I…" I turn to where Liv is looking down, cheeks pink. "This is Liv—Olivia Bankston. She's a lawyer. From Birmingham. We've known each other since we were kids."

"Birmingham?" Maddy smiles brightly. "I'm from Atlanta! We're practically neighbors. It's so good to meet you."

Maddy sticks out a hand, and Liv shakes it. "Nice to meet you."

"Here, hold Baby Pax a second." She hands the baby to Liv and pulls up her bag, propping it on her stomach. "I'll put your number in my phone."

"Sure." Liv shifts the toddler around onto her hip, and she seems pretty natural at holding him. She's even doing that little bouncy thing women do.

He shoves a fat fist into her long hair, and she tilts her head, doing her best to hold his wrist and untangle his fingers.

"Paxy, no!" Maddy drops her phone into the bag again, helping dislodge his fist. "I don't know what I'm going to do when I start showing. My lower back is already killing me."

"You're pregnant?" Liv's eyes widen.

"Can you believe it?" Maddy catches Paxton around the waist and hauls him onto her hip again. "I thought I was just never going to get back to my pre-baby weight. Then I found out I'm pregnant. So what brings you to New York?"

Charlie slaps me on the shoulder. "Let's get started."

He heads to the weight room, but I hesitate, touching Liv's arm. "You okay out here?"

"Of course, she is!" Maddy gives me a shove. "I'll take care of her."

"That's what I'm worried about," I tease.

Still, it's really cute watching Liv rub her hand on Paxton's back and shake his fist, which is now wrapped around her finger. She blinks up at me, and my chest clenches. I remember a time when we were both a lot younger, and I imagined Liv having my babies.

It's funny, because being out here, being frustrated by Ricky's irresponsible attitude really got to me last night. It had me legit angry, and heading to my apartment alone, I was planning to have a few beers and brood about how off-track everything had become. Then she appeared, and it all faded away.

None of that shit matters with Liv here. It's all different. I realize we've fallen quiet, and I look around at everyone waiting on me.

"You can go now," Maddy scolds like a sassy tween, but I'm still looking at Liv.

"That looks good on you, Cherry."

Her cheeks flame, and she blinks away fast. *Shit.* My stomach drops, and I can't believe I said something so thoughtless.

I want to apologize, but Maddy is watching us like a hawk. I'm sure Liv wouldn't want a stranger knowing about her infertility issues. Or if she did, it would be her story to share.

Fuck. My jaw clenches, and I guess my only option is to kick my own ass and apologize later, when we're alone. So much for showing how mature and sensitive to her needs I am now.

Scrubbing my hand over the back of my neck, I clear my throat. "Well, I'll be in the weight room if you need anything."

"We know." Maddy's tone is impatient, and she waves her hand like she's shooing me away. "Now go, so we can gossip about you."

"Right." I nod, forcing a laugh, still feeling like shit, before I turn and follow the way Charlie went.

Ten minutes later, he's spotting me while I hold a bar with 250-pound weights on each side over my chest.

"So that's what you've been thinking about, a tall redhead." Charlie stands at my head while I do my reps. "I thought you didn't want to go out because you were pissed at Ricky. Instead, you've been hiding a very sexy lady from us."

"I wasn't hiding her." I finish with a growl then stand, going around to remove a hundred pounds from each side. "She's an old friend."

Charlie squints up at me like he doesn't believe me.

"She's wearing your jersey." He lies back, positioning his hands on the push-up bar. "Don't tell me she's just a friend."

He does eight reps, and I guide the bar back to the rack as he stands to face me. My shoulders are tense—and not from the workout.

"Liv and I were pretty serious in high school, but that's all over now."

"Doesn't look over to me. It's rekindling season, bro. Get after it."

My jaw clenches. Charlie might be team captain, but he and Maddy love to gossip. Last thing I want is for him to say something to Liv before I know why she's really here.

"It's not like that. She's in town for work, and I thought she might like to see where I play."

"And she just happened to wear your jersey?" He cocks an eyebrow.

"It was the only Pirates merch I had."

"Right." He crosses muscled arms, and I know he's not buying any of this.

"Hey, Bro-skis, you guys are hitting it early." Ricky saunters in the room, and my brow lowers.

I'm not mad at Ricky, but he's just not Logan. After that last game, Logan would've been in here before me drilling.

"You should be hitting it early. We've got some work to do before Monday."

"Always bustin my balls, Grizz. Now I see why Murphy was setting records. He had you on his tail all the time."

"I didn't have to be on Logan's tail. He was way more focused—"

"Hey, I was thinking about this last night," Charlie interrupts before I can go off. "The Warriors' defensive line is killer. We've got enough guys here to do a scrimmage, put some pressure on your receiving game. You up for it, Rick?"

I couldn't have said it better myself, except I might've slipped and called him The Dick.

"Let's go," is all I say.

We spend the next few hours drilling, and every time we take a break, I look up at the box to see Liv standing beside Maddy watching us.

It's not a real game, and only staff and players mill around the stadium. Still, it gives me a feel for what it would be like to have her here, watching me play, wearing my jersey, and cheering when something good happens.

My chest expands, and I gotta say, I like it a lot.

By the time we're done, Ricky has managed to complete a little more than half the passes Charlie fired his way. I don't know what happened to him from the time he was a rising star two years ago. It's like he's too busy being a player to actually play.

Not my business. I'm ready to find Liv and get out of here, when I notice she and Maddy have come down to the field. They're standing on the sidelines like old friends. Paxton is asleep on Liv's shoulder, and as good as it looks, I'm not about to stick my foot in my mouth again.

"Are y'all finally done?" Maddy leans against her husband. "You'd think after playing last night, you'd want to take a break."

"It's how we get to be the best." He wraps an arm around her and leans down to kiss the top of her head.

"Well, I need a nap." She holds out her hands, and Liv passes the sleeping baby to her. "I'm pregnancy-tired, which is the tiredest kind of tired that exists."

"Tell me about it." Liv nods, then she stiffens and exhales a strangled laugh. "That's what I've heard anyway."

"Girl, you have no idea." Maddy puts her hand on Liv's arm. "Charlie is a good daddy, but thank God his mom's here to take Paxton so I can nap."

"Hey!" Charlie gives her shoulder a nudge. "Pax and I let you nap!"

"Sure you do, honey!" Maddy smiles up at him, then shakes her head no at us.

Liv laughs and walks over to me, wrinkling her nose. "You need a shower."

"Give me five minutes." My arms ache, and I want to wrap them around her the way Charlie's doing right now with Maddy. Instead, I remember my goals. "You've been a good sport hanging out here so long. What would you like to do?"

"Oh, I don't know."

"We could take a walk in the park. Or if you want to try and catch a show, I bet we can get last-minute tickets." Man, I hope she doesn't say yes to a show, because I might sleep through it.

Glancing at the clock, it's lunchtime, but I think ahead. "It's probably not too late to make a dinner reservation. I can usually pull some strings, since I'm a local celebrity and all."

"Is that so?" Lifting her chin, she smiles. "Maybe we can order in tonight. I was promised *Dirty Dancing*."

"Yes, you were." I'm doing my best to turn on the charm. "But first, lunch. I'll be right back."

Chapter 13

Olivia

I'M SITTING IN THE LOBBY OF THE PIRATES STADIUM WAITING FOR Garrett to finish showering when my phone goes off.

Mom: Henny Lane is brooding. I had no idea chickens would get broody without a rooster!

What does that mean?

Chewing my lip while I watch the floating gray dots, I think about all that happened today. Maddy is adorable with her Georgia twang and baby boy, and I imagine we'd be good friends if I lived here. Not that I'm planning to move or anything.

Holding Paxton as he chewed on his fist and tangled his baby fingers in my hair over and over, I thought about the possibilities—and decided I needed to get a grip on my fairytale dreams.

Then I nearly outed myself over the pregnancy fatigue. I

swear, I've never been more tired in my life. I could lie down right here and sleep the rest of the day on this couch.

No one seemed to notice my slip, but it's time. I have to talk to Garrett.

Mom: It means she thinks the egg she's sitting on has a chick in it, but it doesn't!

Poor Henny Lane has mental health issues. We must be kind to her.

Mom: Apparently Silkies are very broody. I don't know what to do when 21 days pass and it's a dud.

Buy her a little chick to love.

Mom: I'm not sure I can handle an entire broody flock.

Don't crush Henny's dream.

Mom: Olivia Cherry Bankston! You know I love my chickens, but I can't encourage hysterical pregnancies.

I wonder what she'd do about a real pregnancy. She'd go bananas.

Mom: Dr. Pfefferle thinks I need a hip replacement. This is not a trick, so if there's any chance you might be able to work out a remote situation, I could use your help.

Squinting at my phone, I'm suspicious this is indeed another trick, but I hesitate. I think about the prospect of being in Newhope for eight weeks with so much in the air. So much is unresolved.

> Let me look at my calendar, and I'll find a date.

> Mom: Why does my phone say you're in New York?

Exhaling a swear under my breath, I curse the day I taught her how to share her location with me. Of course, I had to share mine with hers, but that was before my life turned into a Tilt-a-Whirl.

> Taking care of business. Talk soon. Love you 🖤 🖤

> Mom: Love you, Olivia 🖤 🖤

"Everything okay?" Garrett's voice draws my attention, and it takes me a minute to catch my breath and blink away the swoon when I see him.

His dark hair is damp and messy, and he's wearing faded jeans that hug his ass exactly right. A gray T-shirt stretches over his broad chest, and the navy bomber jacket he's wearing makes his blue eyes glow.

I'm lit from within, and I think about pregnancy hormones and all the other things I've heard they do to you, like horniness.

"Henny Lane thinks she's pregnant." I hold up my phone, and his brow lowers.

"What?" Laughter dances in his eyes, and I want to be like we always were.

I want to skip around and hop onto his back, hugging our bodies close together as I wrap my legs around his waist. I want to whisper in his ear things we only share with each other.

Instead, I swallow that down. "Mom says she's brooding."

"How does that work?" He holds out a hand, and I take it, letting him pull me to my feet.

"She thinks her eggs are the real deal, and she won't let Mom touch her or them."

"What's your mom going to do?"

"Play along?" I shrug, slipping my hand into the crook of his arm. "I told her to get a chick, but she's worried the entire flock will get broody. Apparently six chickens is enough."

"I thought eight was enough."

Snorting, I shake my head, and he holds the door. A black SUV waits to take us wherever we want to go. I've never had a car service, but I'm not complaining. I don't feel like walking all the way back to his apartment right now.

"How do you feel about hamburgers for lunch?" He touches my arm as I climb into the vehicle. "I know a place that has the best burgers in town. Or wings if you prefer."

"Sounds good to me. I'm starving."

A short ride later, we're in the middle of Blondie's, a sports bar filled with bar games and televisions blasting every variety of sport available. Garrett leads me to a high-top close to a couple of pool tables.

Sliding onto the stool, I nod at them. "Want to play a round?"

"Nah, I've been banned." He calmly lays it out there, picking up the menu.

"Banned!" My voice goes high. "What the hell?"

"Logan let it slip my family owns a restaurant that's also a pool hall, and now I can't play without being accused of hustling the clientele."

Ducking my head, I cover my mouth with my hand. "We hustled them all the time."

"I know." His eyes dance as they meet mine. "It was so easy!" We say it at the same time, and he leans closer. "Especially for you. No one ever believed someone like you could be so good at pool."

"They had no idea we spent every rainy day perfecting our game."

"Hey." His expression turns suddenly serious. "I wanted to apologize for what I said at the stadium. In front of Maddy."

"What?" My brow furrows, and I can't think of a thing…

"About how holding a baby looked good on you. I didn't mean to make you feel bad or pick at an old wound. I know infertility is a painful thing, and I'm really sorry."

"Oh…" A weight drops in my stomach, and I reach out to take his hand. "No, Garrett, you don't have to apologize."

Looking around the room, I know this isn't the right place to tell him. I consider suggesting we go back to his place when a petite waitress in denim shorts and a black tee skips up to the table, right into a hug with him.

"Garrett!" she cries, and I don't like the way she's holding his arms and smiling up at him one bit. "I haven't seen you in ages. Where have you been?"

She gives him a little shove, and my throat gets hot when I watch her blinking up at him expectantly like they're old friends. Or something more? Jealousy has never been my thing, but wow. Do pregnancy hormones also make you want to strangle flirty waitresses?

"Wendy, hey." Garrett seems to sense the change in my mood and takes a step closer to me. "How's that new husband treating you?"

Okay, *new husband* makes me feel slightly less stabby.

"He's great." She blinks down, blushing a little.

Now I'm feeling a lot less stabby.

Then she turns and smiles at me. "And who is this? Did you finally settle down?"

"I'm Olivia, but everybody calls me Liv." I extend my hand.

"I'm Wendy!" She gives me an enthusiastic shake. "It's nice to meet you, Liv. You must have a lot of patience to be with this guy. He's a character."

"Tell me about it." I decide she's okay. "We've known each other since we were kids."

"Ladies, I have to stop you right there." He holds up his hands. "My one goal is to keep you all happy, and what I know right now, is Liv needs a classic Angus burger. Stat."

Wendy nods, putting her hands on her hips. "My kind of girl. And what will you have, big guy?"

"Bring me some wings."

"Drinks?"

"Yuengling for me, and Liv?"

"I'll just have a Liquid Death. Sparkling."

"And put the game on," Garrett calls as she walks away.

She waves over her head as she goes to the bar. We've just turned to face each other when the television nearest us changes to football.

"Talk about the star treatment." I lean closer, and he reaches for my hand.

"Something else I wanted to say…" Warmth infuses his tone, and I look down to where his large hand engulfs mine. "I'm sorry I didn't call after our weekend. You left in such a hurry, I thought maybe I'd made things weird."

Emotion clogs my throat, and I turn my hand so I can thread our fingers.

Blinking fast, I lift my eyes to his, and when they meet earnest blue, it squeezes my stomach. "You didn't…"

It's not all I want to say, but Wendy's back with our burgers, wings, and drinks. Releasing our hands, we sit back on our stools. My hamburger is massive, although besides being exhausted (and apparently a little horny), I'm also ravenous.

We spend the next hour eating and watching the game. Wendy makes sure we have everything we need, and I'm impressed by how many customers he greets as we have our lunch.

"You really are a celebrity." I lean forward, shouting over the noise. "Everybody knows you."

"Logan and I started coming here when we moved into the city. It's close to our building."

Nodding, I glance around the somewhat basic bar. It's filled with a mix of guys in T-shirts, caps, and jeans as well as a few couples and even some men in button-downs and khakis.

It has a good vibe, and I can't help thinking it's just like Garrett to find a place in Manhattan that has the same feel as his restaurant back home.

The football game is still going strong when he surprises me. Standing, he waves to Wendy for the check and walks around to where I'm sitting.

"You don't want to finish the game?"

"Do you?"

Shaking my head, I look down with a laugh. "Not really."

Wendy walks up with the check, arching an eyebrow. "First time I've seen you leave before the game ended."

"Seen one game, you've seen them all."

My eyebrows rise in disbelief, and I exchange a look with Wendy.

She leans into my ear. "This is more than childhood friendship."

Pressing my lips together, I take Garrett's extended hand. I don't think he heard her, but my chest is still hot. He helps me off the stool, and Wendy stands back with her arms crossed watching us in a way I wish she'd stop.

"Have a good weekend." He gives her a wave and continues holding my hand as he leads me out to the SUV waiting at the curb.

A few guys shout at him when we step out onto the sidewalk, and he waves. I look around and notice we're close to the park. "Want to walk back?"

"Whatever you want." He taps on the window and signals the driver.

Then we stroll the long block, past the Museum of Natural History, until we're at Central Park West. My hand is in the crook of his arm, and I lean into his side as I watch my feet on the un-even bricks that form the hundred-year-old sidewalk.

We're surrounded by people walking or sitting on benches and talking or playing with kids or walking dogs. The city is buzzing with activity, but it feels like we're the only two people on Earth somehow.

We round Columbus Circle, residences turn into businesses, and soon we're walking past Rockefeller Center, then Radio City Music Hall. We continue a few blocks more until we're at his building.

He speaks to the doorman, and I wait as he enters the eleva-tor code. Stepping inside, he turns his back to the wall, smiling down at me as he holds out his hand. "You okay?"

Nodding, I look down at my shoes. "Good thing I wore these boots. That walk was longer than I expected."

"It always is here." He smiles, and I put my hand in his.

His fingers close around it, and my heart beats faster. I think about what Wendy said, about this being more than a childhood friendship, and in a way it is. Our affection has never faded, but so much has changed. We've grown up, and we're both so far apart now.

The elevator dings, and we step out, across the small land-ing, and I wait as he enters the code for his door. It opens, and I follow him inside.

He closes the door, and I continue into the living room, going to the wall of windows and looking down at the crowded sidewalks below. Shadows grow longer, and the seasons are changing, evening comes early, and the air is crisp.

Warmth is at my back, and he's standing behind me looking out as well. My skin prickles with the sensation of his closeness, and my chest tightens.

"What now, Liv?" His voice is quiet, and I turn to face him.

"Now I need to tell you why I'm here." My voice is quiet, and he nods like he's been waiting for this.

"Would you like a drink or something?"

"No." My chest gets tight, and I don't know why I'm suddenly afraid. "But you might want one in a minute."

His brow furrows, and I swallow the knot in my throat.

I didn't rehearse this, and I try to decide the right way to introduce what I'm about to say.

He shifts on his feet, and I'm pretty sure the tension in the air can't get any tighter.

Inhaling deeply, I exhale slowly, then simply say it. "I'm pregnant."

The room goes silent.

I never noticed before, but he has an analog clock somewhere in this apartment. Its *tick… tick… tick* is the only sound, and I have to be hallucinating. New York City is never silent.

Finally he speaks. "That's… great. Congratulations?"

His tone is confused, not happy at all, and my eyes shoot to his face. It's a mixture of frustration and possibly something else. Regret?

My stomach hurts, and I'm trying to breathe normally. "That's it? Congratulations?"

"I don't know what else to say, Liv." He shrugs, starting to turn. "Did you decide to do IVF or something?"

The anger building in my chest breaks, and I lift my hands to my forehead. "No…" Exhaling heavily, I squeeze my eyes shut. "It's not… It's yours. Ours. It happened after the wedding. I got pregnant when we… did it."

Silence again, except for the unbelievably loud clock and its ticking hands of fate.

"But you said…" He starts and stops.

Crossing my arms, I walk away from the windows into the living room. "The doctor said we couldn't get pregnant, and I guess I interpreted that to mean *I* couldn't get pregnant. I mean, if you think about it, we never had a scare after all the times in high school—"

"You were on birth control in high school."

"Yeah, but birth control can fail." My voice is quiet, and

I finally build up the nerve to meet his eyes. "I thought I was broken."

"You've never been broken, Liv. You're perfect." A smile teases at the corners of his mouth, and he takes a step closer. Then he stops, seeming to think twice about it. He swallows, sliding his hand over his mouth. "What do you want to do?"

Pain trickles through my chest, but I won't allow myself to cry.

Diverting my eyes, I take another step away from him. "I've thought about it a lot. You've got your career here, and I'm… there." I have to catch my shaky breath before I can continue. "It's very early. If you do the math, I can't be more than eight weeks along. It's not too late to…"

It's a heavy weight on my chest, a pain in my stomach. My eyes flicker to where he hasn't moved, and my insides twist.

This silence. This oppressive silence presses down on me so hard.

"We don't have to do this if you'd rather I didn't." His forehead tenses the slightest amount, and I can't say it.

"Is that what you want?" It's a low question, tight like his jaw is clenched.

After last night and this morning and today, I don't understand why he's standing there so controlled. It's not how I expected him to respond. I've known Garrett all my life, and he showed more emotion when I told him about Mom's delusional chicken.

All the fears I've had about doing this alone, my impulsive decision to come here, because I was sure of all the men who've ever been in my life, he was different.

I believed he would always have my back.

Breath I didn't know I was holding gulps in my chest, and a hot tear hits my cheek. Pushing it away fast, I lift my chin, finding the strength I know I have.

"No." My voice is thick, and I clear it. "I want this baby very much, only—"

"Fuck me, Liv." The words come out in a rush, and before I can register what's happening, I'm scooped up in Garrett's arms. "I'm pretty sure my heart stopped."

His face is in my hair, and my knees collapse. It doesn't matter. He holds me up, tight against his chest, and a muffled sob escapes my throat. I reach up to put my arms around his shoulders and hold on for a moment, until I get my bearings again.

"Garrett." More tears fall onto my cheeks. I can't stop them. "Why did you do that?"

"What?" He lifts his head, frowning, and I push against his arms.

He releases me, and I take a step back, swiping away the tears and trying to get control. "You stood there like I was giving you the weather report. You didn't even react."

He takes another step forward, and now his eyes are shining. He cups my face in both hands, looking down at me like I'm something precious. My stomach twists, and another tear pops out.

"You have no idea how hard that was for me." Shaking his head, I think I see moisture hiding in his blue eyes. "But I'm trying to change, Liv. I'm trying not to make it all about me."

"Well, you picked a fine time to change!" My voice is pouty, and he chuckles, pulling me into his chest again for a hug.

"Damn, Liv. You're having my baby."

My head is on his shoulder, and I nod slowly. Rotating me carefully, he moves a hand around my waist. His palm spreads over my stomach, and he softly speaks the word *Mine*.

It's pure amazement, and at last, I feel calm.

Chapter 14

Garrett

LIV'S HAVING MY BABY. IT'S LIKE SOME KIND OF CRAZY DREAM COME true. My mind reels, and all I want to do is hold her in my arms. I want to kiss her so bad, but again, it's not The Garrett Show. I have to let her take the lead.

Letting her take the lead is fucking hard as hell. I'm ready to put a ring on it and move her here to New York. We can spend my last year in the city together. I smile, thinking about her in the box all round and pregnant, smiling and waving in my jersey.

Damn, that's good.

"I can't do this alone, Garrett." Her tone almost seems afraid.

What the hell does she have to be afraid of?

"You won't do it alone." I'm pure confidence. "I'll help you with everything."

"But how?" She takes a step back again, brow furrowed. "I can't move here, and you can't move back to Newhope."

So much for my big plan.

We're quiet again, and the sounds of the busy Manhattan

streets echo soft in the air, audible even at this height. I think about what Jack and I've discussed, and how it looks like we'll have to speed up the timeline. I can't wait until next year to retire. Liv needs me now.

"Who says I can't?"

"What?" She blinks up at me, her pretty hazel eyes wide. "But your contract…"

"I'll worry about my contract."

"I just… Mom needs me to be close, and I can't imagine having a baby without her, so far away."

Looking down, I think about what she's saying. I think about all those years ago, when we were faced with our first separation, and it was only college.

"The last time we had a hard decision to make, you asked me to come to you, and I said no." My throat tightens, and I swallow that regret. "I'm not saying no to you again."

Our eyes meet, and another tear falls onto her cheek. She wipes it away fast.

"Okay." Her voice cracks with a whisper, and it hits me right in the stomach.

"No more tears." My voice is gentle, and I pull her to me. "We got this, Cherry. It's going to be good. I promise."

She nods, stepping back. "I believe you."

Looking around, I try to think of something to lighten the mood. "I think it's *Dirty Dancing* time. What's that quote?" Her brow wrinkles, and I explain. "You know, like in *Road House*, he says 'Pain don't hurt,' and it's so over the top?"

"I carried a watermelon?"

"No…" I shake my head, thinking.

"You'll hurt me if you don't trust me?"

"Wow." My chin pulls back. "That's a good line. That's in *Dirty Dancing*?"

"You'll just have to see." Her tone is lighter, and the worry that's been creeping across her face since she arrived is gone.

Maybe I should have more thoughts about this, but I don't.

She's happy. I'm fucking thrilled. It's the easiest decision I've ever made.

Liv is having my baby, and I can't stop smiling about it.

"It's good, but that's not the line. I can't believe you of all people…" I'm about to give her a hard time when I catch a sparkle in her eyes, and I realize she's messing with me.

"Nobody puts Baby in a corner," she groans, and I lean down… stopping short of kissing her.

"No, they don't." I give the side of her hair a gentle tug as I pull up the movie on streaming. "Now get comfortable. Do you want a snack or something? Are you feeling okay?"

"I'm good." She sits on the couch, pulling her feet up beside her. "I'm still full from lunch. That hamburger was delicious."

She doesn't look pregnant at all curling up on my sofa, but she said it's really early. I don't know anything about this stuff, which means I've got some homework to do.

"Man, I should've known something was up when you were only drinking sparkling water the whole time." I grab a pillow and throw it on the floor, sitting in front of her.

"Why did you think I was here?"

"I wasn't sure, but you had that look on your face, like when I saw you the first time in Newhope. I thought I was going to have to bust your ex in the lip. Or maybe your law partners."

"My poker face has never been very good." She stretches out, bending her elbow and propping her head on her hand.

"That's all right. I've got you."

The movie starts with blurry images of couples dancing to the song "Be My Baby." I steal a glance at Liv lying on her side.

Her hazel eyes are fixed on the screen, and as the music plays, I think about the way we always dance. I think about being a teen and watching this movie with her, just waiting for it to end so I could pull her onto my lap.

I think about the nights she'd sneak into my bed, and I'd thread my fingers in her soft hair. I was so sure it was how my life was going to be. That part was settled, and I was happy.

Then I think about all the years I thought it was gone. I remember the night she got married, and I got drunk.

It was over, and I knew I'd never find somebody who made me feel like I did when I was with Liv.

She blinks to meet my gaze, and a smile curls her lips. "What?"

Glancing down, I think about what I said to Jack about telling her I've changed versus showing her.

Meeting her eyes again, I simply say, "This is good."

Her smile broadens, and she slides her fingers along my cheek. "It is."

Dr. Anderson's office is dimly lit and a tiny fountain sits on a table in the corner of the room. Flute music plays softly overhead, and a subtle, herbal scent drifts in the air—eucalyptus? Maybe it's patchouli.

Liv is lying on an exam table with the back raised so she's sitting up. She's wearing a cloth hospital gown, and a paper sheet is over her front. I'm sitting in a chair at her side, ready to be supportive.

When she told me she had to do her first ultrasound, I hopped on the next flight to Birmingham. Reddit said *The Expectant Father* was the best pregnancy book, and it said this is a very important moment—which made me say *No shit* out loud.

Leaning closer, I whisper, "This is the fanciest doctor's office I've ever seen, and I've seen a lot of doctor's offices."

"He's supposed to be the best OB in Birmingham," she whispers back. "Only… I'm not really excited to have a guy down there."

I'm not excited about it either, but see above. *Supportive.*

After she fell asleep during *Dirty Dancing*, and we spent another night with her on the couch and me on the floor, Liv decided she'd better head home. Especially, since she'd only brought a change of underwear and a toothbrush.

I was pretty proud that she'd run straight to me when her primary physician confirmed she was pregnant. I was also pretty smug when I discovered she'd taken my jersey with her. She says it's a comfortable night shirt, and I'm counting that as a win. Getting closer.

Liv is one of the smartest people I know. She's strong and capable. She's a fucking lawyer. She can literally handle anything, and thinking how she ran to me like that, without even packing, has me doing my best to remind myself it's not The Garrett Show.

Internally, I'm strutting around, feeling like a star. Like I'm her own personal bodyguard. Or better, I'm her baby daddy.

Putting her on the plane was tough. Not touching her for more than awkwardly long hugs is tough, but when she kissed my cheek at the security line, I took it as my signal she wants to go slow.

I can do that. I can go as slow as I need to go if it means we'll be together in the end.

While we might be going slow physically, we've been texting pretty much nonstop.

Liv: Another day of toast for breakfast.

I thought you'd stopped barfing.

Liv: I have, but the nausea is real.

Heading to the stadium for training.

Liv: Kept lunch down.

At this point, I'm still working on the details of getting out of my contract. I get paid on a weekly basis, so the worst that could happen is I'd lose out on the rest of the season. But I've been with the team so long, it's possible they'll pay me out—it's my hope, considering my situation.

I need to figure out what to do with my apartment. I could try subletting, but I don't think I could get away with it, considering everybody knows me. One of the pitfalls of being sociable.

"Good afternoon, Miss Bankston!" Dr. Anderson is an older fellow with white hair and glasses. "You must be the husband? Nice to meet you, Mr. Bankston."

My brow rises, but I don't correct him. Liv isn't sold on this guy, so I'm pretty confident this might be our only visit.

"Is this your first ultrasound?" He looks down his nose at us, and I'm not sure why I feel like a teenager confessing I knocked up my girlfriend.

I can't even imagine what it'll be like when we tell our families. They'll go crazy. Hell, they'll probably throw a party for the whole town.

"Yes," Liv answers. "Dr. Beck did the initial testing, but he referred us here for the ultrasound."

"My nurse Arati will handle that, and we'll meet up to discuss when you're done."

With a smile, he stands and walks out of the room, closing the door softly.

Liv's head snaps to me, and she's clearly pissed. "So what is his point? He just sits behind a desk and reads results?"

Yep, I know my girl pretty well. We won't be seeing this guy again.

I don't have a chance to answer when a pleasant young woman in pink scrubs enters the room.

"Hi, there, I'm Arati. I'll be doing your ultrasound." She takes out a half moon-shaped device. "I'll just need to uncover your belly and apply some gel. We'll move this over your stomach and see what we can see. Okay?"

Liv nods, moving the paper blanket aside, and I can tell by her cooperative smile, she likes this young nurse a lot better than that old doctor. I can't say I disagree.

"I got this good and warm…" Arati squeezes blue gel onto Liv's skin then rests the half-moon wand against her stomach.

The room immediately fills with a loud swishing sound like being underwater. A black-and-white image appears on the screen, and we both lean forward.

After a few seconds, the swishing turns rhythmic, and Arati's calm voice cuts through the noise. "That's your baby's heartbeat."

My chest tightens, and a knot forms in my throat. It's a strong, rhythmic strumming, and when my eyes meet Liv's, hers are watery.

"All I do is cry now," she whisper-laughs.

Leaning closer, I take her hand in mine, kissing her knuckles. "It's pretty damn incredible."

What's incredible is how in one moment, your entire life can change in the best possible way.

Chapter 15

Olivia

WE STEP OUT OF THE BEN & JERRY'S ICE CREAM SHOP INTO THE crisp fall air. I'm holding a cup of Cherry Garcia, and Garrett has an Americone Dream.

"I'm moving back to Newhope." It's the first thing I've said since we left Dr. Anderson's office. "I need to be home now."

Hearing the baby's heartbeat then going to the doctor's office and getting an estimated delivery date made it all seem very real, and I decided it was time to make the changes I've been turning over in my mind like pages in a book.

"How can I help?" Garrett doesn't miss a beat.

Reaching out, I squeeze his arm. "I'll hire movers, so it shouldn't be a lot of work. I didn't take much with me when I left Warner's."

"I'll like you being at your mom's better than at your tiny apartment." He frowns, thinking about it. "Or would you get your own place in Newhope?"

"I'll start off at Mom's."

Looking down, I stab my spoon into the ice cream, thinking about the things I've dreamed of doing and about changing course, what that would look like with a baby.

"What about being made partner?" Concern laces his tone, and I almost lean my head against his shoulder.

He's being so good, so supportive. I hoped he would be this way, and having him actually do it, fly down here for the ultrasound, hold my hand the way he did… I'm pretty sure hearing that strong, determined heartbeat changed us both.

"I'm not interested in working for anyone now. I want to have my own practice." I do a quick mental inventory of my open cases. "I can probably keep a lot of my clients, since I'm not leaving the state, but we'll have to send a letter and give them the choice."

He nods, lifting his eyebrows. "It sounds like you've been thinking about this a while."

We're at the car, and I stop, finally scooping out a bite of ice cream and putting it in my mouth. The sweet vanilla mixes with the chocolate covered cherries, and it's so good.

"I started thinking about it after Mom's fall." I squint up at him. "It's just her and me now, and when I was driving home, I felt how far away she was if something happened."

His lips tighten, and he hasn't eaten his ice cream either. "I know what you mean."

He hesitates as if he'll say more, but when I look up, he only smiles. It's a tight smile, and my stomach knots. We're both acting weird, like we've been shaken awake from a fuzzy dream.

"I think I'll wait to tell her about the baby until thirteen weeks. It's just a little longer."

"The book said it's common practice." He nods. "Once you're in the second trimester, there's a lot less chance of anything going wrong. Not that anything's going to go wrong."

"That was a really strong heartbeat." Warmth moves through my chest.

A real smile curls his lips, and he nods. "Strong and steady."

He finally takes a bite of ice cream. "What's this book you're reading?"

"It's called *A Dad's Guide to Pregnancy*. I got it on audiobook so I could listen to it while I'm training."

More warmth. "You're listening to it while you train?"

"I'm listening to it all the time. It says you'd appreciate compliments."

"I don't think a person has to be pregnant to appreciate compliments."

"Yes, but it says you might be especially sensitive about your changing body."

I take another bite of ice cream and inspect my torso. "I haven't changed much yet."

"Not true. You're really glowing since I knocked you up."

A laugh snorts through my nose as I eat more ice cream. "Is that so?"

"And your boobs have gotten bigger."

"Garrett!" I push his arm with my elbow.

"I mean, you've always had a hot body." He points his spoon at me. "But you look especially good growing our baby."

Hesitating, I chew my bottom lip before saying it. "They're going to think we're back together… But of course, we're not," I quickly add. "It was just one night."

"Technically it was two if you count the kiss." His voice is thoughtful, and I dare to glance up at him.

Our eyes meet, and his are serious, studying me like he's considering it. Energy flashes from my chest to my stomach, and my ears get hot. The baby is too small for me to feel, but I wonder if strawberry-sized he or she can tell—something happens when I look at Daddy.

"We've changed a lot since we were teenagers," he continues. "We're different people now."

"Are we?" My nose wrinkles.

"I know I am."

My lips twist, and I toss my ice cream cup into a nearby

trash can. "We're not the type to get back together just because we're pregnant. Those relationships never last."

"I guess not." He walks over and tosses his cup as well.

Is it possible he seems a little disappointed? It's time to drive him to the airport, and my emotions have been on a roller-coaster ride since he got here.

It's not a long drive from here to the airport, and I don't get out at the Departures gate.

He only has a carry-on bag, but before he gets out, he pauses. "About what you said earlier, you're not alone, Liv. You never will be. I told you I'd be there, and I will."

"We hate to lose a good lawyer like you." Bob Semple sits behind his massive, mahogany desk situated at an angle in the back of his oversized, corner office.

"You do?" I can't help the surprise in my voice.

"Of course, Olivia." He has the nerve to act offended. "You've brought in a lot of revenue. I was actually telling the boys we should consider making you a partner in a few years."

Nodding, I hold back from asking him why. I already know why. I'm single, unmarried, and as far as he knows, not pregnant.

Instead, I manage a smile. No point in burning bridges. "I appreciate the consideration, Bob, but my mother isn't getting any younger. She's having some health issues, and well, I've just decided it's time I got closer to home."

"I can understand that." Graham pipes up like a good little lap dog.

I'm standing at the door, but he sits in a small, leather armchair situated in front of Bob's desk. I can't help noticing it puts him at a level much lower than Bob.

My nose wrinkles picturing myself sitting there, looking

up at this guy who might, *in a few years, consider* making me a partner.

"I've learned a lot working here," I continue. "I'll work remotely from Newhope while we make the transition."

"How soon are you leaving?" He sits up straighter in his chair.

"I'm packing up my office this afternoon." My tone doesn't leave an opening for discussion. "Let's say in three weeks, we can send letters to my existing clients giving them the option to remain with the firm or come with me."

Bob leans back in his chair, steepling his long fingers in front of his lips and nodding. "It appears you've worked out all the details."

"Yes, I have." I take a step back. "If you need anything, you have my mobile number, and I can access my email from my laptop. Have a good afternoon."

They actually acted stunned like how dare I leave the firm.

Garrett: I still want to punch that guy in the nuts, but I bet you hit them better than I could.

I smile, thinking about Bob's shocked expression, as if anyone would consider not working there.

It was pretty satisfying to say See ya.

Garrett: Wouldn't wanna be ya.

Although, I guess there was a time when I did want to be them.

Garrett: You're way too good for those guys.

The movers are coming tomorrow morning. This time tomorrow, I'll be at Mom's.

Garrett: Do you want me there when you tell her?

My breath catches, and I realize in that moment I really do.

Is that possible?

Garrett: Anything's possible for my baby mama.

That makes me snort, and I shake my head. No matter what, Garrett Bradford always finds a way to make me laugh.

I'd really like that.

Garrett: Pick a date and I'll be there.

What about two weeks? I know you can't keep flying here on a moment's notice.

Garrett: I'll fly there on a second's notice if you need me.

My eyes heat, and I wonder when I turned into such a cry baby.

Thank you, Garrett.

Garrett: Anything for you, Cherry.

You're a good baby daddy.

Garrett: I've always been pretty competitive.

Another big grin splits my cheeks.

So you're going for the title?

> Garrett: I'm going for a lot more than that.

Heat floods my veins, and I study my phone, wondering how much more and what more he might mean.

How is it possible, after all this time and everything that has happened, the first boy to break my heart turns into the one vying to be my hero? Although, to be fair, the first man to break my heart was my father.

My mind slips back to middle-school me, working so hard to be seen, going to dance camps, determined to be the best. Thinking if I made it to the very top, he'd have to see me. Then he'd love us again. Then he'd come home.

I was so focused, so controlled. I've always been in control. Until now.

My phone hums, and I turn it over to see another text from Garrett.

> Garrett: Get some sleep now. The book says the fatigue should ease up in the second trimester, but you're not there yet.

Another little puff of laughter slips through my lips.

> Goodnight, Champ.

Chapter 16

Garrett

It's ten o'clock at night, and I'm lying on the sofa watching an old episode of *The Wire* and wishing I was in Newhope with Liv.

A week has passed, and I miss her every single day. The book says her body is changing all the time, and our baby is the size of a lime now.

Yesterday, I had a meeting with my coach and the team owner to ask about being let out of my contract. I told them about the baby and how I didn't want to be so far away during Liv's pregnancy.

They weren't sold on the idea, and I can't say I blame them. Guys have babies all the time, and it's not like Liv and I are married.

I also tried to play up the skill of the other linemen. I was actually glad Ricky has been such a disappointment this season, since it hasn't had me in the spotlight as much as I was when Logan was here.

My hope is, since I've been on the team longer than five years, I'd be considered a vested player, in which case, they'd let me go without a fine or legal action. I'd like to think I've got a good enough relationship with them for that.

We left it with them willing to consider it.

I didn't say what I was thinking, which is I've made my decision. There's no room for consideration anymore, only whether we'll part amicably or not. My hope is we will.

I really don't care.

Liv: Spill it, Bradford.

I can hear her playful voice, and it makes me chuckle. Leaning my head against the cushions, I think about the question. It doesn't take long to decide.

I'd like a baby girl, but I'd like her to have a big brother.

Liv: So you want a boy?

Twisting my lips, I decide fuck it. I'm going there.

I'd still like a baby girl, so I guess we'll have to do all this again.

Gray dots appear then disappear on the screen. Then they're back. And they're gone. I start to laugh imagining I threw her for a loop with that one.

The book states emphatically expectant fathers should not talk about having more babies while the expectant mother is pregnant *unless he wants his ass handed to him.* The book doesn't say that last part, but I'm pretty good at inferences.

Liv: Let's just take this one baby at a time.

So you're open to the possibility?

Liv: Goodnight, Champ.

You asked.

"What's this I hear about you leaving the team?" Charlie jogs to catch up with me as we're walking to the stadium for our Sunday night game.

Having this week's game on Sunday is perfect timing for me. Liv wants to talk to her mom this week, so it gives me plenty of time to be there, spend some time with her and not miss my obligations here.

I'm pushing my luck by missing a practice and training session during game week, but I've got one foot out the door as it is.

"Who told you that?" My brow lowers, and I can't help worrying who all knows my business.

The tabloids can be brutal. I saw what they did when Logan and Dylan started dating, and I don't want them breaking a story before Liv's had a chance to talk to her mom. My only hope is I've fallen off their radar.

"I'm team captain, Grizz. Coach told me what you're considering. They wanted my input."

"I'm not considering it. They are. I've made my decision."

His brow lowers and he catches my arm, stopping me. "What's going on, bro?"

My jaw clenches, and I look straight into his eyes. "We

haven't told the fam, and I don't want anyone knowing until they know. Maybe not even then."

"You're making me nervous. Are you sick?"

"Liv's pregnant." I look down, doing my best to keep it quiet as our teammates jog past, pushing and rough-housing and touching our good luck pirate at the entrance to the stadium.

"Hold up." Johnson pulls me away from the large opening leading out to the sidelines, away from the crowd, to where we have a bit more privacy. "Is this for real? You're going to be a dad?"

It's the first time anyone's said it to me out loud, and a sense of pride explodes in my chest.

A smile breaks across my face, and I can't help a laugh. "Fuck yeah, I am."

"That's a big deal—congrats." We high five, doing our touchdown hand jive, and he's smiling now, too. "Liv's the pretty redhead who was here in your jersey? Your high school sweetheart."

"My baby mama." Damn it feels good to say it out loud.

"But you don't have to leave the team to have a baby. We need you here."

"Liv needs me, and I don't want to miss this."

"So bring her here." His earnest plea hits me where it hurts.

Charlie, Logan, and I played together the longest on the Pirates, and I imagine he's feeling the way I did when Logan left—kind of lost, lonely… It's hard to lose your crew.

"Sorry man, I would if I could, but she doesn't want to move here. She has her mom and her career, and I want to be with her." I know he sees my expression change.

I can't help it, it's the truth.

"Are you getting married?"

Dropping my chin, I think about this question. *If I had my way…* "We've got some ground to cover before we get to that point. High school was a long time ago, and I've got to show her who I am now."

"Well, if you need a character reference, you got one right here."

"Thanks, man."

We can hear the announcers, and we look to where the rest of our teammates have all entered the field.

"We've got to get in there." He slaps my shoulder, and we jog to catch up with everybody.

The noise is deafening when we emerge onto the side-lines, and I remember when I was part of the hype. It's pretty addictive.

Although, to be real, nothing is as addictive as Liv's pretty smile or the sound of our baby's strong and steady heartbeat. It's what I want.

The music plays loudly, and the crowd chants as the dancers do their thing. The other guys slap helmets and generally get each other ready, but my heart's not here anymore.

I'm miles away in Newhope, wishing I had my girl in my arms.

> Liv: Did you know the fam watches all your games at C&S?

Tonight was another win for the Pirates, and the talk has turned to the playoffs. Ricky completed three of the four passes Charlie sent his way, and we're in the running for the Big Game.

I've done it all before, and it's a legit adrenaline rush. Few things are as gratifying as being at the top of the game.

Except a text from Liv.

Sitting on the bench in the locker room, I chuckle as I tap a reply.

> I've heard about this. I've also heard Dylan hides behind a post so she doesn't have to see us get tackled.

> Liv: I don't want to burst your bubble.

Gray dots appear, disappear. I shake my head wondering what in the world?

I think back to a tackle in the third quarter when a defensive lineman so big he makes me look like a normal-sized guy caught me off guard. I was trying to create an opening for Ricky, and he threw me on the turf like I was a rag doll.

She knows how it was when we were in high school. They always put me on the line because of my size, and I was usually the biggest guy out there—but not always. Sometimes I'd get hit, and when I did, I was on ice for at least a day or two.

I was also seventeen. It takes me a little longer to bounce back now. The funny thing is, I don't feel a thing.

The thought of seeing her again, seeing how much she's changed in two weeks, warms my whole body. I don't want to let her go, and I'm texting, hoping I catch her before she puts her phone down.

I stand, grab my bag, and head for the door. The guys are all going out, but I'll be in my bed, doing my best to speed up the hours until I see her again.

Liv: I want a healthy baby.

Cut the crap, Cher, which is it?

Liv: 🤪 you sure are being bossy tonight, Champ.

You made me tell, now spill it.

I've managed to slip out with only a few guys yelling at me for being a nun and not going out with them. I flip them the bird, my eyes on my phone as I headed to my waiting SUV.

Fred holds the door as I hop inside. Those players know what it's like to have a lady, and I've seen them all glued to their phones at one point or another like it's an Uncrustable PB&J sandwich.

Liv: I think I'd like a little girl (see no evil monkey emoji) But I'd love a little boy, especially if he's as sweet as his daddy.

Fuck, that hits. Mommy and Daddy.

I'm tight with anticipation, ready for it to be tomorrow. I'm ready for all of this to change. I send her a quick goodnight and shift direction. Up to now, my entire focus has been on Liv and her needs. It's time for me to take care of business.

Jack's probably still with our family at the restaurant if he was there watching the game. Still, I shoot him a quick text. I've been wanting to do this for a while.

Hey, man, making a quick trip home. Got some news, but keep it on the DL, okay?

Back at my apartment, I place my phone on the counter

and pull down a glass. I don't expect to hear from my brother until tomorrow, so I'm surprised when it lights up with a text from him.

Jack: What's up?

Scooping up the device, I hesitate a moment, thinking about how I want to present this.

What's the status of our plan?

Jack: Rodney said Faye Huntington is retiring in March. It'll fit perfectly with your return. If you're still interested.

What are the chances I might start sooner?

Jack: How soon are we talking?

This month? Next?

I'm hoping for sooner, but I still haven't gotten the word from the coaches.

No gray dots. It's like my whole phone goes silent. Was that too much? Chewing my lip, I hate the tightness in my chest. I hate this uncertainty. It makes me angry.

I hate thinking the owners who should have my back won't, and I hate feeling like I'm taking advantage of the kindness of locals I never see anymore.

Still, it's the way of the world. We help each other in the hopes that when it all comes around, like it always does, someone will be there to help us. At least I'm sure of my family, and the goodwill we've built up in the community.

Jack: Let me see what I can find out. Is there some reason you're wanting something so soon? You're still under contract.

Inhaling slowly, I type the words.

> Please keep this between us... Liv is pregnant. It's mine, and I told her I'd be there for her.

Hesitating, I add the last bit.

> I want to be there for her. I want to show her I've changed.

It doesn't take long for my oldest brother, also a single dad, to reply.

> Jack: I'll do everything I can, and G? Congrats, man. I always thought you two made a great couple. It's why I never busted your ass for sneaking her into your bed in HS.

> I'd like to have seen you try.

He doesn't respond, and I exhale a chuckle. He did his best to wrangle four wild siblings after our parents passed. We all loved and respected him for it, especially me, but when it came to Liv, for better and for worse, nobody could tell me a thing.

Chapter 17

Olivia

Henny Lane sits on her nest almost completely flat. Her breast is plucked almost bare, and she looks slightly deranged, like she'll attack anyone who tries to touch the common, ole non-fertilized egg she's trying to hatch.

Poor, crazy bird. I'm sure it's the hormones (*again*), but I actually feel empathy for this mentally ill creature. I want to keep her safe.

"It's okay, Hen." I speak in a low, even tone. "I know how it feels to be growing a baby. I'm growing one of my own right now."

Reaching out, I place a small cup of food on the edge of her roost. It's attached to the side, so it can't be tipped over, along with a cup of water.

Mom said Henny stays on her nest for hours at a time, only leaving for a few minutes each day to eat and leave a large, stinky poop.

The poop part has me a little worried. My nausea is back,

and the prescription Dr. Beck gave me seems to have stopped working. Or my body has gotten used to it. Either way, I don't like how large the swells of nausea have become, and I can't seem to find the trigger.

Something tells me a big, stinky chicken poop might be it.

Glancing at the clock, I expect Garrett any minute.

"It's so nice to have you home." Mom walks out to where I've finished checking on her chickens.

"It's so nice to have you moving around again. Are you sure you want to have a hip replacement so soon? You've just gotten your mobility back."

"I might as well get it over with." She shrugs. "It hasn't been that long since I needed a walker."

"It's been almost four months." Despite what she says, I suspect this might be another ploy to bring me home, but have I got a surprise for her.

As much as I hate to reward her for lying, her trick to keep me here for Dylan's wedding played a pivotal role in making a dream I didn't think was possible come true.

I'm going to be a mother. She's going to be a grandmother, and the father is a person we both care for very much, even if it's really, *really* complicated.

"Well, anyway, I've had this ache in my hip and he said hip replacement surgery is as common now as heart surgery."

"Another very serious procedure," I note under my breath.

She waves a hand over her head, going back to the house. "I'm just happy you're here. Now what is all this important conversation we have to have right now? I'm missing my Dungeons and Dragons session at the senior center, and I'm the elf bard who plays bagpipes and wields a bow and arrow."

"I don't know what any of that means."

"We have to get out of an alternate dimension of our homeland, Olivia! I can't just blow off a session. People are counting on me."

"I have something important I need to tell you, and I didn't know you were on a senior-citizens DnD team. I thought Dungeons and Dragons was for kids."

Her eyes narrow in disapproval. "Olivia Bankston, I didn't raise you to be ageist. DnD is a creative way to keep your brain active."

"Your brain's active enough as it is."

Outside, the sound of a car makes my stomach jump. I've been texting with Garrett all morning, so I know it has to be him, based on his ETA.

"Is someone here?" Mom tilts her head, walking over to look out the living room window. "Who in the world…"

"I'll go see." Leaving her, I hustle out the door, meeting him halfway.

As always, Garrett has my senses tingling. He's in simple black jeans and a brown sweater with a tan suede bomber jacket on top, but my whole body hums at the sight of him.

His dark hair is a little longer than it was in the summer, and I imagine threading my fingers in it. His beard isn't as clean shaven, and my inner thighs tense at the thought of how it might feel. Heat rushes to my core, and I won't lie, the rugged look is working for him.

"Perfect timing." I do my best to distract my lusty brain. "The grandmother is getting restless."

He grabs his duffel from the Uber XL, and I slide my hand into the crook of his arm. His blue eyes are heated when he looks down at me, and it's all I can do not to pull him down for a kiss.

It's been happening a lot more since we found out about Baby.

"How are you feeling?" He holds my arm, lifting it and moving me out as if he's inspecting my appearance. "Still glowing, healthy. Boobs."

"Shut up!" I laugh, pulling him to the house. "Mom's not going to know what to think of you being here. We'll have to tell her right away."

"Lead on."

"Garrett?" Mom meets us at the door. "What in the world? What are you doing here?"

Her eyes move from him to me and back so fast, I know she's scheming. She's smart, and she's already been working on her own plan to put us together since the wedding.

"Come inside." I take her arm, moving her into the living room. "Sit down."

"You are so bossy."

"I learned it from the best. Now, here. Garrett and I have some important news, but I want you to listen all the way to the end without interrupting. Can you do that?"

She exhales a disgusted noise. "Of course, I can do that. Don't speak to me like I'm a child, Olivia."

"No interrupting." I hold up a finger. Another scoff, and I continue. "We've got some good news, but it's not what you think."

Her mouth opens, and I hold up my finger. Instantly it closes.

"I'm going to have a baby… and Garrett's the father." Her eyes bug, but I push on quickly, knowing I've hit her limit on self-control. "We're not getting married, but…"

Her expression melts from ecstatic to confused, but I won't let her start with the pressure yet.

"We're committed to this baby. Garrett's planning to re-tire and move back to Newhope, and we're going to do this together."

Her lips tighten, and I watch as she inhales deeply through her nose.

"Now you can go."

Blinking her eyes, she shakes her head, a smile spreading across her face. "I'm going to be a grandmother?"

That makes me laugh. "Not *just* a grandmother." I drop to my knees in front of her, clasping her hands. "You're going to be the *best* grandmother."

With a little squeak, she pulls me into a hug, and the two of us rock side to side. After a few minutes, she releases me, and I look up at Garrett.

His hand is on the back of his neck, and his brow is furrowed. I almost laugh at his bewildered expression.

"Garrett Bradford!" Mom pushes off me to stand. "Get over here and give me a hug."

I sit back on my heels, watching as he bends down to hug my tiny mom. "One person down, ten more to go?"

Releasing her, he shakes his head. "Nobody knows I'm here. The only person I've told is Jack, and he's sworn to secrecy."

"Why is it a secret?" Mom's tone is indignant. "Everyone knows the two of you belong together. It's the happiest news you could give us that you're back together and having a sweet little baby!"

"Mom, you're not listening. We're not back together."

"Why not?" She seems genuinely confused, and I exhale heavily.

"We can't get married just because we're pregnant."

"People do it all the time."

"And they get divorced all the time. I'm not vying to be the next Kim Kardashian."

"I don't know what that means." She shakes her head, closing her eyes. "When it's right, it's right. And this is right."

I look helplessly up at Garrett, and he gives me a warm smile. He doesn't say a word, and so much emotion is in his blue eyes. My chest squeezes, and I have to look away.

How can we know if it's right so soon? I thought for four years Garrett was right. I spent my entire high school career thinking we'd never be apart. I even went to college thinking we could never be apart. I was wrong.

Mom reaches up to take his arm. "Garrett, are you staying for supper?"

"No, ma'am, I'm taking the next flight back to Manhattan. I can only miss so many practices before it starts to add up."

"What does that mean? You have to pay to miss practice?"

He gives her a little wink. "They like to call it a fine, but it's basically the same thing."

"Garrett!" I push to my feet. "You should've told me. I didn't even think about you getting fined. I'm sorry."

"I told you no more apologizing. You needed me here, and I told you I'd be here when you needed me."

Mom looks from him to me, and she steps back, picking up her oversized bag. "Well, I'd better get going. If I hurry, I might still make my DnD session." Stepping forward once more, she hugs Garrett again. "It's always good to see you, Garrett. Liv, I'll be back later."

She hurries out the door so fast, I almost call foul on her hip replacement ruse. Instead, I look up at Garret. "You can't do this."

The smile that lifts his cheeks almost does me in. "I can do whatever I want, Liv. I only have one chance at getting this right, and I'm not wasting any more time worrying about other people."

"Still, you have to tell me when I'm causing you a problem. I'll understand."

Reaching down, he takes my hand in his. "I only have one problem, and it's scheduling. Now what should we do for an hour that won't get me busted?"

Scratching my forehead, I look up at him. "Want to see a hysterical chicken?"

That makes him chuckle, and the protective shield I've been clinging to so tightly starts to slip.

Chapter 18

Garrett

MY PHONE BUZZES, AND I DO MY BEST TO LIFT IT DISCREETLY AS I sit in the Pirates owner's office.

Logan: WTF, man? You sneak into town without telling anybody?

My brow furrows, and I remember my visit. Liv and I were really careful. We had lunch at her mom's, sitting across from each other at that little table in front of the bay windows looking out over the yard… down to the *bay*.

I said I finally got why they called them that, and she teased me for living on a bay all my life and just getting it. I wanted to pull her into my lap and kiss her.

I didn't.

Her mom said everything I was thinking, but I didn't have a leg to stand on. If we were still in the days when we were just graduating from high school, I think I'd have a better chance of convincing her we should get married—crazy as that sounds.

Instead, she's seen my worst. She knows what a dickhead I can be, and she was right to walk away. Even if that's not technically what she did.

She actually begged me to understand, and the image of her tear-flooded hazel eyes will never, ever leave me alone.

I'm getting a second chance, which is not something everyone is lucky enough to get, and I will not blow it. What's that line from that musical? I am not throwing away my shot?

"We've given this a lot of thought, and we need you on the team." Kurt Lucas is the Pirates' owner, and it's the first time I've ever met with him alone.

Usually, he's jetting around the world on his private jet. Yes, that's redundant, but this guy has more money than God, so I imagine he has a lot of redundancies he couldn't give a shit about. Including me.

"I hate to contradict you, Kurt…" *Lie.* I'm happy to contradict him. "We've got so many great players on the team just waiting for their chance to shine. Most of them are a lot younger than me—"

"Yes, but they don't have your experience." Kurt looks down at his desk. "They don't have your star power, and in this age of influencers, we need all the faces we can get."

Sliding my lips together, I hold back my impulsive swear. Kurt's calling me a face guy? Like I'm filling the seats? It's fucking bullshit, and he knows it.

My eyes cut to Thad Holloway sitting beside me. He's one of the coaches I don't know as well, but he's been around long enough to know I'm not putting butts in seats these days. I give him a silent plea, and he clears his throat.

"My vote is to let him go." Thad flops it out there like a dead fish, no prelude. "We thought Berke could fill the space left by Logan Murphy, but it's not working. I think matching him with another lineman might be the key. Move Bradford to second string."

Wow. He's blaming Ricky's failure on me.

The impulse to defend my record is strong, but I push it down. Thad's taking an unexpected approach, and perhaps this angle will get me what I want. Leaning forward, I exhale my frustration and focus on Liv.

"You're new, aren't you, Holloway?" The near-snarl in Lucas's tone draws my eyes. "Garrett Bradford is *not* the problem here. The fact you would say something so ignorant makes me question your competence. If anyone should go, it should be Berke."

Mother. Fucker. How the hell did I get a superfan for an owner? I mean, it kind of rocks, but it's screwing up everything.

"I'm sorry, sir." Thad drops his chin, looking at his shoes. "I didn't mean to offend you."

"Get out." Lucas tosses a Mont Blanc pen onto his blotter. "Garrett, I appreciate your paternal instincts, but they'll pass. You're not going anywhere. End of discussion."

He turns away, and my lips press into a frown. Thad grabs my sleeve, pulling me to the door. I cut my eyes at him, not interested in his protective gestures.

Still, I follow him out.

"I'm sorry, man. I thought if I came on strong, he'd cave." Thad looks up at me with apologetic eyes. "He's as big of a fan as we all are, and if you go, it'll be the end of the triumvirate. First Logan left, now you. Charlie's contract is up for renewal next year, and we don't want him getting any ideas."

Reaching up, I rub the back of my neck, exhaling a growl. "I want to be with my family."

Lifting his shoulders, he holds out his hands. "I'm sorry."

We're headed back to the locker room, and I take out my phone, remembering the text from Logan. Liv said it would be okay if I wanted to tell the guys. I guess this means she told the girls.

Liv's pregnant.

Hendrix: You didn't wrap it???

It's Liv, dumbass.

Hendrix: Sounds like you're the dumbass. How many wild oats have you spread?

Again, it's Liv.

Hendrix: And I love Liv, but now you've got poopy diapers, no sleep, vomit. Babies carry disease… Always wrap it.

Next time I see you, you'd better run.

Zane: Hey, I'm proud of you, bro. You figured out where to put it.

It wasn't that hard.

Hendrix: They make a pill for that.

Keep digging.

Logan: When are you moving home? You can't miss the good stuff.

Jack: I haven't talked to Rodney yet, but I will.

No worries. I've hit a snag here.

Logan: Jack knew? That hurts, G.

Jack was approved by Liv. He's helping me get a job, but who knew the owner is a superfan? He won't let me go.

Logan: How can I help?

Is it possible to get canceled without any long-term effects?

Hendrix: Make direct eye contact. Say what you want.

Thanks, Yoda. I never tried that.

Jack: Don't do anything hasty. Let's brainstorm.

Zane: It'll work out. Somehow it always does.

Shoving my phone into my pocket, I walk slowly to the locker room. Another whole week has passed. Liv and I text all the time, but it's not the same. At fourteen weeks, the book says the baby is the size of a kiwi fruit, and Liv's in the second trimester. I'm missing everything.

"Am I in a stable?" Ricky walks up to join me on the way to the locker room. "Why the long face?"

Cutting my eyes at him, I've never wanted to punch him in the junk more. "Why are you such a dork?"

He huffs a laugh. "That's better than a dick. Something must really be bothering you."

"I'm working on my team building."

"Keep working." He shakes his head. "Look, I get it. I'm not Logan Murphy."

Stopping, I size him up, thinking about what Thad said. "You're right. Logan and I could read each other's minds on the field. We trusted each other. You can't force that kind of chemistry."

"What are you saying?" His brow lowers, and he almost seems worried.

"Maybe you'd mesh better with a different lineman. Is there someone you'd like to train with?"

Hesitating, he thinks a minute. "How about Huck Holmes? He's about my age, and we've hung out a few times."

Nodding, I look into the locker room. Huck is a new guy, transferred over from the Admirals last year. He's been on the bench, but I think it's time he got off it.

"I'll take care of it." Ricky starts to go, but I grab his shoulder. "Good luck."

Ricky Berke is not dumb. It only took me one conversation with Huck and another with Thad before the starting lineup was shuffled, taking me out. Considering it was my idea, I was not offended.

Jack: Why didn't you play tonight?
Are you hurt?

Working an angle I hope will get me home.
Any word?

I'm sitting on the bench in the locker room, wondering why I haven't heard from Liv. Jack's worried about me. I'm worried about her. If the owners were watching tonight, they have to be weakening.

We won the game. I wasn't on the field once, and Ricky looked like a good trade for the first time in two years. It has to be worth something.

Jack: Rodney can't fit you on the force til March, but animal control needs help.

Like a dog catcher?

Jack: More like a gator catcher, water moccasins in pools, who knows what else. He said you'd get credit for law enforcement training on the job. Might be interesting.

Scrubbing my hand over my chin, I hesitate before tapping my reply.

If it's as close as I can get...

Charlie walks up. "I would never leave you standing on the sidelines. Coach must've lost his mind tonight."

"It's okay. I suggested trying Berke with Holmes. I hope it'll give them some ideas, help them see they don't need me."

My friend's jaw tightens. "You're needed. You're more talented than Holmes. You've got more experience on the field, not to mention your spirit, your enthusiasm."

Another stab of guilt. "You'll find a new guy, Chuck. Before it was me, it was somebody else."

"Dammit, Grizz, I knew you'd say that. I don't want you to retire."

Standing, I pull my friend into a bro-hug. "I know. It was tough on me when Logan left, but you'll adjust. And you've got Maddy and the kids. I want that."

He starts to protest when my phone buzzes again, and I lift it expecting Jack. Instead, what I see makes my blood run cold.

Liv: Something's wrong—I need you!

I don't waste time texting. My thumb is on the call button, and my heart stops when I hear her voice. She's crying. Correction, she's sobbing.

Grabbing my duffel off the bench, I'm practically running to the exit before her first words are spoken. "Garrett?"

"What's wrong, babe?"

I can't stand to hear her crying. A fist is in my chest as I jump into the waiting car.

"I don't know." She hiccups a breath. "I went to the bathroom and… there was blood."

Fuck. My stomach plummets, and I wave at Fred. "Teterboro airport. Fast as you can."

My old driver hops to it. "Yes, sir."

It's a gamble, but Logan's dad had a private jet service at Teterboro when Logan lived here. I have to hope he still does, and he'll let me use it.

"We should never have told anybody." Her voice wavers, and my heart breaks at the fear in her tone. "Now what will we do?"

My throat hurts like I swallowed a bone turned sideways.

"Is your mom there?" Forcing myself to think, I swallow air. "Are you cramping? Having contractions?"

What the fuck did that book say about this?

"Mom's taking me to the hospital. But Garrett…" Her voice breaks, and she exhales another brief sob. "I'm scared."

If I weren't in a car, I'd be on my knees.

"I'm going to hang up and call Logan."

"Don't tell them about this!"

"I'll only say what I have to. I need to see if his dad's jet is available. It'll take me a few hours to get there, but I'm coming, Liv. Hang on, okay?"

Her soft hiccup rips me in two. "Please hurry."

"I'll be there tonight. Try to be strong. We're going to be okay."

I want to say I love you. I don't want to hang up the damn phone, but I have to call Logan.

"Okay." Her voice is small.

"I'll keep you posted. I'm coming." And I press the button.

Chapter 19

Olivia

I'M LYING ON MY SIDE IN THE DIM-LIT HOSPITAL ROOM. A BAND IS around my stomach, and stickers are on my chest, stomach, and wrist. Quietly beeping monitors surround me.

As soon as we got to the emergency department, they took us back. Mom held my hand, her eyes round and blinking fast the whole time. Every now and then, I'd catch her saying little prayers under her breath.

A blond male in magenta scrubs took us to a smaller room to run an ultrasound. Lying on the bed, all I could think about was that day in Birmingham when Garrett and I heard our baby's heartbeat for the very first time.

I think we were both stunned. We were definitely changed.

"That's a good sound!" The technician smiles, moving the wand over my abdomen.

Just like before, a steady, rhythmic whooshing fills the air around us, and my mom's hand flies to her mouth. "Is that the heartbeat?"

"Yes, ma'am." The fellow slides the wand around, and the black-and-white image changes shape. "The doctor will be in soon, but this is a good sign. If you can, try to relax."

He stands, going to the door, and we thank him.

It's quiet as we wait. Mom sits beside me, holding my hand, but we don't speak. I don't want to talk. All I can think about is the apple-sized baby I was told I could never have, and how much I don't want to lose it.

And how much I want Garrett here with me.

I blink, and another tear hits my cheek. I don't care about my trust issues or our past. I need his strong arms holding me. I'll worry about what it means later.

"It's been almost two hours since he texted last." Mom's voice is quiet as if she can read my mind.

My phone is in my hand with all Garrett's texts, from the first one telling me he was waiting on the pilot to file a flight plan to his next one telling me they were boarding. The pilot promised to get him here as fast as possible. His final text said he had to go into airplane mode, but he'd let me know as soon as they touched down at Callahan.

The girls' group chat blew up, but as much as I love them, I just can't right now. For better or worse, I only want one person. Two, if you count the doctor.

Mom seems to understand. She walks to the sink in the sparse room and pulls several towels from the metal box hanging on the wall. Holding them under the faucet, she squeezes the excess water before returning to where I lie.

"Want to put this on your eyes? It might help."

Her expression is worried, and even if it's not at all what I want to do, I smile and nod. Placing the cool brown paper towels over my eyes, I do my best to quiet my thoughts.

With my eyes closed, I picture an apple baby tucked inside me, its heart beating so strongly, so steadily. I think about Henny Lane sitting on her nest, protecting her unfertilized egg.

For whatever reason, since I've been home, Henny and I

have developed a connection. She's so devoted to her plain, beige egg. I can't let her be disappointed. I want all her efforts to be worth something.

I'm sure a therapist would have a field day with that.

"We're getting Henny Lane a chick." My voice is slurry, and I realize I've fallen asleep.

A warm hand smooths my hair off my forehead, and a deep voice answers. "What are we getting?"

Squeezing my eyes, I blink them open, and I hiccup a breath when I see Garrett beside me. Concern deepens the fine lines around his blue eyes, but they're warm with emotion.

"You're here." I don't mean for my voice to break. I don't mean for tears to leak out of the corners of my eyes again.

His smile is so comforting. "The pilot said he probably broke some air-speed records to get me here. I think Logan told him what was up."

Pushing against the mattress, I move to a sitting position. Smoothing my hands over my face, I clear my throat. "You missed the ultrasound. We could still hear the heartbeat."

"Your mom told me it was strong, just like before." He sits back, looking up at me with so much confidence.

"Where did she go?" I look around the space.

"I think she needed to walk around. I just got here, so she might be giving us a minute."

"We've been waiting for the doctor so long." I glance at the door, wondering what's happening.

The door opens slowly, and Garrett and I both look. I'm expecting my mom. Instead, it's a woman with dark brown hair and tan skin, who looks my age or a little older.

"Hello, I'm Dr. Pierce. What's going on in here?" She smiles, and her upbeat demeanor quiets my stress over how long it's taken.

"That's what we're hoping you'll tell us." Garrett's tone is equally upbeat, and I'm glad he's talking to her and not me. I might be less understanding.

"Let's see." She takes a stethoscope from around her neck

and moves it over my chest. "Your heart rate has come down, which is a good thing."

"Is… is the baby…" I can't finish, and Garrett's hand tightens over mine.

"The ultrasound showed a good, strong heartbeat and all of your vitals are good." She sits back, crossing her arms. "We've been watching the monitors over the past few hours, and I don't see any cause for alarm."

"I wish you'd told me that." My voice is quiet.

Dr. Pierce smiles, tilting her head. "Your stress levels all dropped when your husband got here. You were sleeping, and truthfully, sleep is the best thing for this."

Stealing a glance at Garrett, I think about what she said about my stress levels. "So why am I bleeding?"

"Spotting at this early stage can be caused by all sorts of things, from dehydration to cervical changes to sex." We both start to correct her, but she continues. "The baby is healthy. You're healthy. We really only worry if it's heavy bleeding or bleeding with cramping or pain or dizziness."

Embarrassment pricks my cheeks. "I didn't know."

The doctor reaches out to put her hand on my arm. "You've never done this before. It's normal to be afraid when you see blood, but you're going to be fine. I'll schedule a follow-up in a week, and we'll give you the all-clear to resume your usual activities."

She gives us a knowing wink, and my eyes drop to my hands.

"Thanks, Doc." Garrett seems to be taking it all in stride.

I want to die.

When we're finally alone, I drop my head into my hands. "I'm so sorry. I can't believe I panicked. You flew all the way down here—"

"Hell, Liv, I panicked." Garrett sits on the edge of the bed, pulling me into a hug. "It's like the doctor said. We've never done this before, and blood is fucking scary."

Nodding my head against his chest, a frown tugs at the sides of my mouth. "I think… I still don't believe it's happening." Sitting back, I meet his eyes. "It still feels like at any moment, it could be taken away."

I already love this baby too much, and in my experience, loving something too much has always led to loss and pain. For whatever reason, I can't seem to hold onto the things I love. My chest squeezes, and I inhale a shaky breath.

We're sitting on the bed, facing each other. The soft beep of the monitors surrounds us, and my eyes fall to our hands clasped together. Garrett dropped everything and flew here for me. I want so much to believe that changes things. It proves my past doesn't have to be my future.

"I'm not going back to New York." Garrett's tone is final. "I mean, I'll go back to pack up my clothes and my truck, but I'm not going to stay. Next time something happens, I'll be here. You won't have to deal with shit like this all alone ever again."

I don't want to argue. I want what he's saying. "Mom was with me, and she was really great—"

"Next time, I won't be flying across the country dying inside." His blue eyes hold mine, and I know he was as scared as I was.

I know he wants this baby as much as I do, even if it was a huge surprise that changed both our lives. We want it so much, and maybe that's the difference. I'm not the only one this time.

Nodding, I can't help a little smile. "I'll like having you here. The whole time, I really wanted you with me."

"I promised you wouldn't do this alone, Cherry. It's a promise I'll keep."

Sorry, for the wait. I was kind of panicking.

After we left the hospital, Garrett drove us to Mom's and stayed. It was after midnight, and without even discussing it, we climbed into my queen-sized bed together. It's a little small, but it didn't matter. He turned my back to his chest and wrapped me in his arms, holding me close.

One large hand covered my stomach, and the other held mine. As I drifted to sleep, warm lips pressed against the top of my shoulder, sending a flood of warmth through my body. My eyes closed, and I slept soundly through the night.

Now we're lying beside each other. He's still asleep, and I'm replying to the million messages in the girls' chat.

Dylan: Please tell me my baby niece or nephew is okay.

All good. Doc said lots of reasons for spotting, but apple baby is okay.

Dylan: I love that! It goes with your mom being Plum and you being Cherry…

Allie: No, Gwyneth Paltrow!

Rachel: I love the name Apple 🍎

We're just calling it by the weekly fruit. Next week, it'll be avocado.

Allie: Okay, that's cute 🥰

Dylan: I'm so excited to have Grizz home at last. Piggyback rides for all!

Allie: Poor Grizz.

Rachel: I've only known him a little while, but I think he likes it.

I'm happy he's here, too.

"The heartbeat is very strong." Dr. Pierce does her own ultrasounds, and at her encouraging tone, I exhale for the first time in seven days. "You might start to feel a little kicking. It'll be like flutters in your stomach."

Garrett's hand tightens on mine, and I smile. He hasn't left my side the entire week. Every morning, he's up making my half-caff coffee. He said the experts are divided on whether caffeine is dangerous, but all seem to agree two cups a day is okay.

When we were sure I wasn't spotting anymore, he went to meet with Rodney Brewer at the sheriff's office in town. I had no idea he was planning to take a job in law enforcement. He said he didn't want to mention it in case it didn't work out.

He helped me feed the chickens, and I showed him Henny Lane flat on her nest making dinosaur noises whenever we approached. I showed him how I carefully checked her for fresh eggs and slipped them out without upsetting her, always taking care to leave one behind.

Rachel dropped off a casserole, and her younger brother Edward informed us chickens are the closest animals to dinosaurs still alive today—even closer than alligators. I've seen them eat mice, so I believe it. She also invited me to join her at Miss Gina's for water aerobics and yoga, which I'm totally doing.

Tension made the days pass slowly, but suddenly we're back for our follow-up visit with Dr. Pierce, who is now my regular obstetrician.

"If you look right here, you can see the outline of the skull, and down here the fingers have formed." The corners of her black eyes wrinkle with her smile. "We can tell the sex if you'd like?"

My eyes cut to Garrett's, and his eyebrows lift. We didn't talk about this, but I kind of want to know.

"Okay?" I ask, and he gives me a little nod.

"We can never say for sure it's not a boy, but I don't see any indication it is."

A baby girl. Energy blooms in my chest, and I can't hold back a smile. His eyes shine at me, and he lifts my knuckles to his lips for a kiss. I tap the wetness from my cheek, because of course, I welled up again.

Dr. Pierce takes the wand away, wiping it with a towelette. "I'll put these images in the patient portal so you can share them with friends and family."

Her office is not a spa like Dr. Anderson's. It's very basic, and the waiting room is filled with expectant mothers, some with fathers, some with little kids, some alone.

It's all very homey and welcoming, and I like it so much. Probably because I am home, and Garrett is beside me.

"No more spotting?" She turns to the laptop beside her, typing in notes as I answer her questions.

"Not since that night." I shift, covering my stomach and sitting higher in the bed.

She nods, tapping on the computer. "Excellent. I think it's safe to resume all your regular activities. Being sedentary isn't good for either of you, so moderate exercise, walking, swimming, things like that will help with circulation, digestion."

We thank her, and Garrett waits in the hall as I get dressed. Relief is on both our faces as he takes my hand, walking me to my car. When we get there, he stops me before I open the door and pulls me into a hug.

"A baby girl." I hear the smile in his voice, and I hug him closer. Our little girl.

For a long moment, I hold him, and we breathe together. His lips are at the top of my head, and my eyes close as I'm surrounded by his warm clean scent, his strong, protective arms.

After another few moments, he steps back, dipping his chin so he can catch my eye. "I need to go and wrap things up in New York. I'll only be gone a few days—long enough to pack what I need and drive my truck here. Will you two be okay without me?"

My chest squeezes, and I feel so silly having separation anxiety over this. Nodding, I force a smile. "We'll miss you."

"I'd say come with me, but I don't think you'd be very comfortable driving twenty-four hours."

"I think you're right." I cringe, making scared eyes. "I'll hang with the girls and take care of Mom. I still have several cases open, so I need to work."

Sliding his thumb along my jaw, his clear blue eyes are brimming with something deeper, a new emotion we've never shared until now. "Let's wait until I get back to tell them it's a girl."

I reach up to slide my palm against his. "I'll try not to let it slip."

"No worries if you do."

He holds my hand for a long moment, and the energy between us pulls so fiercely. My lips are heavy, and I want him to lean down and kiss me. I want to rise up and kiss him.

We blink, and he lifts his chin, taking a step away. "I'd better get going. I'll see you and Miss Pomegranate in a few days."

Another breath, another wish for a kiss, and I let him go.

"When will you start showing?" Rachel squints up at me standing on the side of the pool in my red one-piece.

She holds Miss Gina's arm, guiding her down the steps into the warm pool. It's fall, but the temps are still in the low eighties during the day here. Still, at night, it's getting cooler. Of course, Miss Gina's gorgeous, cerulean-blue tile pool is heated. Descending into the warm water is luxuriously relaxing.

"I don't know." I put my hands on my midsection. "I hope soon, because right now I just look like a sausage."

"You are not a sausage." Rachel leans forward with a snort.

Her light blonde hair is in two braids tied on the top of her head, and she's in a mint green one-piece.

"None of my clothes fit, but I don't have a bump. I just look frumpy."

"I can't imagine you looking frumpy," Miss Gina interjects, her blind eyes lifted to the blue sky overhead. "You're always so elegant."

Cutting my eyes at Rachel, I huff a laugh as I bounce closer to where they're standing in the chest-deep water. "Miss Gina, how could you possibly know that?"

"People talk. You have a very professional style, and red is your signature color."

"Don't question Miss Gina," Rachel scolds teasingly. "She's always right."

"Well, you're very elegant yourself."

She's in a colorful, Lily Pulitzer one-piece with a bright pink swim cap on her head that's covered in fake, nylon flower petals.

Rachel hands us each "water weights," which are simply foam dumbbells, then she taps the face of her phone.

Dance music begins, and she bounces over to where we wait. "Let's start with eight reps, pushing down and up with control."

"You're going to be sore tomorrow," Miss Gina murmurs, moving her set up and down beneath the surface in time with the music. "I didn't believe it when we used them the first time."

"I believe it." I bend my knees to keep my weights underwater. "I'm already feeling it."

"Now to the back." She turns to the side so I can see the triceps move she's doing.

"How long before the kids have a holiday?" Miss Gina turns her head in Rachel's direction. "I miss Eddie Nashville and all of Kimmie's questions."

"They've only been back a month." Rachel bounces over to adjust her form.

"Children keep you young. I expect you to bring the baby to swim, Liv."

"Okay!" I smile, moving to the next exercise.

"When are you planning to get pregnant, Rachel?"

"I have to get married first, Miss G."

"Not always, but it's probably the best order. I'm ready for Dylan and Logan to have a baby, and then we'll have all these little feet running all over the place." She smiles looking up. "This old house is too big for one little blind lady."

"Now let's do some balance moves." Rachel takes her dumbbells and moves them to the side of the pool.

I follow suit, and as I do, a kitten rolls out from the flower bed followed by another, who jumps on its stomach. Then they both roll around before scampering away, and I imagine our baby girl playing with them. The thought makes me smile.

"They'll love all the kittens."

"Oh, those kittens!" Miss Gina groans. "Is Garrett taking that job in animal control? Tell him he has to help me solve my cat problem."

Rachel leans into her ear and stage-whispers, "It's called getting them fixed."

"Actually, they do have a trap-neuter-release program in town." We all join hands and do a little bouncy move in a circle. "I'm sure he'd be happy to help you with it."

Miss Gina lifts her head and smiles. "I know Dylan loves having her brother home. It reminds me of when you were all here, growing up."

"The stories make it sound so fun, with all the football games and the dance recitals and the ballet." Rachel's tone is wistful.

"It was." My eyes go to where the sun is drifting lower to the horizon. "We had everything we needed right here."

Miss Gina's hand tightens over mine. "No reason you can't have it again."

I blink over to her, thinking about how she always seems to know everything.

"Maybe we can have it again with the second generation of Bradfords." Rachel's nose wrinkles, and we release hands, drifting to the steps. "Can't you just see it?"

Climbing slowly, my hand goes to my stomach, and hope trickles through my chest. The sky is golden, we're back, and even with the tremor in my heart, I think I can.

Chapter 20

Garrett

BEFORE THE WHEELS TOUCH PAVEMENT AT THE SMALL AIRPORT IN New Jersey, I've made an appointment to meet with Kurt and Thad. While I was home, focusing all my attention on Liv and our baby girl, Logan worked behind the scenes to help Thad strategize.

I could use a fucking massage for how tense my muscles have been all week. I've never seen Liv that way, and it activated something inside me, something even more protective than I already felt for her.

She's always been so strong and so damn smart and in control all the time, but when I walked in and saw her in that bed so scared, I knew my days in New York were over. I wasn't leaving her again.

Now I just have to let these guys know, and hope they give me the benefit of our time together.

"Have a seat, Garrett." Kurt doesn't stand.

Thad meets me at the door to the office, leading me to one of the stiff leather chairs facing Kurt's desk.

"How is everything back home?" Kurt actually looks concerned, which is encouraging.

"Better." I don't really want to sit, but I do. "We had a follow-up appointment, and the heartbeat was steady, no more spotting."

"That's good." Kurt nods, resting his arms on his desk.

Thad doesn't say a word, and I'm pretty sure he doesn't have kids. I know he isn't married.

"Did you happen to catch the game last week?" Kurt turns, tapping on the laptop beside him. "Berke and Holmes look like they've been playing together all season."

"I caught the highlights." I wasn't interested in watching a four-hour football game with Liv still restless and worried.

"I'll cut to the chase. We're not letting you out of your contract."

I'm about to tell him I don't give a shit what he *thinks* he's not doing, but he continues.

"Instead, we're moving you to the disabled list." He turns to face me. "You're still on the roster, and we can call you back into play if anything happens. But for now…" He stands, reaching out a hand over his desk. "Go back to Newhope and be with your family."

It's all I needed to hear.

Standing, I shake his hand. "Thanks, Kurt."

Charlie: Maddy wanted to have you over for dinner, but Thad said you're already on the road.

The lights of the city are in my rearview, and I'm setting my own land-speed records when my phone lights up with his text. Lifting the phone, I use text-to-speech to reply.

Charlie: Everything okay?

Charlie: That happened to Maddy with Pax. Don't worry, you'll be fine.

Charlie: We'll set the table for three guests.

Flexing my grip on the steering wheel of my truck, I think about that possibility.

For a week after the scare, we slept every night together in her bed. The doctor said her stress levels went down when I was there, and it was enough. Hell, I'm pretty sure mine went down, too.

Holding her in the darkness, her body would relax. She'd drift to sleep so peacefully, and I'd trace my fingers through her hair, thinking how my entire world was right there in my arms. I'd place my hand on her stomach, and I had everything I needed.

When I was in the city, I'd pull up the images of our little pomegranate on my phone, and energy surged in my chest. She's tiny, but the outline is so bright. Her heartbeat is as strong as this bond growing between us, and I'm already imagining holding her in my arms.

Standing in the parking lot of Dr. Pierce's office, I wanted to kiss Liv so badly. We're so close to being back, it's hard to wait. We've been making small steps with each passing week, and I know now, as I cover these miles in my truck, we're at the beginning.

Our second chance starts now.

"Did you know as recently as colonial times, birds were so numerous, people thought they could never go extinct?" Liv stands inside the chicken coop in that pretty dress with the cherries on it.

Her strawberry hair is back in a ponytail, and she's wearing gloves as she checks on Henny "the goof" Lane. Of course, I don't say that out loud.

I rolled into town after one a.m. and crashed in my bed at the house. I slept hard, but when the sun broke on the horizon, I was up, quickly unpacking, showering, and heading here to her mom's house to brew her morning coffee.

Ms. Plum greeted me at the door with a warm smile and a big hug. She told me Liv was out here feeding the chickens and checking on their crazy little brooder.

"Can't say I did." I've got the garden hose, and I fill the water trough while she prepares individual cups of food and water for Henny.

The little white chicken makes the strangest sounds. They're noises I've only heard on *Jurassic Park*, but for whatever reason, Liv thinks it's so special.

"I was listening to a podcast." She steps out of the chicken coop to where the other birds are pecking around and spreads feed on the small picnic table-trough, along with ground oyster shells. "It said there were so many birds, they would block out the sun at times."

My brow rises, and I nod. "What happened?"

"Ladies fashion. Everybody wanted to wear feathers." She puts a hand on her hip, studying the flock. "I sure could go for some buffalo wings right now. There's a Buffalo Wild Wings in Foley."

Talk about a record-scratch moment. "It's nine o'clock in

the morning, Liv. I'd be glad to get you some, but I don't even think they're open yet."

Her lips twist, and she glances up at me. "Are they open for lunch? I wonder if they deliver."

Taking out my phone, I search for options. "It looks like they have online ordering… in a couple hours."

She walks over to hold my arm. "Buffalo wings and a chili cheese burrito. Doesn't that sound delicious?"

My brow furrows. "Together?"

"I bet Krispy Kreme is open now." Her eyes widen, and she rises onto her toes. "Chocolate glazed donuts would be so good for breakfast."

"You always said Krispy Kreme was too sweet for you. It made you sick."

"Remember when you made those cinnamon rolls for me in New York? That would be even better."

Swallowing my laugh, I slide my finger along her chin. "Give me ten minutes."

It takes less than five to jog back to my house and grab a can of cinnamon rolls out of the refrigerator. I'm on my way out again, when I see Dylan trotting up the hill from the restaurant.

"Garrett! You're home!" She runs straight to me, laughing and throwing her arms around my waist. "What are you doing with the cinnamon rolls?"

"Liv's craving them." Scratching my thumb over my chin, I huff a laugh. "She's kind of craving everything all at once. Buffalo wings, chili cheese burritos, Krispy Kreme donuts…"

"Now I *know* that's the baby." Dylan's eyes sparkle as she skips beside me, holding my arm. "Liv never liked Krispy Kreme. She said it was so sweet it made her sick."

"She wanted chocolate-glazed Krispy Kreme donuts."

"And you're bringing her Pillsbury cinnamon rolls?" She makes a little *tisk-tisk* sound, shaking her head in disapproval.

"She changed her mind halfway through. I'm not sure if she

wants this stuff all at once or if she's just checking them off as they come to her."

"Text me, and I'll see what Thomas and I can whip up for dinner." She laughs, twirling towards the house again. "I've got to get ready for school, but have fun!"

"I already am."

"I can tell." Dylan has a big smile as she walks backwards, her amber eyes holding mine. "You're glowing."

"Garrett Bradford, it really is you!" Aubrey Schiffer walks out of her small, glass cubicle to greet me at the front counter in the animal control office. "I heard you were joining the force."

Once Liv was satisfied with her cinnamon rolls and sat down to catch up on lawyering, I decided I'd better check in with my own "job."

Rodney called Aubrey when I was in his office, and she said to stop by when I was ready to start. Now seems as good a time as any.

She crosses her arms, looking up at me with a grin. "I haven't seen you since you graduated high school. I thought you were the best-looking thing…"

My smile is tight. I guess it's okay to be flattered. Even if Aubrey is my superior officer, she's still five years younger than me.

"You were in what? Seventh grade?"

"How do you remember that?"

"I'm pretty good at math."

Chuckling, she walks around the counter, waving for me to follow her. "Let's go."

We walk down a short hall to a sterile, linoleum-lined lunchroom. It's empty, and the fluorescent lights bathe the space in pale green. Just inside the door is a closet with a lock, and I wait as she stretches out a string of keys from her hip and inserts a bright gold one into the slot.

"I'm pretty confident we don't have a uniform that'll fit you, but you can wear one of these vests." The wire hangers make a scraping sound as she slides them across the metal bar.

The vest is black canvas with *Animal Control Agent* in white across the shoulder blades and a patch that has the law enforcement seal of Alabama on the front chest.

"People really don't care what you're wearing when they have an animal control problem." She leans in as if she's telling me a secret. "They just want you to fix it. Stat."

"I can believe that."

Taking the vest, I pull it on. It's roomy, which means it fits me fine. Aubrey, by contrast, is wearing a full khaki uniform with stripes on the arms and epaulets on the shoulders. She's very official.

"We'll start out doing the rounds together until you get the feel of things." We leave the cafeteria, and I follow her back to the front desk. "After that, you can handle the smaller jobs on your own."

"What kind of jobs are the smaller ones?" This is the part where I'm hoping for dog catcher.

"Oh, you know, the usual stuff, setting raccoon traps, retrieving squirrels from gutters, chasing skunks out from under porches."

"Skunks?" I don't like the sound of that.

"Don't surprise them." She stops abruptly, eyes wide. "*Never* surprise a skunk."

I almost laugh. "You've got experience with that?"

"Nope, but my dog does." She shakes her head. "It took three cans of tomato juice before he stopped howling."

Her phone starts to ring, and she leaves me standing at the front desk while she hustles into her office behind the glass. It has a plastic stack of shelves on one corner, and some papers are strewn across the blotter. Other than that, it's pretty neat.

I rest an arm on the counter, thinking about how I left Liv this morning asleep in bed. She's sleeping later now that I'm back, or at least that's what her mom told me. I was only gone four days, but Ms. Plum said she was up at dawn every day taking care of that silly chicken, almost like it's a soothing mechanism.

Ms. Plum likes to exaggerate things, but she's on my side. I'm not questioning her account, and I know to treat Henny Lane like she's a very special hen. Tracing my finger over the grain in the wood, I chuckle thinking about my serious lawyer lady so focused on a chicken.

"Looks like it's your lucky day!" Aubrey emerges from her office, moving fast. "Or mine. Let's go!"

"What's up?"

"Your brother works with Gloria Fruit out at Second Chance Stables, doesn't he?"

"Zane, yeah." My chest tightens, and I hustle to follow her out to her old-school, brown and tan Chevy Suburban. "Something wrong with the horses?"

"Nah, they'd call the vet for that." She turns the key and it roars to life. "Snakes. Gloria said a black racer decided to hide a nest of eggs in her back stall. Now they're hatching, and she needs us to relocate them. Gloria said she'd handle it, but she's got a class and your brother's at Miss Gina's."

"A black racer *snake*?" *Fuck*. I'm no Indiana Jones, but I hate snakes.

"Yeah, and it's causing a big problem. Horses and snakes don't mix." Aubrey reads my face and starts to laugh. "Don't worry, I'll take the lead on this one. Just help me with the traps. And don't forget your gloves."

Chapter 21

Olivia

"Tell me the truth, Marcus." The phone rests on my shoulder. "Are Putnam and Barnes involved in organized crime?"

A light chuckle meets my ear, but it does nothing to soothe my irritation.

"As far as I know, they're just regular ole Chicago realtors trying to capitalize on mineral rights."

"They sound like money launderers."

"Let me see what I can do, and I'll get back with you." He's so smooth, and I have to hand it to him. Marcus has handled much bigger cases than I have and always comes out on top. I've heard he even got a guy off for murder once.

"How's the baby doing?"

My eyes widen, and I hesitate. "Who told you I was pregnant?"

"I'm sorry, was that a secret?" I can hear the smile in his voice. "The receptionist told me you were working remotely, and when I asked if you were okay, she said you were expecting.

No harm no foul. I'm glad we've reached the point where remote work is acceptable."

I look down, turning the stylus in my fingers. "I don't mean to be guarded. Not everyone in our profession shares your attitude. The baby's doing great. Thanks for asking."

"I'm glad to hear it, and don't worry. I've got your back."

"Thanks, Marcus."

We spend a few minutes more strategizing how we'll handle the latest curveball in our case, and when we disconnect, I sit back in my chair, wishing I had a bag of Funyuns.

Silly pregnancy cravings. Last night I wanted salt and vinegar chips so bad, but not just any. I wanted Zapp's salt and vinegar, and poor Garrett had to drive across the bay to find a bag.

"Olivia, I need to speak with you a moment." Mom breezes into the room carrying a large duffel bag and two suitcases.

She looks like she's going away for a year.

My brow furrows, and I rise to my feet. "What the hell?"

"Language, please." Her lips purse with a frown.

I walk to where she's stacking her bags. "What's going on, Mother?"

"Your cousin Gwen just called while you were on the phone with Chicago. I didn't want to interrupt you because you were working, and it sounded important."

"What's wrong with Gwen?" A cousin of my mother's generation I haven't seen since I was in middle school.

"You're not going to believe this." Mom slaps her hand against her leg. "She really *did* have a hip replacement last week!"

"You're right. I don't believe it."

"And she's all alone in Evergreen with no one to help her. I figured I'd drive up there and stay with her until she's back on her feet. What else can I do?"

"I can't think of a thing."

"I'll have my phone, but I expect I'll be gone for *several* weeks. You should have Garrett come and stay at the house with you."

"You do." My lips press into a smile.

"Well, he's over here so early every morning anyway." She picks up the duffel bag, hauling it over her shoulder. "Tell him I don't mind if he stays in my room. I've washed the sheets."

"Gwen just called, and you had time to do all this packing *and* wash your sheets?" I can't resist poking holes in this very obvious attempt to put Garrett and me in the same house for *several weeks*.

"It's one of my rotating chores, Olivia." She gives me a look. "How often do you wash your sheets?"

"I don't have a schedule."

"Well, you should." She pulls the handle out of her large rolling suitcase, and I take the medium one. "Anyway, I'm only a few hours away if you need me. I'll be back in plenty of time for the delivery."

Following her to the car, I watch as she puts the bags in the trunk.

Turning, she pulls me into a firm hug. "I love you, Olivia." Stepping back, she holds my hands, smiling up at me. "Remember what I've always told you."

She climbs into her enormous Lincoln, and I prop a hand on my hip. "Love you, Mom. Drive safe."

I stand watching as she heads out onto the road. When she gets to the stop, she sticks an arm out and waves. I wave back, knowing exactly what she's referencing when she tells me to remember. It was her mantra when I was in high school.

Garrett Bradford is nothing like your father.

"Holy shit, animal control is wild. I might change careers." Garrett's voice booms from the kitchen as he enters the house. "You're not going to believe what Aubrey Schiffer did today."

Sitting up from where I'd fallen asleep on the couch, I push my hair off my cheek, rubbing my eyes. "Hey…" My voice is thick with sleep. "I take it you had a good first day?"

"I don't want to give you the wrong idea, but I think animal control might be the most important branch of law enforcement."

That makes me laugh, and I move my legs around to the floor. "What happened?"

"First, come with me." He takes my hands in his, gently lifting me to my feet. "Dylan said they've made a feast for you at the restaurant. They have buffalo wings, chili-cheese burritos, Thomas made his version of a White Castle burger, and Allie made her mom's special beignets."

I look around the dimly lit living room. "Am I dreaming?"

"Nope." Garrett puts his arm around my waist. "I mentioned you were having some pregnancy cravings, and my little sister got together with her partners in crime to be sure you have everything you need."

Tilting my head, I smile up at him. "Why are they so sweet?"

"Because you're my girl, and you know Dylan. She loves you, and she loves a cooking challenge."

Pressing my lips together, I silently acknowledge the tingle of pride in my veins at him calling me his girl. I'm hopeless, and I don't even care.

He holds my hand as we take the short walk to the restaurant, and I think about hopping on his back. It won't be long before my stomach prevents that option. I'm wearing a larger size of jeans, and my red sweater hugs my body. Sliding my hand over my stomach, I'm pretty sure I've got the start of a bump.

Dylan meets us at the door. "Look at you!" She steps back holding my hands and lifting my arms. "I think I see a pooch!"

"Do you?" I look down, sliding my hands over my thickening middle. "It's either that or a food baby."

"It is not a food baby. It's little… What fruit are we on now?"

"You're going to love this one." I lean forward. "Bell pepper."

"Craig's going to love it." Her nose wrinkles, but she's laughing.

Rachel skips out of the kitchen to where we're talking "You're here! Let me see that baby bump!"

"It might only be a food-baby bump." Turning to the side, I put my hand on my middle. "You won't believe how much crap I've been eating. Your poor brother has been working overtime."

Garrett puts a hand on my shoulder and leans down to kiss the top of my head. "Gotta keep my ladies satisfied."

We both gulp air, and Dylan squeals, throwing her arms over her head in a V. "You're having a girl?"

Falling back against Garrett's chest, I start to laugh as I nod. His arms wrap over mine, and he leans down into my ear. "Sorry."

"Why are you sorry? I've been dying to know!" Dylan claps.

"Baby girls are so fun." Rachel holds my hand. "We'll dress her up in the cutest little outfits and put ribbons in her hair."

"What am I missing? Is she showing?" Allie bursts through the double doors leading to the kitchen. "Damn, Liv! Your boobs are enormous!"

Her voice is too loud, and heat races to my ears. "Shut up!" I push her arm, glancing up at Garrett.

He gives me that sly grin that makes my entire body hot, but Dylan explodes with a laugh, shaking Allie's arm. "It's a girl! They're having a baby girl."

They're hugging me, and Garrett's standing back, grinning when Zane emerges from the kitchen. "What's this I hear about you wrangling snakes, G?"

"Snakes!" It's a collective gasp, and his gender oops is momentarily forgotten.

"That's what I said," Garrett takes my hand again, leading me to a booth near the large, open windows facing the bay.

"Gloria said Nala almost kicked a hole in the wall, she was so scared."

"Nala did that?" Rachel's eyes widen. "She's the sweetest horse! She's the one I always ride."

"Sounds like you had an exciting first day at work." I scoot into the seat beside him.

"Sorry I wasn't there to help you." Zane slides into the seat across from us with Rachel right beside him.

"I didn't do a thing." Garrett stretches an arm along the back of the booth behind me. "Aubrey handled it all like a freakin pro."

Dylan waves her hands between us. "Hold that thought, because I want to hear all about this, but the food's getting cold." Her amber eyes shine when she looks at me. "Garrett told me about your food cravings, and we had the best time making our own versions. Allie and I'll grab everything. Help yourself to drinks."

Her excitement reminds me of ninth-grade Dylan, three years younger than us, holding my hand and resting her head on my shoulder like I was already her big sister.

"I'll get them." Zane scoots, and Rachel stands to let him out.

Pointing around the table, he takes our drink orders, beers for all and sparkling water for me. He goes to the small bar near the pool-table area, where Edward went as soon as they arrived, and grabs us all drinks.

"Talk about the star treatment," Rachel teases, leaning forward.

I glance up at Garrett, remembering my comment in Blondie's.

He laughs it off. "It's not hard to be a star when you own the place."

Leaning back, I put my hands on the table, taking in his happy demeanor, his relaxed features, the black vest with the law enforcement seal on his chest.

"Aubrey Schiffer is Craig's cousin, isn't she?" Zane puts three longnecks and a tall black can in front of me.

"Yeah, and she's a badass." Garrett takes his arm off the back of the booth, leaning forward to take his drink.

My lips twist, and I do my best to fight the unexpected zing of jealousy at this new information. "What makes her so impressive?"

"Yeah, I'm not sure if I like her or not." Rachel sits back in the booth crossing her arms, and I want to reach out and give her a fist bump. "Is she as cute as Craig?"

"Nobody is," Garrett deadpans, and Zane holds a hand over his mouth.

Forcing a swallow, he shakes his head. "Dammit, G, you almost made me do a spit-take."

Shifting in the booth, Garrett squints down at me. "Are you seriously jealous of Aubrey?"

I study the can of sparkling water. "I don't know."

He leans back, grinning like he won some kind of award. "She's just a kid. She was in seventh grade when we graduated."

My lips part, and my eyes widen. "How do you remember *that?*"

"She told me."

"That was a long time ago. I doubt she's still just a kid."

"Hang on, you two." Zane holds up a hand in a time-out gesture. "Liv, if it makes you feel better, I'm pretty sure Aubrey is on Gloria and Sandra's team. Not to be stereotypical, but they all went to the Indigo Girls concert last summer, and I've never seen her with a boyfriend."

I huff an exhale. "That's hardly proof of anything. Everyone likes the Indigo Girls."

"Not everyone..." Rachel mutters, glancing to the side.

A strong arm wraps around my shoulders, and Garrett pulls me close. "Listen, Cherry, I'm not interested in anyone but you. Hear me?"

Butterflies swoop through my stomach at his bold statement. Zane's eyebrows flicker up briefly as he takes another sip of beer, and Rachel bites back a grin, her green eyes sparkling.

"What did I miss?" Dylan calls as she, Allie, and a young guy I don't know carry all the food to the table.

"A lot." Rachel practically shouts, and I want to kick her under the table.

"No!" Allie cries. "Y'all can't be telling all the good stories without us!"

"We haven't even gotten to the story yet." Rachel winks as she stands to help them pass out the plates.

She gives Dylan a little nudge, and the two exchange a glance. Garrett's expression is smug as he has another sip of beer, and Zane rests his arms on the table with a grin, looking up at his younger brother.

I've known this family long enough to guess what they're all thinking, and after everything that's happened, I'm ready to stop being the holdout.

"Here's what we've got." Dylan sets baskets down the center of the table. "These are the buffalo wings—mild for Liv, but I brought some hot sauce if anybody wants it."

"I do!" Rachel holds up her hand."

"Chili-cheese burritos with extra cheese." She puts the next basket in the middle. "Thomas's version of a White Castle, which is basically his classic burger, slider-size."

"I want that!" I'm already drooling.

"And last, but not least, Zapp's salt and vinegar chips." Dylan hands me my own bag.

"And my mom's beignet recipe for dessert!" Allie puts a basket of golden-brown pastries on the end with a silver, cup-sized shaker. "With powdered sugar. It's not Krispy Kreme, but it's pretty sweet."

Dylan's helper takes the trays to the kitchen while she and Allie pull up two chairs at the end of the table.

"Anybody need more beer?" Allie circles her finger over the group, counting the raised hands.

She runs to the small bar again, while everybody takes a serving of food.

"This is something to look forward to." Zane lifts a chili-cheese burrito from the basket nearest him.

"As long as the cravings aren't too weird." Rachel pours hot sauce over her buffalo wings. "I've heard stories—pickles with mayo, raw onions on strawberries…"

"No!" Dylan cries. "Why would anyone do that to a strawberry?"

Allie returns with the beers. "Tell us about the snake wrangling!"

"Like I said, I didn't do much." Garrett polishes off his tiny

Thomas burger, wiping his fingers with a paper napkin. "Aubrey rounded up a nest of sixteen baby black racers in less than ten minutes, no lie. *Sixteen* snakes, and those suckers are fast."

Jumping straight in my seat, I cover my mouth with a napkin. "Aubrey *is* a badass! Oh, my lord, Garrett…"

"I know!" He shakes his head. "I pretty much handed her stuff when she asked for it and stayed out of the way. Snakes were everywhere."

"Stop—I can't stand it!" Dylan waves her hands, doing a full-body shudder. "I would've run."

"Imagine how the horses felt. That mama snake laid them all right there in the back stall."

Craig walks up with a beer. "Why are y'all having a party back here without me?"

"Share my seat." Dylan hops up, grabbing his arm. "We're discussing how your cousin's a badass."

"Aubrey? Yeah, she's got some stories." He points at Garrett. "She's so excited you're coming to work for her. She's been your biggest fan ever since the incident."

"What incident?" Rachel's eyebrow arches.

"Something that happened back in middle school." Garrett shifts in his seat. "It was nothing."

"Was that when you got sent to the principal's office?" Zane's brow lowers like he's remembering, and now I'm pretty sure we're all on the edge of our seats, glancing between both of them.

"The one time." Garrett nods. "It didn't happen again."

"What happened?" I tilt my head at him.

"I was in eighth grade." Garrett leans closer. "You didn't know I was alive."

Craig points his longneck at Garrett. "This guy was always a foot taller than everyone, and when my parents moved here, I didn't have any friends."

"You had me!" Dylan loops her arm in his, leaning her head on his shoulder. "We danced together and played Barbie vs. Brats together."

"And there were a few high school guys who didn't like boys dancing ballet and playing with dolls," Craig continues. "So Garrett stuffed them in a dumpster. After punching them both in the face a few times."

"Just taking out the trash." Garrett straightens in his seat.

"They were beating you up." Dylan's voice is quiet, and her lips press into an angry frown. "You couldn't dance for a month because of your ribs."

"But they gave me this sexy scar." Craig slides his hand along the side of his hair, and a noticeable scar is on his temple.

My eyes widen. "That looks like it was pretty bad."

"Dad was so pissed you were sent to the principal's office." Zane smiles proudly. "I'm pretty sure he threatened to throw that guy in the dumpster along with the bullies."

Garrett puts his napkin on his plate. "Nobody bothered my boy Cray after that."

"Or anyone else who played with dolls or danced ballet," Craig adds.

"Yeah, I'm pretty sure you were the only fairy doing that," Garrett quips. "Oh, wait. I was dancing with you."

Dylan grins, wrapping her arm around her friend's waist and resting her head on his shoulder. "Those idiots."

Shifting in my seat, I slide my arm behind Garrett's waist and rest my head on his shoulder, too. "Were you always being a hero?"

He turns, kissing the top of my head. "When I wasn't being a dumbass."

Chapter 22

Garrett

W E STAY A LITTLE LONGER UNTIL LIV'S EYES BLINK SLOWLY, AND I know she's tired. She gets tired early these days.

With all of us working together, it doesn't take long to dispose of the trash and put our dishes in the large dishwasher. Tables are cleaned and condiments refilled, and we leave the restaurant ready for tomorrow before telling everyone goodnight.

Being with my family and with Liv this way reminds me of how I always dreamed it would be, and walking back to Liv's house, she catches my shoulders and hops onto my back.

Wrapping my arms under her knees, I love the feel of her body against mine. "Is your mom playing DnD tonight?"

I can't get over Ms. Plum being an elf bard.

"She went to Evergreen!" Liv's arms are around my neck, and she tilts her head to the side. "My cousin Gwen had hip replacement surgery, so Mom packed enough clothes to last a year and went to stay with her. She said you're welcome to sleep in her room while she's gone."

Anticipation tingles my stomach as I think about what she's saying. "Are you asking me to spend the night at your house?"

"You're over so early every morning, I don't see why you shouldn't. Unless you don't want to."

"I want to." My tone is definite, and we fall quiet.

Liv rests her chin on my shoulder as we walk, and the cool breeze touches my cheek. The weather is changing, and we'll be wearing coats and the kids will be having bonfires before long. I think of holding her in my arms, watching the orange embers.

"I'm really proud of you for defending Craig like that."

"I've never liked bullies." It's low, almost a growl when I remember those big boys holding my friend down, punching him in the stomach and face.

"You really are a champ."

That makes me laugh. "Champ of spilling the beans."

Her head tilts to the side and she smiles. "What's your favorite baby girl name?"

"Hmm…" I hold her legs as I think about it. "I don't really have any favorites, but Mom's name was Lucy. My grandma was Grace."

"What was your mom's middle name?"

"Knox."

"Your mom's middle name was Knox?" Disbelief is in her tone, and I chuckle.

"I think that was her mother's maiden name."

"I like that for a boy, but maybe not a girl."

We're almost home, and I give her a little bounce. "What's yours?"

"Angie, Bianca, Lola…"

"I like Lola. She'll be a showgirl."

We've reached the house, and she slides off my back, skipping ahead of me, up the steps and turning to place her hands on my chest. "Our daughter will *not* be a showgirl."

"With yellow feathers in her hair, and her dress cut down to—"

"Garrett!"

I can't help laughing, and I reach up to cup her face in my hands. Tonight when she tried to get jealous about Aubrey Shiffer of all things, I didn't hesitate. I'm tired of holding back, and I want her to know how I feel. So I put my cards on the table—in front of witnesses.

Our eyes hold, and a tentative smile lifts the corners of her mouth. She reaches up to slide her hand over my wrist. "We should get inside. It's chilly."

I follow her inside, stopping to slip off my work boots at the door and hang my vest on the coat rack. She goes to the kitchen and takes down two glasses.

"Would you like some water?"

"Sure."

When she returns, she hands me one, and I look down at her, feeling the humming tension of us being here in this house, all alone.

"I'm not really tired. Want to see what's on TV?" She passes me, picking up the small remote of the end table. "Mom still has cable, so no telling."

She sits on the couch, and I lower myself beside her, watching as she cycles through the channels. Finally, she stops on an old police show with Kyra Sedgwick in it.

"Oh, I used to love *The Closer!*" She sets the remote down, settling into my side.

I can't focus on the show with her beside me, then she shifts again.

"I can't get comfortable in these jeans." She stands. "I'm going to change."

My eyes glide down her body, her full breasts hugged in that sweater, and my dick twitches. "I'd better run back to the house and get some clothes for tomorrow."

She peeks her head back into the room. "Don't be gone too long."

With that, I hustle out the door, jogging quickly to the

house and doing my best to grab a few things and stuff them into my duffel bag before leaving again. The house is dark, and I expect Dylan and Logan will appreciate having the place to themselves. It reminds me, I need to start looking for my own place, for when Ms. Plum returns. Something with plenty of room for a family.

When I get back, Liv is perched on the couch with a bowl of popcorn in her lap. Her legs are crossed, and she's in my old cotton jersey and lounge pants. Fuzzy socks are on her feet, and she looks cute as hell with her hair tied to the side in a ponytail.

"You're wearing my jersey."

"Every night." Her slim brow lowers. "That's not a lot of stuff."

"I'll get more tomorrow." I carry the bag into Ms. Plum's small room.

Frowning, I look at her single bed and decide on the spot I won't be sleeping in it. It's a kind offer, but for whatever reason it feels weird to me. I replace my jeans with the sweatpants I brought and trade out my work shirt for a tee.

When I return, Liv holds out the bowl. "Popcorn?"

Dropping beside her, I exhale. "Nah, I'm good." Reaching down, I lift her foot into my lap and take off her sock.

"What—" Her protest devolves into a moan when I start to massage her foot.

Not gonna lie, that moan is the sexiest sound I've heard in a while. "The book says expectant mothers really like foot massages."

"Everybody likes foot massages."

Kyra Sedgwick is walking around a crime scene in a pretty dress and cardigan set taking pictures, and I reach down to lift Liv's other foot into my lap to repeat the process.

"You're really good at this." She smiles. "You don't tickle or nothing."

I grin. "*Pulp Fiction*."

"You know what they say about foot massages."

Pressing my lips together, I nod. "I wouldn't give a guy a foot massage."

With a quick inhale, she puts the bowl aside and shifts higher on the couch. "What else does the book say about me?"

My eyes slide from her bare foot to her bare ankle, and I slide my fingers around to the back of her calf, gently circling my fingers. "It says a lot of things."

Her tongue slides out to wet her bottom lip, and her eyes flicker to my hand. The back of her calves is another one of her sensitive spots.

When we saw that episode of *Friends* in high school, I immediately made Liv show me all her erogenous zones. It was hot, and I wanted to make Liv moan that way. We spent the summer finding every place—behind her neck, in the bed of her arm, her lower back, the backs of her shoulders… I loved watching her eyes darken and her nipples peak.

"Some pregnant ladies get really horny." Her eyes drift to the screen, but my senses tingle at her words. "I wonder what evolutionary purpose that serves. I'm already pregnant."

"Are you saying you're horny, Cher?"

She shrugs, pushing her hair behind her shoulder. "I think it's important to be able to communicate your level of horniness with your partner. Maybe you're both equally horny, but you don't know it."

"True."

"I've heard women complain they're hornier than their boyfriends, but if they've never shared that information, how could they know? Maybe their boyfriends are just as horny as they are."

"I'm getting horny just talking about it."

She sits forward arching an eyebrow. "Are you?"

"Always for you." My voice is lower, and my eyes drag from her full lips down her neck. "You know how I feel."

"How do you feel?" Her voice softens, and our eyes meet.

"Only ask me if you really want to know."

"I really want to know."

Taking her hand, I give her a gentle pull, helping her straddle my lap facing me. She sits on my erection, and her eyes slant. I know she feels it.

Leaning forward, she speaks in my ear, soft lips brushing my skin. "Tell me."

I put my hands on her waist. "I want to tear this jersey off your body and devour you."

Holding my neck, she hums. "Or you could just slide your hands underneath it."

Tilting her head to the side, she traces her lips along my jaw, getting closer to my mouth. I do as she says, finding her body completely bare.

Groaning, I lift and cup her breasts, squeezing them and sliding my thumbs over her hard nipples. I've been obsessed with touching her for weeks. She's softer, rounder…

She exhales a hushed moan in my ear. "Don't stop."

"Fuck, Liv," I groan, shifting my hips so my dick hits her core. "It's been so long since I touched you."

"I've wanted you for months." Her lips brush mine.

Slim hands cup my cheeks, and our mouths seal together. She exhales a whimper as my tongue invades to find hers. I want to be gentle, but I'm not sure I can.

Her kisses are as hungry as mine, and the way she's sliding back and forth on my lap is making me crazy.

"Let's go." Sliding my hands under her ass, I lift her as I stand.

Her legs wrap around my waist, and I carry her to her bedroom. Lowering her gently onto the bed, I take a knee as I reach up to jerk those cotton pants down her legs. Straightening, I hold her jaw as I kiss her, pulling her lips with mine before opening her mouth and curling our tongues together once more.

Dragging my mouth down her neck, I pause to help her out of my jersey. She lies back, and I lean forward to suck a nipple into my mouth. My hands brace the mattress on either side of her, and I devour her soft skin, inhaling her sweet jasmine scent.

"I want to fuck you til you can't walk."

"Garrett…" she moans, threading her fingers in my hair.

Her body curves up to meet me, and she kisses my head, the side of my face.

I'm moving lower, lingering a moment at her stomach, spreading my hand over the bare skin and kissing just above her navel. Tracing my lips to the side, I move lower to where her lacy underwear rises over her hip.

She hisses my name as I hook my fingers in the sides to yank them down her thighs, past her knees, and she kicks them off her feet.

Rising onto her elbows, she looks down at me between her legs. I push my pants down, allowing my erection to spring free, and her bottom lip goes beneath her teeth.

Hazel eyes darken, and she's so fucking sexy watching me. I palm my cock, sliding my hand to the tip, over the precum leaking, and using it to smooth my strokes as I slowly jerk off for her.

"You make me so hard," I groan, and her hand slides between her legs.

I know my girl likes to watch, and I'm happy to give her a show. A few more strokes, and I have to stop before I come too soon. Moving forward, I spread her thighs wide, so I can drag my tongue over her clit.

"Oh, God…" She falls back onto the bed, her body shuddering as I eat her pussy.

Her ass tenses, and she moans as my tongue moves in circles up and down and all over that hard little bud. Closing my lips, I give her a suck and her lower body shudders. Another flicker of my tongue, and she breaks into jerky spasms, moaning and pulling my hair.

Kissing higher, I trace my lips over her lower belly. Another kiss for our baby, and my hand is on my dick again. Lifting her knees, she holds her hands out to me. I slide my tip up and down her wetness, coating my cock as I thrust firmly into her core.

"Fuck," we both groan, and I drop forward with my arms beside her on the bed.

I'm sheathed, warm and tight in her shuddering body, and it feels so damn good. My face is buried in her shoulder, and I kiss her skin, dragging my lips to her collarbone. Her fingers dig into my back, and she moves her hips beneath me.

"Fuck me, Garrett." Her voice is thick, and I start to move, rocking my hips.

Lifting higher, I meet her mouth for another, messy kiss. Our lips frantically chase each other's, both moaning as our tongues drag together. She drops her mouth to my neck, biting and sucking at the skin, and it's a charge straight to my cock.

"Liv…" I groan, unable to slow my raging orgasm.

It climbs higher in my legs, twisting in my core, driving my movements. I'm fucking her hard, and my ass tightens. Everything twists achingly hotter.

"This pussy is mine."

"Yes," she gasps.

"This pussy belongs to me." She groans louder, and my jaw grinds.

Bracing my hand beside her on the bed, a bead of sweat rolls down my brow. I hold her waist as I thrust faster again and again.

"Say it." It's a primal demand.

"My pussy is yours."

I hold, breaking with a loud groan. My dick pulses, and I'm blinded by the intensity of this one. It's just like before, just like always. For several moments, I can't move. I'm lost in this moment, holding the one thing I know is true.

Until slowly, my muscles release. I shudder with the aftershocks. It's so damn good.

Dropping to the bed beside her, I gather her into my arms, hugging her to my chest. Her hands find my waist before sliding around, and she's holding me equally tightly. I dip my chin and kiss her eyebrow, her hair, the top of her head.

This is my family. She's my home.

Chapter 23

Olivia

GARRETT'S ARMS SURROUND ME, AND I CLOSE MY EYES, LETTING THE high of his kisses vibrate through me. He fucks me so well, stretching and filling me until I can't take any more. He's demanding and possessive, claiming me, and I've missed him so much.

Lifting my chin, I press my lips to his, opening his mouth and swiping his tongue with mine. He rolls me onto my back, taking charge and kissing me deeper before moving his lips to my cheek.

Stretching my body, I moan. "Say it again."

"What do you want me to say?" His voice is so calm, his blue eyes gazing into my soul.

So many things.

"Say I'm your girl."

Exhaling a chuckle, he leans down to kiss my nose as he holds my naked body flush with his. "You're my girl, Liv. Always."

Dipping my chin, I rest my cheek against his chest. I want

to say so many more things. I want to make promises and plans, but right now I'm satisfied in the cocoon of his embrace, basking in this step we've taken.

We're home. I'm in his arms. It's right, and I never want to leave this place. I always want to be his.

"Losing you was the worst thing I've ever done." His voice is quiet, and I tighten my fingers against his back. "You were always so smart and strong and beautiful. I was always so proud to be with you, to be your guy. I wanted everyone to know you belonged to me."

His voice is low, almost like he's starting to sleep, and I hug him tighter thinking about this. I think about how hard I worked to be something special, a girl my father would be proud of.

I don't know if my father was ever proud of me, but this man was.

"Now you're having my baby, and I realize…" His lips trace a line over my brow. "I didn't know what being proud meant."

My eyes squeeze, and my fingers curl as I hold him tighter. "The happiest times of my life have all been with you, Liv."

His hand cups the back of my head, and it's true. Sleep pushes against my eyes, and I curl to the side. Being in his arms is the best place to rest.

The moon glows through my window when I wake to warm kisses sliding up my back. My nipples tighten as his lips move into my hair, behind my ear, pulling the skin of my neck gently between his teeth.

Heat rises in my core, and my insides are slippery wet. It's tingling and electric, and the added scuff of his beard makes me moan. He smiles against my skin and cups my breasts, squeezing and lifting, rolling the tips between his fingers.

"Are you still horny?" He pulls my earlobe, and I nod.

"Yes."

"What do you want?"

"The tip."

"Where?" A smile is in his voice, and my stomach trembles with anticipation.

"In my ass."

His low groan makes me whimper. Large hands grip my butt cheeks, squeezing and massaging, and I rub my knees together with need.

"This sweet little ass wants my cock?" His beard scuffs the side of my neck.

"Yes…" I nod, shuddering as my back arches.

My tingling nipples point to the ceiling, and I put my hand between my legs to stroke my clit.

He dips two fingers into my dripping core then slides the wetness higher, over my tightest hole. Gently pushing a finger inside, I drop my head back against his shoulder with a moan.

"You're so wet," he groans in my ear. "It's not enough for this."

"The nightstand drawer…"

He moves quickly. My eyes are closed, and I hear the click of a cap.

Turning my face to his, I kiss his cheek. "You're the only person I do this with."

"Me too," a dark chuckle. "It's our little secret."

My nose wrinkles, and I breathe a laugh, thinking of us as curious teenagers, believing we were being so bad.

Holding my jaw, he consumes my mouth. Our tongues curl, and his hand slides across my stomach, around my waist as he pulls me closer. Heat ripples out from his touch, and he lifts his mouth to my ear.

"I'd never hurt you, Liv." From the first time we did this, he's always so careful with me.

His lips return to my neck as he coats my ass with lube, inserting one finger, then two. His hard cock is at my hip, and I reach down to stroke and pull it. It's big like everything about him, and my fingers don't meet when I wrap them around his shaft.

Another groan as I cup and circle my palm over the tip. His hand joins mine, coating his erection in lube.

We stroke him several more times as he pants, then I return my fingers to my clit.

Energy tightens my stomach as he approaches me. Guiding his cock to the small entrance, he takes his time, slowly increasing the pressure as the muscle starts to relax.

My eyes squeeze, and my jaw drops as I massage my clit faster. His face is at my ear again, and he starts to groan when his tip pops through the tight ring.

"Fuck, Liv…" It's a husky groan, and my hips bend as sensation radiates through my pelvis.

His thrusts are shallow but fast. He fucks my ass like he's losing his mind, and it shoots thrills of pleasure through my pussy to the arches of my feet.

It's so dirty and so hot, hearing his moans turn to ragged grunts. He swears, gripping my hips, pressing his teeth to my shoulder.

My orgasm twists tighter, irresistibly tight, and wetness is on my inner thighs. His thrusting becomes erratic, his breath shaky gasps. My stomach is tight, and my fingers circle faster.

Another deep groan, another swear, and he thrusts deeper, stretching my ass wider.

"Garrett," I cry, and my body breaks.

Orgasm electrifies my core, shaking my legs, and I bend forward, circling harder as I wail.

Another two pumps, and he lifts his chin, coming with a shout. He reaches down to pull out gently, and hot come spills onto my trembling thighs. He jerks himself off fast, groaning low as he finishes, more hot liquid on my lower back.

We're both panting, like we've just run a mile.

"Fuck, that's so fucking hot." Kissing between my shoulders, he looks down at what we've done. "Let's get you cleaned up."

I'm in his arms, and he carries me to the shower. My head is tucked against his neck as we wait for the water to heat, and he cups my chin, pulling my mouth to his in a devouring kiss.

My lips part, and his tongue curls and strokes mine. He nips at my top lip then my bottom before kissing me again, moving to my cheek and the tip of my nose. "I lost it when you came."

Blinking my eyes, I grin up at him. "I could tell."

"You're going to be shitting come tomorrow, sorry."

"Oh my God." I snort, burying my face in his neck. "I should never have told you that."

He cups my chin, kissing me again, long and slow, before he stands, carrying me into the shower. My eyes consume him. He's a gorgeous statue of male perfection. Broad shoulders are rounded with muscles. Defined biceps, veined forearms, large hands.

Lines of muscle stripe his ribs, his stomach, leading to that luscious V wrapping over his hips to his long, thick cock. His thighs are defined and powerful, and he wastes no time working up a lather and cleaning his dick thoroughly before moving to me.

His talented hands massage my breasts, teasing my nipples before making their way down to my stomach.

Dropping to his knees, he pauses to eat my pussy. Slow strokes of his tongue are followed by quick, little sucks. He holds me to his face, and I ride it, loving the feel of his beard against my inner thighs. He keeps going until my legs buckle, and he has to hold me up through the orgasm melting my knees.

Straightening, he spends a little more time on my breasts, nibbling and sucking them, before lifting me off my feet and fucking me hard against the wall.

I'm completely boneless by the time he carries me to bed again. My back is against his chest, and I'm wrapped up tight in his arms like always.

My hunger is satisfied, and a little smile curls my lips as I drift to sleep, perfectly spent and so happy.

Chapter 24

Garrett

"I SN'T IT INTERESTING HOW WE WERE BOTH INTO SPORTS AND athletics, and we both ended up in legal-type fields?" Liv sits at the small table in the kitchen with her phone propped on her growing midsection.

She's so cute at this stage, wearing stretchy leggings and tight sweaters to show off her small baby bump. There's no mistaking she's pregnant now. Our baby girl is the size of a head of cauliflower, and she's moving a lot.

At night, when we sit on the couch watching *The Closer*, I'll hold Liv between my legs with her back against my chest, and we watch as her stomach morphs into crazy shapes. At times it's like a torpedo, which Liv says is her butt. Then it'll be a small point, which she says is her elbow or knee. Maybe even a foot.

She assures me it doesn't hurt as she holds my hand against the movements. It seriously blows my mind.

"It's probably because we watched all those crime shows in high school."

"We didn't always watch them." She slants her eyes up at me, and my dick twitches.

"Careful, I don't have time to fuck you right now."

Her lip pouts. "Sounds like you're working too much."

That does it, I put my mug down and walk to where she's sitting. Her brow arches, and she stands, turning around and shaking her ass at me.

"Dammit, Liv, what are you doing to me?"

"Do I have to spell it out for you, Sheriff?"

My vision darkens, and I have ideas about handcuffs. "Put your hands on that table and don't let go."

She exhales a little squeal as I jerk her leggings down, and we do it right there, doggystyle over the kitchen table.

I gotta give it up for the horny phase of pregnancy. We've been fucking more lately than we did as teenagers, and that's saying something.

I'm helping her get dressed again, and she laughs softly.

"What?"

"Remember that time Mom went to bed early, and we were alone in the living room, and I climbed onto your lap?"

"You always blew my mind, Liv."

"We could've been caught, and I loved it." Her nose wrinkles as her eyes blink down, almost nostalgic. "Thank you."

"For what?"

Pretty hazel eyes meet mine again, so beautiful and open. "For reminding me what I was like, happy and free."

"It's how I always want you to be." Using my finger, I slide a lock of her hair behind her ear, thinking about a question that's been bothering me a while. "You never told me why you stopped dancing. You were so good at it, and you worked so hard."

A little shrug, and she goes to the coffee pot. "I discovered law in college, and one of my professors encouraged me to take the LSAT. I did really well on it, but I also made it all the way to the finals with the dance team." Her head tilts to the side as she pours another cup. "For so long, it had been my whole purpose. Then I looked around at all these talented women fighting for just a few spots, even after they'd already been on the team… I decided to let them have it and fight for justice instead."

Straightening, I walk over to where she sits at the table and take a knee. "I think it's pretty badass that you're a lawyer. You were hot as shit when you were dancing, but knowing you can shake that ass and practice law…" Lifting my eyebrows, I nod. "Badass."

Her nose wrinkles, and she huffs a laugh. "Not as badass as Aubrey Shiffer."

Groaning, I fall back. "You had to be there!"

"I'm just teasing. You were being sweet." Cupping the sides of my neck, she kisses my lips. "Thank you. Now I've got to get some work done. I can't spend all morning having sex."

Catching her face, I kiss her again, a little longer, a little tongue. Then I'd better get out of here before I do carry her to bed again.

"I think we blew all the excitement on the first day." Going to the door, I lift my vest off the back of a chair. "It's been kind of slow-going ever since."

She stands, waddling just a little as she joins me at the door. "It's pretty hard to top sixteen snakes."

"It's okay. It gives me time to work on my law enforcement materials."

Her eyebrows rise. "So it's a good thing?"

A good thing. I slide my hand along her cheek, thinking about all those months ago when we said being pregnant wasn't a good enough reason to get married.

I think we have plenty of good reasons now.

"I'll see you this afternoon." Leaning down, I steal one more kiss.

Her cheeks flush, and she's fucking adorable.

Hendrix: Garrett, is it true you're never playing ball again?

I'll play at Thanksgiving. If we're still doing that...

Zane: We're doing it. I've done the work.

Hendrix: So what, you're just going to be a dog catcher for the rest of your life?

I'm training to work in law enforcement. Don't make me cuff and stuff you.

Hendrix: That's cool.

Hell, yeah it is. I'm the sheriff in this town.

Zane: Not yet.

Jack: Will you be home for the holiday, Hen? I thought you had a game.

Hendrix: I do, but the Pirates are bound for the playoffs. I thought Grizz would want to be there.

Been there, done that, having way more fun watching Liv's stomach.

Logan: Liv's a cute little pregnant lady. Makes me want to put one in Dylan.

We discussed this, bro. You only get babies from a stork.

Zane: I gotta say, it's giving me some ideas.

Hendrix: Fuck me, I'm def not coming home now. I don't want to catch what you all have.

Zane: What's that, smart guy?

Hendrix: Baby fever. Pass.

Don't knock it til you try it, little man.

Hendrix: I'm surprised Liv was brave enough to have your baby, Sasquatch.

Liv's a badass, and our little girl will be perfect.

Hendrix: I guess Dylan's a shrimp. There's hope for recessive genes.

Jack: I saw the Tigers are also headed for the playoffs. Good work, bro.

Hendrix: I don't like The Dick saying Grizz was holding him back. That's a bunch of bullshit if I ever heard it.

I confess, it gets my back up, too, but what am I going to say? I didn't like him either.

I needed to get out of there. If it helps him build his legacy, so be it.

Hendrix: He's messing with your legacy. It's fucking bullshit.

I care about my family more.

Hendrix: You might care one day, when you get your head out of your ass.

Jack: Take a beat, Hen. Grizz is doing what he loves now. It's all good.

Hendrix: Fuck that. Y'all might've drunk the Kool-Aid, but I'm not buying it. Grizz and Logan worked hard for what they built, and that little shit isn't taking it away from them.

Logan: I'm only a BIL, so while I thank you, being out of the game kind of changed my perspective. There's more to life.

Hendrix: So you don't care either?

Logan: I care about different things now.

Hendrix: Like I said, I don't want what y'all have.

The chat falls silent, and a weight is in my stomach. I don't want to tell my little brother he might feel differently one day. He won't believe me until it happens—I don't think I would've believed me until it happened.

At the same time, I love his protectiveness. I love his family loyalty. He's looking out for all of us, even if we're not so worried about it anymore. Hendrix can be a little shit, but he's my brother. His heart's in the right place, and one day Cupid's going to kick his ass.

Scrubbing my hand over the back of my neck, I don't know what to do. Liv would probably have some good advice, but for now, I have to trust Jack to take care of him like he does all of us. I can't stand in the parking lot any longer or Aubrey will think something's wrong.

"Hey, girl." I pull the glass door open. "Sorry about that. Brother stuff."

Her lips press into a smile and she walks over to stand behind the counter. "I can only imagine, with all the star power in that bunch."

"Yeah, it's a laugh a minute." My tone is flat, and I go to the desk. "Anything interesting today?"

"Not much. An out-of-towner just called the 800 line. She's staying down near the pier, and apparently there's a cat in a tree."

"Isn't that what the fire department's for?" I'm teasing, and she laughs.

"We trade off based on who's busier. Feel like taking a drive?"

Shrugging, I pluck the Post-it with the address off her finger. "Might as well. It's not sixteen snakes, but…"

Shaking her head, she waves me away. "Sixteen baby snakes is nothing. Go be a hero for some little girl."

Little girl. I think about our baby and how one day, she might have a cat who gets stuck in a tree. I'll be her hero. Not going to lie, that makes me feel all sappy. "See you in a little while."

"I'll call you if we have any gator encounters."

"Thanks." I laugh, heading out to my truck.

It's a short drive to the big hotel south of town. I pass the large city pier and the marina, out to where the vacation cottages line the road with their bike and walking paths. Specialty shops and small restaurants are sprinkled among them, and it's a popular vacation spot.

The address leads me to a small cottage with white wooden siding, window boxes full of flowers, and a screened-in side porch. An ancient, enormous live oak tree is out front with thick, black limbs reaching down almost to the ground.

I can't help thinking if a cat is in this tree, it will have no trouble climbing right back out again.

Pulling onto the shoulder of the road in front of the house, I put my truck in park and step out, slowly walking to the door. I'm wearing my *Animal Control Agent* vest, so there's no mistaking why I'm here.

When I get closer, a woman with shoulder-length silver hair steps out to meet me. She looks about five to ten years older than me, and she's well-dressed. Pretty fashionable for the beach. It kind of reminds me of how women dress in the city.

"Thank goodness!" She calls, jogging to meet me at the road. "Are you here about the cat?"

"We got the call, but I have to say…" Scratching my thumb over my chin, I look up at the tree. "I think a cat can get out of this tree on its own."

"It's been a while since I saw it, but it was crying and crying." She chews her finger, staring up into the branches. "Perhaps I overreacted. It seemed so pitiful."

"No worries." I reach out to pat her shoulder. "It probably hoped you'd feed it. You know how cats are."

Her brow crinkles, then all of a sudden she jerks, her eyes widening. "Wait a minute… Are you?" Her mouth opens, and she covers it with her hand. "Are you Garrett Bradford? Number 50, starting offensive lineman for the New Jersey Pirates?"

I clear my throat, a mixture of pride and embarrassment in my chest. "That's me."

"What the heck are you doing down here? I heard you'd been injured or something…" Squeezing her eyes, she scrubs her fingers over her forehead like she's trying to remember. "I read you were on the disabled list. Were you hurt?"

"Ahh, well, you see…" Fuck, this hasn't happened before, and I didn't think about what to say if it did. "I had some family issues I had to take care of, and I couldn't really be in the city full time."

I'm not convinced any of that makes sense. At the same

time, why am I explaining myself to a random vacationer in south Alabama?

She seems to read my expression and takes a step back. "It's none of my business, is it?" She exhales a laugh. "You probably have a sick mother or sibling with cancer, and I'm the worst possible fan, prying into your personal life. I want to die. I'm so sorry."

Now I feel guilty. "No, it's not like that. My girlfriend is expecting, well, my fiancée actually…" *I hope.* "She was having some complications with the pregnancy, and I needed to be here with her."

"Is she okay now?"

"Yeah," I nod. "She's a lot better."

"But you're still here. Are you quitting the team?"

"Ahh… still working out the details there." My throat tightens as I say the words, and I decide I'd better go.

This woman has a weird way of getting me to say more than I want to say, and I'm not sure how much Liv would want me telling strangers about our plans.

"Anyway, looks like the cat's gone. Enjoy the rest of your visit."

The woman smiles, and her voice turns into something a little more sly. "Thank you so much, Mr. Bradford. You've been a big help."

Narrowing my eyes, I don't like the feeling of fingers pinching the back of my neck as I walk away from her.

I'm not sure where this is coming from, but I feel like I just made a critical error.

Two nights later, I'm sitting with Liv in an incense-scented room with yoga mats and large pillows scattered across the floor.

"Sit with your back against your partner's chest, knees bent." The woman at the front of the room is dressed in black yoga pants and a white shirt with bell-shaped sleeves. Her brown hair hangs in one long braid down her back, and she looks like one of those gurus with all her beads and leather bracelets. "We're going to start with acknowledging our fears."

Liv signed us up for our first birthing class last week. She wants to test out every method, so tonight we're trying HypnoBirthing. I'm 100 percent skeptical, but Liv makes the point we're both athletes. She says she wouldn't run a marathon without training, so I'm here for whatever helps her feel ready.

"Let's talk about FTP, which stands for fear-tension-pain." The teacher's voice is soothing. "When you're afraid, your body tenses. Adrenaline spikes, and you feel pain more intensely. So our first step is to face your fears ahead of time and release them. Now speak your fear to your partner."

Liv turns her face to whisper in my ear. "I'm afraid my stomach will keep getting bigger and bigger until the baby's the size of a watermelon, and it's going to tear my vag to shreds on the way out."

"Jesus!" I hiss, tightening my hands on her arms. "Could that happen?"

"I mean, look at you. It's like a Chihuahua mated with a Great Dane."

"Now, partners, I want you to help your partner work through these fears and find peace."

Our eyes meet, and all I can think about is Hendrix's crack about her having my baby. "You're a lot bigger than a Chihuahua."

Liv's eyes grow rounder, and my throat goes dry. I can't tell if she's about to cry, and if she does… Her eyes glisten, and all at once a laugh bursts through her tight lips.

She covers her face with her hands and leans forward, her shoulders shuddering with laughter.

My eyes fly to the instructor, who's walking slowly around the room. A high-pitched shriek comes from my expectant partner, and the woman's eyes narrow. A few of our classmates check us out, and I reach forward, rubbing the center of Liv's back.

She shakes her head, laughing more, and I don't know what to do.

"Everyone responds to fear differently." The instructor continues walking slowly through the pairs, but when she gets to us, an edge is in her tone. "Perhaps you two would like to get some water?"

Moving quickly to my feet, I catch Liv's hands, pulling her into my arms. She's wiping her eyes and shaking her head, but she snorts another laugh.

I make the most apologetic face possible, doing a little wave as I lead my girl into the hall. As soon as the metal door closes behind me, she collapses into my chest.

"I'm sorry!" Her voice is high, and she looks up at me. "That wasn't funny at all!"

As she says it, she breaks into another fit of crying laughter. I have no idea what to do right now, so I say the first thing that comes to mind.

"We're not too far from Miss Gina's. Let's go for a swim. She must've invited us ten times by now, and I think floating in a pool might help."

"We don't have our suits."

"You're wearing a jog bra. You can just wear your underwear and take them off for the drive home." Wrapping my arm around her shoulders, I lead her out to my waiting truck.

"Are you trying to get me out of my underwear?"

"Always, Liv." Holding the door, I help her in then run around to the driver's side.

Minutes later, Miss Gina is greeting us at her front door in a robe, and I feel like shit again. "Were you in bed? I'm sorry, Miss G."

"Nonsense!" She waves a hand in front of her face. "I was listening to an audiobook about a maid in a big mansion where her boss might be trying to kill her. I'll probably be awake all night."

"Miss Gina!" Liv's voice is hushed. "Why would you listen to something like that when you're all alone in the house?"

"FOMO." Her flat response almost makes me laugh. "Everybody's talking about it, and I couldn't resist. If you two would like to sleep over in the guest cottage, I wouldn't mind at all. In fact, I'd welcome it."

Liv glances up at me, and I shrug. "We didn't really bring anything to sleep in."

Miss G's lips twist with a frown. "I probably have something that would work for Liv, but you're a special size, Garrett."

"Wow…" I pat her narrow shoulder. "That's the nicest way anyone's ever called me huge."

She instantly frowns, crying out in protest. "Garrett Bradford, you are not huge. You're simply taller than the average man, and from what I understand, you're very fit. Liv's a lucky girl."

She arches an eyebrow, and I glance at Liv.

Liv only smiles, slipping her hand into the crook of my arm. "I definitely am, Miss G."

"Well you don't want to stand here talking to an old blind lady all night. The pool should still be warm from our water aerobics class, but you know how to adjust the control?"

"Yes, ma'am." Liv steps forward to hug our hostess. "Thank you, Miss G. You're the best."

"Just remember, you promised to bring that baby to see me when she gets here."

"Be careful what you wish for," I tease, but she only waves her hand as she leaves us at the ornate, wrought-iron and glass door leading out to the flagstone patio.

Liv's sweet voice is calmer than during her laughing fit at the birthing class, still I feel like I got a little peek behind the curtain. Stuff's brewing behind her super-controlled façade, and it's stuff she hasn't shared with me.

I'm ready to hold her close and get to the bottom of it.

Chapter 25

Olivia

TWINKLE LIGHTS ADORN THE DELICATE TREES LINING THE PATIO, AND dim lights shine in the depths of Miss Gina's Italian, blue-tiled pool.

I've been doing water aerobics with her and Rachel twice a week for a month, so this is the first time I've been able to relax and appreciate its luxury.

The moon is a fingernail overhead, and I'm floating in perfectly warm saltwater, with my back against Garrett's chest and his strong arms around me.

My insides are way less jittery, and after my breakdown earlier, I feel like I could crash. "Maybe we should spend the night here. I'm exhausted."

"I have no objections." His voice is quiet beside my cheek. "I'm sure it'll be as elegant as everything else here."

My eyes are on that sliver of yellow hanging in the vast expanse of blackness overhead. I wish we could see the stars.

Garrett's hand slides down my arm, and he kisses the side

of my head. "Talk about birth-class backfires." I can tell from his tone, he's approaching with caution. "What happened back there?"

"I don't know." I feel so foolish saying these fears out loud.

"Come on, Liv. You can't keep this stuff from me. I'm here to help."

Moving out of his arms, I go to the side of the pool, resting my eyes against the back of my hands as I confess. "I'm a freaking whale. I know it's mostly baby, but after so many years of being in complete control of my body, all through my dancing days, to see it changing this way is really disorienting. I wonder every day if I'll ever be the way I was before, and I'm pretty sure I won't."

Quiet falls around us. The waterfall at the opposite end of the pool typically creates a restful ambiance, but tonight it feels very far away.

Garrett drifts closer to where I'm standing with my back to him. "Would you believe me if I tell you you're adorable?"

My shoulder rises in a shrug.

He slides a finger down the side of my arm. "Well, you are. You're actually giving all the guys baby fever. All except Hendrix, of course. And Jack, I guess."

"I'm not thinking about them." My voice is quiet, and I hate the twist of anxiety in the middle of my back.

"Who are you thinking about?"

Another beat of silence. I'm not accustomed to saying stuff like this out loud. I've always been strong, managed my emotions, and placed feelings like these in their appropriate boxes.

My chin dips, and I cringe so hard. "My vagina will never be the same after I have this baby. My breasts are going to be all full of milk…"

The finger on my arm turns to a hand sliding across my back. "It'll be different for a little while, but that's okay."

"It'll be a lot different." I rest my forehead on the back of my hands again.

"Come on, Liv." His voice is warm, and he moves closer. "I've never seen you like this."

"I'm never going to be the same, and you're never going to want to have sex with me again."

He moves back slightly, looking at me like I've lost it. "Are you serious right now?"

"Yes." My voice is pouty. "You want me tight and muscular and young, and after I give birth to this giant watermelon baby, my body will be all stretched out and ruined, and you'll never want me again. It won't feel the same, and—"

"Stop." His tone is firm. "Look at me." Touching my chin, he lifts my head so I have to meet his fierce blue eyes. "I would never say this to you, Liv. You know how much I respect you, and how much I think you're smart and a badass…"

"Just say it." I'm feeling shame, fear, loss, and I can't stop the tear that hits my cheek.

"You've lost your fucking mind if you think I'll ever stop wanting to fuck your brains out. Are you kidding me? You're having my baby, Liv. It's the most incredible thing I've ever been a part of."

"You say that now…"

"I'll say that always, even when we're on baby number five."

"Number five?"

A hint of a smile curls his lips. "I gave up believing I'd get a second chance with you when you married that douche in Birmingham. I went out that night and got so drunk…" His chin drops. "Logan didn't know what the hell was wrong with me. Nobody did. But I knew it was my fault, and I'd lost the best thing I ever had."

"You never lost me." My voice is quiet. "I never stopped loving you, Garrett. As much as I thought I could move on with my life, I knew if I ever saw you again… I don't know what I would've done."

"Hey." Large hands cover my shoulders, and he pulls me closer. "All that's past now. We're here. We made it, and I'm so fucking happy. I'm not going to let you be afraid to have my baby."

Pressing my lips together, I don't know how to break it to him. I'm terrified. I'm not just afraid of the tearing. I'm afraid I'll barf everywhere when the first contraction hits. I'm afraid I'll poop myself when the baby comes out.

I'm afraid of all the horror stories I've heard, and I'm certain they're all going to come true in the most humiliating way possible.

"I'm afraid you'll never think I'm sexy again."

His lips part, and he exhales a laugh, shaking his head and looking up at the trees. "I don't know how to tell you I can't even imagine what would have to happen for that to be true. If anything, you're more beautiful to me every day."

"Stretch marks and all?"

"Come here." He pulls me close, turning my back to his chest again and wrapping his arms around me. "We should try that class again. I was skeptical, but I think it's helping us already. For starters, you were the most beautiful woman there. They'll want you for the publicity photos."

A laugh snorts through my nose, and I tuck my nose against his jaw. "Compliments will get you everywhere."

"Will they get me in your pants?"

"You've never had to worry about that."

"I'm ready to take you to that guest cottage and remind you how hard you make me."

Warm lips cover mine, and while anxiety still twists in my chest, while I'm still terrified my body will never be the same, I'm a little less terrified it's the end of our sex life.

At least not when Garrett lifts me out of the water and

carries me to the pretty little house on the edge of the premises overlooking the bay, and proceeds to make me scream.

"I thought your mom said no more chickens." Garrett's voice greets me as he crosses the backyard to where I'm standing right outside the henhouse, introducing Henny to her new baby chick.

It's been longer than twenty-one days, but she doesn't seem to care. She's making soft little clucks and doing her best to scoot the little chick under her body.

"It's called chicken math." I keep my voice low and calm. "If Mom didn't want it to happen, she shouldn't have left."

Garrett stands just outside the perimeter watching as Henny guides her baby around. Every time the baby black silkie tries to come to me, she clucks over to it, lightly touching it with her beak.

I put a handful of chicken feed in the small cup Henny's been using, and she shows the baby chick how to eat. The little black puff ball runs over, and she nuzzles it with her beak.

"Look how happy she is," I coo, sliding my finger down the soft feathers beside her neck to her back. "She has a baby girl now, just like our... Gina Grace? Gigi?"

Garrett's brows furrow as he thinks about this, then he rests his hand on the roof of the henhouse, leaning attractively as he watches me. "I like it."

"Miss Gina has always been like a sweet grandmother to you and your siblings, and your real grandmother is no longer with us..."

"I think Gigi's a good name." He's grinning now. "I even like Gina and Grace alone, if she wants to be more traditional when she gets bigger."

"I don't know if Mom will be annoyed. I didn't name her Persimmon or some other fruit."

"I don't care for Persimmon."

I go to where he's standing, watching me in a way that lights all my nerve endings. He's watching me like he wants to put his mouth all over my body, and I'd let him.

"What are you thinking?" My voice is suddenly shy.

"Just you, worrying about that silly bird."

"She's not silly." I pretend to pout, which makes him laugh. "I'm also a little worried about you."

"What?" He frowns.

"You haven't watched a single football game since you got here. It's always been such a huge part of your life and your family. Don't you miss it?"

"Not really." He lowers his hand, standing straighter. "I guess it seems strange to watch the games when I'm not play-ing anymore."

"But you love football."

His voice drops, turning softer. "I love you."

Energy floods my body as he takes my hand. We've said similar things to each other, more and more lately, but this is the first time he's saying it in a way that feels like he's saying something more.

I meet his possessive gaze. "You do?"

He traces a lock of hair off my cheek with his finger, tuck-ing it behind my ear. "Don't you already know it?"

He doesn't have to ask me. "I do."

"I wanted to show you I'm not the same guy who only thinks about himself." Lifting my left hand, he studies my fin-gers. "I'm not the guy who hurt you in college."

"I loved that guy, but you're right. You're a better man. A man I love."

"Do you think I might be a good dad?"

The earnestness in his tone squeezes my heart, but I'm able to say with complete honesty, "You're going to be the best dad." Wrinkling my nose, I step closer. "You're the champ."

"One day, I'll be a good sheriff." His hand covers mine, and he lifts it to his lips. "And a good husband…"

My breath catches. "What are you saying?"

"I want you to marry me, Liv." My lips part, but he stops me. "Don't answer me now." He looks around with a chuckle. "Not here in the henhouse."

Lifting my chin, I rise onto my toes, ready to kiss his face off. "So you're *not* proposing to me?"

His thumb touches the line of my jaw. Electric blue eyes hold mine, and I'm about to get my answer when I hear the sound of footsteps approaching fast.

We both turn to see Dylan marching across the lawn like she's about to commit murder.

"Dylan?" I step away from Garrett, going to meet her. "Are you okay?"

"No…" Her voice trembles. "I am not okay, and we need to talk."

"What's wrong?" Garrett's right behind me, reaching for his little sister.

"This." She holds up the iPad she uses for recipes when she's cooking, and I don't understand.

On the black screen, in large, blocky white letters reads "They Say Disabled. He says Pregnant!!!" My jaw drops, and I look up at Garrett.

His lips tighten, and he shakes his head, muttering, "Shit."

Chapter 26

Garrett

"THIS IS MY FAULT." WE PASS DYLAN'S IPAD BETWEEN US, SCROLLING through the "exclusive exposé" on the *TMI* website.

"Garrett Bradford Leaving the Pirates???" The headline is typed in all caps with three question marks like it's screaming at us.

"What do you mean?" Dylan's tone is sharp. "How can this be your fault?"

I quickly fill her in on the mysterious call we got about a cat in a tree, and how it turned out to be a woman pretending to be a fan and asking a lot of personal questions.

"The way she asked the questions made me feel like I needed to explain." I feel like such an amateur. "My spidey senses were tingling, and I did my best to be nice and get out of there."

"You can't be nice to these people." Dylan stomps ahead of us in her jeans and yellow Cooters & Shooters tee. "It's just like the guy who came here asking about the restaurant and pretending to be so interested in the Dare Nights and my spicy dishes."

Her arms are crossed, and she's fuming. She kind of reminds

me of one of Ms. Plum's chickens when they decide to peck at each other. *Mad as a wet hen.*

I quickly scan the article before putting my hand on her shoulder. "Yours was much worse. They said a lot of shitty things about you. This is at least mostly about me."

Dylan squeezes my hand on her shoulder. "It's not your fault. These people are evil."

We're walking with Dylan back to the restaurant. My little sister is fuming and moving fast.

But Liv's attention is focused on the article. "It's so amateurish. Do people really read this? Why do they use so many exclamation points?"

"It's garbage." Dylan's tone is sharp. "It's hearsay and guessing what they think is going on based on the tiniest sliver of a fact, yet it's presented as coming from a reliable source."

"I guess talking to me is kind of talking to a reliable source." I rub the back of my neck feeling like I'm the real problem. "I can't believe how much she got me to say."

"I'm sure you did not make Liv out as a manipulative clinger, faking pregnancy complications to get you home."

"I only wish those complications had been fake." I groan, putting my arm around Liv's shoulders. "Flying back that night took ten years off my life."

"I don't really care what they say about me." Liv's face is lined with worry. "But will it make them call you back to New York?"

"No." I shake my head, although I don't know for sure. "I worked out this deal with the owner himself, and we made sure Homes was a solid replacement. They're headed to the playoffs. They don't need me there."

"Logan said he can tell you're not playing this season." Dylan's nose wrinkles.

"Logan's biased. The truth is, I was at my best when he was on the team." I try to sound reassuring. "They must be having a slow news cycle if they're scraping the bottom of the barrel worrying about what I'm doing."

"That's not true!" Dylan cries. "The fans love you. I'm sure they want to know what you're doing now."

She's being nice, but I want to tell her she's not making the situation better.

Liv is still frowning, and she's chewing her bottom lip. After all the shit we've been working through lately, the last thing I want is for her to be worrying about this kind of bullshit.

"Are you okay?" I take her hand, slowing her pace as my sister continues on ahead.

"Yeah." She blinks up to me, and the little smile she gives me is somewhat reassuring.

At least the article isn't a hatchet job like the one about Dylan. I'd like to think it's because they learned their lesson with how Logan handled it, but I doubt that's the case. We're at the restaurant, and Dylan trots up the steps leading to the back entrance to the kitchen.

"Why don't you two stick around and have dinner?" Dylan holds the screen door as we enter. "The guys are all set up to watch Hendrix play. Go join them."

"Why don't we all join them?" I can't help teasing my little sister now that I know she stopped watching our games.

"Maybe in a minute." She grabs Liv's hand. "First, I want to show Liv my new recipe!"

Liv smiles up at me. "I'm good. Go hang out with your brothers."

With that, I let them go. If I know Dylan, she's going to keep Liv in the kitchen all night talking and getting all the news.

"Wait!" Dylan hands me a large platter of Thomas's spin on White Castle burgers. "Take these out to the guys."

"Are those my White Castle burgers?" Liv cries. "I want one."

"Don't worry." Dylan taps her shoulder. "I've got more for us back here."

And my suspicions are confirmed. I won't be seeing Liv again until it's time to go.

"Hey, look who's here." Zane stands when I round the corner with the tray of sliders. "Need some help?"

"Dylan sent these." I pass my brother the tray, and he carries it to the table where Jack and Logan sit facing the large-screen televisions all on the same channel.

It's a Monday, so the restaurant is pretty empty. Most people are at sports bars watching the game or they're home getting ready for work and school tomorrow.

"Did you see the article?" Logan's expression is somber and he hands me a beer out of the silver bucket in the center of the table.

"Yeah." I take the drink. "Thanks. It's not as bad as what they wrote about Dylan."

"Still, it's pretty shitty." Logan pulls out a chair, and we sit together.

"It's my fault."

"What?" All three of them turn to look at me, and my jaw tightens.

I quickly fill them in on what happened with the phony cat in the tree, and my big mouth.

"It's really suspicious how she knew you'd take the call." Jack's brow lowers. "I'll ask Rodney if he can look into it. I'd hate to think we have a mole at the municipal complex."

"Wow." My brow rises. "I never even considered that."

"They pay people to help them, and these so-called reporters are sneaky." Logan's tone is simmering anger, and I know it's as much about how they treated Dylan as the situation with me. "She probably asked around to see how she could get you out there. I don't expect it would take much in Newhope."

"You know that's true." Zane nods, sipping his beer. "People talk to everybody down here."

"And those assholes take advantage of it." Logan's jaw is tight, and he shakes his head.

The televisions flicker with the start of the game, and we put the conversation to rest while we watch my youngest brother on the field. Throughout his professional career, Hendrix has played wide receiver and running back, and now he's starting tight end for the LA Tigers.

"This is the best he's played all year." Jack's arms are crossed, and he watches like a coach.

"He's fast," Logan agrees. "And his instincts are good."

"There he goes!" I shout when he shoots through an opening, running thirty yards for a touchdown.

We all yell and high five, and I laugh with pride. It feels good to be here with them watching the game. The time passes, and I like it more when Liv walks out to join us for the final quarter.

She sits on my lap, and my hand is on her round belly. The baby pushes against my hand, and for a few minutes our baby girl steals the show.

"That's crazy," Logan laughs, putting his hand over the small point pushing right out of the middle. "I never knew they did that."

"Neither did I," I laugh, rubbing the spot and giving Liv a squeeze.

I think she's doing better with how her body is changing. I know the birthing class has helped. We've started doing more of the HypnoBirthing, and they're pretty good at relaxation and working through her fears.

Jack lets out a yell, and we all snap our attention in time to see Hendrix strutting into the end zone for another touchdown right before he's surrounded by his teammates and lifted off his feet. It's a great sight, and it leaves me feeling better than I did when I arrived.

"What did I miss?" Dylan scampers out of the kitchen, amber eyes wide like she had no idea a game was happening.

"Nice try, faker." I pull her ponytail and she elbows my side.

"Don't mess with my lady." Logan pulls her into his arms,

kissing the top of her head. "She doesn't have to watch the games if they stress her out."

"Because you're not playing anymore." Zane pipes up from where he's sitting by Jack.

"I want you guys to come to the station on Thursday so we can record the show." Logan nods at the four of us.

"I should be able to do that. It's been pretty slow lately."

"Jack? You in?" he calls to my brother, and Jack stands, walking to where we're talking.

"Can't do it. We're getting ready for Homecoming Friday."

"Oh! I love homecoming." Dylan tilts her head to the side.

"Me too," Liv coos. "We always had so much fun decorating the field and having bonfires."

"The girls in ballet class are so excited."

"Hold up." Zane stands, moving closer to the large television screen. "Garrett, you'd better come take a look at this."

"Oh, shit!" Logan's voice rises, and we all go to where Zane is standing.

They're replaying highlights from the Pirates' game, and my throat tightens when I see one of those massive defensive linemen slam hard into Huck Holmes. Flags rain all around them, but my replacement isn't moving. *Fuck.*

"What are they saying?" Jack's tone is somber as he returns from tossing our trash.

"Not sure yet." Zane reaches up to increase the volume. "Looks like a concussion. He's not getting up."

Liv walks to where I'm standing, putting her hand in the crook of my arm. I lift it at once, wrapping it around her shoulders and pulling her into my side. Dylan has already returned to the kitchen, and I know it's because she hates concussion injuries.

She wants us all to retire.

"How long ago was this?" Logan asks. "They should have an update by now."

"Here we go." The screen changes to talking heads breaking down the injury just as my phone starts to vibrate in my pocket.

I know before I even lift it whose name is going to be on the screen. *Kurt Lucas*. Liv sees it, too, and round hazel eyes meet mine.

Leaning down, I kiss the top of her forehead. "I have to take this. Don't worry."

Walking to the back of the near-empty restaurant, I take the call. "Kurt? Hey, man, how's it going?"

"I was going to say the same to you. How's the family?"

"Good." I nod, even though he can't see me. "Doing good."

"I don't suppose you caught the Pirates game?"

"Ah, no, we were actually watching the Tigers—"

"Your brother Hendrix. Killer tight end."

"Yeah, but I just saw the highlight reel. What's happening, Kurt?"

"Well, that's why I'm calling." His tone changes to somber, and I remember that day in the office when Kurt nearly fired Thad. "We need you back here."

My chin drops, and I scrub the back of my neck. I've been doing it so much lately, I'm starting to get a burn. "How is he?"

"Doctors say he'll be out for at least nine days." It's the standard protocol following a concussion. "It was pretty mild, so we're thinking two games tops."

"And after two games?" My chest is tight, and I'm worried he'll make me stay. "I don't want to stay, Kurt."

"I know." His tone is quiet. "We can make that call when we know more."

I don't like it, but I also know I can't leave my team hanging. He let me go with the understanding I could be called back, and I agreed. At this point, Liv is doing well. She's not having any problems, and the family is all here with her. Still, I know she wants to be near her mother. Dr. Pierce is here, and I'm not missing the birth of my baby girl. Hell, we still have more HypnoBirthing to learn.

"Two games."

"I need you here in time for practice." His tone has switched to all-business. "I want you and Berke on the field drilling A-sap. We're headed for the playoffs, and we can't lose momentum over this."

We disconnect, and I turn to see Liv standing at the back of the group, chewing on the side of her finger and watching me.

Going to her, I pull her into my arms, smiling down. "How would you feel about going with me to New York for a few weeks?"

Chapter 27

Olivia

"OLIVIA! YOU'RE HERE!" MADDY WADDLES OVER TO ME AS SOON AS I step into Charlie's box at the stadium.

She's wearing Charlie's jersey, modified to cover her pregnant belly. She's even bigger than I am, which somehow fills me with a sense of relief.

"Just look at us," she laughs. "You're adorable. I look like I'm having twins."

Garrett left for New York on Tuesday, but I stayed behind and finished up some work. I called Mom to let her know what was going on, and no surprise, Cousin Gwen was perfectly able to take care of herself.

She returned home Tuesday soon after Garrett left for the airport, so while I missed him being in bed with me, I wasn't alone.

Mom burst into tears as soon as she saw me. I've gotten big since she left, and we spent pretty much all of Tuesday night and Wednesday watching for Gigi to move and discussing all my fears.

I had to fuss at her for not being here to talk me through all my first-time pregnancy fears. Truthfully, I wasn't angry at all. She was only ever a phone call away, and it meant I was forced to be honest with Garrett about how I was feeling, which I think drew us even closer.

Which I also think was her plan all along.

Not to mention, if she'd been here, Garrett and I would never have been able to have sex all over the house at the drop of a hat. Or a coffee cup.

Logan was able to get me on his father's private jet service from the small airport outside Newhope to Teterboro this morning. It was the first time I'd ever flown on a private jet, and I felt like a true celebrity—or like a *WAG*, the girlfriend of a famous football player.

I wasn't able to have any complimentary champagne, but I did have a warm, chocolate-chip cookie. Even better, it was lovely to be so pregnant and to be able to walk straight out to the small plane and have it to myself. The flight attendants were sweet, the plane was cozy, and I slept the whole way.

Touching down, my emotions caught me off-guard. We've only been apart a few days, but when I saw Garrett waiting on the tarmac, so tall in his dark jeans and light brown bomber jacket, hair ruffling in the breeze. Need twisted in my chest, and I couldn't get down the short flight of stairs fast enough.

He met me at the bottom, pulling me into the tightest hug. "I missed you so much, Cherry." His warm breath at my temple sent chills down my back.

We only had time to drop me at his apartment before he had to be at the stadium for the game, but I expect we'll make up for lost time tonight if all goes well.

I packed the cotton jersey I've been sleeping in, but he was two steps ahead of me. A brand-new navy and red Number 50 jersey was lying on the bed when I got to the apartment. It was even altered to allow room for baby.

Garrett's driver Fred helped me into the SUV and drove me here. He even walked me all the way to the elevator leading up to Charlie's box.

A blast of camera flashes and yelling reporters shocked me when we arrived, but Fred had me covered. Now we're here, ready for the game, and I'm so happy to see Maddy again.

"You're adorable," I argue. "What are you talking about?"

"I'm a whale." She groans, waving her hand. "They say you get bigger with every pregnancy, but this is too much. My body will never be the same again."

My cheeks heat, and I'm embarrassed to say, "I literally had the same conversation with Garrett a few weeks ago. We had our first HypnoBirthing class, and I was supposed to say my worst fear… I completely lost it. We had to leave the class!"

"Wait." She holds up her hand. "Two things, first, HypnoBirthing? Second, you were kicked out of class?"

"The instructor suggested I might need to drink some water."

"What did you do?"

I cover my face with my hands. "I guess I'd been sort-of, I don't know, letting my feelings build up, and when I told Garrett my fears about tearing, I lost control and couldn't stop laughing. Only it was more like shrieking, crying, laughing."

"That is so valid." Maddy's eyes are wide. "I was terrified of tearing and episiotomies and all of it my first time."

Reaching out, I grip her forearm. "What did you do?"

"I had a little tear." Her upper lip curls. "My doctor worked with me during my delivery, but it still happened."

"It did?" I can't help a cringe.

"Yeah, but she stitched it right up, and it healed pretty fast." She shakes her head. "I promise, it's really not as bad as it sounds."

"Okay…" Chewing my lip I turn to look down at the guys

on the field, thinking how great it is to have someone my age to talk to about this. How I feel way less embarrassed by my fears.

Charlie isn't as big as Garrett, but he's still probably six-foot-two, two hundred pounds. "How big was Paxton when he was born?"

"Eight pounds." She rubs my shoulder. "If your doctor's any good at all, she'll help you."

"My doctor's pretty good."

Garrett looks up at us from the field and does a little salute. Lifting my hand, I wave, forcing a smile.

While I'm not feeling terribly confident, it helps to know she's done it and survived… and is actually doing it again.

"So what's this HypnoBirthing? Tell me all about it."

I fill her in on the details while we watch the guys on the field. It's a different experience being up here instead of on the sidelines dancing. When I used to be at every game, he'd walk over and we could hold hands a minute in between turnovers.

He was as focused then as he is now, and we all erupt into cheering screams when he turns to stop a cornerback at the last second, creating an opening for Ricky to complete the pass and score the winning touchdown.

The sports announcers go crazy, shouting that The Bear is back. It seems like every time I look at the jumbotron, Maddy and I are on it. All of this is new and exciting, and baby girl is kicking like crazy.

Confetti rains down on the field as the guys flood out to pick Ricky off his feet and slap Garrett's shoulders. He and Charlie do their fist-bump routine, and Maddy grabs my hand.

"Come on!" She pulls me out of the box and to the elevator.

In just a few minutes, we're out on the field, and Garrett's the first one to meet us. He's a sweaty mess, but he pulls me into a hug that makes me laugh.

"Wasn't sure I could pull that off after such a long break." A smile splits my cheeks, and I hold his face when he kisses me long and hard. "Were you okay with Maddy?"

"Yes!" It's all I'm able to say between the noise and the hustle of the guys.

Garrett has to speak to the reporter on the field. She asks how it feels to back, and he shakes his head.

"It's always great to play with the Pirates." He smiles, holding out his hand, which I take. "I'm glad to be going out on a high note."

"There's been a lot of talk about your legacy with Logan Murphy and now Berke and Holmes picking up where you left off. What do you think about that?"

"It's how football dynasties are made. I can't be out here forever, so it's good to know the team's in good hands."

She nods, and Ricky's right behind him, ready for his turn on the mic. "Good game, Grizz." He slaps Garrett's back before stepping in front of him.

I'm annoyed, but Garrett's eyes are fixed on mine. "Let's get out of here."

He's smiling big as we leave the field, and I look back ready to call Ricky out for being ungrateful.

"How are you feeling?" We're at the large entrance leading to the locker rooms, and Garrett's hand is on my shoulder. "Are you tired?"

"Not right now." Reaching out, I take his hand. "Feel this."

We stop walking, and his palm spreads flat over my large midsection. His brow rises as he starts to laugh. "She's going crazy in there."

"I think we have a football fan on the way."

"She's cheering for her Papa Bear." Leaning down, he holds my jaw as he kisses me slow. "Or maybe she'll be a dancer like her mama when she gets here."

"And her aunt Dylan."

"Don't look now. We're on the Jumbotron."

"Again?" I look over my shoulder, and the cameras are right on us again.

"What do we do?"

"Go with Fred to the car, and I'll do a quick change and meet you there."

Standing in Garrett's apartment, I look out at the lights of the city. From this height, we can see the courtyard at Rockefeller Center, where people are ice skating and sitting at the café tables.

Garrett walks up behind me, placing his hands on my shoulders. "It's a pretty good view, don't you think?"

"It is." Turning, I look up at him, a new fear bubbling in my chest. "Do you wish you were still here?"

His eyes are on the street below, and he frowns lightly. "No."

"You don't?" My eyes narrow, and I'm not sure if he's saying what I want to hear.

"Two years ago, I probably would've said yes, but I'm really far away up here. I love my teammates, but I miss my family. I like being in Newhope." His blue eyes lift to mine, and a half-smile curls his full lips. "I like being there with you."

My chest aches with joy, and I step forward to hug my arms around his waist. He presses his lips to the top of my head, inhaling deeply, and it's another rush of emotion through my body.

"I like being there with you." My voice is quiet.

"You don't miss being a high-powered lawyer in Birmingham?"

Exhaling a laugh, I shake my head. "No." I step back, lifting my chin to meet his eyes once more. "I'm right where I want to be."

He cups my cheeks, and our mouths unite. Lips part and our tongues curl together as heat surges in my lower body. Holding my hand, he leads me to the bedroom.

He takes a knee to remove my leggings and underwear. I'm about to take off my top when he rises, stopping me.

"We'll keep the jersey on for now." His voice is lusty, and he takes my hand, leading me to a low dresser with a large mirror in front of it. "Put your hands here and don't move."

Lifting the jersey over my lower back, he squeezes my ass in his large hands, lifting and spreading before dropping to one knee and burying his face in my pussy.

His beard scuffs my inner thighs as he licks and sucks, and I almost lose my grip on the dresser when I come so hard. Rising fast, he slides his cock into my fluttering core, thrusting fast and hard while he holds the front of my neck.

"That's it… Come on my cock, Cherry." He kisses behind my ear, making me shriek and come harder. "Feels so good."

I can't stop with him behind me, and I start to lift my ass, pushing back against him. His head drops to my shoulder with another deep groan. A little more, and I feel him break inside me. Holding his body to mine, we sway forward and back as he finishes, wrapping my body in his strong arms.

Bonding us even closer, sealing our words with promises too deep to break.

Chapter 28

Garrett

L IV IS BY MY SIDE AS WE STEP OUT INTO THE BRISK FALL MORNING. I put my hand over hers, tucked in my arm, as we make our way south from my apartment to Fifth Avenue.

I haven't told her where we're going, because I've been trying to figure out how to get away with this since I looked up and saw her standing beside Maddy in the box at my game.

Seeing her there, wearing my jersey, waving and smiling after every play cemented what I want in my chest. My feelings for her couldn't be more certain, and I have a plan. And I really don't want to spoil it.

Dylan: You're going to propose ON THE FIELD??? 🏟️

It's a big risk, but I think she'll say yes.

Dylan" I'm crying rn 😭 😭 😭

How can I get her a ring without her knowing?

Dylan: A push present!

WTF is a push present?

Dylan: You are so lucky you have me. Husbands always get their wives push presents for after they have the baby.

Why have I never heard of this?

Dylan: IDK, but you'd better share this information with your brothers

Yeah, I got you, but is a push present a diamond ring?

Dylan: No, but you can tell her you want it to be a surprise. Get her to pick a bunch of things she likes, and make one of them a diamond ring.

Liv's too smart for that.

Dylan: Of course she is, but it'll still keep her guessing about when…

I guess that's the best I can do.

Dylan: I'M SO EXCITED!!!

This means you have to watch the next game or you'll miss it.

Dylan: OR! I can get Logan to call me when it happens.

You can watch with Thomas on his little TV in the kitchen.

Dylan: His lucky TV.

Maybe it'll make me lucky.

Dylan: You don't need luck. She loves you. I'm so happy!!!

Dylan's confidence boosts mine. Seeing my girl is in love with me in print makes it feel more official somehow, even if it is just a text from my little sister. Also, Dylan's plan is pretty solid. I'll have to remember how sneaky she is next time I have to pull off a surprise.

"I thought we were going to brunch?" Liv's brow furrows when I take a turn on Fifth Avenue away from the restaurant.

"Just need to make a quick stop." I lead her to the brass and glass, art deco front doors of Tiffany & Co.

"Garrett…" She hesitates, pulling her hand out of my arm. "What are we doing?"

Her reaction fans the anxiety simmering in my chest, but I push through it and smile, focusing on Dylan's ruse.

"Come on, Liv. Apparently I'm a bad dad if I don't give you a push present." Tilting my head, I act disappointed. "Are you trying to make me a bad dad?"

Her lips tighten against the smile trying to break out, and her pretty, pretty hazel eyes mist. "I would never do that. It would be impossible."

"Then get in here." I take her hand, leading her into the iconic jewelry store.

It's a surprisingly low-key establishment. Other than the stunning arched windows lining the walls, it's just a large room full of glass cases arranged around the center. Clerks stand behind them wearing suits and smiles, and I lead her up to the closest one.

"How may I help you today?" The man almost sounds British, he's so formal.

"We're looking for an assortment of gifts for my lady here." I motion to Liv.

"An assortment?" She leans into me, hissing a whisper.

"It's for what you might call a push present." I use a fancy accent when I say it—two can play at this game. "But I want it to be a surprise."

"Of course, sir."

"I don't want her to know exactly what she's going to get, so I'd like her to pick several things for me to choose from."

"Very smart." His expression is placid. "How would you like to proceed?"

Leaning my arm on the glass case (yes, I see him wince), I look up at Liv. "Would it be possible for her to walk around and note the items she likes, then you can give me the list?"

"Absolutely."

"Garrett." Liv's expression is flat. "I can't walk around pointing out things."

"Sure you can. Put a Post-it on whatever makes you happy."

Her eyes narrow, and I swear, I love this woman. She's the same girl I fell in love with in ninth grade, but with so much more strength and a little edge. I love that she keeps me on my toes.

"Do it." I wave my hands at her. "I'll just sit over here scrolling social media."

"I thought we were having brunch." She leans closer.

"Mr… Statler is it? Would Tiffany's happen to have a snack for my lady? To help her concentrate."

"Indeed, we do." He motions to a minion standing at the back, who quickly steps forward. "Snack."

"Yes, sir." It's a hushed whisper.

Liv is furnished with a tiny box of robin's-egg blue macarons. She takes one out and bites it carefully.

"It's vanilla!"

"Tiffany vanilla, Miss," the kid supplies with a smile.

She ducks forward, covering her nose with her fingers. "Thank you."

Liv wanders away, and I motion to Statler. "Be sure she picks out a diamond ring in her size. Something I can pick up this week."

I give him a wink, and he places his finger on the side of his nose. Then I walk over and sit in a gold, satin-covered chair and pull out my phone.

A half-hour later, we're at the door. Statler emails me the list of her choices, including item numbers and colors, and I scan it quickly, looking for rings. I'm happy to see she picked out a few oversized statement rings and one delicate square-shaped diamond with smaller diamonds down the sides of the band. It's simple and elegant, just like Liv.

I give the clerk a brief salute. "See you soon, Stat."

"Yes, sir." He withdraws as formally as he appeared.

Liv slips her hand in my arm, looking up at me with sparkling eyes. "That was fun. I felt like a princess."

"Good." Lifting my chin, I kiss her forehead, happiness brewing in my chest. "Whatever you want to do, just let me know."

"Right now I'd like to get some lunch. Baby girl is starving."

"You've got it."

"It's been fun playing with you again." Ricky stands at the edge of the field in his uniform. "You know, we could've had something out here."

"I already have a girlfriend, Rick." I'm doing so well at this whole evolution thing. I really wanted to call him *Dick* just then.

"Yeah, I know, you're a family man now." He lifts his chin in the direction of Charlie's box. "Can't say I blame you. I did a little googling and Olivia Bankston was some hot shit when she was a dancer."

"Yes. Still is." Anger tightens in my throat.

He's not as dumb as he looks, because he quickly raises both hands. "No offense—I meant it as a compliment!"

I size him up a second. If I kick his ass, I'd probably have to stay here longer or something worse, and I know Liv wants to get back to Newhope. "We'd better head out."

As we jog onto the sidelines, I look up at her in the box beside Maddy. They both wave, and the swell of joy in my chest helps me forget about The Dick.

Instead, I think about getting her down to the field after the game. Maddy and Charlie are both in on it, and Fred is actually holding the ring for me, which I picked up this morning.

My muscles are jittery thinking about it. It's one of the crazier things I've done. I hope she says yes. I hope it makes her laugh, because nothing is better than Liv's laugh.

Charlie jogs up to me, bumping his fist on top of mine, and he looks up to blow a kiss to Maddy in the box. "She doesn't have any idea?"

I filter through our day, shaking my head. "Not that I can tell."

"You are one brave motherfucker. Everybody is going to be watching. Tonight's game is on CBS."

It's a tough one. We're playing Texas—Jack's old team.

The whistle blows, and we all jog onto the field. One thing about playing the Mustangs, they're historically great, so we'll have to work tonight if we plan to win.

We line up, and in the seconds while we wait for the snap, Number 59, the defensive lineman across from me is already shit talking. "Thought you'd retired, 50, started having babies."

I've faced this guy many times in the past. He's a good player, about two inches taller and fifty pounds wider than I am, and I'll be doing good to hold him in place.

"Did you cry? Did you think you'd get the sack?" I've never been one to back down from some good shit-talk.

"I'll get your Johnson."

That does it. I snort a laugh as the ball snaps, and we all charge forward. I hit him as hard as I can with my shoulder to his torso, doing my best to keep him from drilling straight through the line and sacking Charlie.

Almost as soon as it starts, the play's over, and he pushes me back. "I thought you were tough. You hit me, and I didn't even move."

We're standing face to face. "That's right, you didn't move."

He didn't, and Charlie got the pass off. We gained a few yards, but it's not enough.

The refs blow the whistles to break it up, but we're not really fighting. Looking up as we jog down the field, I see Liv in my jersey bouncing Paxton on her hip. He's in a baby version of Charlie's jersey, and Liv smiles, waving his little hand. It makes me laugh, and I blow them a two-finger kiss, which she pretends he catches.

The game feels long and short somehow. I do my best to create openings for Ricky, but the Texas D-line is a wall. At one point we snap, and neither side even moves.

"Have you lost weight?" Fifty-nine is still going. "You look like you've been dieting. Must be why I can't feel you at all."

It's a low-scoring game, and by the third quarter, we've only made one field goal. Texas has scored, so they're up by four. We're all the way at the end zone, three yards to go, and Charlie pulls me to him.

"We're not going to win this without that opening, Grizz."

"I'm doing my best, Chuck."

"I'm going to send it to Ricky." He slaps my back, and we jog to the line. "Make it happen, then you can focus on your plan."

Shaking my head, I go to the line. I'm thinking about my plan, but it's not keeping me from playing well. It's the fucking truck across from me.

I take a few steps back. Maybe if I get a little speed before I hit him, I'll actually move him out of the way.

The ball snaps, and I dig in with my feet, charging towards my guy. His eyes are lit when he sees me coming, but something happens. I don't see what it is, but he goes down right in front of me.

I'm flying on momentum, and I throw up my legs, jumping clear over him when I realize I'm across the goal line. I spin around, and my eyes lock with Charlie's. Guys are scrambling all over the field, it's chaos on every side, but I'm wide open.

Charlie's under pressure. A big guy is headed straight at him, but he pulls back and fires the ball, fast as a bullet to where I'm standing. Time stops, silence falls around me. I'm solid in my stance, but in my peripheral vision, I see 59 is up and barreling at me.

My chest is tight. When he hits, it's gonna hurt, but I've got this. He's behind the ball, and I only have to stretch out my hands… and pluck it out of the air as the clock runs down.

The minute it hits my chest, 59 plows into me, sending me to the turf, but I don't drop the ball.

It's the winning play of the game, and the stadium explodes.

I'm only on my back long enough to catch a breath when two guys grab my arms and haul me to my feet. One of them actually tries to lift me.

Fans are screaming, jumping up and down, and hugging each other. Blinking around, I get my bearings just in time to see Charlie running to jump onto my back.

I take a staggering step forward as he laughs, yelling in my ear. "Whatever else happens tonight, that play's going in the books!"

It's true. Linemen pretty much never score touchdowns. It's not our job.

Charlie laughs, pulling my shoulder pads and doing a dance. Shaking my head, I'm still getting over that last-ditch effort by 59. It's going to leave a bruise.

His helmet's off, and he's holding up a hand and smiling. "Glad I could send you home a hero."

"Did you trip?" We slap hands, and he shakes his head.

"Stepped on one of my guys."

Navy and red confetti falls thick onto the field, and I'm surrounded by sports reporters. It's a full-on celebration, and while that was a historic play, it's seriously fucking with my plan.

A mic is in my face, and they want to know if Charlie and I planned it. *No.* When did I know I was going to score the winning goal? *When it landed in my hands.*

I'm taller than everyone, and I'm straining, looking for Fred, trying to see if Liv is down here, searching for Charlie. He steps up beside me, slapping me on the back right when I spot her on the sidelines smiling big.

Fred stands behind her, and I push through the throng to where she's standing, one hand on her stomach. When I get to her, I bend down so she can hug me. Our teeth bump as we smile through the kiss, and I take a step back.

"You are amazing!" she yells.

Fred holds out his hand, and I take the blue box from him. Going down on one knee, I'm still at Liv's waist. When I look up at her, her eyes are wide.

"That day in the henhouse, you asked me when…" I have to shout over the noise, and it's making me second-guess my plan.

Too late to change it now.

"What are you doing?" She steps forward, putting her hand on my shoulder.

At this point, the players around us notice what's happening. I don't have much time before all eyes and cameras will be on us, and I need to say this.

"I know you can't marry me because we're pregnant." She's close enough, bending down so I don't have to yell as loud. "Marry me because I love you, Liv. Because you love me, and these past months have been the best months of our lives. We got it back, Liv…"

Her eyes shine, and a tear falls onto her cheek. Still, she's not giving me a yes or a no.

My throat is tight, and I open the box. "What do you say?"

She swallows hard, holding my gaze. "I'm afraid." My brow furrows, and she continues. "I already lost you once. I can't do it again."

Moving closer, I drop my chin to catch a breath. "We were kids, Liv. Kids make mistakes. I was too insecure. I'd lost so much myself, and I was afraid to trust." She's nodding, and I keep going. "I'm a man now, and I know who I am. I know who you are, and I know what I want. You won't lose me, and I won't let you down."

The field has fallen quiet. Only some people at the other end of the stadium are still going, and I know the cameras are on us.

"I was married before, and it didn't work."

My eyes hold hers. "You were married to the wrong guy. You were never his to kiss. Never his to have a family with. You're mine, and nothing is going to change that." It's my turn to swallow the ache in my throat. "If you need a little more time to see who I am, I can wait. But you're it for me, Liv. You're the mother of my children. You're my wife. All you have to do is say yes."

A trembling hand lifts to her mouth, and her eyes flood with tears as a smile splits her cheeks. Nodding, she leans down to wrap her arms around my neck.

Her soft voice is in my ear, and it's a rush of joy in my chest as she says the only thing I want to hear. "Yes."

"I'm so glad I was able to come with you." Liv sits beside me in the SUV holding my hand. "I loved watching you play, wearing your jersey, and it's been great having Maddy to talk to about baby stuff."

It's our last night in the city, and we're headed to Charlie and Maddy's for an intimate farewell dinner—*finally*, Maddy said.

"I had a feeling you'd be friends." I lift Liv's hand to my lips, kissing right under the engagement ring. "I really loved having you in the box, watching me. It was kind of a dream I'd always had."

"Like catching the winning touchdown pass in the final seconds of the game?"

Exhaling a laugh, I shake my head. "I never even imagined something like that could happen."

"It was the greatest moment." She exhales a giggle. "I was screaming so hard I'm surprised I didn't go into labor."

"All I could think about was finding you." I look down at our entwined fingers. "I had that whole proposal planned out to the minute."

"Garrett." Her eyes shine as they hold mine, and I'm the luckiest man alive.

Charlie's place is on the Upper West Side, which isn't too far from my apartment. Fred stops at the entrance, and I step out, reaching for Liv's hand to help her out of the car.

Riding in the elevator to the penthouse, she threads our fingers, pulling me down for a kiss. "It was the cherry on top of your football career, and I'm so grateful I was there to see it."

The doors open, and I'm about to say *she's* the cherry on top, when Liv drags me out of the elevator and skips across the small foyer to do a little rhythmic *tap-tap-tap-tap* on the door.

"What's that?" I chuckle as it opens.

Liv cups both hands over her mouth when I see twinkle-lights shining inside the dim apartment. My brow lowers, and I move closer, stepping just inside as all the lights blaze on, and loud voices yell *Surprise!* all at once.

My heart nearly jumps out of my mouth as my teammates gather around to slap my back, shake my arms, and pull me in for bro-hugs. Music cranks louder, and I see a banner hanging over the fireplace that reads *Congratulations, Grizz!*

Looking around, I see Charlie standing beside Maddy, who

is openly crying. I let out a yell when Logan steps forward with Dylan.

"You didn't think we'd let you retire without a party, did you?" He's dressed in a suit, and my little sister is wearing a pretty, short cocktail dress.

"I'm so proud of you." Dylan wraps her arms around my waist. "I've never seen anything like it—you scored the winning touchdown!"

"Then 59 cleaned my clock."

"We're not talking about that part."

I laugh, hugging my little sister. Looking around the room, I spy Liv in the corner with her hands clasped in front of her nose. Her eyes shine, and I mouth *I love you.* She mouths it back, and I can't believe they got me. I had no idea this was coming.

"That's my big brother!" Hendrix steps out of the crowd, and my eyebrows shoot up.

"What?" I yell, pulling him in for a hug. "Are you kidding me?"

He laughs, slapping my back in a tight hug. "And I was over here worried about your legacy. Fuck me."

"Not this guy." Ricky walks up, gripping my shoulder. "Garrett Bradford is a legend."

Hendrix and I exchange a glance, then we both laugh, shaking Ricky's hand and letting it be water under the bridge.

"I can't believe you're here, and Logan and Dylan." I thought I couldn't get happier, but damn, this is just what I needed.

My teammates line up to shake my hand and swap old stories from all the years we've played together. There's food and drinks, and the music plays. On the televisions, they're running highlights of all the years I was a Pirate, most of which include killer plays Logan and I pulled off together.

The time passes so fast, but it's a great night. It's the best party.

At one point I end up on the sofa with my siblings, thinking how good this feels and how infrequently it happens.

"When are you coming home again?" Dylan presses Hendrix. "We miss you."

"Looks like I have a few more weddings to attend," he teases. "But I had fun last time. What's up with your friend Raven?"

"I'm not sure." Dylan's brow furrows. "I need to check on her. We kind of lost touch."

"She was fun." Hendrix looks around the room, his voice taking a tone I've never heard before. "She's the kind of girl…"

Logan leans down, slapping my palm with his. "Get up here for the toast, big guy."

I stand, going to where Charlie and Logan are waiting for me beside the cake table. I'm not one to get all sentimental, but these two guys have been a big part of my life for a long time.

"To the best of O-line, the best of friends, and soon to be the best dad." Charlie holds up a glass. "Garret Bradford, the man, the bear, the legend."

Shaking my head, I laugh as the room bursts into yells and applause.

It quiets down, and Logan adds, "To a guy I've always called my best friend, and now I call my brother."

Another big cheer, and fuck, I'd better not cry.

It's my turn, and I look around the room at the group of athletes and friends I've spent almost a decade of my life encouraging, working, and winning games with.

"You guys are like my family, and you know for me, that's everything." Tight smiles, a few nods. "I'll always be a Pirate at heart. I'll always be with you in spirit, and I can't wait to see where you go from here."

"To Garrett." Charlie holds up his glass, and as we all toast, I see this chapter close.

I'm leaving on a high I never imagined, but it's been a great part of my life. If I were going to leave the game for my wife and daughter, I'm really thankful I had the gift of leaving them with a smile.

Chapter 29

Olivia

GARRETT IS ON THE BAR IN HIS BLOND WIG, DANCING WITH CRAIG to "Work It" by Missy Elliot as the line of Thursday Night Dare customers slowly makes their way to the front. Tonight, Dylan's testing out one of her honeymoon recipes made with Guajillo, which she promises is one of the milder hot peppers.

Behind them on the big screen televisions is the recording of the Jumbotron blazing in red letters, "She Said Yes!" after Garrett proposed to me on the field on repeat. Balloons and streamers are all over the place, and tonight I'm wearing a white sash emblazoned with "Same Dick Forever" in gold across the front.

We've been home a little more than a week. Garrett wrapped up everything in New York, had his things moved into storage, and while that was happening, Dylan was busy planning this whole surprise engagement celebration for the following Thursday Dare Night.

"Does this mean I'm not getting a push present?" I pretend to pout.

I'm in a booth with Miss Gina, Mom, Clint, and Rachel, and Dylan has just walked over with two additional servings of chips and pico de guajillo for Mom and Rachel.

"You'd better get a push present!" She sits on the edge of the booth across from us, beside Miss Gina. "That was a cover story, but Garrett knows what to do."

I look over at my fiancé shaking his sexy ass on the bar beside Craig, and a smile spreads across my face.

Mom puts her hand over mine, and leans closer. "I knew you'd learn to trust again."

I glance at her frowning. "What do you mean?"

"After your father left, I was so worried about you. You cried for him every day, and I didn't know how to explain to you it wasn't your fault."

My chin drops. "I used to think if I were only good enough at something, he'd love us again." I study the diamond ring on my finger. "Now I'm afraid none of this would be happening if I weren't pregnant."

"I don't know about what-ifs and hypotheticals," she sighs. "But what if this baby is divine intervention, correcting a past mistake?"

Wrinkling my nose, I look up at her. "I'm afraid to reach for too much happiness. I should be thankful for having the baby I thought I never could."

"*Pfft!*" Mom shakes her head. "When has my daughter ever let fear stop her?"

"Not often enough."

"Well, don't start now." She wraps her arm around me. "I knew your father so much better than you did, Olivia. It's how I can tell you with complete confidence, Garrett Bradford is nothing like your father. He will give you the love you deserve."

My eyes go to him again, standing beside the bar with Craig and looking up at the television screen showing us hugging and kissing with *She said yes!* in a banner across the top. His smile is filled with satisfaction and pride, not smug acquisition, and peace settles in my chest.

He's my family. He always has been.

"I don't know about push presents, but I gave Craig a stuffed chicken for our nesting phase," Clint volunteers between bites of hot salsa. "I would've loved to give him a silkie, but we don't have room for a real hen."

"You'll get there, just give it time." Mom pats Craig's boy-friend's arm. "I wasn't able to have chickens until Liv moved out for college."

"That was hardly the reason," I huff beside her. "The only thing you changed was the yard."

"I was very focused on you," Mom fusses. "I couldn't have cared for my hens the way I do now with you at home."

"How many hens did you start with?" Clint has Mom on her favorite topic, and I push out of the booth, needing to walk around.

"You okay, babe?" Allie scoots up beside me. "I know when I was pregnant with Austin, the third trimester was the worst."

"I can't get comfortable." Holding the side of my stomach, I take her arm, and she walks with me to the screen door lead-ing to the playground on the bay.

"I hated being pregnant," Allie laughs, counting off on her fingers. "I got the rash, the hemorrhoids… you name it. It was like being handicapped for nine months, with a nightmare at the end."

"How big was Austin when he was born?"

"Gosh, let me think." Her chin drops, and her dark brown hair falls over her cheek. "He was around eight pounds?"

"Did you tear?" I'm still struggling with my old anxiety.

"I'm not sure. I wanted all the drugs," she laughs. "Oh, wait—yes! I must've, because I remember the doc saying she gave me an extra stitch. She did it right there on the spot."

"What does that mean?" My brow furrows.

"An extra stitch." She elbows me, leaning closer and arching an eyebrow. "You know, to make it a little tighter."

"Does that work?" A whole new possibility crosses my mind.

"I don't know." She shrugs, looking down. "Jessie was in jail before I even brought Austin home."

"Oh." Embarrassment heats my neck. "I'm so sorry. I had no idea."

"It's okay. I was pretty dumb when I was younger. Throw a bad boy in my path, and I thought it was *so* exciting." She shakes her head. "I've come a long way, baby. Now I'm just trying to get Austin through school and into college. Jack has been really great with that." She sighs, looking up to where Garrett's oldest brother stands with Zane watching the boys playing pool. "He's just been really… great."

My eyes narrow, sliding between her and him, and I'm ready to say more when a voice I never expected to hear again sends ice through my veins.

"Hello, Olivia. My goodness, you've been busy."

Turning slowly, I look up to see Warner Oberon III in the flesh, looking down at me with those cold blue eyes like a greedy cat finding a fat mouse.

"What the hell are *you* doing here?"

"I'm checking on my wife, of course."

My head juts forward, and Gigi kicks hard in my stomach. "What are you talking about?"

"I must be out of the loop." Allie blinks between us, and she shifts her stance to a defensive pose. "And you are…?"

"Hey, you okay back here?" That deep voice has me wanting to crawl into his arms for safety.

"Garrett," I exhale relief, reaching for his hand.

He takes mine immediately, stepping up beside me.

"You must be Garrett Bradford." Warner holds out his hand. "I've heard so much about you—and what I haven't heard, I've read online or seen on TV!"

"That's odd." Irritation is in Garrett's tone. "I haven't heard a thing about you. Who is this, Liv?"

"Warner." My voice is quiet fury. "Oberon. The third."

"Aw, my bad," Garrett laughs. "I have heard about you. You're the dickhead who treated Liv so badly."

"Even better, friend." Warner leans forward as if he's telling the most hilarious joke ever. "I'm her husband!"

The music ends, and the next song is quieter, one of those country ballads Craig likes to throw in. Nausea burns at the base of my throat, and I'm scoping out the nearest trash can.

"I'm sorry, *friend*..." Garrett's voice takes on an edge. "What did you just say?"

"I'm her husband" Warner is more pompous, slapping Garrett on the shoulder. "Surprise!"

Now I'm really about to barf. Swallowing hard, I force my breath to steady. I force my brain to think as I trace through the possibilities of what he's saying. I left Birmingham without another thought. I had all my mail forwarded here. Mason would've told me...

"What have you done?" Lifting my eyes to Warner's I see the truth in his slimy smile.

"I haven't done anything." He takes a step closer to me. "You, however, have been a very bad girl."

Garrett's hand shoots out, and he grips the top of Warner's shoulder, almost lifting him off his feet as he moves him away from me. "Unless you want to know what the inside of a dumpster looks like, you'll back the fuck up."

Warner starts to chuckle, and I wonder if he's on drugs. Garrett is a head taller than him, and from the look on his face, two seconds from beating him to death.

"Hang on." Holding up my hand, I turn away, digging my phone out of the pocket of my pants. "Just hold that thought."

I don't waste time on texting, and Mason answers on the second ring. "Hey, girlfriend!" His voice is cheerful. "You've been all over the news lately. I see best wishes are in order—"

"They're not in order, Mason." I can't hide my anger. "Warner just showed up in Newhope. He says we're still married."

"What?" Mason hisses a whisper, and I hear him shuffling in the background.

"That's what I said." My voice grows louder. "What the fuck, Mason?"

I hear laptop keys ticking. "I gave the contract to his lawyer months ago. He said he'd take it from there."

"Did he?" My chest is caving in on itself, and I know the answer before he even finds it.

"I'm not seeing the filing."

"Mason!"

"Why wouldn't he file the papers?" My friend's voice sounds genuinely confused, as if he thinks we're dealing with normal people.

"Call his lawyer. Let me know as soon as you know something."

Hanging up the phone, I turn back to my smirking... ex? "You didn't sign the divorce papers."

"My little pet." Warner smiles down at me. "Why in the world would I want to divorce you—especially now that I know you might be having my baby."

Another jerk back. "*Your* baby?" My voice goes high. "You mother—" At the last second, I remember we're in a family restaurant. Shaking my head, I turn. "I can't do this right now."

"Come here." Allie puts her arm around me. "Want me to drive you to your mom's?"

Garrett is right at my side. "She's staying at my place tonight."

"What's going on here?" Jack walks up, followed closely by Zane.

"You okay, G?" Logan is right behind them, and I want to die.

"Looks like the gang's all here." The sound of Warner's voice turns my stomach.

"Garrett?" I look up at him, and he reads my expression.

His jaw is tight, but he takes a breath. "This is Warner Oberon, Liv's ex."

"Not quite." Warner smiles, holding out his hand for a shake. "I'm here for my wife and a paternity test."

"I'm not taking a paternity test, you smug asshole. I haven't slept with you in… I don't even remember." Several people around us turn to look, and heat flashes in my face. "Garrett, please."

His fists are clenched, but he takes my hand, leading me away from Allie and his brothers in the direction of the door.

"I'm staying out on the Island when you're ready to talk, babe!" Warner calls after us. "I hope we don't have to do this the hard way."

Garrett's hand tightens on my arm, but I hold him close. "Don't."

It's a short walk from the restaurant to the Bradford house, and as soon as we enter the back door, I rush to the guest bathroom, dropping to my knees as I barf the pico de gallo and Liquid Death I had at Cooters & Shooters all in the toilet.

My shoulders heave, and angry tears burst from my eyes. Garrett squeezes into the small room with me, sliding large hands along the sides of my face and holding back my hair.

"It's okay…" His voice is soothing, but I'm a wreck.

"Oh, God." I gasp, reaching for tissues off the back of the toilet as I flush. "I hate throwing up. I hate Warner Oberon the third."

"Come here." He pulls me into his arms, and I lean my cheek against his chest. "Looks like Gigi hates him, too."

"I can't believe I married that guy." Sitting up, I blow my nose, anger burning in my chest. "I can't believe he's doing this. And trying to say Gigi is his? What the fuck?"

"I wish you'd let me stuff him in a dumpster." Garrett traces the hair off my cheek behind my ear, and despite my anger, I huff a laugh into another handful of tissues.

"I would love for you to stuff him in a dumpster." His brow rises excitedly, but I shake my head. "It would only make things worse."

"But think how good it would feel."

Pushing off the floor, I hold Garrett's hand as he helps me to my feet. "It really would."

Leaning over the sink, I scoop a handful of water into my mouth before following Garrett to the stairs.

I've just finished washing my face and getting ready for bed when my phone lights up with a text.

> Mason: Warner took the papers and said he'd file them himself. Then he fired his lawyer, who didn't follow up.

> I'm so sorry, Liv. I should have double checked everything. We can request a default judgment. You've been separated a year, but you'll need to come to Birmingham.

Exhaling heavily, I walk across the hall to Garrett's bedroom, where he meets me at the door wearing flannel pants and no shirt.

He lifts my chin. "What's that face about?"

"Mason says we can get a default judgment, but I need to go to Birmingham to appear before the judge." Looking down, I slide my hand over my stomach, dreading a three-hour road trip followed by hours in court.

"Is that the only way?" He leads me to the bed, turning back the covers.

"Short of Warner signing the papers." I arrange the pillows so my back is elevated, which is the most comfortable way to sleep right now. "He fired his lawyer."

"Does Mason have the papers?"

Frowning, I shift onto my side. "What are you thinking?"

"Ask him to fax them to you at the restaurant tomorrow. There's a notary on staff at the clerk of court's office. I'll pick her up, and Zane and I will pay a visit to Mr. Oberon."

"Garrett…" My chest tightens, and as much as I want this, I don't want him getting in trouble. "This is my mess. I should handle it."

Reaching up, he slides his thumb along the line of my hair. "You've wanted a partner for a long time." Blue eyes meet mine. "Now you have one."

"Yes, but…"

"You've got your hands full here, growing our little lady, taking care of yourself. Let me take care of this."

"I don't want this to hurt you." My eyes flicker down, and I trace my finger along the line of his chest. "You've had such a great two weeks. I want you to have your time, and something like this could ruin it."

"Nothing will be ruined." Reaching forward, he scoots me around so my back is tucked against his chest. Large hands slide over my baby bump. "It'll be a friendly visit. We'll be *nice*."

"Nice?" My eyebrow arches as I thread my fingers over his. "Who are you? Dalton?"

He exhales a chuckle, pressing a kiss to the top of my shoulder. "I thought you slept through *Road House*."

"I fell asleep that one time in *Road House*. It was hardly my first viewing."

"We'll be nice until it's time to not be nice. Now get some rest."

Chapter 30

Garrett

IT'S A FORTY-FIVE-MINUTE DRIVE TO THE SMALL BARRIER ISLAND situated in the waterway between the Alabama and Florida state lines. Rhonda Peachtree rides in the backseat of my truck and Zane is up front.

When we reach the guard shack at the base of the tall bridge leading from the main road to the island, I flash my badge, and the guy waves us through the gates with only a glance.

"That's an animal control badge, right?" Zane huffs a laugh.

"Yeah, I'm not the sheriff yet."

"Animal control officers aren't law enforcement, but they work under state and local government," Rhonda calls cheerily from the backseat.

"Right here, Rhonda." I hold my fist up, and she bumps it.

Rhonda's the notary public at the municipal complex, which houses the clerk of court as well as the sheriff's office. She's a few years younger than me, moved here from Georgia to live on the water like everybody else, but she's good people.

I've been on a low simmer since that dick Warner showed

up at Cooters & Shooters running his big mouth. He made my lady cry and my baby barf. I scan the road as we get closer to his address, looking for a dumpster just in case.

Liv's eyes were so weary last night. Holding her in my arms, I kissed her head as she slipped into a fitful sleep, and it took all my strength to promise I wouldn't come down here and kick this smug dipshit's ass. Having my brother here will help me stay *nice.*

I hope.

Following the main boulevard, I take a right on River Road, which leads all the way to the point. We turn left onto Key Drive and park in front of a large, white home with sea-green trim and a screened-in, wrap-around porch.

"It's more modest than I expected." Zane's low voice is calm as he steps out of the truck. "Isn't this guy supposed to be some kind of gazillionaire?"

"Something like that." My jaw is set, and I close the door, climbing the wide steps leading to the front door.

Rhonda is behind me, and Zane stands to the side in his flannel shirt over a navy tee. I picked him up at the stables, so he's in his work boots and baseball cap turned backwards. He crosses his arms, and while he's not quite as tall as I am, with those cool blue eyes and dark hair, he has his own imposing presence.

Knocking on the door, I put my hands on my hips, turning to my brother and Rhonda, carrying the papers and her notary supplies in a messenger bag. She's wearing jeans and a waist-length pink blazer, and she looks like a petite professional standing beside us.

The door opens, and it's the man himself. Warner Oberon in light blue shorts and a pink polo. I didn't think I could hate this guy more.

"Oh, hello." He has the decency to look startled, taking a step back. "I wasn't expecting… How did you get through the gates?"

"Cut the crap, Oberon." I put my hand on the door, opening

it wider and pushing him back so we can enter. "What do you want? You can't be after money."

"I don't understand."

"Why are you here bothering Liv?" I repeat.

"I want my family."

My fist tightens. "Then go make your own. Liv and the baby are mine."

"That's what you say."

Zane steps to me quickly, catching my forearm before I punch this guy in the nose. "I think Liv would agree with us." His tone is level, and Warner's eyes flicker to him. "We have the divorce papers that state you were unfaithful to your wife, and you share no children."

"Who are you, a lawyer?" Warner jerks his chin, and I don't like the way he curls his nose at my brother.

"Zane Bradford." Zane extends his hand. "I'm Garrett's brother, and I've known Liv a long time."

Warner's jaw clenches, and he nods. "Then you know she's high-spirited and flighty. You can't believe a word she says. She was a dancer, after all."

"I've only ever known Liv to be very thoughtful about her decisions." Zane's tone doesn't change. "Except for perhaps one, and even then, she owned it."

"The one where she ran off with my baby to come down here and marry this guy? We're not even divorced!"

I can't take much more of this. "Dude, are you cracked? Liv filed for divorce before she even came here—and she came to take care of her mom. I was in New York."

"Exactly, which means it can't be your baby."

Huffing air through my lips, I turn to Zane. "I'm doing my best here…"

"She humiliated me in front of our friends." He walks to the end table and pours a tumbler of clear liquid.

"She humiliated *you*?" My tone sharpens.

"We were married in front of a large group of witnesses. Half of them don't even know we're separated."

"Do they know you were fucking around on her?" Heat rises in my tone. It burns in my chest. "Do they know she hasn't let you touch her in over a year?"

"They know she's my wife." His eyes blaze. "I am not treated this way. I have an image, and her place is at my side. If she comes home now, all will be forgiven."

"This guy reminds me of a snapping turtle," I say to Zane before turning to look down on him. "You know what we do when we find an old turtle who won't let go? We get a stick."

"Look…" Zane steps between us. "This can get a lot more humiliating, or it can be over pretty quick—"

A door slams in the kitchen, and we all look up. "Honey, I'm home!" A petite blonde in a bathing suit and a caftan walks into the room wearing a cheery smile. "Oh, hello, there. I didn't know we were having company! I don't think we've met."

She's obviously pregnant, and I exchange a glance with my brother. "I'm Garrett Bradford. This is my brother Zane, and this is Rhonda."

"I'm Maren Oberon, Warner's wife!"

We all step back, turning to catch Warner's stunned expression. "Maren, what are you doing here? You were supposed to be at the pool all day."

"I got tired. You know how it is when you're pregnant."

"I've heard." I nod, stepping forward to take her hand. "I'm just curious—is this Warner's baby? I was told he couldn't have children."

"Yeah, we did the IVF and *voila!*" She exhales a little laugh. "I'm only a few months along. We're having twins."

"Congratulations." I nod, feeling even more confident than before.

"So you and Warner are… married?" Zane asks the next question for me.

"Not officially." She goes to the kitchen, pouring herself a glass of water. "Warner has some shrew of an ex who won't give him a divorce. So we did the whole *Cold Mountain* thing... I'm sorry, can I offer you something to drink?"

"Maren, you don't have to tell them—" Warner starts.

"I'm good," I interrupt quickly. "What's the *Cold Mountain* thing?"

"You know, from the movie! I love that movie. Nicole Kidman and Jude Law?" She holds her chest and gushes. "They couldn't get married either, so they said three times 'I marry you, I marry you, I marry you.' And that was it!"

"Maren." Warner's voice sharpens. "These men are not interested in our personal life."

"Oh, I'm sorry! Are y'all not friends?" Her blue eyes blink wide, and she looks between the four of us.

"It's like this, Maren, we're actually here on behalf of the 'shrew' ex-wife. She's ready to get that divorce, and we just need Warner here to sign the papers." Motioning to Rhonda, I smile. "We even brought our own notary public."

"You did!" Maren's voice is an exuberant squeal. "Warner, did you know this? Were you going to surprise me?" She tilts her head to the side, slanting her eyes as she smiles.

I take the papers from Rhonda and go to where Warner's standing helpless. "Here you go." Lowering my voice, I level my gaze on his. "Sign the papers before I break your jaw."

With a disgusted glance at me, he takes the pen. I motion to the three places he has to initial, and Rhonda squeezes her seal over the last page and signs it quickly.

"How about that?" I can't resist once she has the papers securely in her briefcase. "I divorce you, I divorce you, I divorce you."

"But you're not..." Rhonda laughs, looking from Warner to me, then her eyes widen. "Oh! I need to pee. Twins are no joke."

She scurries from the room, and I clap hands with Zane. "Have a nice life, Oberon."

"This isn't over," he hisses, and I break.

Turning quicker than Zane can stop me, I grab him by the neck, lifting him off his feet and shoving his back to the wall. "Yes, it is." My voice is a low growl.

"Put me down!" His face is red, and he claws at my hand as his nose starts to run.

"Look at me, Warner. This is me being *nice*." My eyes laser into his. "If you ever bother my wife again, if you ever make her angry or make her cry, I'll rip your throat out." Lowering him to his feet, I straighten his shirt as he wipes the snot off his lip and gasps for air. "And if you ever bother my baby girl, you won't have to worry about taking a paternity test ever again."

"Are you threatening me?" His voice is hoarse, and his weasel eyes meet mine.

I take another step closer, and he shrinks away. "That's a promise."

Zane pats my back, chuckling. "Okay, Papa Bear. We're done here."

My chest is heaving, and fury cycles hot in my blood. "I still want to take out the trash."

"I know." Zane gives my arm a gentle pull. "If this guy's ever stupid enough to come around again, I'll help you. Now let's get these papers filed."

Chapter 31

Olivia

"THAT ONE LOOKS LIKE A LEG OF LAMB," GARRETT SAYS LAZILY.

We're sitting in the hammock on the back porch at Cooters & Shooters on a crisp spring day. My head against his chest, and we're rocking gently back and forth.

I'm wrapped in a fuzzy blanket as we watch the clouds slide by in a clear blue sky, finding shapes in the towering bales of white. "I think it looks like Henny Lane."

So much has happened since my divorce papers were filed with the judge here in town. The clerk said it could take up to ten weeks to get the final decree, so I put it out of my head. I don't care how long it takes. I only know it's done, and this guy made it happen.

He told me I wouldn't believe him if he told me how it went down, and I said I didn't care. All that matters is we're together, and our baby is healthy

We had a lovely holiday season with the family. It's been so long since I was on the coast full-time. I forgot about the parades and the lighting of all the trees downtown and *The Polar Express* in the park with blankets and popcorn.

We rang in the new year with a kiss as fireworks went off over the bay. It's been our time to get established in our hometown, get reacquainted with the community, and get ready for the baby.

The only problem now is I'm overdue.

Nobody ever talks about being overdue, and I can only think it's so rare. After my first week, I started researching. I researched how often it happens—only 5 percent of pregnancies. *Five.*

Then I started combing everything I could find to make her come out. I've tried foot massages… There's supposed to be a spot on the foot that induces labor. *False.* I've tried acupuncture… Nope.

Nipple stimulation is another trick, and while having Garrett spend time gently rubbing, teasing, and sucking on my breasts ultimately led to many toe-curling orgasms—another supposed labor-inducer—baby girl still hasn't budged.

I've reached the point where I don't care about the pain. I don't care about pooping or tearing. I don't care about anything except getting her *out of me.*

Even Kimmie Joy did her best to help. She rested her little head on my stomach, petting me softly and cooing, "Come out, Baby Gina, I want you to play with me!"

"Liv's just so warm and cozy," Garrett teased, goosing his little niece to make her squeal. "She's too comfy in there."

"Really?" Kimmie's eyes were wide as she studied me.

"Time to make it a little uncomfortable," I grumbled.

Now we're at the restaurant waiting on Dylan to whip up a spicy eggplant parmesan dish, and I'm pretty sure Garrett's hungry.

"That one looks like Lindsey Cluckingham." I point to a large, fluffy cloud with what looks like an arched tail.

"I think it looks like a rack of ribs."

"You think every cloud is food."

"You think they're all chickens!"

That makes me snort a laugh, and I roll into his chest. His arms go around me, and it's warm and safe and home.

"I'm hungry," he groans.

"I can tell." I push into my spot again, taking the pressure off my belly.

Our feet are on the ground, and we're swinging slowly. "I've got one." Garrett picks up my hand, threading our fingers together. "What's the corniest love song you'd dedicate to me?"

"The corniest?"

"The absolute worst. The cheesiest love song you could long-distance dedicate to yours truly."

"I actually have one." I don't even have to think, and my lips twist in embarrassment. "It's too sappy."

"That's the point. The sappier the better. Tell me how much you can't live without me, Liv."

I put my hands over my face to hide as I say it. "A Thousand Years."

"Which one is that?" He frowns.

"You know, the one about dying every day…"

"Waiting for you?"

"Yes." My cheeks flame, because it's true. "One time I was listening to it, and I started to cry."

His eyes warm, and he catches the back of my neck, pulling me closer to kiss my lips. "That's really hot, Liv."

"It's not hot. It's sappy."

"It's giving me a boner. We should try nipple stimulation again."

"No." I shake my head. "I could die."

"Every day, waiting for me?" His brows rise, and I give him a playful shove.

"Your turn, and it better be sappy."

"Easy—'Don't Want to Miss a Thing' by Aerosmith."

"From that Bruce Willis movie?"

"Yep, *Armageddon*. Don't want to close my eyes or fall asleep or anything."

Warmth spreads in my chest, and I reach up to pull his lips to mine again. Our mouths open, and our tongues curl. His hand is on my breast, moving under my shirt when Dylan interrupts us.

"Whoa! Sorry!" She turns around on the landing, grabbing at the screen door to get it open again. "Pretend I'm not here!"

He looks into my eyes, and we both laugh. "That's a good game. We should play it again after lunch."

"If I don't have this baby…"

Holding my hands, he helps me out of the hammock, and we go into the restaurant. Dylan has plates set on a table, since I can't fit in a booth anymore, and Garrett holds the chair as I ease into it.

"Gigi, come out!" I cry, resting my elbow on the table. "What are you afraid of?"

"Are you kidding?" Craig puts a glass of milk beside me. "Have you seen the world we're living in?"

"Stop!" I hold up my hand. "I can't carry this baby inside me until the world improves. I'll explode."

"Did you know elephants gestate for two years?" Dylan puts a platter of eggplant covered in a peppery red sauce in front of us.

"Dylan…" I cut my eyes up at her, and she starts to laugh. "Sorry."

Garrett is already serving me an eggplant medallion, and I have my milk on hand. "I'm really desperate. I hate spicy food. It burns my tongue."

"The milk will help."

I've just taken my first bite when the door opens, and Rhonda Peachtree hurries into the room.

"Garrett, I've been looking for you everywhere. It's here!" She's waving a brown envelope over her head.

"Hey, Rhonda, what's up?" Garrett rises, meeting her halfway.

"Olivia!" She hurries over to where I'm sitting, unable to stand. "This is perfect. This…" She hands the envelope to me. "Is actually for you."

My eyes widen, and I turn to the side, fingers trembling as I unbend the bright gold fastener holding the envelope closed.

"I don't think I can open it." I feel excited and anxious and expectant… and finally, the flap opens, and I reach in to pull out the thick set of papers."

Divorce Decree is typed in all-caps at the top, and it proceeds to state that it's over. Warner Oberon the Third is officially out of my life once and for all. Holding a moment, I take a few breaths, waiting to see how I feel.

"It's so odd," I whisper. "I don't feel anything."

Lifting my gaze, I meet Garret's smile. "That chapter is closed."

"It is." I nod, reaching up to him.

No tears, no regret. The feelings are so far in the rearview mirror, and I'm completely over it.

"Hey." Garrett gives me a nudge, and I look up at him. "Will you still marry me?"

Pressing my lips together, I pretend to consider this. "I only just got divorced. I might want to play around a little."

"Play being my wife."

A smile breaks across my lips. *I love that.* "My husband."

He hugs me close again, pressing his lips beside my ear as he whispers, "I'm never letting you go again."

"I can't take another day of this." I'm standing in the kitchen at the Bradford house eating pineapple and drinking licorice tea.

I'm on the verge of tears.

"I wish there was something I could do!" Dylan holds my hand, her face scrunched in a frown.

Her hair is up in a bun, and she's dressed in her ballet leotard with nylon pants over it. She's headed out to school to teach her P.E. classes, and I'm facing another day of waddling around like a whale.

"Are you kidding? You've done everything! You made shrimp quesadillas, lemon drop cupcakes, spicy eggplant parm…"

"It only gave you heartburn." She tilts her head to the side sadly. "I've got to go, but can I get you anything?"

"No." I sigh heavily. "I think I'll walk to Mom's. Maybe being with the chickens will coax her out."

She laughs, giving me a hug before skipping out the door. I put my hand on my lower back, making my way out to the wide concrete path along the water that leads down to Mom's small cottage on the bay.

Signs of spring are all around me. Pink flowers sprout on the redbud trees. Butterflies flitter over the small, white bloodroot flowers. A biker zooms past when I take a break to pick a bright orange calendula.

"Aren't they beautiful?" An older lady in a straw hat stops to pick one.

She has a small dog on a leash, and it's wearing a little plaid jacket.

"Yes," I nod, smiling. "I like your dog. Is it a Yorkie? I've never seen one that color."

"It's actually a Biewer Terrier." Her eyes sparkle, and I hesitate.

"Did you say a Beaver—" I don't finish when a squirrel pops its head up, and the little black-and-white dog goes crazy barking.

"Oh!" The lady reaches down to try and catch him, but he bolts.

My heart jumps, and I reach out to try and help her, when a hollow thump sounds inside me and a gush of water rushes down my legs. All at once, I'm hit with a contraction so hard, I almost have to take a knee.

"Oh no…" I gasp, reaching out for a skinny tree growing alongside the path. "Why, baby girl?"

Another contraction hits, and cold sweat breaks across my forehead. I've had stomach cramps before, but this pain is like my insides being clamped in a vise.

"Oh, no…" I cry this time, squeezing my eyes shut as the twist keeps going.

It feels like it won't let up, until it finally does.

Gasping for air, I look up to see the woman is down the way, still trying to catch her little dog. "Help…" I try to call to her, but it comes out as more of a yelp.

The contractions are coming so fast, I can't walk. I'm starting to panic. I'm looking all around for anyone, but on this mid-morning in March, the path is pretty deserted.

Tears are in my eyes, and I hold my stomach, doing my best to keep moving forward through the pain. "You couldn't have waited until I got to Mom's?"

Another blast of pain stops me, and I bend forward, putting my hands on my upper thighs as I cry out. My mind spins, and when it finally stops, I fumble to get my phone out of my pocket.

I can't believe this is happening. After all this time of waiting and trying and everything I did, I'm going to have this baby right here on the sidewalk. Terror strangles my throat, and my hands shake as another contraction starts.

Again, I can't help a loud groan, which is what they taught us to do in birthing class rather than scream. Blackness starts to lower over my eyes, but I try to fight it. I can't faint right now. I'm trying to remember… HypnoBirthing, what's my mantra?

None of it matters as I reach for the nearby bench, using it to lower to my knees…

Chapter 32

Garrett

"HOW BIG IS SHE?" I CLIMB OUT OF MY TRUCK, WEARING MY ANIMAL control vest and walking slowly up the narrow, two-lane road to where a group of older men stand around with their arms crossed.

Aubrey is with me, and she hesitates, taking out her gloves. "Looks like an eleven-footer, which means it's probably a male."

It's the most excitement we've had since the snakes, and I'm pretty much as terrified now as I was then.

The alligator lying across this little country road all the way south of town is bigger than me, and he's not going anywhere.

I grab the cooler Aubrey packed from the bed of my truck, and now the question is who's going to get close enough to handle this situation?

"It looks like he's asleep," I whisper as we stop beside the old-timers.

"It's been there all morning," one of the fellows says. "Didn't even move when we drove off the road to go around."

"Did you call Jeff over at Alligator Alley?" I suggest.

"He's in the middle of doing a show for a bunch of preschoolers."

"It's all right. He couldn't have gotten here as fast as us anyway." Aubrey is as calm as she was dealing with the snakes. She opens the cooler and takes out a medium-sized chicken breast. "Get this on the loop, Garrett. I pumped it full of Diazepam."

"Okay…" I take the chicken and fasten it to the heavy steel pole. "Then what do we do?"

"Duct tape his jaw and load him in the back of your pickup." A different old guy nods at my shiny, practically new Chevy.

"Not in my truck." I shake my head.

"My son-in-law has a dually, but he's out on Fort Morgan Road."

"Can you give him a call?" Aubrey squints up at him, and he nods, pulling out a cell phone.

"I guess I'm going fishing." I grin, walking out to where the massive reptile is napping on warm asphalt.

"If it hisses, just back up slowly," Aubrey advises me.

My eyes are fixed on the creature, and I approach carefully, dangling the chicken from the metal pole in front of me. "Should I whistle or something?"

"They're not really domesticated."

"Tell me about it."

Naturally, my phone starts vibrating as soon as I'm five feet from the gator. Whoever it is will have to give me a minute. I take a few steps closer, monitoring the beast for any signs of irritation. As big as these creatures are, I've seen how fast they can move.

The sound of a phone ringing goes off behind me, and I hear Aubrey answer quietly.

"Here, boy," I say gently, lowering the chicken near its head. "Have some chicken."

It doesn't move, and I'm not sure what to do now.

"Garrett?" Aubrey's voice is level. "I'm coming out there to take over."

"It's okay, I've got it." I swing the pole slightly, so the chicken bonks the reptile in the head.

That gets its attention. It lets out a low hiss, and my stomach drops.

"Garrett?" Aubrey tries again, but I shake my head.

"Don't come over here…"

All at once, the big guy lunges, and I toss the pole, digging in my toes to sprint back to the truck like I'm on the football field. The old-timers all do the same, darting in every direction, and I run straight to my truck, grabbing the side and jumping into the bed before looking back to see the alligator finishing the chicken in two big chomps.

I take off the gloves, muttering a *damn* when I see Aubrey in the cab behind the wheel.

"Get in the truck, Garrett," she shouts, and I frown. "We're leaving!"

Glancing at the alligator, I see it's lying on the road again in the same position, and I climb out of the back of my truck to get in on the passenger's side. "What's up?"

Aubrey gives me a worried look, and my stomach drops. "What is it?" My voice grows louder.

"Nothing to worry about, but we need to get to the hospital. Your wife's having the baby."

I grab the seatbelt, pulling it over my shoulder. "Step on it, Aubrey."

She floors it, and we squeal tires. "That was your brother Jack. An old lady found her on the walking path having contractions."

"The walking path?" My head hurts, and I grip the top of the dashboard. "Is she okay?"

"She seemed fine, but he said the baby was coming fast. Olivia was calling for you, and they were searching for you everywhere."

"I should've stayed home today."

"To be fair, you've been staying home a lot of days."

"Of course we're as far out in the country as we can be."

"We could be a little farther."

My neck is tight. My stomach is tight, and all I can think of is Liv there alone with all her fears, calling for me. "Is anybody with her?"

"I'm sure her mom is." Aubrey reaches over to squeeze my arm. "We're almost there."

She hesitates through a four-way stop before barreling up the last stretch of highway before we turn onto the main drag. We're headed south when the large hospital comes into view. Flipping on the turn signal, she slows down as we enter the hospital parking lot.

"Let me out." My hand is on the door, and I don't have time to wait while we creep through the hospital lot or worse, try to find a parking spot.

Aubrey stops the truck, and I'm out, running at top speed to the front entrance.

As soon as I enter, a male nurse recognizes me. "This way, Mr. Bradford!" He leads me through a door marked *Staff Only*, and we dash down the back way to a stairwell. "The birth center's on the fourth floor."

Of course, it is. "Thanks." I grab the rail and take the stairs two at a time.

Adrenaline drives me, and when I finally reach the top, I crash through the doors.

Jack is there, and his brows rise when he sees me. "You made it!"

"I did?" I'm about to collapse, but I don't have time.

"This way!" He takes off down the hall with me right behind him and pulls up short at a room. "She's in here."

Looking around, I guess it's okay for me to go right in. Again, there's no time to hesitate. Pushing through the door, I hear the beep of monitors mixed with the sound of Dr. Pierce giving orders and Liv's low groans—until her voice goes high. "Garrett?"

Rushing to her bedside, I lift her hand gently in mine. "I'm here."

"Thank goodness!" Ms. Plum sighs, passing me the cup of ice chips and backing away. "I don't know how to do any of this. I took the drugs."

Liv's face scrunches when she sees me, and a tear falls onto her cheek. "It's not working." She sniffs, and her eyes squeeze as another contraction tightens her stomach. Then she yells, "It hurts like hell, Garrett!"

Wincing, I try to remember what they told us in the birthing class. "That's okay, that's okay. Don't panic… Remember the acronym…"

"Fuck the acronym!" she yells again. "This baby's the size of a Buick, and I'm never getting her out of me!"

My wide eyes meet Dr. Pierce's, and she shakes her head, pressing her lips together, I guess so she doesn't laugh at me.

"Oh, Liv," Ms. Plum whispers. "Is it too late to give her something?"

The doctor nods, and she puts a trembling hand on her forehead. "My poor girl."

"No shame if you want to wait in the hall, Ms. P." I give her mom an encouraging smile, hoping to get her out of here, and she blinks at me wide-eyed before nodding and quickly scurrying to the door.

"You're going to have this baby today." Dr. Pierce has a smile in her voice. "You're almost to ten centimeters, and I've got a warm compress on your perineum."

"Hear that?" I try to stay upbeat. "It's almost time."

Liv's head falls back, and she whimpers. "I'm so tired, Garrett."

Her hair is slick with sweat and stuck to her forehead, and her cheeks are wet with tears. My heart breaks a little, but I can't let her give up. We've trained for this.

I put my arm around her, behind her shoulders, and her face falls against my neck. "Why didn't I take the drugs?"

"Come on, Liv, remember the script. Relaxing your jaw relaxes your pelvis." I rub her arm, kissing the top of her head. "Release the tension in your face as you release the baby."

Her jaw begins to tremble, and I hold her tighter. "That's it. What's the script? Do you remember the words?"

"No," she whimpers, shaking her head. "I completely forgot my mantra."

"You're doing really good, Liv." Dr. Pierce's voice is strong. "Whatever you're doing, keep doing it. The baby's moving."

"I feel her!" Liv's eyes squint, and her jaw begins to tense again.

"Stay with me, Liv! What are the words? Soften… You know them. Say it with me. Soften…"

Her teeth unclench, and she blows air out through her lips. "Soften…"

"Settle…" We say the second word together, then I give her a gentle nudge. "You know the rest. Say it."

"Relax…" Her eyes squint, and she pushes against the stirrups, sliding higher in the bed.

My body tenses, and I know she's feeling the pain. "You can do it."

Her voice trembles as she says it again. "Relax…" Another huff of breath. "Release."

"That's it."

"We're ready to push. Are you ready?"

"Long breaths, Liv. Remember to hum."

Our eyes meet, and she nods quickly. Inhaling for three, I watch her relax her shoulders and her jaw. Tears flood her eyes, and my heart rips. Still she's doing it. She's following the script, and I rub her shoulders, doing my best to keep her encouraged.

Low groans, measured breathing, I've lost track of time, but we're getting there.

Dr. Pierce is at the foot of the bed, and she looks up at us. "I see the head! Do you want a mirror?"

Liv shakes her head fast. "No!"

I know her fears of tearing and poop, and I grab her hand. "Remember the process."

She nods, fixing her eyes on mine again, and inhaling slowly. Her eyes close, but she keeps her jaw loose. Her hand grips mine as she hums low, and Dr. Pierce calls out.

"She's crowning!" Excitement enters her voice. "One more time."

Liv rises up, inhaling for three, squeezing my hand, and humming down for a count of eight. One more low groan, and we hear the first, annoyed squeal from our little girl. Liv's face breaks into a smile, and fresh tears flood her eyes.

"One more time," Dr. Pierce calls, and she does it again, another long push, and Gigi's out.

Dr. Pierce lifts her quickly, moving her onto Liv's stomach, dark pink and pouting with perfect little rosebud lips. Her eyes squeeze shut, her tiny mouth opens, and another grumpy cry fills the room.

"Oh, no," Liv's voice is a weepy laugh. "Don't cry, baby Gina."

I'm officially in love. While I wash my hands, the nurse quickly weighs and measures her then wipes her eyes with the antibiotic ointment.

Gigi puckers her little mouth again before letting out another little angry cry. Liv pulls her to her breast, and she's already nuzzling. It takes her a minute, but Liv keeps pulling her in close, sliding her baby mouth to the nipple. She tilts her head back, until finally Gigi settles into feeding.

"I'll give you three a minute." Dr. Pierce pats my arm as she goes to the door.

Worried hazel eyes meet mine. "I'm not very good at any of this."

"Hell, Liv..." Leaning forward, I kiss the top of her head. "You look like a pro to me."

"You didn't see what I was like before you got here. I was

a complete spazz. I couldn't remember the script. I couldn't re-member what I was supposed to do…"

"You were just a little shook up." I lean back, squeezing her hand. "Jack said you went into labor on the path?"

"I was walking to Mom's." Her eyes blink wide. "This lady had a dog, and my water broke… I think I fainted. I don't know how I got here."

"Jack said someone called 911. It must've been the same person."

Gigi makes a little grunty noise, and we both look down to see her watching us with round, dark eyes. "Did my baby girl just snort?"

Liv exhales a smile, carefully lifting her and moving her to the other breast. This time, when she pulls the baby close, she latches much quicker.

"See?" I grin, sliding a finger over her soft, round cheek. "You're a fast learner, little G."

We both watch her eating and blinking at the two of us. "She's so pretty," Liv whispers.

"Just like her mama."

That gets me a kiss. Liv lifts her chin, leaning closer. "I'm so glad you made it."

"Me too."

I'll save my gator-fishing story for another day. For now, I'm happy to watch my baby girl nuzzling into her mama's breast, my beautiful family growing closer.

"Whatever happened to the alligator?" Dylan has baby Gina snuggled against her shoulder while Kimmie stands beside her stroking her cousin's small hand with her finger.

My brothers, Logan, Ms. Plum, Allie, Rachel, the kids and,

of course, Miss Gina are all with us at the family house for Gigi's first official meet and greet.

Even Hendrix sent her a pink cashmere baby cardigan. Liv only laughed, saying she'd save that for when she was out of the spit-up stage.

We've only been home a week, but Liv has bounced back so fast. She didn't have any tearing, which the doctor said was a miracle. Liv said it was because I was there to help her relax. I know better than to take any credit, but that tracks. Apparently, nursing also helps. Either way, Liv is happy and getting back to her old self.

"Aubrey said the old guys were able to load it into a truck, and they drove down and released it somewhere around Week's Bay."

"Aubrey Schiffer was always very resourceful." Miss Gina nods from where she's sitting beside Dylan, holding the baby's little hand. "I still can't believe you named her after me."

"We decided that night we showed up to swim," Liv explains. "You've always had the kindest heart. I hope Gigi grows up to be the same way."

Her wrinkled hand rises to her lips, and it's the first time I've ever seen Miss G cry.

Dylan leans her head on her shoulder. "It's true. I'm mad they beat me to it."

"She's holding my finger!" Kimmie looks up at us with wide eyes, cooing. "She's so cute."

"She loves her cousin," I say from where I stand behind Liv.

"Can you believe everything happened at the same time?" Liv shakes her head, exhaling a laugh.

"Yes," Allie groans. "It's always the way it happens. Nothing, nothing, nothing, then *Boom!*"

"I honestly thought I was going to have the baby right there on the walking path. Those contractions were coming so hard and so fast."

"I can't believe I let you walk off like that all by yourself."

Dylan shakes her head, looking down at the baby. "If anything would've happened—"

"It all worked out just fine." Wrapping my arms around Liv, we bask in the warmth of our friends and loved ones welcoming our baby girl into the family.

Liv's wearing a pretty V-neck dress in a red, handkerchief pattern, and her long hair is loose over her shoulders. Her push present, a 24-karat gold necklace from Tiffany's with a heart engraved with Gina Grace's birthdate (and room for a few more) hangs around her neck.

She's so beautiful, and I'm so proud of them both.

"I'm just glad you finally got there," Ms. Plum laughs. "I've only done it once a long time ago, and I was out of it the whole time."

"Same here," Allie leans into her shoulder.

"You forget how little they are." Jack stands beside me watching.

Gigi lifts her wobbly head and lets out a huge baby-sneeze, which provokes a chorus of oops and ahhs. I can't help but laugh, because it's pretty much what Liv and I do all day every day. We're all so amazed by her. Everything she does is new and adorable.

"She sneezed, Daddy!" Kimmie runs over to where Jack's standing. "Did you see her sneeze? Wasn't it funny?"

"It was." He chuckles, glancing at me. "Pretty sure it's the first time she's been around a newborn."

"It's been a while for all of us." Allie walks over to pat the baby.

"You set the bar pretty high." Zane's low voice is at my side, and I hold up my hand for a fist-bump.

"I didn't do anything you wouldn't do."

Rachel is on Dylan's other side, sliding her hand in small circles over Gigi's back. "She's just perfect, Liv."

"Can I hold her now, Aunt Deedee?" Kimmie scoots closer to her aunt.

"Let's sit on the couch, so I can help you."

The two of them go to the couch, and Dylan helps my niece hold the baby in her lap. She puts a pillow under her little arm to lift Baby G's head, and Rachel sits on the other side of her.

"Good work, bro." Logan grips my shoulder. "I knew you could do it."

"Hell, I didn't do anything." I exhale a laugh.

"It's not true. He did a lot." Liv argues, lifting her chin and kissing the side of my jaw.

Pride tightens my chest, and I lean down to kiss her lips briefly, holding her pretty hazel eyes and feeling like the king of the world.

Eventually, it's time to feed her. Gigi gets fussy, and Jack scoops up his obsessed little girl.

"You need to marry Miss Allie, Daddy, so we can get a baby, too!" Kimmie announces, and Allie nearly does a spit-take in the kitchen.

"I think that's a great idea," Dylan calls from where she's standing beside her, adding fuel to the fire.

"Night, everybody," is all Jack says as he carries his waving daughter out the front door.

"Do I get a vote?" Allie teases when he's gone, and Dylan points at her.

"I already know your vote."

She wraps her fist around my sister's finger, and pulls her in. "I've got to get home, troublemaker. School starts early."

"I can't wait for her to be big enough to stay with Granny." Ms. Plum stops to give her daughter a hug. "You're so strong and brilliant, Liv. I couldn't be more proud of you."

"Thanks, Mom." Liv kisses her mom, giving her a squeeze before starting for the stairs. "Night, everybody. I've got to feed the baby bear and put her to bed."

We all say goodnight, and soon the house is quiet. Logan and Dylan retire to their room, and I climb the stairs to the second floor.

We're snuggled in my bed together with Gigi right beside us in a bassinet, and I scroll through pictures of the house I'm planning to buy for our family. It's a sweet little cottage not too far from Ms. Plum's, but closer to downtown. It has three bedrooms in case we decide to do this again, but I know the rule, no pressure.

Liv is asleep at my side, and I look at our sleeping little baby. I'm not ready to sleep yet. I think about our sappy songs, and how I don't want to miss a thing. I trace my finger lightly along the side of Liv's hair, and I've almost forgotten the time when I was alone, unhappy, missing her. Even more of a distant memory are those days when I thought I'd never get her back, when I thought I'd never again feel the way I felt when I was with Liv.

By some miracle, it happened. My beautiful wife, our beautiful baby girl.

I miss my parents at times like these. They really liked Liv and me together, and I know they would love her even more now.

They gave us the best gift in each other. We'll never be alone as long as we have our family, and with each new member, this tree, made strong by our love, continues to grow.

Epilogue

Garrett

Six months later

FLASHING LIGHTS CIRCLE AROUND US. WE'RE BACK AT COOTERS & Shooters, and Liv is hugged against my chest as we slow dance to a song about Levi Jeans by Beyonce. We might even grind a little, but it's not a Dare Night. So we keep it PG-13.

Dylan has the place decorated with balloons and streamers, and a banner hangs over the small bar that reads, *Congratulations, Deputy Sheriff Garrett!*

It took me forever to read the manual, so I wound up getting an audiobook. After watching me struggle for a month, Aubrey, the official badass, asked if I'd ever been tested for dyslexia. Frowning, I told her no. I wasn't really sure what that was.

Well, wouldn't you know, I have it, but according to the doctor, my brain made adjustments for it through the years. Still, that's why I read so slow.

"It doesn't mean you're dumb," Liv was quick to note. "It

has nothing to do with intelligence. It just takes you longer to finish."

"I was told a gentleman always lets the lady finish first," I couldn't help teasing.

All jokes aside, it's something I wish I'd known in high school, because all those years ago when my baby sister would be flying through one-thousand-page romantasy novels, and I struggled with *Frankenstein*, I wouldn't have felt stupid.

Water under the bridge. It's been an incredible year. Liv and I have officially moved into our small house, Baby Gina is sleeping through the night, and we're both getting established in town.

Liv put out her shingle as a small-town, country lawyer doing wills and estates and all kinds of small jobs, and I'm officially a member of law enforcement. I even have a uniform that fits.

The song ends, and I look down into the bright hazel eyes of my gorgeous bride-to-be. "When are we setting a date for the wedding?"

"My schedule's wide open." Her nose wrinkles, and she rises onto her toes to kiss my lips. "I'm finally getting my figure back."

"I'm ready to mess it up again."

She laughs, turning as she leads me off the dance floor to where our friends and family are milling around with cake and champagne.

"It's not going to be the same at animal control without you, Deputy." Aubrey holds up a beer. "Still, congratulations to you."

"Thanks, Aubrey," I chuckle. "I really learned a lot working with you. Hell, I wouldn't have known what to do in half those situations."

"Sheriff Grizz!" Craig walks up, clapping my hand. "I hope this doesn't mean you're not going to dance on the bar with me anymore."

"When I'm off duty, what happens at Cooters & Shooters stays at Cooters & Shooters."

Zane walks over to where we're standing, Rachel at his side with Baby G on her shoulder. The minute my little girl sees me, she starts fussing and reaching, which of course, makes me smile with pride.

"Garrett!" Rachel pouts. "I just got her!"

"Shouldn't have walked over here, then." I reach out, taking my little girl from my future sister-in-law and holding her against my chest.

She's getting so big, she sits up and looks around at everyone with those big blue eyes. Her hair is pink like her mom's, and she still has perfect little rosebud lips. She still squeezes them in an adorable little pout before she cries, too, which is not very often.

Liv says I'm spoiling her, but I don't even care.

Zane pulls Rachel into a hug at his side. "Jack said Rodney is looking to retire now that you're on the force."

My brow lowers, and I glance over to where the old sheriff is talking to my brother. "I hope he waits until I know where the bathroom is at least."

Zane chuckles. "I'm sure he'll wait until you know the ropes. I'm just saying, it won't be long before we're changing that sign."

"Sheriff Bradford." Rachel lifts her chin. "That's really cool, Grizz. You'll be a great sheriff. You're already a great daddy."

"Thanks, Rach." We're getting to be good friends, and she fits right into the family. "Say, when are you two planning to set a date? I'm ready to tie the knot with Liv, but I don't want to steal your thunder."

"If we can get all the excitement to die down," Rachel teases. "I'd love to have a winter wedding. She looks over to where Clint is leaning against the bar beside Craig. "What do you think, Clint? Could we pull together a wedding in three months?"

He pushes off, walking over to where we stand. "I think a December wedding would be divine. We could have horse-drawn carriages, little ballerina girls lighting candles, maybe do it at the stables. Would Gloria allow that?"

Zane shrugs. "I don't see why not."

Rachel's eyes widen, and her cheeks flush. "Oh, Clint! It's like you read my mind!"

He takes her hand. "Let's get it on the books. Come on."

The two of them walk away, and I look down at my brother, exhaling a laugh. "You're welcome."

Zane only smiles, shaking his head. "I've got what I want. Signing a paper is only a technicality."

The music starts up, a perkier song this time, and the baby starts to sway in my arms. My eyes widen, and I turn to Craig, pointing at the baby. "You're seeing this, right?"

"That's right, baby girl!" He walks over to take her from my arms, moving his hips and dancing to the song. "You're going to be up on that bar with Uncle Craig before long."

Gigi laughs, patting his shoulders with her fat hands, and he makes a happy face, rubbing his nose against hers. "That's right. You're just our little dancing girl."

"I told Liv we should've named her Lola."

We're walking across the room to where Liv is holding a glass of champagne and chatting with Allie and Dylan when the door opens, and a face we haven't seen in more than a year enters the room.

She's dressed in jeans and a loose sweatshirt, and she's holding a baby girl who looks about the same age as Gigi on her hip.

"Raven?" Dylan's voice goes high. "Is that you?"

She runs over to her friend, pulling her into a hug.

"Dylan..." Her voice is hushed, and she seems embarrassed, like she might turn around and bolt out the door again. "I didn't know... It's not Thursday!"

"Oh, we're celebrating Garrett's promotion. He just joined the sheriff's department." She holds Raven's hand, and she's slowly leading her into the restaurant. "You dropped off the map! I thought something had happened to you!"

"Ahh..." She shifts the dark-haired little baby on her hip, and my eyes widen. "I should probably come back another time."

I look at Jack and Zane, and they're walking closer to where I'm standing as well. We're the only ones who remember, because we're the only three who are still around from when he was a baby.

"Who is this?" Dylan leans closer to the baby. "Aren't you just a little cutie!"

"This is Haddy." Raven's eyes blink fast. "She, uh…"

"Raven?" Jack's the first one of us to speak, stepping closer carefully. "Is this… Hendrix's baby?"

Raven's face flushes, and she visibly gulps air. "I can come back another time."

"What?" Dylan's voice goes high, and she looks from Liv to Raven. "Did everybody get pregnant at my wedding?"

"I have an implant." Rachel holds up a hand from where she's standing with Clint.

"IUD." Allie holds up her hand.

"I'm sorry, I didn't mean to crash the party. I wanted to talk to you… I don't know how to get in touch with him, and I thought… he should know." Her chin drops, and she almost seems ashamed.

"Hendrix doesn't know?" Dylan's voice is gentle. "You did this all alone?"

"Technically. My sister was there."

"But she's only, how old is Amelia now? It doesn't matter…" Dylan waves her hand, leaning closer. "Hi, Haddy! I'm your aunt Dylan!"

The baby rocks the same way Gigi does before leaning into her aunt's arms. Dylan fawns happily, lifting her onto her shoulder and bouncing her side to side.

"It's like she knows." A tentative smile appears for the first time on Raven's face since she walked through the door. "I wasn't trying to hide her. I just had such terrible morning sickness—I was sick all nine months. I actually lost weight while I was pregnant."

"Oh, Raven, that's horrible!" Liv takes her arm.

"I wish you would've texted us," Allie adds.

"Then after she was born, I was so busy taking care of her," Raven explains. "And I guess, maybe I was afraid—"

"You don't have to be afraid." Dylan hugs her close. "We love babies!"

"I wasn't sure Hendrix would think that…"

The girls surround her, leading her over to where the cake and champagne are waiting. Jack meets my eyes, and I'm pretty sure we're all thinking the same thing.

Bending my elbow, I cover the grin threatening to split my lips. "Looks like I'd better get working on that cross-stitch."

Zane's chin drops, and he's smiling big as well. Mr. "No Marriage, Babies, or Poop" is about to get a big surprise. "Looks like we have a new family member."

Jack has his phone out, and I can't wait for the brothers' chat that's about to begin. If only Mom and Dad were here to see this…

Thank you for reading *The Way We Score*!

Be sure to download your **Free Bonus Scene** here:

Up next is *The Way We Collide*!

Football is my life. I'm not interested in marriage or babies or poopy diapers. Yet here I am, standing in front of a judge saying "I do," with a six-month-old on my hip and an aspiring storm-chaser on my arm...

Hendrix & Raven's small-town, surprise baby, marriage of convenience, football player meets storm-chaser romance is going to keep you on your toes, laughing, and cheering for this unlikely pair...

Available in ebook, paperback, and on Audio!

Learn about all of my books on TiaLouise.com/Books, and get your downloadable Reading Guide.

The Way We Collide

Football is my life. I'm not interested in marriage or babies or poopy diapers. Yet here I am, standing in front of a judge saying "I do," with a six-month-old on my hip and an aspiring storm-chaser on my arm.

From the time I was a little boy, sleeping with my head on a football, I've had one goal: carrying on the Bradford-family legacy.

Our famous father trained all my older brothers and me to be star athletes, just like he was, but seven years later, I'm the only one with my head still in the game.

Until Raven Gale storms into my life.

She's smart, sassy, curves for days, and lightning in the sack. When I met her at my little sister's wedding we bonded immediately over our dedication to our dreams, and our determination to let nothing stop us.

She wants to make a name for herself in the world of high-stakes meteorology—if Raven Gale shows up in your town, you're going to have a bad night, weatherwise.

We had a great night, non-weatherwise. We did things I've never done before, including breaking right through the protective barrier I always use and scoring a winning goal.

A baby girl is a surprise neither of us expected. To make matters worse, Raven's overprotective, billionaire dad threatens to revoke her trust fund if we don't make her legit. So we hatch a plan— get married, secure the nest egg, then shake hands and walk away.

The only problem is the longer Raven and Haddy play house with me in LA, the more I like having them around. And the more nights I spend with my wife, the more times I rock my baby girl to sleep, and yes, change her poopy diapers, the more I want our pretend marriage to last.

It never rains in LA, and there's no football for me in south Alabama. But when you collide with a cyclone, everything changes, including your plans.

(THE WAY WE COLLIDE is a small-town, surprise baby, sports romance with a marriage of convenience, close proximity, poopy diapers, an over-protective alpha, a feisty FMC, and a few twisters. No cheating. No cliffhanger. No third-act breakup.)

Prologue

Hendrix

I REMEMBER IT LIKE IT WAS YESTERDAY. I WAS BACK HOME IN NEWHOPE, Alabama, standing in the kitchen of Cooters & Shooters, our family's restaurant on the bay, freshly graduated from USC, on my break before returning to Los Angeles to be the starting tight end for the Tigers.

Everything was coming together for my brothers and me. We were the stars our father molded us to be. I imagined the four of us walking into awards ceremonies, meeting up on the field, ruling the league like a band of Marvel superheroes.

It was the culmination of my childhood dreams, looking up to them, taking my place beside them, and my oldest brother Jack had just announced he was retiring.

In my mind, I'm right back in the moment…

"Retiring?" I stare at him like he sprouted a second head.

"Why would you do that? You're a star. Hell, you're on track for the MVP!"

Jack's grin is tight as he messes the front of my hair. "There's more to life than football, little brother."

He's trying to play it off like it's no big deal, but his smile doesn't reach his eyes.

I don't know why he's saying this, and I'll be damned if I believe him. I can't.

"What about Dad?" My tone is sheer disbelief tinged with hurt.

"What about Dad?" He says it through a chuckle.

"Dad dedicated his life to training us. He taught us everything he knew. He opened the doors, paved the way. You inherited his legacy." My mind trips back to all the Saturdays we scrimmaged in the park; all the Sundays we sat in front of ESPN.

"Dad taught us the only path he knew to a better life, but there are other paths." Jack's tone is calm, reasonable, and it's pissing me off.

"I don't believe that." I push back. "Not for you."

For a player like Jack Bradford, there's nothing more to life than football. It's the same for my brother Garrett, and it's the same for me, the youngest of the "Bradford Boys." We're the sons of legendary quarterback Arthur Bradford. We're special.

The only one of us I could honestly believe would walk away from the game and never look back is Zane, the brother I understand the least. He likes to read and take walks and be alone and disappear.

Not me.

I've been sleeping with my head on a football since I was old enough to carry one. I've been busting my ass to be as good as my three big brothers since the first day Dad told me to get out there and play with them.

At six-foot-two, I've always been the receiver to Jack's quarterback. Garrett is a born lineman at six-foot-four, two hundred pounds. Dad guided Zane to being a kicker, and for a loner, had the most natural talent of all of us.

Zane was the first-round draft pick for the Admirals, and after five successful seasons, he even seems to like it now.

Jack has always been our constant.

When Dad died, Jack kept us on track like the team captain he was taught to be. He finished school and went to Texas where he became the star quarterback on our dad's old team, carrying on the legacy.

From there, he made sure we all followed the path. Garrett is making a name for himself in New York, and Zane is in Baltimore. We have talent, and our places are secure.

Now this.

"What will you do if you're not playing football?" My chest is tight as I try to understand.

"Mrs. Laverne asked me to coach at the high school." He slides his hand up and down his sleeping daughter Kimmie's little back. "I'll start this fall."

"High school?" I can't keep the disgust out of my tone. "You've got to be kidding."

"It's what I want to do, Hen. It's what I've done since Mom and Dad died. Taking care of all of you changed my priorities. Then Kimmie changed them even more."

Now it makes sense. Now I understand the hurt in his eyes, the smile that isn't completely there.

"This is because of Danielle." I flat-out say it. No point beating around the bush.

Jack's first wife was a two-bit country singer from Fort Worth who caught his eye somehow. I only met her once, but I couldn't figure out why he was with her. He never dated girls like that in school. Then she turned up pregnant. Then she ditched him for a singing career in Branson.

"It's not because of Danielle." His voice is low, but I catch a growl.

"She ruined Texas for you, and you think this place will make it all go away."

Don't get me wrong, I love our hometown on the coast. When Dad decided he couldn't play anymore, he and our mom came back here and opened this restaurant and raised us all in this tight-knit community.

It's a tight-knit community that rallied around us when we were orphaned, but as sweet as it might be, nobody's getting famous in Newhope, Alabama.

"Sometimes I forget how young you are." He says it in that dismissive tone like he's done with this conversation.

"Don't listen to him." Our sister Dylan pushes past me as she reaches for the baby, her amber eyes shining. "Come here, Kimmie! Come see your favorite aunt."

"Her only aunt," I grouse.

Dylan is eighteen months younger than me, and she'd love nothing more than all four of us giving up football and moving back here.

"I'm so happy you're home." Her voice is soft and high as she talks to the toddler, shaking her head and rubbing their noses. "You're going to love it here. We'll take baby swim classes at the Y, and I'll get you in at the preschool—"

I can't take any more of this baby talk, and *I'm* not finished with our conversation. "You want me to believe that being a high school football coach is better than being the best quarterback in the league? Better than winning the Big Game. Better than getting your championship ring?"

"Being with my daughter, being here with my family, and yeah, coaching the next generation of star players is better than the grind." Jack's tone grows firmer. "Maybe Danielle did spoil Texas for me, but my goal has always been to save enough money to be able to walk away and do what I want."

"I'm so glad you did." Dylan shifts the baby onto her hip and takes his hand. "I can't wait for all of you to retire."

"Don't hold your breath waiting on me," I grumble. "I'll never throw away my career for a woman."

"Never say never unless you're hungry," Jack chuckles. "You'll end up eating those words."

"Not me. I know what I want, and it's not quitting."

"I'm not quitting, little brother." He puts a strong hand on the top of my shoulder, and gives it a squeeze. "I'm doing what I want to do, and one day, you might find something you love more, too."

"Doubtful." I walk over to where Thomas is mixing seasonings into ground sirloin to make his famous burgers.

Thomas Jones has been the head cook at the restaurant since it opened. He and Dad played ball together in Texas, although Thomas kept playing after Dad retired. When our parents opened Cooters & Shooters, Dad offered him a place to land, and he's been with us ever since.

Dylan runs the restaurant now, but Thomas is still head cook. Next to Jack, he's the closest thing we have to a father.

My siblings drift away, talking about setting up the house Jack bought, getting settled, enrolling Kimmie in all the baby stuff in town, and I sit on the stool beside our old friend with my arms crossed.

I watch his dark hands skillfully shaping the meat, and my mouth waters just thinking about how delicious it will be.

"How can he do this, T? How can he walk away with so many good years ahead of him?" Anger is hot in my chest. "If Dad were alive, he'd never let him retire this young."

Thomas's dark eyes hold sympathy with a touch of amusement when he looks at me. He knows me. He knows us all. I can't remember a day of my life without him in it.

"Your dad would want Jack to do what he loves."

"He loves football—just like Dad."

"Your dad loved the game, but he also loved his family." Thomas speaks low, continuing to work. "One of the two is always more important, and Jack decided to make it his family."

My jaw is still tight, but I hear what he's saying. I know one is going to dominate, and I appreciate Jack being a single dad now. It doesn't make it an easier pill to swallow.

"Football is life." I meet his eyes. "He might say it's not, but how can anything be more important?"

A smile curls Thomas's lips as he rolls out the patties for the day. "Life is long. What you think is important now will change. You'll understand when you're a dad."

"*You'll* understand it's time for me to get my head examined."

I have no intention of ever giving up my career for anybody. I've worked too hard to get where I am, and I've been careful. Sure, I have a good time, but I'm always in control.

That was seven years ago…

My brother retired in September of that year, and my career took off.

I put my head down and stayed focused, and it got better and better. With every contract renewal, my salary increased until I was setting records for pay in the league.

Seven years later, I'd just wrapped the best season of my career when I got a text that started the countdown.

The events that changed everything.

August is the hottest month in LA. The Santa Ana winds blow dry air, and we're in the final weeks before preseason begins. Before it's time to start another year. I can't wait.

Satisfaction unfurls in my chest as I stand on the balcony of my prairie-style mansion. It's concrete and metal beams built into the side of a hill, and I look down over the city like an emperor surveying his domain.

I'm alone, but I'm content as I contemplate the year ahead.

I finished last season going all the way to the playoffs. We fell short of the big game, but this year will be different. Adrenaline beats in my chest as I think about it. I'm so ready to get started, because I can feel it—this year we're going all the way.

Every sportscaster is talking about it. It's going to be my best year yet, and I'm ready to get started. Then my phone lights up with a text.

Jack: You got time to come home for a few days?

My brow furrows. It feels like a loaded question, and I quickly tap back a reply.

Is something wrong?

Jack: Nothing wrong—just family business. We need you here.

My jaw tightens, and I look around the place. I have plans with friends tonight, but I can bow out and book a flight to south Alabama. I don't know what "family business" means, but Jack never asks me to come home. I decide it must be important.

I can be there tomorrow.

Jack: Plan to stay a few days.

I always do.

In a few taps, I arrange for the team jet to fly me to the small, private airport ten miles south of Newhope. It takes about an hour for the pilot to file a flight plan, and a few more for me to pack and catch a car to the airport.

Traveling from the West Coast to the east sets me back a bit, and it's after midnight when I arrive at the hotel I always reserve when I'm in town for a visit.

Dylan and her husband Logan live in our old family home up the hill from the restaurant, and I like to have my own space in case I meet someone or just want to lie around all day in my boxer briefs and watch football.

Besides, Dylan and Logan are newlyweds. They don't need me lurking around the house, interrupting their marital bliss. They should be able to have sex on the kitchen floor if they want.

I send a brief text to the brother's group chat that I'm here, then I crash for the night.

Eight hours later, I open my eyes to a string of texts telling me to come to breakfast at Cooters & Shooters. The restaurant doesn't open to the public until eleven, but when the family is all home, we have breakfast together.

At this point, I'm the only brother who hasn't retired from the game and moved back to Newhope, which makes me shake my head at the waste.

Zane gets a pass, since he was taken out by a horrific injury trying to fake a field goal. He's lucky he can still walk.

Garrett retired last season after reuniting with his high school sweetheart at Dylan's wedding and getting her pregnant. I can't believe he could be so careless. He keeps saying it's Liv, and I get it. They were inseparable in high school. Hell, I grew up thinking Liv was my big sister.

None of us could believe it when they broke up in college, and we never got the whole story on what happened. Garrett just kept saying he blew it. Then they saw each other again at the wedding, and it was back on like Donkey Kong.

It sounds romantic.

It's not.

Never have unprotected sex.

I park the truck I rented at the house and walk down the pea-gravel path leading to the long, tin-roofed white-wood restaurant with the oversized, shuttered windows wide open to catch the bay breeze. It's a steamy August morning, like every other August morning down here, but the wind never stops moving.

Somehow it makes it tolerable. The briny sea air touches my tongue, and I do love this place. One day I'll come back here and retire. I'll be an old, old man at that point, and I'll sit around and fish and talk shit with the other old-timers. I'll be too old to play football, but I'll have a legendary career to look back on with pride.

"Hey, bro!" Garrett meets me at the door, pulling me in for a hug. "Good to see you."

He almost seems smug about me being here, and my antennae go up. "Good to see you, too."

Garrett towers over everybody, and today he's in his Deputy Sheriff's uniform. It's made of thick khaki, and at his height and build, with the heavy, black leather gun belt on his waist and all the stripes and badges on his chest, he looks pretty badass.

"Busted any criminals lately?" I tease.

"Just the usual—kids acting up, tourists getting drunk, folks driving too fast." His brow arches. "We've had some excitement, but nothing illegal."

"Oh yeah?" I'm intrigued, but Jack catches me by the arm.

"How was your flight?"

"Easy. I slept most of it."

"Come with me to the kitchen."

I'm a little confused as he guides me in the opposite direction of our family and friends, but okay.

Zane and his fiancée Rachel sit at a booth watching us. Liv is with them, holding their new baby on her shoulder, patting her back. I give them a wave. My spidey senses are definitely tingling now.

Dylan is in the kitchen, I assume, and Logan's probably with her—if he's not at the radio station he bought and has been busting his ass to make the premier sports destination on his dad's communications network.

Maybe this is something about that?

"What's going on?" We're just approaching the kitchen when the doors open on their own, and out steps a girl I haven't seen in more than a year.

She stops me in my tracks. "Raven, hey…."

My chest tightens. After all this time, Raven Gale is the one woman I haven't been able to compartmentalize away. She's petite and pretty with brown hair and golden highlights around her face.

She has a great smile with a big dimple in her left cheek, and her body is banging. She's soft and curvy, and fuck me, her boobs look even bigger than the last time I saw her.

Heat surges below my belt, and my mind jumps back to the night we shared after Dylan's wedding. We had a lot of fun and a lot of sex.

But it wasn't just the sex I remember. We really got to know each other, and it was cool how much we have in common. We both have big plans and big dreams, and we're committed to achieving them. She also really digs in and enjoys life. Hell, the night we spent together was some of the best sex I've ever had. We did things I've never done before, and I came so hard…

It left an impression.

And I've got to stop thinking about it before I pop an inappropriate boner right here in front of my whole family. Glancing around, they're still watching us, and it's a nice bucket of cold water on that train of thought.

Clearing my throat, I extend a hand. "It's been a minute, but wow. You look great."

Her brown eyes widen, and she seems flustered, which is new. When we were together, she was so confident and bold. She was funny, and our chemistry crackled in the air.

"Is he here?" Dylan emerges from the kitchen, with a dark-haired baby on her shoulder.

My brow lowers, and I'm confused. No one told me Dylan was pregnant. Has it even been nine months since I've seen her? Last time was at the party for Garrett in New York.

"Yes." Raven's voice is quiet. "I didn't know you'd be here so fast."

"Who is that?"

My sister bounces the little girl on her hip, smiling up at me brightly. "This is your daughter!"

"What?" My chin pulls back in surprise.

"Yes, she is!" Dylan leans forward, rubbing their noses and making the little girl smile. "This is Hayden Gale Bradford, and she is *adorable.*"

"My…" A knot is in my throat, and I'm having trouble swallowing. "How…"

The room falls silent. My eyes move quickly over the crowd of spectators all watching me. Garrett looks like he's fighting a burst of laughter.

"I thought we might have a chance to talk first." Raven's tone is apologetic. "I didn't plan to do it this way."

"Want to hold her?" Dylan passes the chunky baby to me.

I'm holding her like Rafiki in *The Lion King*, trying to re-start my brain, and the small human blinks at me with wide blue eyes, just like mine. She's cute. She's weirdly like looking in a mirror. Her head is covered in shiny dark hair that ends in soft curls around her chubby cheeks, and the longer I hold her, her rosebud lips press into an angry scowl.

I don't know shit about babies, but I'm pretty sure she's about to scream in my face. Raven steps forward quickly, taking her out of my hands and hugging her little body close to her chest.

"It's okay, Haddy." The baby girl puts her head on Raven's shoulder and two fingers in her little mouth.

"What's this about, Rave?"

If I were anywhere else, I'd push back on this. I remember every time we had sex, and every time I used protection. But my family wouldn't play a game like this with me. At least, not with a little baby involved, and hell, even if I wanted to argue, I don't have a leg to stand on. There's no doubt this little girl is mine.

Raven catches my hand, pulling me with her through the double doors into the kitchen. The sounds echo in the spotless room, and she turns to face me, fixing her eyes on my chest.

"I didn't know how to get in touch with you. I didn't have your number, and I had the worst morning sickness the whole time I was pregnant. I actually *lost* weight." She's talking fast. "It took me a minute to get back on my feet after she was born, and the longer I waited, the harder it seemed. I knew I had to tell you, but I don't have your number and…"

"You got pregnant." I'm a little dizzy, and my brain is having a hard time processing this information.

"I did." Brown eyes finally meet mine along with bright blue ones framed in thick dark lashes.

She's curious, sucking her fingers and watching me like she's wondering what I'll do next.

I have no freaking idea.

"Haddy is…" The words get stuck.

"Haddy is our daughter."

The Way We Collide is available in print, ebook, and audio.

Books by
TIA LOUISE

ROMANCE IN KINDLE UNLIMITED

THE BRADFORD BOYS
*The Way We Touch, 2024**
*The Way We Play, 2024**
*The Way We Score, 2025**
*The Way We Collide, 2025**
*The Way We Win, 2025**
(*Available on Audiobook.)

THE BE STILL SERIES
*A Little Taste, 2023**
*A Little Twist, 2023**
*A Little Luck, 2023**
*A Little Naughty, 2024**
(*Available on Audiobook.)

THE HAMILTOWN HEAT SERIES
*Fearless, 2022**
*Filthy, 2022**
For Your Eyes Only, 2022
*Forbidden, 2023**
(*Available on Audiobook.)

THE TAKING CHANCES SERIES
*This Much is True**
*Twist of Fate**
*Trouble**
(*Available on Audiobook.)

FIGHT FOR LOVE SERIES
*Wait for Me**
*Boss of Me**
*Here with Me**
*Reckless Kiss**
(*Available on Audiobook.)

BELIEVE IN LOVE SERIES
Make You Mine
*Make Me Yours**
*Stay**
(*Available on Audiobook.)

SOUTHERN HEAT SERIES
When We Touch
When We Kiss

THE ONE TO HOLD SERIES
*One to Hold (#1 - Derek & Melissa)**
*One to Keep (#2 - Patrick & Elaine)**
*One to Protect (#3 - Derek & Melissa)**
One to Love (#4 - Kenny & Slayde)
One to Leave (#5 - Stuart & Mariska)
*One to Save (#6 - Derek & Melissa)**
*One to Chase (#7 - Marcus & Amy)**
One to Take (#8 - Stuart & Mariska)
(*Available on Audiobook.)

THE DIRTY PLAYERS SERIES
*PRINCE (#1)**
*PLAYER (#2)**
DEALER (#3)
THIEF (#4)
(*Available on Audiobook.)

THE BRIGHT LIGHTS SERIES
Under the Lights (#1)
Under the Stars (#2)
Hit Girl (#3)

COLLABORATIONS
*The Last Guy**
The Right Stud
Tangled Up
Save Me
(*Available on Audiobook.)

PARANORMAL ROMANCES
One Immortal (vampires)
One Insatiable (shifters)
***

GET THREE FREE STORIES!
Sign up for my New Release newsletter and never miss a sale
or new release by me!
Sign up now!

Acknowledgments

I'm pretty sure second-chance, accidental pregnancy might be in my Top 3 romance tropes. I love going on the journey with characters through their difficulties, back to their one true love. It's ultimate romance and so much *Swoon!*

From my alpha readers to my beta readers to you, we've all been swooning and drying tears and fanning ourselves and consumed with Garrett & Liv. I adore my people, my incredibly supportive team, and really, this whole world of The Bradford Boys.

Huge thanks and so much love to my husband "Mr. TL" for everything, including checking my fictional legal skillz…

My amazing PA Kat is invaluable in keeping the wheels turning while I write, and the incredibly talented Laura Moore literally knocked it out of the park with this illustrated cover!

Thanks so much to the BEST alpha readers on the planet, Jen DeJong and Leticia Teixeira. Huge thanks to my *incredible* betas, Maria Black, Corinne Akers, Amy Reierson, Courtney Anderson, Jennifer Christy, Heather Heaton, and Michelle Mastandrea. So much **LOVE** for you ladies.

Thanks to Jaime Ryter for your eagle-eyed edits and to Lori Jackson and Kari March for the incredible cover designs, to my dear Wander for the *perfect* photography, and the amazing Stacey Blake, who helps me make my gorgeous paperback interiors!

Thanks to my dear Starfish, to my Mermaids, and to my Veeps for keeping me sane and organized and helping me spread the word. And all the incredible BookTokers who I've come to think of as friends.

Finally to my author-buds Kandi, Laura, Suzy, and Elizabeth. Thank you so much for being sounding boards and support. Old friends are the best friends.

And to my readers everywhere, thank you for helping me do what I do.

Love, small towns, and spice,
❤*Tia*

About the Author

Tia Louise is the *USA Today* and #4 Amazon bestselling author of (*primarily*) small-town, single-parent, second-chance, and military romances set at or near the beach.

From Readers' Choice awards, to *USA Today* "Happily Ever After" nods, to winning Favorite Erotica Author and the "Lady Boner Award" (*lol!*), nothing makes her happier than communicating with fellow Mermaids (*fans*) and creating romances that are smart, sassy, and *very sexy*.

A former journalist and displaced beach bum, Louise lives in the Midwest with her trophy husband, two young-adult geniuses, and one clumsy "grand-cat."

Sign up for her newsletter and never miss a new release or sale—and get a free story collection!

Signed Copies of all books online at:
https://geni.us/SignedPBs

Connect with Tia:
TiaLouise.com
Instagram—@AuthorTLouise
TikTok—@TheTiaLouise